# Second Chances

## Karsyn Joy

# CONTENTS

# DEDICATION

To my very best friend, you know who you are. You have been with me on this new journey of writing my first book, and I couldn't have done it without you. You have kept my secrets, supported my dreams, and encouraged me when I felt discouraged. You have shared my tears, my laughter, and my anger at some of these characters. You are more than just a friend, you are my soulfriend, my confidant, my partner in crime for the last 37 years. I will always love you.

# Acknowledgments

I am grateful to my cousin, for her encouragement when I told her about my book. She was thrilled for me and introduced me to Denise.

I am grateful to Denise Cassino for taking on my project and helping me make my book better. Your support and encouragement have been invaluable throughout this exciting process. Denise, I look forward to working with you on my other books.

I would like to express my gratitude to the artist who created the cover of my book, @Yaksukii on Instagram. Thank you for your hard work and patience in accommodating all my little changes.

Last but not least, to my very best friends who kept me encouraged throughout this process. Thank you for helping me fix inconsistencies in my book and keeping me motivated.

# PROLOGUE

My name is Brinley (Winter) Jameson. I am the youngest triplet of Alpha Zane and Luna Estelle Winter. My older brother, by five minutes, is Jaxon, and my older sister, Brooklyn, who is also my identical twin, by three minutes. We are twenty-five years old and the only children our parents had. I am very close with my siblings and we tell each other everything. Because we are triplets, we've been able to mind-link each other since we were old enough to talk. Most wolves can't mind-link until they shift for the first time at eighteen years old. I think we could mind-link before we could talk because my parents would always tell us we would know what each other was saying and thinking when we were just babies.

My siblings haven't found their fated mates yet, and my parents are still going strong running our pack. My parents found each other shortly after they turned twenty and two years later, we were born. My dad doesn't want to hand the pack over to my brother until he finds his mate, but my mom wants him to step down so they can travel while they are still young. My dad is old-fashioned in the sense he feels the alpha needs to have a mate before he takes over, but truth be told, my brother has been doing most of the work for him for about five years, ever since... well, I'm not going there, I'm not ready to talk about it. My Dad's not opposed to either myself or my sister taking over the pack, but neither one of us wants the responsibility. We don't mind stepping in and helping out, and we were training for the position too, but we, as siblings, decided Jaxon should take it.

On our eighteenth birthdays, we were so excited to get our wolves and what they looked like that we decided to go to our favorite hiding spot so we could shift together instead of shifting with the rest of the eighteen-year-olds. All three of our wolves are white. We are a little extra special. Jaxon's wolf, Branson, has a blue tint, Brooklyn's wolf, Maya, has a crimson tint, and my wolf, Amanda, has a lilac tint. We didn't know why we were a little different but knew we couldn't keep our color a secret from our parents. Not that we ever keep secrets from them, we just didn't know what it meant at the time.

When we turned nineteen, I met my fated mate, Jerod Jameson. He was twenty-three years old and an elite warrior from the Timberline pack. He came to our pack because he wanted to train with our enforcers so he could get stronger and be a better warrior. The moment we laid eyes on each other, we knew we were fated mates. He didn't want to separate me from my siblings, so he asked my dad if he could join our pack. About a year after our mating ceremony, Jerod asked me to be his wife. It's not traditional for wolves to get married, but we wanted each other every way we could and four months later, we welcomed our baby girl, Cassandra Mae Jameson, into the world. Three weeks after that, my life changed... forever.

# Chapter 1 The Nightmare

BRINLEY

My siblings and I grew up in a home where love was abundant, and and laughter was constant. Our pack land is a haven for our kind, a gated community hidden in the woods. The packhouse is the heart of our territory but there are also cozy apartments for singles and mated couples without children and spacious homes for families. Within our gated community, we have a small town with shops and amenities so we don't always need to shop in human towns. It is a secret sanctuary for wolf shifters, far from the prying eyes of humans who do not know we exist.

Our packhouse is a five-story home with a grand driveway entrance and wrap-around porch, it's painted light gray with black trim. Double wood front doors open to a large foyer. When you enter there is a massive staircase winding up to each floor with an elevator off to the side. The first floor has a game room, movie theater, industrial kitchen, and a communal dining hall for all the pack members to eat in if they don't feel like cooking at home. There are also small studio apartments for each of the omegas and warriors who work primarily in the packhouse, a laundry room, a mud room, and a locker room with showers.

The second story is the Delta floor which includes three bedrooms each with an en suite bathroom, a kitchen, a dining room, and a great room. The offices for the Alpha, Luna, Betas, Gammas, and Deltas are also on this floor. Each of those offices has a bathroom inside and there is also a bathroom in the hall as well. We don't currently have a delta and my dad has never expressed wanting or needing one since my siblings and I can fill that role if needed. We have also been trained to fill in for the beta and of course, the alpha since we will be expected to take over that role in the future. We are trained for the gamma position too, except for their primary role which is to bring comfort to the luna, that is something they are born with and can't be taught.

The third story is the Gamma floor. They have four bedrooms each with an en suite bathroom, there is also a small kitchen, dining room, and bonus room. The fourth story is the Beta floor. Same setup as the Gamma floor except they also have six guest suites on their floor as well for visiting packs ranked leaders. The fifth story is the Alpha's floor. There are four apartments with three of them each having two bedrooms with en suite bathrooms, a small kitchen, a dining room, a great room, and an office.

The alpha apartment has three bedrooms, each with en suite bathrooms, a full kitchen, a great room, two offices, a main dining room, and a private dining room. All bedrooms in the packhouse are soundproof and the alpha floor has a panic room attached. There is a panic room located on the first floor as well that takes the occupants to a secure bunker underground. When the panic button is activated, hidden steel doors automatically roll out covering all doors and windows for extra protection.

The backyard has an Olympic-sized swimming pool with three springboards at different heights, a smaller pool with slides, and a wading pool for the younger pups. Three large hot tubs. An outdoor full kitchen with five large smokers and BBQs and a large screen TV. Behind that and down a hill are three training pitches, a grand meeting room that is also used as a gym for indoor training, and an enclosed arena for us triplets to train in.

There is another building for daycare pups ages infant through five years old during school and when school is out, pups ages infant through ten years old unless they are in junior warrior training. The pups start public school with humans at six years old. They need to learn how to interact with humans at an early age since the majority of our money comes from our businesses in the human world. There is a large garage off to the side of the packhouse that can house fifteen vehicles.

When we were little, our training started by playing games such as wrestling, martial arts, hide-and-seek, Battleship, Risk, and Monopoly. They all played a role in teaching us proper fighting form, using all our senses, preparing us for battles and pack perimeter security, and, of course, money management. My mom also had us helping the omegas around the house doing chores, cooking, cleaning, gardening, etc. She wanted us to be well-rounded in our lives and also said it would help us later in life. She drilled into us we shouldn't always rely on the omegas to do everything for us. I love my family, friends, and the home we grew up in, but I'm ready to heal my heart.

It's the first nice day we've had in April since Spring started a month ago. I'm hanging out watching the elite warriors train, as I have done for the past five years. I've been encouraged to join them but I haven't felt like it. My parents had us training with the warriors as soon as we started walking. My dad always told us since we were the children of a double alpha bloodline, we needed to know how to protect ourselves. He didn't want us relying on anyone else for protection if we were ever in a bad situation by ourselves. The three of us are not only enforcer training but we are master elite enforcers.

When we were younger, we always tried to see who the strongest of us was. Sometimes my sister and I would gang up on our brother and hold him down until he'd submit to us and other times he'd grab his friends, and they would gang up on us and hold us down until we'd submit. It was all in good fun. We never hurt each other, we were all best of friends, even though a few of them were a couple of years older than us. There I go again, I keep digressing to when things were simpler, and I felt free.

Sometimes it's easier to live in the past because living in the present is where all the pain is. I haven't been able to do anything since that fateful day five years ago. I'm still connected to my wolf, Amanda, but because I'm so traumatized from what happened, I've been too afraid to shift. Amanda, or Andi, as I like to call her, keeps telling me she understands, but I know she misses her wolf siblings and wants to run and play with them. I just can't, I'm too afraid of what might happen and to be honest, I'm afraid to heal. I know I need to for both of our sakes, and for that reason alone I feel I'm finally ready. I'm also afraid I'm not able to shift anymore because I haven't done it for five years, but I've kept that to myself.

I know Amanda, Branson, and Maya talk to each other. I can feel them in my head, I usually block them out so I don't hear them. I don't like to sleep because of the nightmares. Doc gave me some medication to help, but when I'm too tired, I forget to take them. I usually stay up until my body gives out, which is why I forget to take the meds. My sense of smell has been wacky and because I haven't been shifting, I can't sniff out pack members or my own family so it's easy for them to sneak up on me and scare me. It's all in good fun but it's annoying too.

My powers are still intact, but I don't use them very often, they drain me more quickly when I use them. Everyone tries talking me into shifting saying it will help, it will heal my heart, my body won't tire as quickly when I use my powers, and I will be able to smell everyone again, but I'm not sure I believe them. Andi has tried healing me but I told her I'm just not ready.

I've been thinking about asking my dad if I could stay at Uncle Samuel's pack for a while, just to get away from here and the memories, but I haven't gotten up the courage to do that yet. I stopped picking at the grass and looked over to the training pitch, the warriors were standing around talking. Training is pretty much over and I'm tired and need to lie down. I haven't slept in three days and I'm feeling it. I don't want to fall asleep on the training field otherwise Beta Michael might carry me back to the packhouse, that's not gonna happen again... not ever.

The last time it happened, he put me in his son's bed. He's hoping Matt will be my second chance mate. I'm hoping not because he's like a brother to me, but I wouldn't know if he's my second chance mate anyway since I can't smell his scent. Matt tells me I'm not and I need to trust him. I made it to my room, curled up in my bed, and fell asleep.

## BROOKLYN

"Jaxon!"

"What's wrong!"

"Get Mom, Dad, and Doc! They need to get to Brinley's room immediately!" I was so scared seeing her thrashing around and screaming in her sleep. I'm tired of this happening to her, my heart is pounding in my chest, and I can't stop the tears from sliding down my face.

"Brinley! Brin! Wake up!" I've been desperately trying to wake her by shaking her for fifteen minutes, but she hasn't even acknowledged I'm there yet. She just keeps screaming, "No, no please goddess, please let them be okay." She always screams the same thing. "Jaxon, hurry up. I can't wake her this time!"

"Brinley, please wake up, it's a bad dream, you're safe. It's just a bad dream. Please Brin wake up." I'm sobbing now, my shoulders are dropped, and I propped my face in my hands and just let the tears flow. When I heard Mom running down the hall, I wiped the snot from my nose and dried my tears, although my eyes were red and puffy.

"Brooke, what's wrong," she asked, frantically running into Brin's room.

"She's having another nightmare. I was walking by her room when I heard her screaming in her sleep. I can't wake her this time. I'm so scared, what if she doesn't wake up? I wish we could take the pain away from her so she doesn't have to keep reliving it. I just don't know how to help her."

"Jaxon was supposed to get Dad and Doc too, where are they? They need to hurry, Dad and Jaxon can usually get her to wake up, maybe Max can help?" I said through tears.

"Honey, you need to calm down, they are getting Dr. Carter. I was in the kitchen when Jaxon linked me. Your dad was in a meeting in his office and his link was closed, I had to break through the block. Dr. Carter is in surgery with an omega's son who broke his arm. Jaxon and your father went to get him and Max is busy." she said, rubbing my back and kissing me on my head.

"No! No! Where are they!" Brinley cried out, her thrashing around was getting worse.

"Brinley, Sweetheart, wake up, it's Mommy."

"You're safe, you're home, it's going to be okay." The look on Mom's face breaks my heart. "Brooke, hold her down so she stops thrashing, I don't want her to hurt herself."

"Mom, Doc Carter needs to hurry up and give her something to calm her."

"I know Honey, but always giving her medication isn't the answer, she needs to shift so the natural healing abilities we have can work. She refuses to let Andi shift. She won't even let us talk with Amanda. Has Maya or Branson tried reaching out to her?"

"Yes, they told us she wants to shift, but every time she talks to Brinley she pushes her to the back of her mind and closes her off. Andi doesn't want to force the shift because she knows it will be more painful for her. She told Maya and Branson she has come to terms with what happened but Brinley hasn't. She said Brin doesn't want to shift because she's afraid of healing her heart."

"She believes if she heals, she'll forget about them, and she doesn't want to forget. Mom, I think she needs to talk with someone. She needs to move past this and know that healing is okay, and she won't ever forget them. If she allows herself to shift, then Andi can help her get stronger."

"I agree with you, Honey. We have all been able to move past it. Hopefully, your father, Jaxon, or Dr. Carter can help pull her out of this nightmare. Once we can wake her up, we will sit down and talk with her."

I twisted my hair around my finger, "*Maya, I have my doubts Brin will want to talk about it, she never does, and it breaks my heart.*"

"*It breaks my heart too Brooky. Can you call Max, maybe he can get here more quickly?*"

"*Good idea. Max, can you come to Brinley's room, it's urgent.*"

"*I'll be right there.*"

"Mom, I linked Max, he's on his way, maybe he can calm her."

"You shouldn't have bothered him, I told you he was busy today," she patted my hand.

"I had to try, Mom. I can't stand this, I feel like my heart is being ripped from me."

## JAXON

When Brooklyn yelled at me to get our parents and Doc, I could hear the fear in her voice. I had been helping a couple of omegas get two guest rooms together when I heard her. I knew my dad was in a meeting with a visiting Alpha and Beta from the Black Diamond Pack and it was getting late; I assumed they would be invited to stay over. I dropped what I was doing and told the omegas I'd be back as soon as possible.

I linked Mom as I was running to my dad's office. Just as I was rounding the corner to his office, I saw him walking out with the alpha and beta behind him instructing a warrior to escort them to their guest rooms. I waited out of sight until the warriors had escorted our guests out of earshot before speaking.

"Dad, we need to get to Doc, something is wrong with Brin," I was frantically rubbing my hand through my hair.

"I know, your mom broke through my block and told me. He's just finished up surgery. Let's get over to the clinic, grab him, and head to Brin's room and see what's going on." He put his hand on my shoulder, "Son, she'll be okay. Tobias will look her over and we'll figure this out."

We threw the doors to the clinic open an, andd Doc Carter was standing there. "Alpha, Jaxon? Is everything okay? I've been in surgery, what can I do for you?"

"We need you in the packhouse immediately, it's Brinley."

"I'll grab my bag and be right there. What's going on with her?"

"She was napping, Brooklyn walked past her room when she heard her screaming in her sleep. We think it's her nightmares again."

"I just got a link from Luna Estelle, Brinley's starting to come out of it."

"Let's check her out and see if there is anything I can do for her. Do you know if she took any of her medication?"

"No, we don't," my dad and I replied at the same time.

*Branson, I wish we could help her but she is the only one who can decide when she's ready. Can you reach out to Andi and find out what's going on?"*

*"I'll try but whenever Brin gets this way, I usually can't reach her because she's focusing on Brinley."*

*"Okay, buddy, I get it, but please try."*

## BRINLEY

*"Andi, I'm so tired, I need to sleep. Why are people talking to me?"*

*"You need to wake up."*

*"I can't, please tell them to leave me alone."* I feel like I've been running around keeping busy, well, I have been actually. I need to keep my mind busy otherwise I dwell on what happened to my life. Andi is trying to help me through this. She has already processed it and wants to move on but I'm having a hard time doing that. I feel disconnected from her, mostly because I haven't let her shift.

The last time I shifted and went for a run was the day our lives changed, forever. Every time she talks about shifting and healing from the pain, I push her into the back of my mind. I don't want to shift, and I don't want to heal, if I shift and heal, I'm afraid I'll forget and I don't want to ever forget. At the same time, I know I need to heal. It's all too confusing for me.

Maya and Branson like to talk with her, I try pushing them out of my head but sometimes I can't. I know they want to see her. They are triplets too. She hasn't forced the shifting issue with me... yet. I know it's just a matter of time before she does. I'm not looking forward to it, I know it's going to hurt like the first time because it's been a long time.

I hear my sister screaming my name and shaking me frantically. I just can't seem to wake up. I'm thrashing in my sleep to get her off of me. I just want to sleep, please let me be. I wish I would be swallowed up in a deep hole and disappear. I tried taking my own life but Amanda wouldn't allow that to happen. The nightmare is consuming me and I can't shake it. I'm hearing voices, my parents, brother, Max, and Doc too. They are talking but I can't understand what they are saying, I need to wake up but at the same time, I don't want to.

## TATE

I was visiting the Winter Moon Pack on official business with my beta, Benjamin. We were meeting with Alpha Zane to set up an alliance. I recently took over as alpha of the Black Diamond pack because the former alpha, Alpha Fredrick, was running the pack into the ground. His allies revoked their contracts with him because he violated them and rogues were attacking all the time. Along with him not acting like a proper alpha should, I also had personal reasons for challenging him for the position.

With the approval of the council, the challenge was set to end by submission or death. I won, and he lost his life. Alpha Fredrick lost his chosen mate and unborn baby about fifteen years earlier during childbirth leaving him to raise his then ten-year-old daughter by himself. Since she was a chosen mate, it didn't affect him as it would usually affect a wolf.

With a fated mate, unless you have strong family support to help you through it or find a second chance mate shortly after, they will go mad and need to be put down. I know first hand, my fated mate died five years ago but I had support to help me through it and we never got the chance to mark each other. So here we are, sitting in Alpha Zane's office, talking about being allies. He has a lethal reputation and his pack warriors are just as lethal as his reputation. This is why I want to become one of his allies. Our pack is smaller since the rogues took out many of our people, I want to try and grow our pack again but I can't do that without allies.

"Alpha Zane, thank you for meeting with me and Beta Benjamin today, we greatly appreciate it."

"Alpha Tate, I'm happy to be sitting across from you. I know you've only been in the alpha position for a short time but I'm sure you will bring your new pack to where it needs to be. Your previous alpha was a piece of shit and letting his pack fall to the rogue attacks was very disheartening. So, what brings you here today?"

Benjamin and I stared at each other for a few minutes before responding. "Well Sir, I was hoping we could become allies and was wondering if some of your elite warriors might be able to come to my pack and help me train our warriors? We could use all the help we can get. I can only train them so much, and on top of my new alpha duties, I just don't have the time I want to put into it."

I'm sitting there staring at Alpha Zane, in hopes he'll help us when Benjamin links me, *"You holding up okay? You're tapping your feet again."*

*"Yeah, but it's still nerve-wracking. If he won't help I don't know how long before we lose the pack to the rogues."*

*"I'm pretty nervous too but from what I've heard about Alpha Zane, unless you're his enemy, he's a reasonable person."*

*"If we can secure an alliance then all will be good."*

I turned my attention back to Alpha Zane, he had a concerned look on his face, "Well fellas, I think we can work something out. I would like to talk more about it but I've been notified of an urgent matter. It's getting late, I would like you to join us for dinner and stay the night if you don't mind. We can finish the details in the morning. I will send a few of my elite warriors to your pack tonight to help with security while you are here if you agree."

I looked at Benjamin and he nodded at me. "I think that will work, I appreciate your time and hospitality. Benjamin will need to call his mate and let her know we'll be staying over and she can inform our warriors Winter Moon will be sending some of their elites tonight." I'm happy we packed an overnight bag just in case. With our meeting concluded a warrior came to show us to our rooms so we could freshen up for dinner. As we left Alpha Zane's office, I got a scent of something that intrigued Chase, my wolf, but I wasn't sure where it was coming from.

## BRINLEY

I barely had my eyes open, everyone was in my room staring at me. Dr. Carter was taking my blood pressure, "Brinley, did you take your meds before taking a nap?"

"I don't recall. I remember watching the warriors train and wanted to lie down before I fell asleep on the training grounds, I was so tired. I wanted to close my eyes for a few minutes. I didn't want Beta Michael to carry me to Matt's bed again so I came in here to lie down. I must've fallen asleep longer than I thought."

"When was the last time you slept?"

"It's been about three days, I think."

Doc looked concerned and Mom was stroking my hair away from my forehead, "Do you want to talk about your nightmare?"

I rolled my eyes at her and shook my head, "No, I don't. It's the same thing over and over again." Doc took out a syringe and gave me some anxiety meds to help ease my thoughts. Amanda was trying to talk with me too but I blocked her out.

"You know Brinley, you can't keep closing your wolf out like you do, she wants to help you heal and move on. It's a full moon in two weeks. I want you to shift with your siblings when we have the pack run. If you want to talk with someone, I can set it up. It would be good for you," I stared at Doc with a blank look on my face.

"I'm not ready to talk with anyone about this, please let me be."

"At least consider letting Amanda out, it will be good for the both of you. I know you have been disconnected from her for a long time."

I looked down at my hands, wrang them tightly, and bit my lower lip. I know they're right, I'm just so scared to do it. I don't know if I'm ready for that yet.

*"I'm sorry Andi, I just can't right now."*

*"Brins please remember I also went through that tragic day. I need to be let out as much as you need to let me out. I feel trapped inside you and I miss Branson and Maya,"* she sounded so sad, my heart broke for her.

They were all getting ready to leave my room when I grabbed my dad's hand, "Dad, will you sit with me for a little while?"

"Of course Pumpkin, whatever you want." My mom, siblings, Max, and Doc left my room. I just lay there quietly listening to my dad breathe. He and Jaxon were always able to calm me down. As I got older Max was able to calm me too.

I fiddled with my fingers trying to process everything that just happened. I decided I needed to do something for myself and Amanda. I want to get away from the pack for a while. Maybe getting away will do us some good. I kept my head turned down, lifted my eyes, and looked at my dad. In an almost too quiet voice, I asked him, "Dad, how did your meeting with the Black Diamond alpha and beta go?"

"It went well. I agreed to an alliance. I'm sending some of our elite warriors to his pack tonight while they stay here overnight. The elites will stay at Black Diamond to help train their warriors too."

"That's great, um, do you think I could go with them? I think a change of scenery would do me and Amanda some good," I hurried out before he could cut me off.

My dad stared at me for a minute before responding, "Let me talk with Mom and Dr. Carter to see if they think it's wise. If they agree, then I will talk with Alpha Tate and Beta Benjamin."

"Thank you, Daddy, I love you," I wrapped him in a hug. "Thank you for always being there for me, protecting me, loving me, guiding me, and training me. I appreciate everything you have ever done for me. I know I don't say it often, but I do appreciate and love you and Mom."

"Pumpkin, we will always be here for you, and your brother and sister. We love you, we just want you to get better."

# Chapter 2 Deciding Her Fate

**ALPHA ZANE**

My little girl wants to leave and go to Black Diamond to get away. I'm not sure I'm comfortable with that especially since they have a new alpha and are still seeing rogue attacks. I need to talk with Estelle and Tobias before I approach Alpha Tate and get their thoughts on this. I can see where it might be good for her, she might be able to move past what happened here if she's not surrounded by it all the time.

I walked into our room, my beautiful, sexy wife is in the middle of changing her clothes. She's been working in the kitchen again and has chocolate covering her... hmmm, maybe that talk can wait another hour or two or three. I have some chocolate to lick off her and my cock is pressing so hard against my zipper, I think I may have a permanent indent in it.

I walk over to her with a glint in my eye, grab her around the waist, and whisper in her ear, "Hi Baby, can I help clean that chocolate off of you?" I licked her throat and sucked her mating mark. She shivered in my arms then reached down and caressed my cock.

"I won't say no when you kiss me like that."

I slowly turned her around, she grabbed my hair and held my mouth over her mating mark as she moaned. That's all I needed to hear. I picked her up and threw her on the bed. "Baby, you are so beautiful" I trail my mouth down her neck and circle my tongue around her hard nipples.

"Zane," she moaned, "why do you still have clothes on?"

I don't need to be told twice. I ripped my shirt off and shredded my pants and underwear so my cock could spring from its confines. I continued my way down her belly and before I reached my destined spot, I scraped some chocolate off her arm and rubbed it on her opening. She moaned and I kissed up her thighs before settling in her folds. I lick all the chocolate off her folds before plunging my tongue inside and using my finger to rub her clit.

"Zane, don't stop. Oh, my heavens, please keep doing that," she moaned. "Zane I need you, please, I need you inside me."

"Not yet my Sweet, I haven't been satisfied with dessert yet. I want you to cum all over my face and tongue first." I remove my tongue and insert three fingers, finding her G-spot while sucking on her clit.

"Zane, don't stop, just like that, oh yes, yes, yes!" I can feel her walls tightening around my fingers and I know she's on the edge of her orgasm so I lightly bite down on her clit and she gushes all over me.

With a smile on my face, I lap up her sweet juices, "Sweets, are you ready for me?" With a nod of her head and a moan of want, I adjust myself and push into her. I take her body until she orgasms three more times.

"Zane, you make me feel so full, I can't get enough of you."

"I know my Sweet, but we need to get cleaned up because we have company for dinner tonight and I need to talk with you and Tobias before dinner."

I pick her up bridal style and carry her to the shower where I take her again two more times and she goes down on me and gives me one of the best blowjobs of my life. She always gives me the best blowjobs of my life, who am I kidding. I'm so glad all of the rooms in this packhouse are soundproof. I don't want anyone to hear my wife scream and moan, that is for my ears only.

After our little escapade in our bedroom and making sure Essie was completely satiated, I mind-linked Tobias and asked him to meet us in my office. I sat behind my desk with her on my lap, where I preferred her to be. There was a knock at my office door, *"Come in Tobias."*

"Alpha, you wanted to see me?"

"Yes, please have a seat."

"What can I do for you, Sir? I'm assuming this has to do with Brinley?"

"Yes, it does."

"I want to talk with you and Luna Estelle because I need both of your opinions on this subject. When I was sitting with Brinley after everyone left, she asked me how the meeting with the Black Diamond alpha and beta went. When I told her we were going to enter into an alliance agreement, she asked if she could leave with them and stay in their pack for a while."

"She feels a change of scenery might help her and Amanda since she's surrounded by the memories of what happened. I told her I would talk with both of you first and if you agree I would speak with Alpha Tate and Beta Benjamin. They will be responsible for her safety and needs. We would also send more elite warriors to Black Diamond with her. What are your thoughts?"

I first looked at my mate since she is very protective of our pups, even though they are grown. Then Toby to see who would speak up first. Essie was wringing her hands together before speaking. "I don't like the idea of her being so far away but I do understand where she's coming from. I think it would be good for her too."

"Brin being somewhere where no one knows her, what she's been through, or her special powers, will be good for her. It might give her and Amanda what they need to finally heal and shift. I think she should go as long as the fear of the Goddess is put into the alpha and beta. If anything happens to my baby girl, they and whoever harms her will suffer the consequences."

Toby was staring at my wife with wide eyes and mouth open. "I don't think I have ever seen or heard you speak like that Luna."

"Well, Toby, no one has ever had to take care of my pup in another pack before. Don't cross a mamma wolf and her pup," she looked stern.

"Good to know. I also think it would be a good idea. She's been hurting for five years and anything that might pull her out of this will be helpful. Maybe she'll even start to train again. It would be good for both her and Amanda. I know she's been training on her own a little here and there but not how she had been. I can send medication with her and talk with the head doctor at the Black Diamond to make sure they are abreast of her situation."

"I would appreciate that Toby," Essie said reluctantly.

I looked at both of them and took in a deep breath, "We have an hour before dinner is served, do you both want to sit in on the conversation with Alpha Tate and Beta Benjamin?"

Essie looked at me, crossed her arms over her chest, and glared at me, "Of course I do. I need to make sure the fear of the Goddess is put in them and make sure they know I'm serious about keeping my baby girl safe."

"I would also like to be in that meeting in case they have any questions about her, medically speaking."

"So be it, I will have them brought to my office now."

## TATE

There was about an hour before dinner so Benjamin and I met up in my room after he was finished talking with his mate, Quincy. We were just going over logistics as to where Quincy was going to house the Winter Moon elite warriors when there was a knock at my door. There was an omega standing there, "May I help you?"

"Alpha Tate, my name is Mary. Alpha Zane and Luna Estelle request you and Beta Benjamin's presence in his office. Please follow me."

We looked at each other with a concerned look, *"Ben, do you think he changed his mind?"*

*"I hope not."*

We were both a nervous wreck when Mary, knocked on the alpha's door. When it opened Alpha Zane had two other people with him, his mate and another guy.

"Please come in and have a seat. You've already met my mate, Luna Estelle and this is our head doctor, Dr. Tobias Carter. I asked you both to come here before dinner so we could run something by you."

"By all means, what is it you need?"

"We have a delicate situation with one of our daughters. Without going into detail, she has had a very difficult time over the past few years. She's been having nightmares and thinks a change of scenery will be good for her."

"May I ask why she's having nightmares?"

"Gentlemen," Essie stepped in, "We will defer to our daughter to disclose that information. It affects her, she is in control of choosing who she talks with about it and when. What I will tell you, she has not shifted in five years. She had some major trauma happen to her and everything around our pack reminds her of it. Honestly, she needs a break and I'm hoping this might help her."

"From a medical perspective, she has been on medications to help her sleep. She must take them before naps or going to bed at night. She has insomnia due to the trauma and sometimes will go three or four days without sleeping. Oftentimes her body will just give out and she'll fall asleep wherever she is and the nightmares haunt her," Tobias said.

"If this happens, is it very difficult to wake her out of the nightmare? Will her wolf not heal her?" Benjamin asked.

"Her wolf has come to terms with the trauma but Brinley will not allow her to shift."

"Alpha Tate, Beta Benjamin, Brinley is my baby girl. You need to understand, that if you decide to allow her to stay with you, I will hold you both accountable for her. If a hair on her body is harmed, you both, along with whoever brings her harm, will suffer the consequences. Do I make myself clear?" My mate looked sternly at them.

"Yes ma'am, you make yourself clear. Would it be okay if Benjamin and I have a quick mind-link regarding this?"

"Please do, my daughter's life will be in your hands. This is not something to take lightly."

*"Ben, what do you think? We just took over the pack and are trying to keep the remaining pack members safe. Do you think we could keep her safe too?"*

*"I don't know, but it sounds like their daughter could use a change of scenery. I don't know what happened to her but if her family is willing to let her go to an unknown pack with new ranked leadership and rogue attacks then they must be at a loss as to how to help her."*

*"I think you're right. They will have some of their elites in our pack too who can help keep an eye on her. One more thing to consider, what do we do with Maribel? You know how she is and what she's capable of. If she sees you with another she-wolf, she will go berserk. She thinks you are going to take her as your chosen Luna."*

*"I know, she is a concern. She needs to realize she is not going to get anywhere near being a chosen mate for me. I'm hoping the Moon Goddess will still bless me with a second chance mate. Also, if we do this and help their daughter with whatever trauma happened to her, our alliance with Winter Moon will be secured."*

I looked at all three of them, "We agree to have your daughter stay with us for as long as she needs to be there."

Dr. Carter stood up, "I will need your head doctor's contact information so I can send Brinley's medical file to her. Your doctor will need it to understand who Brinley is and what she's been through." He handed me a piece of paper to write Doc Crystal's contact information on.

We stood up to leave after giving Crystal's information to Dr. Carter but Alpha Zane stopped us. "We will provide whatever Brinley needs while in your care. Her mother and I will speak with her in the morning. She's resting now and will not be joining us for dinner tonight. We will also have a conversation with our other two children to let them know what will be happening. We ask you not to mention this at dinner. Our beta family will be joining us l and I don't want anything getting out before talking with Brinley first."

## LUNA ESTELLE

We walked down to the private dining room with Tobias, Alpha Tate, and Beta Benjamin and met Michael, Sylvia, and Matthew on the way. "Alpha Tate, Beta Benjamin, I would like to introduce you to our Beta, Michael, his mate, and our Beta female, Sylvia, and their son and future Beta, Matthew." The three of them reached their hands out to the men and shook their hands.

"It's nice to meet you. I apologize on behalf of my mate and son for not meeting you when you arrived today. We had some issues on the training pitch which took our attention away from greeting you properly."

"No need to apologize, we're still learning the ropes as alpha and beta."

"Please gentlemen, Sylvia, let's head into the dining room for dinner. Jaxon and Brooklyn will be joining us shortly. Brinley will be resting in her room."

Michael tried reaching for Sylvia's hand but she glared at him and moved away, taking my hand, squeezing it lightly saying, "Was it another nightmare? I do hope she gets better soon."

"It was pretty scary but she was able to come out of it. I'll fill you in later. I see Michael is still trying to get in your space."

"He thinks because we have visitors, I'll allow him to touch me... not happening."

To this day I have no idea what happened between Michael and Sylvia, but whatever it was must've been pretty serious. I didn't want the conversation to linger on about Brinley at dinner, she doesn't need to be the topic of conversation so I quickly changed the subject. "Micheal, you said you had an issue on the training pitch today, what happened?"

"Sylvia had some of the younger pups out on the playground and two of the boys took off running. One of them landed right in the middle of the training pitch and got between Matthew and Gunther as they collided in their wolf forms. His arm was in the wrong place at the wrong time and it broke. Can you believe it?"

I looked at Tobias, shocked, "Was this the boy you were in surgery with when we needed you?"

"Sure sounds like it. It's nice to hear the whole story of what happened. All I got from the boy was he was playing, he fell and broke his arm. His mom was in hysteria and the warrior who brought the pup in didn't see what happened."

"Michael, Matthew, why didn't either of you bring the boy in and tell Dr. Carter what happened."

"We weren't able to. Where the pup was standing when Gunther and Matthew collided with him, the force of the hit knocked the wind out of both of them. All three of them dropped and stopped breathing for a few minutes. By the time they came around, the warrior was already on his way to the clinic and Sylvia was mind-linking his mom."

"Is he going to be okay?"

"Oh yeah," he chuckled, "he was already coming out of anesthesia when I left. He was excited to hear he'll have a scar, and said he didn't want the triplets to touch his arm either."

We all laughed, well, except for Alpha Tate and Beta Benjamin, they looked at each other and shrugged their shoulders confused.

# Chapter 3 Family Meeting

**JAXON**

Brooklyn and I were heading to the private dining room when we caught Doc Carter laughing and saying something about us not touching a pup's arm. I looked at my sister with a quizzical look and she shrugged her shoulders and made a funny face. Walking in, I asked, "What did we miss?"

"Yeah, what did we miss?"

"We heard something about not wanting the triplets to touch someone's arm and all of you laughing."

"Son, daughter," Dad said, "I'd like to introduce you to Alpha Tate and Beta Benjamin from Black Diamond."

"It's nice to meet your acquaintance. I'm Jaxon and this is my sister, Brooklyn, I hope your accommodations are good. If you need anything, please don't hesitate to ask. I kinda ran out on Mary when we were getting your rooms ready."

Alpha Tate gave me a questioning look, "You helped get our rooms ready?"

"Yes Sir, I did. Our mother raised us to help around the packhouse. She said it would help us stay grounded and not become egotistical jerks like some of the other alphas."

"Well, that is very admirable. I agree with her. I think it makes a person well rounded and to have empathy for others."

I looked at Brooklyn and waggled my eyebrows, "See, I can play nice."

"Oh brother," she rolled her eyes, "I know you can play nice," and she kicked me under the table, "but sometimes you don't play nice and leave things for me and Brin to do. You may be our older brother, by a few minutes, but sometimes you think you can boss us around because of it," she stuck her tongue out at me.

"You're acting like a five-year-old sticking your tongue out, no wonder I need to act older." I grinned and kicked her back.

My parents gave us their, 'Do we need to take you to the arena' look, we smiled and started eating.

"Congratulations on taking over Black Diamond, Alpha Tate. I heard you challenged the old alpha and won. I was wondering when someone was going to put that alpha dickhead in his place. Weren't you just a warrior when you challenged him?"

"I was but I was also training to be an elite warrior."

"Can I ask why you decided to challenge him? I mean someone was bound to but what made you decide to be the one? If you don't mind me asking?"

"It's a long story, and it's personal so I'm not ready to talk about it. But I will say a change needed to happen and no one was doing anything about it. The rogue attacks were getting worse and taking out more of our pack almost daily. When I challenged the alpha and he accepted, Benjamin was going to challenge the beta, but he stepped down before he could. He said he was ready to retire, but the old alpha wouldn't allow him to. He's been a big help in getting us up to speed with everything, but there is still a lot to learn. I've always admired your father. That's why I asked him for an alliance and his assistance."

"I'm glad to have met you and look forward to working with you when you take over your dad's pack. We will be working closely with you though because I help my dad with ninety percent of the alpha duties. I'm assuming you both will be leaving tomorrow?"

"Yes, we will be, although we have not decided what time yet." He gave my parents a look that had my skin tingling. Something was up, and I needed to find out what it was.

## ALPHA ZANE

After dinner, I asked our kids to meet us in my office so we could discuss Brinley staying at Black Diamond. As soon as Essie and I entered my office, we saw them lounging on the couch. I shut the door and locked it. I didn't want anyone else entering my office without permission, especially Michael, he thinks he should be involved in all topics of conversation lately including our personal family matters.

They looked at us with questioning eyes as they always do, and at the same time asked, "Why did you need to talk with us and why did you lock the door?"

"This conversation is between the four of us. I do not want nor do I need Michael's opinion or commentary on it. He already thinks he's being sly when he puts Brinley in Matt's bed when she passes out, but he's not. Brinley and Matt have both told us every time it happens and it irritates them. Matt knows Brinley isn't his mate, Brinley doesn't know for sure because her senses are all messed up so she's relying on us and Matt for the truth in that. Besides, she looks at Matt as a brother, not a lover."

"Now, the reason you're here. Your sister has asked to spend time at Black Diamond." Jaxon was about to say something so I raised my hand to shut down any conversations. "Before either of you say anything, I need Branson and Maya for this conversation too." They called their wolves forward.

"Your sister feels it would be best for her and Amanda to have a change of scenery. She feels being surrounded by the trauma day in and day out keeps her locked up inside. I'm giving you the courtesy of letting you know your mother and I, along with Doc Carter have agreed. We want your thoughts on this, all four of you."

"Dad, first, I'm shocked, I didn't ever expect her to want to leave but maybe this will be good for her and Andi. I mean I can always pop in on her and see how she's doing right?"

"Yes, Brooke, you can visit your sister anytime you want."

When would she leave?"

"Tomorrow, she will leave with them when they head out."

"How long will she be there?"

"That will be up to her, so as long as she feels she needs to stay."

"Who's going to take care of her and protect her, what about her nightmares?"

"Alpha Tate and Beta Benjamin will be responsible for her. I told them if a hair on her body is touched, they and whoever touched her will be dealing directly with me," my mom smirked.

"Ouch, I would hate to be them if anything happens to her," Brooklyn grinned.

"Doc Carter is working on getting her medical file sent over to Black Diamond's head doctor. I would expect her to be taking good care of Brinley as well or she'll be dealing with my consequences too."

"Yikes Mom, talk about bringing out Mamma Wolf," she laughed.

"She's my baby girl and I have a right to be protective of her just like I would if it was you or Jaxon."

"Okay, well, tell me how I can help."

"You can help by helping your sister pack tomorrow."

She raised her hand to her head and saluted, "Yes ma'am."

"Mom, Dad, thank you for taking the time to talk with us about this. What does Doc Carter say about her going?" Essie looked at me with a shine in her eyes before looking back to Jaxon. I think she was on the verge of crying.

"He thinks it's a good idea too. He's been in contact with their pack doctor explaining everything."

"Wait, hold up, did you say everything as in 'ev... 'ry... thing?'

"Yes son, 'ev... 'ry... thing' and he sent her medical file over. Their doctor needed all the information to take care of her."

"So their doctor knows what happened and about her powers?"

"Yes son, the doctor needed to know. Their doctor is under doctor-patient privilege and knows if any of this gets out without it coming from Brinley herself, she will be held accountable to us."

"Goddess help her if she doesn't stay true to that. If you and Dad don't put her in her place then Brin will," he laughed.

"So what can I do to help?"

"You, my son, need to assemble a security detail who will be going with her. Aside from the elites we've already sent to help their border patrol, we want about four elite enforcers to be your sister's protective detail. Since our master elite trainers are also enforcers, I want you to put four of the best we have on her as their assignment."

"I'm on it, may we be excused?"

"Yes you may, one more thing before you go, don't say anything to your sister yet, we want to inform her."

"Are you telling her about her security detail too?"

"Yep."

"Well, have fun with that conversation," he smirked, "I wouldn't want to be near that conversation with a ten-foot pole."

"Me neither."

"Let's go Little Sister, I've got some work to do."

"So do I but I can't help her pack until Mom and Dad talk with her."

He reached for her hand but I stopped them before they left. "Son, who are you thinking about sending with her as her detail?"

"Probably Erik, Jacob, Phillip, and Max. Since they aren't mated we don't need to worry about sending any mates with them."

"Good choices, she should agree to the security detail since it will be them. Besides, they are some of the only ones who can match her strength and skill when she gets her strength back."

Brooklyn gave him a funny look, "Have fun telling the boys they're on Peanut duty."

"Thanks, Little Sis, I'm sure they'll be thrilled about it."

"Can we be dismissed now?"

"Yes, goodnight you two. We love you."

"We love you too." Brooklyn bounced out of the room as Jaxon chased after her making her laugh as he caught up with her.

"We have some pretty great kids."

"Yes, we do. Thank you for giving them to me," Essie leaned in and kissed me.

## BRINLEY

I was so exhausted from the nightmare, I was happy to stay in my room for dinner. Although I did want to meet the alpha and beta, I was happy for the reprieve. Before falling asleep I took my meds and had a much-needed restful sleep. I woke up to someone knocking on my door.

"It's us Baby Girl."

I rolled my eyes at myself wishing my senses were working, I would've known it was them. I grabbed a hair tie and wrapped my long blonde curly hair in a messy bun, threw on some shorts, and padded to the door.

"Good morning."

"Good morning."

"May we come in for a conversation?"

I nodded my head and stepped aside as a big yawn hit me.

"How did you sleep?"

"I slept very well, no nightmares," I said with a huge smile on my face.

"That's so good to hear," my parents wrapped me in a warm hug.

"Brin, why don't we sit down so we can talk," Dad said gesturing to my couch.

I led them to it while wringing my hands together. I had a feeling I knew what they were going to talk about. I'm hoping they and the alpha and beta have agreed to let me leave with them. I must have had a worried look on my face as my mom reached out to me and patted my hands, "It's going to be okay Baby Girl."

I took a deep breath in and blew it out ready for whatever outcome and decision had been made.

## ALPHA ZANE

Looking at my daughter with her worried look, I feel all these emotions rising inside me. I know what we are about to tell her will bring her joy in the sense she will be able to step away from the daily reminder of what happened to her, to us, and hopefully bring her healing. I also know she's going to be a pissed-off she-wolf as soon as we tell her she's going to have a security detail assigned to her.

"Pumpkin, your mom and I have talked with Doc Carter, we have agreed to let you go with the alpha and beta," her mouth dropped open in shock. "We have also talked with Alpha Tate and Beta Benjamin, they agreed you can leave with them."

She looked between us, "Are you serious! I can go, you're going to let me leave?"

"Yes, we have. It's something you want to do and we feel if this will help you heal then we will do everything we can to make that possible."

"You need to know we asked Doc Carter to send your medical file over to their head doctor. Doctor Stevens knows everything about you, what happened, and your powers. She is under doctor/patient confidentiality and will not share your information. She will incur the wrath of your mother if any of that information gets out."

She looks at her mother and smirks like her siblings did, "Poor woman if she messes up, wouldn't want to be in her shoes."

I chuckled at that then got serious again. "Pumpkin, there are a few things you need to know."

"What?" she asked cautiously.

"They have been getting hit with rogue attacks almost daily and because of this, we are sending a security detail with you." I cringed after I got that out because I knew what was coming next.

"What... the... hell... Dad! I don't need a fucking security detail on me while I'm there! I can take care of myself! I'm strong, I've been training, and I still have my wits and powers! Who the hell is going to be my detail!?"

"Calm down, Jaxon is working on it." She got up and stormed around her room and started throwing things, tossing things out her window, then stalks to her punching bag. She starts hitting the punching bag she has hung up there then turns her icy blue eyes on me, but I'm not looking at Brinley anymore, I'm looking at Amanda.

"*I don't want to scrap with you daughter,*" my wolf, Charlie, says as he pushes forward. Amanda uses Brinley's body and stalks over to me, so I push my alpha aura on her to calm her down. I don't like to use my aura on my kids and have only needed to do it a few times. I can visibly see Amanda calm down and bow her head.

"*I'm not going to scrap with you Father, I'm sorry. I was able to push in front of Brinley, shove her back, and block her. I don't like forcing her to relinquish control but I want to let you know I appreciate the security detail. Brinley likes to think she's stronger than she is, but she isn't. She hasn't been training except with the juniors, she's lost a lot of strength because of the trauma, so thank you for allowing us to go.*"

Amanda gave control back and Brinley was pissed off, "what did she say?"

"Amanda and Charlie had a conversation, that is between them. If you want to know, you can stop blocking her and ask her."

She crossed her arms and humphed.

## BRINLEY

Amanda took over, shoved me back, and blocked me. I didn't appreciate it and was pretty pissed at her for doing it. I guess I kind of deserved it though, that's what I've been doing to her for the past five years. She doesn't deserve it and now that I've had a taste of it, I need to apologize.

*"Andi?"*

*"Yes?"*

*"I'm sorry I've blocked you out for so long. I didn't realize how much I was hurting you until you did it back to me."*

She was lying down in my mind and I could see and feel the tears in her eyes. *"It hurts me so much, Brin. You get to see my brother and sister in human and wolf form all the time. I can only watch from the inside when you let the block down. Imagine how it would feel to you if you could never be with them."*

I cried and it felt so damn good to let those tears I've bottled up inside me slide down my face. I felt arms around me and forgot my parents were still with me. "Baby Girl, we want everything to be okay with you, we will move mountains for you if we can. We will miss you but know we are only a few hours away. Your brother and sister can pop in anytime to see you too."

"Thank you for trusting me to go with them. Although I'm more than pissed about the detail. I do understand where you're coming from."

My mom squeezed my arm, "We just want to keep you as safe as possible, especially since they are still having rogue attacks."

My dad kissed my head, "Your sister is going to come help you pack and your brother is setting up your detail as we speak.

It's 8:00 am, how about you have breakfast, call Brooklyn to help you pack and you guys can head out after lunch, say 1:00 or 2:00 pm. We'll let Alpha Tate and Beta Benjamin know when you'll be ready."

"Thank you for letting me do this. I feel deep in my heart and soul this is what we need. I don't know why, but I do."

"You're welcome, we love you so much."

They left and I linked my sister. *"Hey Sis, wanna come help me pack?"*

*"Hell yeah, I do!"* I hear her say and she bursts through my door. I cling to her and tell her how much I love her for supporting me in this journey I feel I need to be on. Although I have no idea why or what was in store for me.

# Chapter 4 Leaving Winter Moon

**TATE**

I was getting my stuff together when there was a knock on my door, "Alpha Zane, Luna Estelle, what brings you here this early?"

"May we come in?"

"By all means. I was just packing, but please come in."

"Thank you," Luna Estelle said. "My mate and I just finished speaking with our daughter. We told her we agreed to let her go with you and Beta Benjamin. She's packing her bags now, but we wanted to let you know we will be sending a security detail with her for her safety."

"That's fine, I would expect nothing less."

"I'm happy to have your support in this regard. When my daughter is firing at full capacity, she is a force to be reckoned with and they are pretty much the only ones besides her siblings, who can match her skills when sparring. She is the youngest of our triplets, aside from us and her siblings, the men on her security detail are very protective of her."

"We are hoping for two things while she's there. One she will heal and two she will start training again. Her detail will consist of four of our master elite enforcers. They all grew up training together so they know how to push her boundaries. We don't want anyone else training her and we ask that she train in a private building, if you have a location available on your pack land. If you don't have a secure enclosed building, we will have one built for you," Alpha Zane smiled.

"We do have a building she can train in but I'll need to check if it's secure. Can I ask why she needs a secure location?"

"You can, but we are not disclosing that information right now. If she wants to disclose it she can."

"Ben and I were thinking about heading out right after breakfast. Is that alright with you?"

"We'd like her to stay through lunch to be sure she has everything she needs and give her time to say goodbye to her friends and some of the younger pups she is close with."

"Maybe around 1:00 pm then?"

"I think between 1:00 – 2:00 pm would be good."

"I will let Ben know we'll be heading out at that time. Will her security detail follow us there or will they come later?"

"They will be following behind you and she'll be with them."

"We will see you for lunch," they turned to leave but before they exited Luna Estelle turned with concern on her face, "Alpha Tate, her senses aren't working properly so she won't know when someone is approaching her from behind, hence the importance of her detail, please keep that in mind while she's in your pack."

"Yes ma'am, we will take every precaution we can."

"Thank you, that is all I can ask." They walked out and closed the door behind them.

*"Ben, can you come to my room?"*

*"Sure, what's up?"*

*"I'll tell you when you get here."*

He walked in a few minutes later, "The Alpha and Luna were just here. They confirmed their daughter will be coming with us and she's bringing four enforcers with her as her detail. Can you call Quincy and ask her to prepare a room for their daughter and her security?"

"Sure, anything else?"

"Yes, I want them on the alpha floor since it's the most secure floor in the packhouse. They also asked if we have a secure enclosed building for her to train in. I was thinking about the meeting hall since it hasn't been used in several years but wasn't sure what condition it's in or if it's even secure. Can you have one of our warriors check it out?"

"Yep, anything else?"

"No, I think that's all."

"Okay, I'll get right on it."

"Thanks."

"You're welcome Alpha."

"Wait two more things, we'll be leaving after lunch between 1:00 –2:00 pm, and her senses aren't working properly. She can't even tell when someone is walking up behind her."

"That's very odd. I wonder if it has to do with whatever happened to her and her not shifting."

"Maybe," we both shrugged.

"We'll be meeting her at lunch so I guess we'll see if she notices us walking in the dining room."

"I guess we'll see what she's all about in a couple of hours then. I hope she's as nice as the rest of her family." With a shrug of my shoulders, I left him to pack. *I need to call Quincy and give her a heads-up. I know she'll want to latch on to her as soon as she arrives since she doesn't have anyone close to her in the packhouse besides Doc Stevens.*

## BRINLEY

After spending the morning with Brooke packing, we were getting ready to head to the dining room for lunch when Jaxon came running into my room. "Can't you knock first? I could've been in the middle of dressing!" I yelled at him.

"Seriously Baby Sis, like I care what you look like naked, it's not like we haven't seen each other without clothes on before." This is true because we shift so often, nudity isn't anything to us. Granted, we don't walk around the packhouse or pack lands naked but people are always shifting to and from their wolf forms so you always see someone naked any given time of the day. We just don't pay it any attention.

"I want to let you know who your security detail is going to be. I'm assigning Erik, Phillip, Jacob, and Max," he grinned. "I thought you would prefer guys we grew up with, who know your powers, and who you could kick their asses when you're back up to strength."

I ran to him and jumped in his arms, "Thank you, I love those four guys and I love you too," I gave him a big sloppy kiss on his cheek and ruffled his messy hair before he put me down.

"I love you too, Baby Sis," he kissed my cheek. "One more thing, and before you say 'no' I want you to hear me out."

I rolled my eyes at him and put my hands on my hips "What do you want?" He looked at Brooke with pleading eyes, she nodded at him.

"Branson and Maya want to say goodbye to you and Andi," he said with a scrunched-up face like he was waiting for me to punch him in the face.

I dropped my head, heaved in a big breath, and blew it out, "Give me a minute to talk with her. *Andi, do you think you can take over without shifting and not blocking me out this time?"*

*"Brins, I love you, and I love that you are giving me a chance to be with my siblings. I would love to be able to shift and be with them but I know you're not ready for that yet. Do you think we could go to our hiding spot so we don't get interrupted?"*

*"Mom and Dad are expecting us for lunch so we can meet the alpha and beta and get some lunch before we leave, but if you promise to not block me, then I can let you have this moment with them."*

*"Thank you Brins, you are the best human a wolf could ever have. I love you."*

*"You're the best wolf I could ever have. I love you too, I wish I could give you more right now."*

*"It will come in time, I have a feeling this will be a good move for us."*

*"I do too."*

My eyes cleared up, I looked at my siblings and with a smirk on my face, "I'll race you to our spot!" and I took off running. I heard my brother and sister running behind me as we raced out of the packhouse and into the woods. When we reached our spot, I linked our parents, *"Mom, Dad?"*

*"Yes, Baby Girl?"* Mom said. *"Your triplets won't be at lunch, we wanted a little bit of time together to say goodbye to each other, all six of us."*

*"Are you letting Amanda out?"* Dad asked excitedly.

*"No, she agreed to come forward but not shift."*

*"I'll put a lunch together for you so you can eat on the road."*

*"Thank you, Mom, I would appreciate it."*

*"You're welcome Baby Girl."*

## WOLF TRIPLETS

I was so excited Brinley was going to let me see Branson and Maya. I haven't seen them in five years, not since that tragic night. I pushed forward and saw Branson and Maya in their wolf forms. My heart aches because I can't run and play with them but I will take anything at this point. I know leaving will be good for us, I can feel it in my bones.

*"Andi? Are you with us or daydreaming again?"* I heard them say at the same time. *"Sorry, I was lost in thought, not daydreaming."* I rolled my eyes.

*"I wish you could come out fully and play with us, we miss you,"* Maya says as she lays her head in my lap. I reached out and petted her between her ears. She was always so soft there. Branson came over and laid his head on my lap, too. He prefers to have his ears massaged so I rubbed his ears.

*"Oooh, Baby Sis, please don't stop. I always love it when you massage my ears. You always know just where to pet and how to soothe us."*

I'm going to miss them so much. Looking down at them with love in my eyes and heart, *"How often do you think you might be able to visit me?"*

*"We can visit as often as you want, well, Brooky can just pop in anytime, but Jaxon will need to check with Dad first since he's pretty much running the pack without the title."*

*"I'm sure Dad will hand the pack over soon. Mom's been hounding him for a long time about retiring."*

*"I know, he wants us to find our mate first, he says we'll be stronger with a mate by our side. I'm glad Mom hasn't tried to play matchmaker with other she-wolves."*

*"You are lucky in that regard, she's been trying to match Brooke with some of her friends' sons,"* Maya said with a laugh. *"She knows Brooke's time will come eventually, but she mostly does it to get her friends off her back. They want their sons out of their hair and are trying to bypass the mate bond to do it."* She puts her paws over her eyes and shakes her head.

*"Hey kids, it's one o'clock, you need to start heading back to the packhouse,"* Mom linked us.

*"We'll be there soon."* Branson and Maya shifted back and Amanda gave control back to Brinley.

*"Thank you for letting me spend time with them."*

*"You're welcome, thank you for honoring my wish. I love you, Andi."*

*"I love you, too Brins."*


### BRINLEY

I looked at my siblings and grabbed their hands in mine, "One last time before I leave?" I questioned them with a smirk on my face and my eyebrows lifted.

"Absolutely."

We held each other's hands and in a short second our hands were glowing and a white light appeared between us. An image of a woman formed in our circle. She has long white hair with a billowing long dress. Her icy blue eyes, just like ours, are shining down on us. Then a sweet, melodic voice spoke to us.

"My children, my special triplets, my chosen ones. It has been a while since you have called me."

Jaxon spoke for us, "Brinley and Amanda will be parting soon, and we wanted to thank you for giving us to each other and our wolves to us."

"No need to thank me, you are precious to me and blessed by me. Brinley has endured a lot over the last several years. It is time for her to heal but she needs to do that on her own. As she and I discovered, I cannot help with that. This time away will allow her to do so. If you need me while you are separated, you know how to reach me."

"Thank you, Moon Goddess."

"I love you, my children." Then she disappeared. The white glow vanished in the middle of our circle but the glow of our hands was still there when a bright white light appeared to be wrapping itself around our wrists. In a whisper on the wind, we heard, "I bind you together, you will be strong apart but stronger when you are together." The bright white glow on our wrists vanished and the glow on our hands left as we unclasped them, I also felt warmth spread through me.

"Well, that was weird," Brooklyn said as we all rubbed our wrists. They didn't hurt but there was a white tattoo on our wrists that looked like the stages of the moon with each of our wolves next to them. "She gave us matching tattoos," we said in unison.

Jaxon looked at me with shock in his eyes, "Brooklyn, look," he pointed at me.

"Oh, my goddess." Her eyes were big and round and her mouth was hanging open.

"I'm freaking out here, guys. What are you staring at?"

"It's your mating mark, it's gone."

"What!? How can it be gone? I need a mirror so I can see." My mating mark had been fading over the last five years but to have it completely gone, how did that happen?

We looked at each other, "Selene removed it."

"Not much can be done about it now, I wish she would've asked before just removing it, though."

"You didn't feel anything when she removed it?" Jax questioned me.

"I felt a warm sensation run through me, other than that, no. I wonder why she would remove it."

"Not sure Baby Sis," Jax shrugged his shoulders, "we better get going before Mom sends someone to find us." Brooke and Jax got dressed and as we left our special cave, I looked back, hoping I was making the right decision.

# CHAPTER 5 FIRST IMPRESSIONS

**BRINLEY**

By the time we got back to the packhouse, the guys were already loading my luggage and theirs into the SUV. We walked over to my parents and I embraced them in a tight hug and cried. "I'm going to miss you so much," I sobbed with snot running from my nose.

"Pumpkin, we are only a phone call away or a three-hour drive. Your brother and sister can pop in anytime to see you and you'll have the guys there to keep you company too plus some of our warriors."

"I know Dad, it's just, the reality of me leaving is hitting harder than I thought it would."

Mom wiped the tears and snot from my face, "We love you and only want what's best for you. You want to try this and see if it helps you heal so that's what we want for you too. You can always come back home."

I just nodded my head, "I know, I can be strong, I can do this."

Mom looked at all three of us and then noticed our wrists, "what are these marks on your wrists?"

My eyes found my siblings and we looked around cautiously before deciding to mind-link, we didn't want anyone overhearing us. *"The Moon Goddess visited us while we were out. She blessed us, she said we are strong apart but will be stronger together then these tattoos appeared binding us to each other. We have no idea what it means though."*

*"She also removed Brin's mating mark,"* Brooke told them.

*"Well, isn't Selene full of surprises,"* she said in our link while chuckling out loud.

"Well Pumpkin, are you ready to head out?" Dad asked.

"Yes, I am."

"We put a cooler in the SUV with some lunch and snacks for you."

"Thank you, I am getting hungry. Please thank the kitchen staff for me."

"Where's Alpha Tate and Beta Benjamin?"

"They'll be out in a few minutes, they wanted to give you a few minutes alone with us before they came out."

"That is very sweet of them to consider my feelings."

"Yes it is, but I may have threatened them with castration if they didn't give me some time to say goodbye to my youngest pup," Mom said as she held me tight in her arms. She reluctantly let me go so I could hug my dad, Jax and Brooke. I climbed into the SUV and shut the door with tears running down my cheeks.

Erik climbed in the driver's seat, Phillip climbed in the passenger seat, and Jacob and Max flanked me in the back seat. After we got settled in, Alpha Tate and Beta Benjamin made their way outside. I still have yet to meet them but I guess I'll meet them when we get to their pack lands. I saw them saying their goodbyes to my parents and siblings, they climbed in their car and took off.

"Are you ready to leave Peanut? It's just after 2:00 so we should be arriving there around 5:00," Erik said while looking back at me in the rearview mirror.

"Ready as I'll ever be, Cracker Jacks," I laughed. I grabbed the cooler and pulled out my food. I fell asleep shortly after fending off extra fingers from trying to take my cookies.

## TATE

As we got closer to pack lands Quinn linked me with an irritated and aggressive voice. *"Alpha, there is an issue on the alpha floor, we need you and Benjamin to handle it as soon as you get back."*

*"What the hell is going on, why do you sound like you're ready to punch someone?"*

*"Probably because I am, in about two seconds. Fucking Maribel, she noticed we were setting up the guest rooms on the alpha floor and poked her nose where it didn't belong and someone, I don't know who let it slip you were bringing back a female she-wolf."*

*"After we left your floor, I decided to put a vase of flowers in her room. When I got back up there, all the rooms were a total disaster and that fucking bitch had a sadistic look on her face. I scowled at her, called "all hands on deck" to fix the rooms, and locked the doors behind me. I'm still trying to figure out who let her on the alpha floor and who told her you were bringing a she-wolf back with you."*

*"We'll deal with that issue when we get there. We're about ten minutes out from the gate. Try to keep her in the packhouse please."*

*"Oh, don't worry, she's parked in front of your suite and isn't moving for nobody but you."*

"Fucking great, the last thing I want to deal with is that bitch. She needs to be put in her place and since she isn't taking the hint that I don't want to be with her, then maybe alpha commanding her to stay away will work," I growled.

"Hey, you okay?" Benjamin asked.

"No, I'm not fucking okay. That bitch of a whore, thinks she can do whatever she wants just because she has beta blood. I haven't even had a chance to meet Brinley yet and she's going to be walking into a tornado with Maribel." I took my frustration out by hitting the steering wheel and putting a little dent in it.

"Sorry Tate, I wish I could help you with that situation."

"Oh, don't worry, you're helping me. You're going to keep me from ripping her head off. If she doesn't know what's good for her, she will stay away from the packhouse while Brinley is here. I wish I could banish her but she hasn't done anything yet that is punishable by banishment."

When we pulled up to the front of the house, I put the car in park, jumped out, and ran up the stairs to the alpha floor to deal with Maribel. Goddess help me from going batshit crazy on the bitch. I had steam coming out of my ears when I reached the top of the stairs and could feel Chase right on the surface and Benjamin not too far behind me.

"Maribel!" I yelled with ferocity in my voice. "What the hell are you doing on my floor!" She dares to try and look at me with innocent eyes.

"What do you mean Tate, I'm not doing anything wrong," she says with a sweet voice that felt like claws scraping on a chalkboard and batting her eyes at me.

"It's ALPHA to you, do not EVER call me by my first name AGAIN!" I roared at her with the help of Chase. This time with my alpha voice I got in her face and yelled, "What the hell are you doing on MY FLOOR! Answer me!"

"I uh um heard you were bringing someone back with you and wanted to greet them and make them feel welcome."

I glared at her and with a low growly voice, "How do you expect to make them feel welcome when you destroy their rooms!"

"I... I... I didn't destroy their rooms, I don't know how that happened," she tried to say with a shaky voice.

"MARIBEL!"

"Fine, you want to know why?" She put her hands on her hips, pointed a finger in my face, and yelled back. "I did it because you are mine and no one else's! You can't bring another she-wolf into this packhouse and put her on YOUR fucking floor without ME letting HER know that YOU belong to ME!"

Benjamin stepped in, "Maribel, you will watch your tone with Alpha Tate if you know what's good for you!"

She turned her pissed-off gaze to Benjamin and just screamed in his face. "YOU ARE NOT A PART OF THIS CONVERSATION, SO STAY THE HELL OUT OF IT ASSHOLE!"

Ben was about two seconds from strangling her. So much for him keeping me from ripping her head off, looks like I need to keep him from doing it. "Maribel, listen and listen closely. I DO NOT need YOUR permission to bring ANYONE, regardless of who they are, into MY packhouse. Let alone, into the guest rooms, ON MY GODDAMN MOTHERFUCKING FLOOR! DO I MAKE MYSELF CLEAR?"

"I DO NOT belong to you, we are NOT in a relationship, nor do I want to be in one with you, EVER!" She's cowering at this point, her lips pouting and tears running down her face, I don't give a shit though. "Get out of this packhouse and back to your home Maribel! If I see you on my floor again, without invitation, you will be punished severely! DO I MAKE MYSELF CLEAR!"

"Yes Alpha," she said as she was skirting herself to the stairs.

"One more thing Maribel, when you leave, go through the back entrance. I do not want our guests to feel unwelcome with your presence and you will leave our guests alone, in fact, I don't want you anywhere near or inside the packhouse while they are here!"

After that confrontation, I needed a stiff drink, shower, and a little time to decompress before finally meeting Brinley and her security detail. "You want to head to my office for a drink?"

"After that, yes I do."


## BRINLEY

"Hey, time to wake up Peanut," I heard Max saying as he shook me slightly. I slowly woke up rubbing my eyes. I stretched with a big yawn and lay back down on Jacob's lap. I'm so exhausted from the morning's events, that I just want to sleep. "Hey Peanut, you need to wake up, we've just arrived at Black Diamond. You fell asleep about thirty minutes into our drive, and you didn't have a nightmare."

With a groggy voice, I looked up at him, "Really?"

"Yes. Now, will you sit up please so we can get out of the SUV and unload everything?"

"Fine, but I'm helping to carry our stuff inside."

"We figured you would," he grinned. Once we exited the vehicle, we went around back taking our luggage out and a couple of people came running over to our car, grabbing our stuff.

"Hello, my name is Sheila, I've been assigned to help you get settled, can I take your things for you?"

"It's okay Sheila, we can handle it."

"Please let me assist, it's the least I can do."

"Thank you, that's very kind of you." She tried to grab my backpack but I took it from her and put it on, "I'll keep this with me if you don't mind," I smiled at her. We walked around the side of the car and I noticed the alpha and beta were nowhere in sight but two other people were waiting at the bottom of the steps. One of the women looked relaxed and the other looked like she was about ready to jump out of her skin.

"Hi, I'm Beta Quincy, Beta Benjamin's mate, and wife but please call me Qiunn or Q for short, it's nice to finally meet you."

Quincy seems very nice, she has short black hair, brown eyes, and a smile that reaches her ears. She's on the shorter side for a she-wolf, about 5'3. I reached out and shook her hand, holding it a little longer than I needed to. "It's nice to meet you too. I'm Brinley, this is Erik, Phillip, Jacob, and Max."

"I'm sorry Alpha Tate and Beta Benjamin weren't able to stick around, they needed to take care of something as soon as they returned. I'm sure you'll be meeting them later," Quincy says as she then points to the other lady. "This is Doctor Crystal Stevens."

"It's a pleasure to meet you, you and I will be getting acquainted in the next few days."

"It's nice to meet you too," I shook her hand a little longer than I should have. They guys shook her hand next and I noticed Max and the doctor's body language change as soon as they touched and looked at each other and she blushed. I need to ask him about that later. I have a hunch about those two.

"Why don't you follow me and I'll show you to your rooms and you can freshen up," Beta Quincy pulled me from my thought.

"Thank you, that would be great." All five of us went into the packhouse and were escorted to our rooms. Entering the packhouse, I was impressed, it's not as big as the one I grew up in but it's a good size for the smaller pack. It's three stories and the foyer is large with a staircase leading upstairs and at the top of each floor it splits to the left and right. We were escorted to the alpha floor on the third level.

"Brinley, this is your room, I hope it will be satisfactory for you."

"Thank you, I'm sure it will be just fine."

"If you men follow me, I'll show you to your room next." She led the boys to their room, across the hall from mine. "I'll be back in about thirty minutes to give you a tour of the packhouse, in the meantime, why don't you get settled and put your belongings away."

I nodded at her, looked at the boys, shut my door, and started to put my stuff away. My room is beautiful, it has a large bed, en-suite, and balcony with a view of the pool with the hills behind it. It's breathtaking. As promised, Beta Quincy came back thirty minutes later. As we were leaving our rooms she pointed at the end of the hallway.

"That's Alpha Tate's suite, if you need anything you can go to him or come to our suite on the second floor. He also has a private dining room on this floor as well." We headed to the second floor and it felt like I was being watched but I didn't see anyone so I shook it off. "This is our suite and down the other corridor are the gamma and delta suites, we don't have a gamma yet but are hoping to find one soon and we've never had a delta, at least not when Alpha Fredrick was alpha."

"Didn't you have a gamma before the takeover?"

"We did, but he stepped down just the same as our former beta did. He didn't want his good-for-nothing daughter taking the position so we are currently looking for a new one," changing the topic, she added, "We also have all of our offices on this floor with a private dining room."

"The first floor is where all the action is."

I looked at her curiously, "all the action?"

"Yep, all the action. Our kitchen, communal dining hall, warriors and omegas' rooms, locker room, gaming room, and entertainment room including a theater are all on this floor. Hence 'all the action.' Let's head outside and I'll show you our training pitches and where you'll be training." The compound grounds were beautiful, with lots of trees, and a huge swimming pool, and down the hill were the training pitches and a run-down building.

Quincy dropped her voice, "Even though we've only just met, I like you. I hope we can become friends, it sure would be nice to have another woman around here who isn't trying to get into the alpha's pants. I can't speak for Crystal, but I'm pretty sure she'd welcome you into our two-person group with open arms too."

"It would be nice having friends here since my siblings can't be here all the time."

"I've had fun showing you guys around. The small talk we've been having is nice and comical too. You wouldn't think the banter coming from the five of you would be acceptable with an alpha female but you're digging at them as much as they are giving it to you."

"Don't let it fool you, we've been friends for years. We know each other and we don't hold rank over our pack members unless we are amongst outsiders."

"Good to know. We're heading toward the building we believe will work for you but I have my reservations. The building hasn't been used in years and it's kind of run down. You don't think it will work either, do you?"

"Why would you say that?"

"Because of the look on your face," she laughed.

"This is the only building we have for you to train in. We weren't sure if it would work for what you need."

I barely heard what Quincy said, because as we were approaching the building, I could still feel a set of eyes digging into my back. I looked around but didn't see anyone. "Peanut," Max says in a low voice, "what's going on? you stiffened up."

"I'm not sure Roo, I felt someone watching me when we were in the packhouse but brushed it off and it feels like that same person is digging daggers into my back."

He stopped and stared at me, "what? You sensed something... that's amazing, maybe getting off pack lands is already helping you."

"Maybe," I shrugged.

"Keep vigilant and let's check this dilapidated building out."

"Yeah, good idea. It doesn't look secure enough though, Dad said he'd have a new one built if I needed it and I think I need it." I linked the guys, *I think I need to contact Brooklyn. Roo, can you stay inside with me while the three of you take Quinn outside and secure the perimeter.*

*"Will do Peanut,"* Erik says. I watched him step over to Quincy, "Do you mind if we step outside for a minute? Brinley needs to get a 'feel' for the building."

"Sure," she said as they stepped outside.

## BROOKLYN

I'm sitting and stewing in Jax's apartment. "So, do you think sending Brin to Black Diamond truly was a good idea?"

"I don't like being separated from her, but if she feels that deeply about this helping her then I'll support her in it."

"I will too, it's just that I'm getting some odd feelings from her."

"I was beginning to wonder if it was just me because I'm getting some odd feelings too."

I felt that familiar tingle in my head and now in my wrist where Selene bound us. "Uh Jax, is your wrist tingling?"

"Yeah, it is, it's really weird."

"I think Brin's is trying to contact me because my head is tingling and then my wrist started to. Didn't Selene say we're now stronger even when we're apart?"

"She said something like that."

"Okay, hold my hand and concentrate on our bond, I want to try something."

We close our eyes and focus on our bond. When we opened our eyes, we were standing inside some kind of building, looking at my sister and Max. My eyes are wide open, "I can't believe that worked, how did that work?"

"Brooky!" My sister yelled and ran to me, "Wait, how were you able to bring Jax with you?"

"We were in his room when you were reaching out to me, our wrists started to tingle so I thought I'd try to bring both of us to you." Max is just staring at us with his mouth open. "Close your mouth, Max, it's not like you haven't seen me apparate before."

"I know, but I've never seen you bring someone with you."

"That, my friend, is something I didn't know I could do either. I think I'm only able to do it because of the binding Selene did," Brooklyn had a huge smile on her face. "Brin, why did you call us, are you hurt, are you okay, do you want to come home?"

"Brooklyn, it isn't anything like that. I need you guys to ask Dad to build a training arena for me. This is the only secure place they have and as you can see, it isn't very secure."

"No, it's not, I'll let him know when we get back." Jax is looking at me with a weird look on his face, "Something is different about you. What changed in the few hours you've been gone?"

"Nothing has changed, I'm still me."

"No, there's something."

"She fell asleep about thirty minutes after we left pack lands and didn't have a nightmare. When we were on the tour of the packhouse and grounds, she said it felt like someone was shooting daggers in her back," Max told them.

"Are you serious!" Both my siblings said at the same time.

"It's nothing, I'm sure it's a fluke, I haven't had my senses about me in a very long time."

"Brin, seriously, this is a HUGE ass deal, maybe Selene started the healing process when she gave us these," she said as she held up hers and Jax's wrists, "and removed your mating mark."

I shrugged, "Maybe."

"Hold up," Max says, "your mating mark is gone?"

"Yes, it is," I pulled my shirt collar down for him to see.

"You didn't think we needed to know about that?"

"I didn't see a reason why I needed to tell you."

"Seriously? We need to watch for guys who could be potential mates to you or who try to tell you they're your mate since you can't smell them."

"Oh, I uh, didn't think about that," I grimaced.

"Hold up Baby Sis, you said you felt someone staring at you?" Jax asked.

"Yes, but I looked around and didn't see anyone."

"You need to be careful, don't go anywhere without one of the guys."

"Jax, seriously, I'll be fine."

"Baby Sis, you need to remember, this pack gets hit by rogues often. Just be safe and be careful please."

"Okay, fine, I'll make sure someone is with me all the time."

"That is all I ask."

"We need to go, I hear Mom and Dad calling for us. We'll let Dad know about the building. We love you, Brin."

"I love you too."

"And watch your back, if you're having those feelings, reach out to us if and when you need us."

"I will," I smiled.

"By Max, you guys take care of our sister."

"You know we will."

Max and I left the building and walked to Erik, *"all good?"* he asked.

*"Yep, all good, Cracker Jacks. We'll talk about it when we get back to our rooms."* With a nod of his head, he got Quinn's and the other two guys' attention and we continued the tour.

# CHAPTER 6 GETTING READY

**QUINCY**

*"How's it going with the tour?"*

*"It's good, Alpha, we're at the training building right now, Brinley is inside with Max and the rest of us are outside waiting for them."*

*"That's weird, why would she need to be alone in there?"*

*"Not sure and I wasn't about to question an alpha she-wolf."*

*"She's harmless Q, you don't need to walk on eggshells around her."*

*"Who says I'm walking on eggshells!? I'm giving her the privacy she asked for without questioning her!" I yelled. "They're on their way out, I'm closing the link."*

*"Hold up, it's almost 7:00 pm, we're having dinner in my dining room at 8:00 pm. Why don't you guys head back to the packhouse so they can freshen up for dinner."*

"Aye, aye captain," I salute even though he can't see me.

"The alpha just linked me, he says dinner will be at 8:00 pm in his private dining room. We'll head back to the packhouse so you all can freshen up for dinner. If you're feeling up to it, we can finish the tour tomorrow."

"That sounds great, I would love to see the rest of the grounds and I would like to shower before dinner," Brinley says with a bright smile on her face, "and I'm looking forward to finally meeting the alpha and beta."

"You haven't met them yet?"

"Actually, no I haven't, extenuating circumstances prevented me from doing so while they were at my pack."

"Well, let's get cleaned up and I'll introduce you."

"Fantastic!" She linked arms with me and we headed back.

*"I do like this girl, Kaylee. Do you sense anything from her wolf?"*

*"No, I don't. She's either holding their aura in or she's not well."*

*"I hope she's just holding in their aura. Brinley seems like a very nice person and I'll bet her wolf is just the same."*

*"I can't wait to meet her, maybe once she gets settled you can see if she and Crystal want to shift so we can go for a run and show her the pack border."*

*"I think that's a wonderful idea, I will ask her once I get to know her better."*

## TATE

I was heading to my private dining room to make sure everything was set up for dinner when I ran into Crystal. "Hey Doc, have you had a chance to meet Brinley yet?"

"Just briefly when they arrived, I'm hoping to set up a meeting with her tomorrow so I can get to know her better. Reading about her in her medical file isn't the best way to know who she is as a person."

"That's very true, anything in her medical file I should be aware of?"

She gave me a stern look, "Nothing I'm allowed to disclose to you or anyone else for that matter. I'm under strict orders from her physician and her parents. If Brinley wants to talk then that's up to her"

"But I'm the alpha and she is a guest in our pack, I should know everything about her," irritation was creeping into my voice.

"You don't get to know everything medically about people just because you're the alpha. You still have a lot to learn and I'm not disclosing anything about her. If you want to know then ask her yourself, Alpha. Besides, didn't you get a chance to get to know her before agreeing she could stay with us?"

"I've not met her yet," I rubbed my hand down my face. "She didn't show up to any of the meals we had there and pretty much stayed in her room the entire time for reasons I do not know."

"Well mister, I guess you'll be meeting her now."

When we stepped inside the dining room, I smelled burnt marshmallows, *Maribel.* Chase growled as we walked in and there she was in the skimpiest black dress. Her tit's hanging out of the too-small top and her ass peeking out from the bottom of it, leaning against the bar with a smile on her face.

Crystal gave me a questioning look, *"No, she was not invited to this dinner I told her to stay away from the packhouse."*

*"She is such a spoiled little bitch, who does she think she is anyway, thinking she's yours."*

*"I don't know, she has this idea that I'm going to make her my chosen mate, and luna, I never did anything to give her that idea."*

*"Hopefully she gets the hint and stays away. That girl is trouble, and I heard she's been sleeping with just about anyone who has a dick between their legs. She needs to be put in her place and I hope someone calls her out on her bullshit actions and knocks her off her pedestal."*

*"You and I both hope that happens, Crystal. She doesn't like to obey my requests, since she's currently in MY fucking dining room."*

*"Hey Ben, where are you guys?"*

*"We're running late. Q and Brinley are having 'girl time' getting ready together for dinner. I think those two are going to be fast friends."*

*"I'm happy to hear that. It will be good for her to have another female to hang out with since Crystal is usually in the clinic."*

*"Yes it will, it will also keep her out of our hair too,"* Benjamin laughed. *"We should be there shortly."*

*"Can you stall for a few minutes? Maribel is in my dining room looking like a whore. I need to get a couple of warriors in here to escort her out the back way, I don't need her to see Brinley or her detail."*

*"Sure, we can hang out in my suite for a few before we head that way."*

*"Thank you, Ben."*

## BENJAMIN

I was getting ready in our suite when Quinn said she was heading to Brinley's room to help her get ready. I wasn't opposed to it since she's been starving for female company and if she stayed in our suite any longer we would've been late for dinner because I would've taken advantage of her nakedness. I love my mate and I've been trying to put a pup in her belly, taking every opportunity to try and do that too. I can't wait to see her rounded belly with my pup growing in it.

If I don't stop thinking about it, this dinner will be cut short and we won't be making it to dinner. Speaking of dinner, Tate and I still have yet to meet Brinley and I'm looking forward to it. From what her family and her detail have said, she's a very nice person, very down to earth, smart, strong, can be a smart ass, doesn't put up with shit, and will call someone out on their bullshit. She sounds like someone we can use around here.

*"Q?"*

*"Are you ladies almost ready?"*

*"Yep, we're on our way."*

*"Can you hurry, I'm starving."*

*"Don't get your panties in a bunch, we'll be there in a few minutes."*

*"I'm going to punish you later for saying that."*

*"Bring it on Mr. Beta, I like being punished by you."* My cock hardened in my pants and I wish we could skip dinner.

*"I will take great joy in punishing you too. Now, can I tell you what I need please?"*

*"Fine, what is it?"*

*"Tate wants us to hang out in our suite for a few minutes, and before you ask, he and Crystal found Maribel in the dining room not wearing much of a dress. He doesn't want her to see Brinley or her detail so she's getting escorted out of the packhouse."*

"Oh wow, she is such a bitch. Who the hell does she think she is? She destroys their rooms, then acts like she's still welcome here. Let me at her, I'll give her a piece of my fucking mind."

"Sweetheart, I appreciate your beta attitude but we don't want Brinley to be in the middle of whatever Maribel is up to."

"Benjamin, she's already in the middle of it. The difference is, she doesn't know it," she screamed.

"Well Sweetheart, let's try to keep it that way.."

"Fine, I don't agree with it. I think Brinley and her detail need to know but, whatever. If this blows up, I'm blaming you and Tate for the consequences and those consequences better not be her leaving. I like her and I want her to stay!" she yells again. "Brinley and I will grab the guys and head to our suite. You get to figure out how to entertain them until that bitch is thrown out of the packhouse."

"Yes Sweetheart, I'll see you in a few minutes."


## BRINLEY

Beta Quincy and I were getting ready for dinner in my room. It reminded me of when Brooklyn and I would get ready for parties together. It was nice having girl time. She was going through my closet, "I think you should wear this," she said coming out of my closet with my yellow sundress.

"That is one of my favorite dresses," I took it from her and slipped it on. "Beta Quincy, is Crystal involved with anyone?"

"Please call me Quincy, Quinn, or Q, no need for the formalities and, no, she's not. Why do you ask?"

"When we arrived today, I noticed she and Max held each other's hands a little longer than they should have and they both seemed to be conflicted."

"She isn't involved with anyone right now. She recently ended a three-year relationship about six months ago with one of our warriors, she found out he was cheating on her. Good riddance to him, that's all I gotta say. He was an asshole and didn't deserve her."

"She would be getting a great catch with Roo. I hope they are fated mates, he's been looking for his mate for a few years."

"Can I ask why you call him 'Roo'?"

I laughed, "When we were kids, his favorite character was Roo from Winnie-the-Pooh. He even dressed as Roo for Halloween three years in a row. I've been calling him that ever since."

"And he hasn't told you to stop?"

"Nope," I said, popping the p. "I have nicknames for all of them for various reasons and they call me 'Peanut' since I'm the youngest of my siblings."

"That's cute," she said, as her eyes clouded over.

# Chapter 7 Mate! Part 1

**QUINCY**

"Benjamin just linked me. He said Tate and Crystal were waiting for us. I told him we'd be there shortly."

"Let's get the guys and head to your suite."

I opened Brinley's door and her detail were about to knock on her door. "Perfect timing, let's go to my suite, get Benjamin, and head to the dining room."

"Ben, this is Brinley. Brinley, this is my mate, Benjamin but you can call him Ben."

"It's nice to meet you, Ben. This is Erik, Max, Jacob, and Phillip."

"It's nice to meet all of you. I hope your rooms are satisfactory."

"Our rooms are just fine, thank you. Quincy was able to show us around a little bit outside and gave us a quick tour inside the packhouse. We are hoping to finish the tour up tomorrow."

"That sounds like a great idea. We are nowhere near the size of your pack but it suits us. Shall we head to dinner?"

"Yes, please. I'm very hungry," Brinley giggled.

*"Q, she is so nice. Probably one of the nicest women I've met in a long time. I can see why you like her."*

*"I told you."*

## TATE

As soon as they got near the alpha floor, Chase was restless, *"Chase, what is wrong with you, settle down."*

*"Mate, I smell our mate, go to her, she needs us, she needs me to help her."*

*"What are you talking about, 'you need to help her,' what does that even mean?"*

*"I don't know. I can scent our mate but I can't feel her wolf, I need to help bring her forward."*

*"Chase, not sure how that's going to happen. She's suffered some trauma and hasn't shifted in years."*

*"What do you mean, what kind of trauma, why hasn't she shifted?"*

*"Weren't you listening when Alpha Zane and Luna Estelle were talking to us?"*

*"No, I was sleeping, I didn't want to hear about some she-wolf, boring."*

*"Well, that she-wolf was and is our mate,"* I said, matter of factly.

I can feel Chase getting agitated and an agitated alpha wolf is not a good thing. *"Chase, you need to calm down. I don't know what the trauma was but whatever happened it must've caused her wolf to recede. The only one who knows what happened right now is Doc Stevens and she's not talking."*

*"Stupid human, you're the alpha, command her to talk so we can help our mate."*

*"Chase, it's not that simple, and don't call Crystal stupid. I have to earn her trust for her to open up to us and I haven't even met her yet. I can't ask Doc Stevens to disclose medical information without permission, and I do not have permission."*

*"You better not mess this up or I won't ever talk with you again and I'll keep you blocked. We lost one mate and I will not let us lose another one. You need to keep her protected."*

*"Chase, she has master elite enforcers as her detail, they aren't going to let anything happen to her. Besides, she's one herself."*

*"Fine, but I'm going to try and keep her safe whether you like it or not."*

*"Whatever,"* I rolled my eyes. Right about that time, I smelled her fresh strawberry scent, I stiffened and was trying to calm Chase down.

## BENJAMIN

The second we entered the dining room Tate stiffened but he didn't turn around to greet us. I noticed his hands fist in his lap. I thought it'd be best to link him. *"Boss, are you okay? You stiffened up, fisted your hands, and look like you're about to lose control of Chase."*

*"Shit, shit, shit... that's because I am."*

*"Why, what's going on?"*

*"She's my mate,"* he said with gritted teeth.

*"Who? Brinley?"*

*"Yes, Brinley, who else would I be talking about?"*

*"I'm trying to keep Chase from saying anything because she doesn't know."*

*"Well, shit, I need to tell Quinn."*

*"Don't you dare say a fucking word to anyone, especially Q, she'd be all over this like bees on honey. I don't want anyone besides you and me to know. The last thing I need is for this to get out to the pack and for Maribel to get wind of it. She's such a dumbass, who knows what she would do. Besides, Brinley can't smell my scent and other things are going on with her I need to know about. I want her to discover the mating scent on her own,"* he sounded distraught.

*"Tate, you're going to need to talk with Chase to rein it in if you want her to discover this on her own."*

*"I know, and I will if I can get through this dinner."*

*"Otherwise, how are you feeling about getting a second chance mate?"*

*"Not sure yet, let me digest it first. We'll talk later in my office about it."*

*"Let's try to get through this meal,"* I said before closing the link.

## BRINLEY

When we reached the dining room, Alpha Tate nodded to Quinn and the guys before he stood up, shook my hand, and introduced himself. He held my hand a little longer than normal and sized me up, which I thought was weird, but whatever, it gave me a chance to feel him out too. Not to mention, I was more interested in what was happening between Max and Crystal. They were staring at each other, then I heard a very faint "mate" coming from Max's lips. Crystal was just staring at him with her eyes wide open.

## TATE

I stood and took Brinley's hand to introduce myself and as soon as our hands touched, there was a spark that shot up my arm and straight to my dick and it didn't help that she looked hot as hell in that dress that I'd like to rip off of her. Looking into Brinley's eyes, I noticed no recognition on her face. Chase laid down, covered his muzzle with his paws, and whimpered.

*"See, I need to help our mate,"* Chase said but I ignored him.

"Hi, you must be Alpha Tate?" She said in the sweetest voice and my name rolling off her tongue just made my dick stiffen more.

"Please call me Tate, no need for formalities."

She giggled, "Okay, Tate it is." She sat down looking between Crystal and one of her men, Max I think his name was.

*This is going to be the longest fucking dinner of my life.*

## MAX

When we entered the dining room, that unmistakable scent of vanilla and jasmine hit my nose again. Doc Stevens was sitting there staring at me. I knew she was my mate the second I scented her when we arrived but I needed to keep my focus on Brinley. She is who I'm here for and if I don't do my job protecting her then Alpha Zane will have my hide. So all I could do was acknowledge her for right now.

When I whispered "mate" I didn't think anyone heard me, but of course Brin would since I was pretty much standing next to her. With the look Doc Stevens gave me, she heard me too. Now she's staring at me with her eyes wide open. I'm not quite sure where to go from here.

"Roo," Brin said while elbowing me, "did you just say 'mate' to Crystal?"

"Uh, yeah, I didn't mean for that to come out of my mouth but Hudson couldn't contain himself."

"So are you going to sit and talk with her or just stand there staring at her?"

"Oh, um, well, I'm here for you so I should probably stay by your side."

"I'm pretty sure I'll be safe enough with a room full of capable men. Go sit next to your mate and get to know her."

"If you're sure."

"Oh, I'm sure, now git."

Walking over to Crystal, without my eyes leaving her sight, I sat down and Hudson pushed his way forward. I could tell his golden eyes were shining through by the way Crystal was looking at me. I could see her wolf peeking through too.

"Hi, Max, right?" Her voice was like an angel talking. My dick pulsated and I got uncomfortable quickly.

"Uh, yeah, Max."

"What's your wolf's name? I can see him trying to get through."

"Hudson, what's your wolf's name?"

"Kiara"

"Beautiful name, both of your names are beautiful," I'm sure my face was as red as hers was turning. "What do you say we get to know each other more after dinner?"

"That sounds good," she smiled.

We turned to the table and started eating with the rest of the group.

## CRYSTAL

"Brinley, are you available tomorrow for us to meet?"

"Uh, yeah sure, what time would you like to meet?"

"That depends, would you prefer to come to my office at the clinic or would you like to meet in the packhouse?"

"If you don't mind, can we meet in the packhouse? We didn't get a chance to tour the other buildings so I'm not sure where the clinic is. Quincy will be taking us around tomorrow to finish the tour."

"Do you want to meet around 10:00 am?"

"That would be perfect. Quincy, would you be able to show us around after I meet with Doc Stevens?"

"That would be just fine."

"I'll be sure to bring your medical file with me too."

Tate looked at Crystal before speaking up, "You're welcome to use the luna office if you'd like, it's not being used for anything."

*That was a strange offer.*

"Thank you Alpha, are you sure," I raised my eyebrow and gave him a questioning look.

"It's not like it's getting used. I'll have Sheila get it cleaned up before your meeting"

"Alright. Brinley, I'll stop by your room tomorrow morning at 10:00 and we can head to the luna office together."

"Sounds perfect," she smiled.

# Chapter 8 Getting Aquainted

**TATE**

After dinner, I pulled Benjamin into my office and locked the door. "So Brinley, huh?" Ben said with a smirk on his face before I could even say anything.

"That would explain the faint smell of fresh strawberries I picked up on at her packhouse."

"So what are you planning on doing?"

"I have no idea," I ran my hand over my face, "all I know right now is I'll have a lot of cold showers in my future. It's going to be so fucking hard keeping my distance from her and not having my way with her. I'm glad she has a protection detail, she's going to need them to keep me away from her."

"Don't you think you should let the guys know you're her mate?"

"Probably, but I'm not going to."

"Good luck with that. You don't tell them and they see you trying to corner her every chance you get, all four of them may jump you."

"Then I'll avoid her."

"Good luck with that too Alpha, she's living on your floor," he laughed. "So you're letting her use the luna office? Think that's a wise decision?"

"Why not, it's her office, she just doesn't know it yet."

"Maybe because Maribel has staked claim to it, unofficially."

"Maribel can fuck off, she's been informed to stay away from the packhouse."

"True, but Diane still frequents the packhouse. I'm sure word will get back to her faster than a fire could spread. Not to mention, she did make her way into your dining room this evening."

"Damnit, I forgot about that freeloader"

"Probably because you were thinking with your cock and not your brains," Ben muttered. "On another note, the pack is going to be over the moon when they find out we have a luna."

"Beta," my voice stern.

"I know, I know," he held his hands up, surrendering, "no one is allowed to know. You know me better than that, I can keep my fucking mouth shut."

"I want to find out what is going on with that woman. She's a mystery and Chase says we need to 'help her.' I have no idea what that means. Crystal knows everything, but she can't disclose it to me on the order of Alpha Zane and Luna Estelle and the doctor-patient confidentiality."

"So where does that leave us?"

"I have no idea."

"Maybe one of the guys will disclose some information or one of the elite warriors?"

"I don't think so, they all know Brinley and how her parents operate. Not sure we'll get anything out of them regarding the alpha's daughter even if I tell them she's my mate, she can't corroborate it." Feeling dejected, I sat down in my chair and placed my face in my hands.

"All that aside, how are you feeling about having a second chance mate?"

"Not sure. Chase is getting protective of her. I know I'll need to keep her safe without letting on anything is different, otherwise, Chase may try and push forward. I want to get to know her and find out what makes her tick."

"I could get Quinn on it, she could ask whatever questions you want answers to."

"I want her to open up to me and tell me on her own. The last thing I want is a one-sided mate bond with secrets. That's just asking for trouble, not only from her but her parents, siblings, and all their warriors currently on our pack lands. Please, don't say anything to Quincy."

"I won't, but Q might come to you instead. The way your presence changed didn't go unnoticed by anybody in the dining room."

"Great, just fucking great."

"Quinn didn't get a chance to show her the clinic, daycare, or village. Why don't you offer to show her the rest of the grounds tomorrow, it might give you the time you need to ask her questions about herself. You know, get her to open up. Trust has to start somewhere and since she doesn't know you're her mate you might want to tell her about you first and maybe about Emberly."

"That's a great idea, except it will take a lot of self-control to keep my hands off her."

"Sounds like you're going to be dealing with blue balls for a while Alpha, I don't envy you," he chuckled as he patted my shoulder.

I needed to change this conversation or I was going to drop my pants and take care of myself in front of Ben. Talking about Brinley has my cock so hard I'm surprised it hasn't punched out of my pants yet. I may need to go for a run before going to bed to get rid of some energy "Alpha Zane won't be checking in for another few days," I tried ignoring my phone when it rang but it wouldn't stop. I finally answered it. "Alpha Tate," I said as I answered the phone without looking at the caller ID.

"Alpha Tate, Alpha Zane here."

"Hello, what can I do for you at this late hour Sir?" I cringed.

"I apologize for calling so late, it's been brought to my attention that the training space you have for my daughter isn't adequate for her. I will be sending my construction crew to your pack tomorrow morning so they can tear it down and build a new one for her to use. My crew will be leaving Winter Moon around 5:00 am and should get to you by 8:00 am, will that work for you?"

I must've looked shell-shocked, Benjamin stared at me, his mouth agape. Since we have wolf hearing, he was able to hear what Alpha Zane was saying on the other end of the phone. "Yes, that will be fine. I will let my border patrol know, Sir."

"Thank you for your cooperation with this. She must have a private building to train in. By the way, how is my Pumpkin doing?"

I looked at Benjamin, "She's settling in, Sir."

"I'm glad to hear that son."

"Alpha Zane, how long can I expect your crew to be here?"

"They'll probably have it built in about six months."

"How many crew members can I expect so we can have rooms ready?"

"About forty. Alpha Tate, it's been a pleasure speaking with you, but it's late so I'll let you go. Have a good evening."

"You too, Sir," and I disconnected the call.

"Why didn't you tell him his daughter is your mate?"

"I'm not ready to go there. As I said, I don't want anyone to know until I know what's going on with her. Once they find out, they'll need to know she's my second chance mate. I'm not ready to tell a stranger about what happened to Emberly."

"I understand, it's a lot to rehash and relive."

"Yes, it is. I need to blow off some steam, I'm letting Chase out for a while. I'll see you tomorrow, Benjamin."

"Have a good run and try to get some sleep." Benjamin headed to his suite, and I headed outside.


**MAX**

After dinner was over I gave a side glance to my mate and caught her eye. She gave me a slight smile and looked away, but not before I saw her face turning pink. I walked over to Brin, "If you're good, I think I'm going to head up to my room." With a gleam in her eye, she leaned into my ear and whispered, "Why don't you take your mate and get to know her."

"You think I should?"

"Absolutely."

"You don't think that's moving too fast?"

"No."

"Okay, I can do this."

"Yes, you can, now go because I think her wolf is about to surface with me leaning into you and I don't need Amanda trying to make an appearance."

"Yeah, that would not turn out in my favor or hers." I hugged her and kissed her head before linking the guys.

*"Hey, I'm going to see if my newly discovered mate will go for a walk with me, so don't wait up."*

*"No problem,"* they linked back, *"just take your time, get to know her before you pound her brains out."* I waved them off and closed the link.

Hudson was jumping around so excited, *"Calm down buddy or I'm blocking you."*

*"Fine, but don't screw this up."*

*"Don't worry, I won't."* I walked to my mate, and put my hand out for her, "Would you mind taking a walk with me?"

## CRYSTAL

When Max glanced at me when dinner was over, I gave him a small smile and could feel my face warming up so I looked away quickly. I saw him walk to Brinley and she leaned into him, I could feel Kiara getting agitated, *"Kiara, what is your problem, calm down."*

*"She is touching our mate!"* She growled.

*"Chill out, they are friends, he is part of her security detail, and she's an alpha, so keep your growls contained."*

*"No one touches what's mine!"*

*"Kiara, if you don't want Brinley's wolf to surface, I suggest you reel it in or I'll block you."*

*"I don't feel her wolf, I'm not afraid of her,"* she said with a snotty attitude.

*"I think you'd lose the attitude real quick if you knew what I do about her,"* my voice was stern. She curled up and lay down.

I saw him walking towards me and the butterflies in my stomach flew around. He put his hand out, "Would you mind taking a walk with me?" He asked, nervously.

"Um, okay."

"I noticed on our tour this afternoon there was a nice garden out back with a gazebo, would it be okay if we walked in the garden and sat and talked?"

"That would be nice, thank you for asking." The butterflies in my stomach were calming down and I could feel Kiara settling too.

## BRINLEY

After dinner, I watched the alpha and beta leave, and then Max and Crystal left. That left Quinn, Erik, Phillip, and Jacob in the dining room. "You guys can head to your rooms if you want, you don't need to stay with me in here. I'm going to help the omega's clean up the table."

"If you're sure you'll be okay, we are pretty wiped, with driving and checking out the grounds, and everything," Jacob said as he stretched and yawned.

"I'm sure, I'll be just fine, now out with your ugly asses," I chuckled and I pushed them out of the door. They each leaned over and gave me a quick kiss on my cheek.

"They sure are attentive to you aren't they?" Quinn asked me.

"They always have been. I remember once when we were little, they all came up to me as a group and told me I was going to be their mate. That didn't turn out how they wanted it to," I laughed. "When I finally...," I stopped talking and changed the subject "you don't need to stay in here with me."

"When you finally what, Brinley?"

"I'm sorry, I was caught up in a memory," I shook my head clearing the memory away. "You can go to bed Quinn, you look tired and I don't sleep very often. My sleep is pretty non-existent actually."

"Why don't you sleep very often?"

"It's nothing you need to worry about," I shrugged her off. "I've got these dishes," I said as I cleaned up the table, "please, you don't need to stay up with me, I promise I'll be fine."

"If you insist, I'll head down to my suite."

"I'll see you tomorrow Brinley. Goodnight."

"Goodnight Quinn."

I grabbed an empty bowl from the table and scraped the food scraps from the plates into it when I heard a howl outside. It piqued my interest so I walked over to the window and looked outside. It was dark out but I got a brief glimpse of a silver streak before it disappeared into the trees. "Hmmm, I wonder who that was," I said quietly.

"What who was?"

I jumped and a small scream left my mouth as I turned around and saw a woman standing there. I put my hand to my chest and tried to calm my breathing. "I'm sorry, I didn't hear you come in." I walked over to the woman and put my hand out, "Hi, I'm Brinley," I smiled.

She scowled at me, looked at my hand, and crossed her arms in front of her. "My name is Maribel, that wolf you saw was my mate, Alpha Tate, you need to mind your business and stay away from him," she said angrily.

"I don't know who you think you are coming into MY packhouse and trying to seduce MY MATE!"

"I assure you, I was doing no such thing. I would never get between mates." At this point, I could feel Amanda push to the surface, *"I don't like her Brin, I get bad vibes from her."*

*"It's okay Andi, she's just being protective of her mate, we would be the same way."*

"I'm sorry you weren't able to greet us when we arrived today, it would've been lovely to meet you earlier," I said, trying to calm both Amanda and Maribel down.

"I was busy with luna obligations, I wasn't able to get away," she growled at me.

*"Amanda, if I knew my aura would work on this luna I'd use it."*

*"We should use it anyway, she has no right to speak with you like that."*

*"I don't want to start anything. I'd rather try and be her friend,"* Amanda curled up and kept growling at her.

"I assure you, I will not get between you and your mate. I have no interest in having a mate. If you'll excuse me, I'll help the omega's finish cleaning up so they can leave and get to their families if they have one."

She dropped her jaw and stared at me and the table. "You can leave those dishes for them to take care of, you don't need to waste your time helping those lowlifes," she turned around and stormed out.

*I have never seen a luna act that way before. Maybe she was just having a bad day. I'm going to try and remember to ask Crystal about the luna when we meet. Oh shit, I should have asked her if it was okay to use her office, it must be okay if Alpha Tate said we could use it though.* I finished scraping the dishes, stacked them, and then took them to the kitchen.

When I entered the kitchen, the omegas assigned to the alpha's dining room were gawking at me. "Ma'am, you shouldn't be helping us with our job, we will get in trouble."

"Why would you get in trouble if I'm helping you?"

"Because you're a guest, our guests do not do the grunt work."

"Well, I was raised differently. Now, do you guys have a compost bin for the food scraps?"

"We do, you can just scrape them in that bucket over here."

"Thank you." After scraping the dishes, I grabbed a cart, took it to the dining room, and picked up the dishes that still had food in them. Again, I jumped from being startled, this time there was another figure standing there.

"Hello, I'm Brinley."

I heard her growling, "I'm Diane, I'm the luna's beta."

*That's weird, there's already a beta female. Oh my goddess, maybe she's going to challenge Quinn for the position.* "It's nice to meet you Diane," I said hesitantly. She didn't say anything, just kept glaring at me. Amanda pushed her aura forward and saw her falter just a little before she composed herself.

"If you'll excuse me, I'm going to finish picking up these dishes so the kitchen staff can go home early."

"I can't believe you, a guest in our packhouse, would even consider helping the low-life omega kitchen staff. That is insufferable, but, you do you bitch. Stay out of my way, the luna's way, and stay away from the alpha and everything will go just smoothly," she glared at me and walked away.

*"Amanda, I can feel you getting agitated."*

*"I'm beyond agitated, those two need to watch themselves. We are here to heal and when we're healed, Goddess help them if they cross us again."*

*"Andi, they are the luna and beta female, we can't exactly do anything to them."*

*"Wanna make a bet!"*

*"I love you, but I need to ask about that Diane person. She can't be the beta if Quinn is unless she's planning on challenging her. I'm going to finish picking up these dishes and once they are put away, we are going to bed. Crystal is going to be knocking on our door at 10:00 am and I think after today and the confrontations we just had, I might try and sleep. I think Doc Carter put some sleeping meds in my medicine bag I'm going to take one. How does that sound?"*

*"That sounds like a fantastic idea!"*

## MAX

I was so nervous, I mean, I've dated before but nothing serious. I always told the girl I was dating there would be nothing serious between us and they were good with it. But this, this is different, she's my fated mate and I pray she accepts the mate bond because I've been looking for my mate since I turned twenty. I kept stealing glances at her and finally got the courage up to ask, "So, how do you feel about the mate bond?"

"Surprised, shocked, excited, and nervous."

I could get lost looking into her chocolate-brown eyes. We reached the gazebo and sat on the bench inside. "I want to put everything out there, so ask me anything you want," I told her with hopefulness in my voice.

She was rubbing her hands together. "I don't even know where to start."

"Okay, well, I'll start then. I'm twenty-six years old, I'm an enforcer but also a master trainer for our elites. I grew up with the triplets and I'm only one of the few who can hold my own when sparring with them. My parents live in a cottage near the packhouse with my younger siblings."

"What about you? What got you into medicine?"

"Well, for starters, I'm twenty-five and the head doctor here. I got into medicine because I always enjoyed volunteering my time in the clinic growing up and had a knack for it. The doctors and nurses took me under their wing and showed me the ropes. I was eighteen when I graduated high school and immediately went to medical school. I was on the fast track since I pretty much learned everything I needed to in the pack clinic. I was able to get through medical school in four years. I've been working in the pack clinic ever since and as head doctor for a year now."

"Wow, that's amazing, I'm assuming you've had boyfriends?"

"I have, I recently ended a three-year relationship with one of our warriors. I caught him cheating on me with the town whore.

I dumped his ass when he was balls-deep in her pussy. Can you believe he decided to fuck her in one of my exam rooms? I was supposed to be out of town that day but I left something in my office. When I entered the clinic I heard some noise coming from one of the exam rooms so I went to investigate... I didn't need to see them fucking but I'm glad I did."

"The funny part is he ran after me saying it wasn't what it looked like. He said he was helping her get something out of her eye. I turned around, put my finger in his face, and said 'Oh, and your dick just happened to slip inside her?' He looked at me dumbfounded until he realized he was still butt-ass naked, and his face turned red, I turned around and stormed out of the clinic."

"Wow, I would've paid money to see that," I laughed.

"What about you, have you had girlfriends?"

"I've had a few, nothing like what you went through. All the girls I've been with knew it wasn't going to be serious because they all knew from the beginning I wouldn't settle for anything but my fated mate."

"So where do we go from here? Normally when a fated pair is matched they can't keep their hands off of each other."

"True, but a lot of fated mates are from the same pack and already know each other. It's different with us because I'm here on security detail for Brinley. Besides," I said looking at her seductively, "I want to get to know you as a person before I get to explore your body." I could visibly see her body shiver and immediately smell her arousal. "It's getting late, would it be okay if I walked you home?"

"That would be nice, I have a little cottage near the clinic."

"Lead the way." We got to her door, "would it be okay if I gave you a kiss?"

Blushing, she nodded her head, "I would like that."

I leaned in and followed her tongue as she moistened her lips. I pulled her chin up towards me and touched my lips gently against hers. I pressed my tongue against her mouth asking for entrance, she gave it to me and my cock pulsated and a growl left my throat. I needed to end this before it got out of hand. As I pulled my mouth away from hers, she whimpered, I looked at her, "you taste so good," I said before stepping away. I ran my hand down the side of her face, caressing her cheek with my thumb. "I'll see you tomorrow," I turned and walked away wishing I could stay.

# CHAPTER 9 COMING TO TERMS

**CRYSTAL**

Max left me with the equivalent of whatever blue balls are for women. That kiss was amazing and I felt my wetness pooling inside me. I'm sure he smelled my arousal because my panties were soaked. I will need to take care of myself tonight now that I'm all hot and bothered. I'm shocked, to say the least, that he wants to get to know me as a person before anything else.

All the other men I've ever been with, it was sex first then talk. I kind of like this, at least I know he isn't in it for the sex, even though it didn't take much for him to get me all riled up. I don't know how long I'll be able to hold out if he kisses me that way every time. It's 1:00 am, I didn't realize we were out so late. I hopped in the shower with my trusty vibrator and chased my orgasm while thinking of Max. Now that I'm coming down from the high of the kiss and my orgasm, I think I'll head to bed.

I have a feeling tomorrow is going to be emotionally draining for both Brinley and myself. I drifted off to sleep with Max on my mind. I'm also thinking I might ask Brinley about him tomorrow since she grew up with him. I'm hoping she'll disclose some information about him.

**BRINLEY**

I woke up the next morning to knocking on my door, I rolled over, looked at my clock, and sprang out of bed. *Oh shit! I'm late, it's 10:30*, I threw the covers off and scrambled out of bed. "I'll be right there," I yelled, assuming it was Crystal.

I heard a muffled laugh, "It's okay, I've only been knocking for fifteen minutes."

I grabbed the water on my nightstand to take a drink and noticed my meds were untouched. I could've sworn I took those last night then realized I slept without nightmares, that's weird, not normal, and the second time that's happened on this trip. I'm not sure what to make of that. I threw on some clothes, tossed my hair in a messy bun, and opened the door.

"I am so sorry Crystal, I overslept."

"It's fine, I don't have anything on my books today except for you so I'm yours for as long as you want. Why don't you lock your door and we'll head to the luna's office for our meeting."

*Lock my door, that's weird, I'm on the alpha floor*, but shrugged it off. "Are you sure it's okay to use her office? I wouldn't want to offend anyone."

"Alpha said we can use it, he doesn't need anyone's permission, so we're using it."

"Okay, lead the way." As we were heading towards the stairs, Alpha Tate opened his door, looked at me, and then slammed it shut without even acknowledging me. *That was weird, maybe his mate told him I was trying to seduce him or something. I would never do something so stupid.*

The offices were on the second floor between the beta and gamma/delta wings. The luna office was next to the alpha office and the beta offices were on either side of those and the gamma and deltas offices were on either side of those. I'm assuming it's set up so the alpha and luna each have the male and female beta's, gamma's, and delta's next to their offices. After we entered the office, Crystal closed and locked the door. I naturally gravitated to the luna chair behind the desk, Crystal was watching me.

"Have a seat Brinley so we can talk."

"Huh, what?" I realized I was going to sit in Maribel's chair, changed my mind, and sat on the couch. "So what do you want to talk about, Doc?"

"Please call me Crystal or Crys for short. Anything we talk about will be confidential and this room is soundproof so no one can hear us. I only locked the door because I didn't want anyone walking in on us. As for what I'd like to talk about, that is up to you."

"I know you came here to try and heal from the trauma of the past and you were having a hard time doing that at your pack. Doc Carter gave me your entire medical file and filled me in on what he knows happened. There are holes he wasn't able to fill in and I'm hoping you'll trust me enough to fill them in."

I lowered my head into my hands and had a conversation with Amanda. *"I haven't told anyone everything that happened that day, I'm not sure if I'm strong enough."*

*"Brins, you are my best friend, I love you, I know you can do this. You need to do this for you, for me, and for them. You can heal from this without ever losing the memories or the love you have for them."*

*"Maybe I need to have Brooke and Jax with me, what do you think?"*

*"They don't know everything that happened either. If you feel you need them then they should be here. You and I both know they will be supportive of you."*

*"I want them here Andi."*

"This is very difficult for me to talk about. Everyone who was there only knows what they saw, they don't know what happened leading up to it or after it. I know I need to talk about it, and it's been eating me up inside. I think that's the reason I have nightmares, why I haven't been able to shift, why I've lost the ability to smell people whether they're in their human or wolf forms, and why my powers are pretty useless. I'm not very confident in myself right now. I know what I need to do, I'm just not sure I can do it."

"Take your time," her voice full of concern. "We can talk about anything you want, you don't need to jump right into what happened but I do want you to find somewhere to start. Maybe with how you met your mate and worked up to it?"

"I think I can do that, but when it gets to the hard stuff, I want my siblings here with me."

"If you would feel better having them here, we can arrange for them to come."

"There's no need," my voice quiet, "my sister can apparate herself and my brother here."

"She can do what?"

"She has the power to aparate."

"I have never heard of a wolf doing that before."

"Then you are in for a huge awakening," I laughed. "My siblings and I have some interesting powers, unfortunately for us, those powers didn't show up until we turned twenty-one." Sitting in this office was giving me some kind of strength, not sure why, but I'll take anything I can get. We've been sitting here for an hour, although it feels like it's been five hours. Crystal's being patient with me.

"I met Jerod when I was nineteen, he was twenty-three. He was an elite warrior from the Timberline Pack. He came to our pack because he wanted to train as an enforcer, or so he told us. The moment we locked eyes, we knew we were fated mates. We had our mating ceremony and a year later we were married." She encouraged me to keep going. "He used me as the excuse for us not going back to his pack, he said he didn't want to separate me from my siblings."

I choked up and my eyes welled up with tears, "is it okay if we take a break? I need a moment to compose myself."

"By all means, take as long as you need."

"Do you think we can pick this up later? I don't think I can talk about it today."

"Of course, why don't you let me know when you're ready and we'll continue. I don't want to push you to talk when you're not ready."

"Thank you for understanding. Would you mind walking me back to my room?"

"Sure, I'd be happy to."

***** Two Weeks Later*****

I've been lying low around the packhouse. I haven't been going outside and so far the pack hasn't had any rogue attacks either. My dad sent his construction crew about two weeks ago to start on the arena and I've been trying to come to terms with what happened and finally have the strength to talk about it. I asked Max to have Crystal come and see me, I was sitting here waiting for her when there was a knock on my door, "Hi Crystal, please come in."

"Max said you wanted to see me?"

"I do, I think I'm ready to continue our talk. Is the luna office open?"

"It is, Tate told me we could use it any time we needed. Do you want to head there now?"

"I would if you have time."

"I have all the time you need me to have, come on." She took my hand and led me downstairs.

"Would it be okay for me to see if my siblings can join us? I thought I'd be strong enough but I need them with me. Do you mind if I link them?"

"You can link them this far away?"

"Yes, I can. Give me a second please." I concentrated on my brother and sister, *"Guys, are you available?"*

*"Baby Sis we are always available for each other, you know that,"* my brother said.

*"Good, I need you. I'm talking with Doc Stevens and I need your support. Brooke, do you think you and Jax can*

*apparate here? We're in the luna office and it's secured and soundproof."*

*"We can do that, give us a few minutes to let Mom and Dad know."*

*"Thank you, see you soon,"* I closed the link. A few minutes later, they were in the room with us.

"Hey Baby Sis, it's so good to see you. Why'd you need us?"

"I'm telling Crystal what... um, what happened." Brooklyn let go of Jax's hand, walked over to me, and hugged me.

"Wait, how is he still here when you're not touching him and how am I feeling you touch me?" I asked, astonished.

"Well Baby Sis," Jax said, "we've been experimenting too. It seems we have enhanced powers since Selene blessed us, which means yours are probably enhanced once you can use them again."

"Enough of us though, we are here for you so start talking," Brooke nudged me.

"The truth is, the Timberline Pack alpha was not a good person. He wanted Jerod's mom as his mate so he killed Jerod's father and sister in an ambush. He tried killing Jerod too but he was able to kill the alpha first. By all rights, Jerod should've taken over the pack as alpha but the former alpha's right-hand men were just as horrible as he was and told the pack Jerod attacked the alpha without provocation.

Those men killed his mom in retaliation. Jerod fled and ended up in our pack. We didn't know what happened within his pack when he arrived but he checked out so my dad welcomed him into our pack. Shortly after that, we found out we were fated mates. Before our mating ceremony, Jerod told us what happened. He wanted a clear conscience before we were officially mated."

"After our ceremony, we moved into a little house just inside pack land borders. We were happy, safe, and very much in love, and even talked about marriage. Shortly after that, our pack started having problems with rogues but because we have a lot of enforcers and elite warriors we were able to kill some of them and ran the rest off."

"Jerod recognized one of the wolves as a former pack member but he never said anything to my dad. He thought maybe they bribed some rogues to help find him. In the meantime, the rogue attacks stopped so we went about our life. I was pregnant when we got married and four months later we had our daughter, Cassandra Mae."

"Everything was great, he was a doting mate, husband, and father. Everyone loved the baby and we couldn't keep people away from our house to see her. After a week of every pack member showing up at our home, we had to ask them to give us a break. It was a much-needed break too." I started to cry at this point. My brother and sister didn't know some of the stuff I just said nor do they know some of the stuff I'm about to say.

"The night before the fire, Jerod and I were talking about moving back into the packhouse because he wanted me and Cassie to be kept safe when he was on the training pitch or patrol. I had just delivered her three weeks earlier so I was getting back into running. I wanted to get my body used to running before my training started back up."

"We were hearing what we thought were rogues in the trees but they were staying far enough away so we weren't too concerned about it, but in hindsight, we should've been. I woke up that fateful morning, fed Cassie, kissed Jerod, and told him I was going for a run and blocking the link. I needed some 'me' time with no one jumping into my mind and then when I got back we would start packing the house to move."

"I put my running clothes on, yelled to Jerod and Cassie 'I love you', shut the door, and took off to the tree line. I had been running for about an hour before stripping my clothes and letting Amanda take over. We ran for another hour when Amanda stopped abruptly, let out a blood-curdling howl, turned around, and headed straight for the house. It was then a pain shot straight through my chest and I had a sickening feeling in my stomach. I'm glad I was in wolf form otherwise I wouldn't have been able to move."

"I knew in my heart they were gone but I didn't want to believe it. I unblocked the link and tried contacting Jerod, knowing he wouldn't answer me, but prayed I was wrong. As we got closer, I saw black smoke in the air and realized our home was on fire. I opened up my pack-wide link and told everyone to get to my house. As I approached the house, it was engulfed in flames and half our pack was trying to put it out as more pack members were showing up to help." I was sobbing now, my siblings were rubbing my arms, crying, and Crystal was crying too, but I continued. They needed to hear the rest.

"I was screaming and even tried to run into the house but someone held me back. The fire could not be extinguished, it had to die out on its own. By the time the fire was out, everything was gone. I walked through the rubble and found their bodies, Jerod was holding Cassie, he was cradling her in his arms, almost like he was trying to shield her from the inevitable."

"Ever since we were little our parents have been training us, training us to look for things out of the ordinary, to be strong, to do our best, and to look outside the box. I took that training and looked through the debris. I found bolts where the doors and windows would've been. They had no way of escaping. I took the bolts and as I was leaving the house, I saw an envelope stuck to a tree. I walked over to it and found a note with photos inside."

"When I opened the envelope there were pictures of me and Jerod and pictures with us and Cassie along with a letter. I memorized every word of that letter," a tear slipped out of my eyes and I took a deep breath before recalling it "He got what he deserved, he killed our alpha and ran like a coward. We spared your life because you had no part in this. Your daughter was collateral damage, but his family line did not deserve to be continued. Don't bother looking for us, we are dead. If you need proof, the bolts you found will have our prints on them and if you walk thirty feet beyond your territory you will find our bodies."

"We are the last of the alpha's faithful, we killed all the other pack members before coming after Jerod. He was the last one who needed to go. There is no more Timberline pack. We also killed the rogues that helped us attack your pack lands, we needed to verify Jerod was there and where he was living on the land. This is why the rogue attacks stopped. Your father is a strong alpha and runs a tight ship, it was very difficult getting past patrol to start that fire."

"I still don't know how they were able to bolt the doors and windows shut without Jerod hearing the noise and they didn't say how they did it, that's just another part of why I have nightmares and can't sleep. I've been trying to figure that out."

"OH, MY GODDESS!" my sister cry yelled. She held me while I continued to cry. It felt so liberating to just... cry. I've been holding that in for five years and I can finally release it.

"Brinley," Crystal said while wiping her tear-streaked face, "I'm going to step out for a few minutes so you and your siblings can have some time and I'm going to bring us back some food and drinks, okay?" I nodded my head and sobbed.

# CHAPTER 10 CONFRONTING TATE

**JAXON**

"Brinley, why did you hold this in all these years?"

"I don't know. I was distraught I had just lost my family, and reading the note just further pushed me into depression. I blamed myself, if only I'd not gone for a run that day, if we would've moved into the packhouse sooner, or if I wouldn't have put my block up. Would it have made a difference, would they still be here!?" I yelled and cried.

Brooklyn and I just held her, "Brin, let it out, let all the frustration, anger, depression, what-ifs out, expel it from your body. You can't live with the would've, could've, should've, it's been eating you up inside." Brooklyn said as we held her as tight as we could as she sobbed in our arms.

All of a sudden she scrambled away from us, it looked like she was looking for a bathroom. She tore open the office door and ran out. We followed her as she ran into the bathroom across the hall and vomited the second she hit the toilet. Brooklyn held her hair out of the way and I rubbed her back. She always does this when she gets worked up. "It's going to be okay Baby Sis." When I was sure her stomach was empty, we helped her get cleaned up and went back to the office.

It was then I noticed a bathroom in the office and Crystal was waiting for us with the alpha. Brin looked shocked to see him there, but I also caught her body reacting to him. She seemed to relax a little, not sure if Brooklyn or anyone else noticed but I sure as hell did. He was sweating and looked like he was seething in anger. I heard Brin very quietly say, "Maybe he changed his mind about us using his mates' office."

*That's weird, he told my parents he didn't have a mate.* "Alpha, I'm sorry, we can move to another office if it's a problem for us to be in here," Brinley was timid and didn't make eye contact.

"You don't need to move from this office Brinley, you can use it whenever you want. I was at the training pitch when Crystal linked me. There was an issue I needed to take care of. I heard you crying, I came to see if you were okay," his anger turned to concern.

As I was watching the exchange between him and my sister, I noticed how his demeanor changed toward her. My eyes flew wide open as realization slammed into me. "Um, Alpha Tate, may I have a word with you?"

"Yes, we can go to my office," his eyes not leaving my sister. He left reluctantly and I followed him out of the office.

Once inside his office I closed the door and locked it. I stared at him, "Are you gonna tell me what's going on between you and my sister or do I need to guess?"

He looked at me dumbfounded, "Not sure what you're talking about Jaxon."

"Really," I said with raised eyebrows and a growl, "try again, I wasn't born yesterday and I'm not stupid."

"Look, there isn't anything going on. I'm not sure why you think there is, so drop it. I have other things to contend with and don't need you making accusations of what may or may not be going on. So if you don't mind, I'll be getting back to the training pitch and then heading over to check on the construction crew and the arena. When did you and Brooklyn get here anyway, I wasn't told were coming," he was getting defensive and his anger was flaring again.

He walked towards the door, "So you don't care for my sister then, you don't love her, you're not her mate?" Just as I thought, he stopped abruptly and his breathing increased. I could feel the anxiety building inside him.

"Jaxon, stay out of it, she doesn't know."

"How the hell do you expect me to 'stay out of it' she's my twin sister! She's been through more shit than anyone else I've ever known, and it's MY job to protect her!" I yelled and my alpha aura was rolling off me.

He shuddered when my aura hit him. He turned around, looked me dead in the eyes, and said, "It is no longer YOUR job to protect her, it's MINE!"

"Then how the hell do you plan on protecting her if SHE DOESN'T EVEN FUCKING KNOW YOU'RE HER GODDESS DAMN MATE!"

He looked defeated, walked to his chair, and slumped down. He buried his head in his hands, and mumbled, "I want her to discover the bond on her own."

I sat down next to him, "her body knows, she and Amanda don't."

He popped his head up looking hopeful, "how do you know that?"

"I started putting things together. First, the guys said she fell asleep on the drive here, without taking her meds, and she didn't have a nightmare. Then she's been sleeping without meds and hasn't had any nightmares. The most important part, is when she saw you in that office, I could see her body relax and I can guarantee the reason she's sleeping, not having nightmares, and her body relaxes around you, is because her body senses you're her mate."

"She and Amanda can't sense it because of all the trauma but once she forgives herself for what happened she'll be able to move on and finally heal. Once that happens, you will be seeing a much better person."

"Not sure how much better she can be, I've only been around her for short periods over the last two weeks and I already love what I see."

"Tate, you need to spend more time around her. I think you and your wolf, sorry I don't know his name, will be the key to helping her shift. Just make sure it happens after the arena is built please."

"Chase, Chase is my wolf's name. Why is that damn arena so important for her?" he asked while running his hand through his hair.

"I'll let you in on a little secret, my sisters and I are special and have been blessed by the Moon Goddess, see this mark," I raised my wrist to him, "before Brinley came here, we went to our spot in the woods, Selene showed up and blessed us. We were already blessed as triplets but when we turned twenty-one we were given special powers. We don't talk about them because we don't want to be exploited so we train in private."

"Our pack knows what we can do and the only one in your pack who currently knows is your doctor because she has Brin's file. When you see what we can do, you will not be able to tell anyone, not even your beta. When Brin has her powers back, she will be the only one to decide who will be informed, not you, Brin only. I need to know you understand this."

"I got it, I won't say a word to anybody."

"Good, because she will know if you do. Since you are her mate, I think you need to know what happened to her that caused her to be who she is now. I will need to talk with them alone first and Brin needs to agree without me telling her you're her mate. Tate, I trust my construction crew to do what needs to be done so you don't need to check on their progress all the time. Can I trust you to wait here while I talk with my sisters?"

He nodded his head, "before you go, how would your sister know if I speak to others about this?"

I smirked, left him there, and went back to the other office where both my sisters were clinging to each other while Brin was still trying to come down from her body going haywire.

"Hey Baby Sis, how're you holding up?" I tucked her loose curls behind her ear.

"I'm okay," she hiccupped. She always gets those damn things after crying. "Why did... you need to... talk with... the alpha?" She asked through her hiccups.

"No reason, I wanted to check in with him to see how things have been with you here."

"I haven't seen much of him but I did run into his mate after dinner that first night I was here."

"What do you mean you ran into his mate?" I gave Doc Stevens, she shrugged and looked as confused as I was.

"When we had our first dinner together, I sent the boys and Quinn to bed because they all looked tired and since I usually never sleep, I decided to help the kitchen omegas clear the table. I heard a howl coming from outside and was drawn to it when his mate said something to me. I don't know what I did but neither she nor her beta like me very much."

"You said the alpha's mate came in the dining room, do you have a description of her or did she happen to say her name and what about the beta, do you know what she looks like or her name?"

"She said her name was Maribel and her beta's name was Diane. I didn't mean to cause any trouble, I was just hoping to get a break from my pack and heal. When am I going to get a break, I just want to be normal again. I told her I would never come between a mate bond." Brin wrung her hands in her lap, looking dejected.

"I need to ask you a very important question that only you can answer, okay?" She nodded her head, "Can we let the alpha know what happened with Jerod and Cassie Mae and about everything you disclosed to us?"

"Jax, I don't think I can explain it again."

"My dear sweet sister, you don't have to explain, remember, we can show him what happened and since you haven't said exactly what happened that night, Brooke and I can be the conduit between you and him for the details. Would that be okay?"

"Yes."

"Come on," I grabbed her and we went next door.

## TATE

After fifteen minutes of sitting I was getting tired of waiting. I was about to walk out the door and into what would be Brinley's office when Jax walked in with the three girls in tow. I gave Jax a questioning look, "What?"

"I thought it was going to be you and Brinley."

"I need Brooklyn for this to work."

"And don't think I was going to be left behind," Crystal said, narrowing her eyes at me and pointing her finger in my direction.

I held up my hands in surrender, "Okay, okay, come in and sit down." I had to play this cool, my mate is in my office and she has no idea. Chase is going crazy, he wants to be near her. I keep telling him we need to take this slow but he wants to mate, mark and claim her.

"So, who's talking first?"

"We aren't going to talk, we are going to show you."

"How will you show me?"

"We need to hold hands for this to work, close your eyes and clear your mind."

*"Chase, are you participating in this with me?"*

*"Of course I am, I want to see what happened to my mate."*

I felt a pulling sensation and all of a sudden everything went black then it was almost like a movie playing. It's the weirdest thing I've ever experienced. I know this all took place five years ago but it feels like it's happening in the present. As the events unfold I can feel my emotions reacting.

*"Tate, we have to help her, she lost a mate and a pup. No wonder she's been lost within herself. She needs to know about Emberly, she will understand."*

I can't respond to Chase, I'm focused on what's happening. I'm glad I'm holding Jax and Brooklyn's hands, I don't think I would be able to hide my emotions from her.

Jax closed the link we were sharing, we dropped hands and I had no words for what I just watched. I looked at Brinley, she had curled herself into a ball on the couch and sobbed. I wanted to reach for her, to comfort her, but Jax got my attention and shook his head no. I stopped in my tracks because he knew her better than I did. I backed away even though everything in me told me to go to her. I have to keep reminding myself she doesn't know we are mates, I have to keep my distance.

Jax motioned for us to leave the office, but before he walked out, he placed the blanket on my couch over her, kissed her head, and whispered something in her ear. Then he walked out and shut the door. "That was," before I could say another word Jax ushered us back into the other office, "intense," I finished. "Your sister has been through hell and back."

"I know she has, this is why she's here. She's hoping the change of scenery will help her heal," Brooklyn said.

"Brooklyn and I need to leave, we've expended a lot of energy being here like this. I'm going to talk with my parents to see if we can come to your pack for a little while. I think it will help if we're near her. You know, that whole twin/triplet thing and all."

"Wait, you're not here in the physical body?"

"Uh, nope, Brooklyn and I have similar powers. She can apparate whereas I can duplicate myself and be in two places at the same time. However, this time around Brooklyn brought me with her. Ever since Selene blessed us with our powers we have gotten stronger. Brooklyn never used to be able to take someone with her but now she can."

"That's incredible, what can Brinley do?"

"That, Alpha, is for her to tell you about. Brooklyn and I do need to leave. Crystal, you need to tell Tate what happened in the dining room that first night." She nodded her head and before we left I linked the guys to take Brinley to her room.

Crystal and I looked at each other after they left. "Did you know they could aparate?"

"I did, we were in this office when it happened, it was the oddest thing to see too."

There was a knock on the door when I opened it, Brinley's security detail was standing there. "Jax linked us, we need to take Brinley to her room and stay with her until she wakes up. Did you do something to her!? If you touched a hair on her body, you will regret it!"

Crystal was trying to contain a giggle, I put my hands up, and gestured toward my office, "She's asleep in my office." I watched as they opened my office door and very gingerly picked her up and took her upstairs.

*"Tate, why are you letting them touch her, let alone carry her, they need to get their fucking hands off her,"* Chase yelled.

*"It's okay, they aren't going to hurt her. They are going to stay with her and make sure she's safe. It was emotionally exhausting for her today."*

*"Fine, but don't let it happen again."*

*"No promises buddy."*

## CRYSTAL

I'm still processing everything, I was not expecting to hear and see what I did. I can honestly say, speaking to Brinley and hearing the full extent of what happened was an eye-opener and heart-wrenching. Not to mention watching her siblings just appear out of nowhere, that was crazy.

*"Crys?"* Kiara asked, I could feel her crying.

*"Yeah?"*

*"I'm sorry I said mean things about Brinley when she was near our mate. I know now she would never do anything to jeopardize a mate bond, will you forgive me for thinking that way?"*

*"Kiara, of course, I'll forgive you."*

*"Thank you, I love you."*

"*I love you too,*" she laid down and covered her face with her paws.

I can understand why Brinley withdrew into herself, that is more than anyone should have to shoulder. Now more than ever, I want to help her heal "What's going on in that head of yours," Tate's voice startled me out of my thoughts.

"I was thinking about what Brinley went through, losing her mate and pup that way. I can't even fathom the emotional toll that took on her body," I sat down and cried. Tate walked over to me, put his hand on my back, and cried with me.

"It was rough when I lost Emberly but it wasn't anything near what she lost, I'm surprised she survived after her loss. It goes to show she has a very strong family bond for them to keep her grounded and help her mentally and emotionally through this," he hung his head and tears dripped from his eyes.

There was a frantic knock on the door, I didn't have the energy to get up, but knew I needed to answer it. "Hey Max, come in please."

He rushed in, "Is Peanut okay? I was linked, she needed me."

"Brinley told me what happened, all of it. She was distraught, that's probably why you were linked."

He looked at me with sad eyes, "That day was the worst day of our lives. She was so broken, we wanted to fix it but we couldn't. That day will be burned into my memory for the rest of my life. When she found Jerod and Cassie in the ashes, to watch this strong woman who could take on the world and beat the crap out of everyone who went against her, just crumble and fall, I can't even explain the devastation."

"How did she get through it? How did she move on and start living life again," Tate asked.

"She didn't, she crumbled inside that day. Her nightmares started up a couple of days later. Her brain was trying to come to terms with what happened but she kept it so bottled up inside that everything started to shut down. She became a shell of herself. She tried so hard to show us she was better but we knew her, she was not better."

"She wouldn't allow Amanda to shift and sometimes her nightmares were so bad she'd stop breathing. The only ones who could pull her out of them were her dad, brother, or me. That's when Doc Carter had her take meds before sleeping, but she was afraid to sleep so she'd stay up for days on end and then crash without taking the meds. That's when her nightmares were the most scary," Max said remorsefully.

"What do you mean they were the most scary?"

"She would thrash around in her bed, she'd cry out for Jerod and Cassie, nothing we did could wake her from them. One time, I tried wrapping my arms around her, she punched me so hard in the nose, she broke it."

"So what can we do for her?"

"Just be there for her, let her talk when she's ready, don't force it. This is a good thing, she's never talked about it. She also doesn't know that the guys and I read the note that was left for her. That's why we are so protective of her. When Jax asked the four of us to be her security detail, it was a no-brainer."

"I'm glad you are here."

"Tate, there was something else you were supposed to be shown you need to know about and it has to do with Maribel and Diane," I told him before Max and I left his office.

## TATE

I was angry when Crystal told me about the confrontations Brinley had with those two insolent girls. I wish I had been told sooner, especially since I already told Maribel to stay out of the packhouse. Brinley was pretty much staying either in her room or with her security detail when she was outside her room so I know those two girls haven't had a chance to interact with her outside of that incident, I know it's just a matter of time though. I was ready to rip their heads off and feed them to the wolves, no pun intended. Before I could call them both to my office, I was linked by our border patrol.

*"Alpha, this is Jason, we're on the south side and we need backup. There's about fifty rogues heading our way on a full run, they'll be here in about ten minutes."*

Well, shit! I linked all pack members. *"All available warriors to the south border immediately, we have incoming rogues! All pack members who are not able to fight, get to the packhouse safety bunker immediately!"*

Crystal and Max ran into my office. "Crystal told me your pack is being attacked. I need to get Brin to the safety bunker. Once she's there the guys and I will help fight."

"I appreciate the offer but I need you guys to stay by her side."

"Not gonna happen Alpha. If Brin finds out we were in the bunker with her, she will have our hides. Have you ever seen a pissed-off alpha she-wolf? It is not a good sight. I'd rather go up against a hundred rogues on my own than go up against her when she's pissed... no thank you," Max said shuttering

"Fine, get her to safety. Crystal, show him where to go and stay with her."

"Alpha, you know I can't do that. My responsibility is to be in the clinic for injuries. She'll be fine there, other pack members will be inside with her."

"Fine, but we gotta go, we're running out of time. Max, do you think any of the Winter Moon wolves working on the arena will assist?"

"I already linked them, they're heading there now as we speak."

I stripped and shifted, Max and Crystal ran upstairs to get Brin to the bunker. I prayed to the Moon Goddess she could stay safe down there. I wanted someone with her because Maribel and Diane couldn't fight. They thought it was beneath them to fight so they never learned and they'd be in that bunker with her. I can't think about it right now, all I can think about is killing these fucking rogues.

## MAX

*Ten minutes, ten fucking minutes is all we have to get Brin to safety before racing to the south border. I'm pissed these rogues are messing with this pack all because their previous dickwad alpha didn't care. I'm pissed because they have no warning system set up around their perimeter, if they did have something in place we would've had more than ten minutes.*

*Now these assholes think they can just attack them whenever the hell they want. They are in for a huge awakening when they are met with over forty Winter Moon pack members. These motherfuckers will wish they never stepped foot on these grounds and I can guarantee they won't be back for a long time. They'll go back to their hideout licking their wounds.*

Alpha Tate isn't aware of it, but all of our pack on the construction crew are master elite warriors, trained by Brin, Jax, and Brooke and that's only because they are sent to different allied packs to help repair buildings left in ruins from rogue attacks. We wanted to make sure they could protect themselves in case an attack happened while they were onsight, kinda like now.

Crystal and I race to Brin's room. The guys are waiting for us, Phillip has Brin wrapped in a blanket. "She's still out and I don't think she's waking up anytime soon." This is good on two accounts, one, she desperately needs the sleep after the day she's had, and two, she would want to join the fight even though she's not strong enough yet.

"Follow me," Crystal says as we run to the bunker entrance.

The bunker is on the first floor inside the kitchen. Looking at it you wouldn't suspect that behind the freezer is a bunker. The door was open and pack members were still filing in. "How does this get closed and securely locked?" I asked, looking at Crystal.

"There's a panel on the inside with the control system for the lockdown of the bunker. There's also CCTV to watch what's happening outside. The previous alpha had this installed so he could hide out whenever we were attacked. He, his beta, and the gamma were the only ones with the code."

"What an asshole, he wouldn't even fight with his pack!?" I yelled, questioningly, "Un-fucking-believable!"

Phillip took Brin inside the bunker. I heard him growling out, "If you know what's good for you, you will not disturb her or touch her. You will answer to me if you do and you will wish you would've been in the battle instead!"

Phillip came out in a hurry, "There was a couch inside, I laid her on it and hopefully I put the fear of the goddess in them if they disturb her or touch her."

We stripped, shifted, and headed to the south border while Crystal waited for the bunker door to be secured before heading to the clinic.

# CHAPTER 11 BUNKER

**BRINLEY**

I was hearing a lot of crying and talking. Then I felt little hands on my face poking me. I slowly woke up and when my vision cleared I was confused as to where I was and why there were a bunch of people around me. I turned my head and a little face was just inches from me. "Momma," I heard a sweet little voice giggle, "she not dead, she sweeping."

"Shhh, okay Honey, let the nice lady sleep."

I sat up slowly, my head pounding, "where am I?" I asked no one in particular while holding my head.

"You in bunker whiff us, come pay whiff me?" that sweet little voice asked.

I looked over and saw what must've been three or four dozen people in here. Looking where the voice was coming from, a young woman was holding a cute little toddler of about two years old. I smiled at them, "I'm sorry, why are we in a bunker?"

"There was a rogue attack, we came in here for safety. I'm Rose by the way and this little guy here is Brayden."

"I'm Brinley."

"You're visiting from Winter Moon, right?"

"Yes, I am." I heard a commotion coming from the back of the bunker, but I was still not completely coherent so I ignored it. Then I heard someone screaming.

"I don't care who the fuck you think you are! You know exactly who we are so you better not cross us! We are in charge while in this bunker and we outrank every person in here! Do I make myself clear!"

I cringed, *great, Maribel and Diane are in here, just what I don't need.* I noticed people starting to part and saw them walking toward me.

"Well, well, well, who do we have here?" Maribel asked with her hands on her hips. "If it isn't the person trying to take my mate," she said snidely.

"I'm not trying to take anyone's mate. I told you I would never do that." She raised her hand and hit me across the face. *My junior warriors hit harder than she does. It probably didn't even leave a mark on my face. I'm going to have a talk with Tate about his luna. He needs to reject her, he can do so much better. If this is how she treats people, I'm glad I was able to avoid her these last couple of weeks. Although it was kind of strange not seeing her around the packhouse.*

"You will not speak to me unless I ask you to bitch!" and she hit me again.

"What the fuck, why did you hit me, there was no need for that."

"You need to learn your place little girl, don't play with the big girls until you're ready."

"Seriously?" She was getting ready to hit me again when we heard someone screaming and pointing at the TV screen.

We all crowded around to watch. I gasped when I saw what was happening. I needed to be out there fighting but I'm locked in here and can't do anything about it. Not that I can at this point anyway, it's not like I can fight yet. I saw eight rogues surrounding Tate when all of a sudden three familiar wolves stalked up to them.

They are a part of my construction crew. A smile grew on my face when I watched one of them shift back to human. It looked like he was talking to them, and then he shifted back and took out three of the eight rouges without issue. The other two took out two each and Tate took out one. The people in the bunker were cheering, and so was I, on the inside though because I trained them and knew what they were capable of.

I turned to sit back down, Maribel grabbed my arms behind my back and Diane punched me. *Here we go again.* *"Brin, can we end them please, they have no idea who they are dealing with,"* Amanda asked.

*"Let's not do anything right now, let's let them think they have the upper hand. When we have our strength back, then we'll end them."*

*"That is going to be so much fun."*

I slumped over and pretended to be hurt. Diane doesn't hit any harder than Maribel does, I would expect more out of ranked she-wolves. After three hours, we were finally able to leave the bunker. I could see the look on Phillip's face, he was pissed. He stormed over to me and looked at my face.

"Who the fuck touched you, Peanut?"

I guess they did leave a little mark on me. I didn't want to cause a scene so I linked him instead. *"Maribel and Diane are what happened. Maribel thinks I'm trying to seduce Tate. They thought they would 'teach me a lesson.' Scout, my junior warriors hit harder than they do,"* I chuckled.

*"I told everyone in that damn bunker not to disturb you or touch you or they will suffer the consequences,"* he growled and fisted his hands.

*"Leave it alone, Amanda and I already had a conversation, we'll handle it."*

*"If you say so, come on Peanut, time to get you back upstairs."* When we reached my room, it was ransacked. "What the hell happened here?" Phillip asked angrily. "Rogues didn't do this otherwise the rest of the packhouse would've been destroyed. This was targeted."

Erik stepped into the room next, "what the hell! Why does it smell like burnt marshmallow and burnt toast in here?" My room was a disaster, it looked like a tornado went through it. I ran to my bag to make sure my meds were still in it along with the viles of wolfsbane and silver I brought with me. Thank the goddess it was still there.

"Rogues didn't get in the house, but we did manage to capture one and put him in the dungeon until Tate can get down there to interrogate," Jacob said coming up behind us, eyes wide open when he saw the damage.

*"Jacob, that burnt marshmallow scent is our mate."*

*"Are you serious right now Aries?"*

*"Yes, I don't think I like her."*

*"I agree, if she can do this to Peanut, then she's not worthy to be our mate. Let's keep an eye out for her scent so we can see what she looks like. Then we can keep a vigil watch on her so we can see what kind of a person she truly is."*

Skipping over what Jacob said, "I think I know what happened, those two asshats were the first ones out of the bunker. I came out last because I wanted to make sure everyone got out safely. My best guess, is they came up here and ransacked my room, why? I have no idea. I think they believe if they mess with me I'll leave, but they don't know me or who I am."

"Amanda wants to teach them a lesson, and we will, but not until after I'm back to full strength. In the meantime, we decided to play their game. We're going to let them think they have the upper hand and I want you guys to play along with it. I also need to speak with Tate regarding them. I have some questions that need to be answered"

I turned to Jacob, "You said a rogue was captured, I want to interrogate him."

"You sure you're feeling up to it, Peanut?"

"I'm feeling better and a little more energized actually, not sure why, but I am. I've been sleeping and haven't had a nightmare since we left our pack. It's kinda weird, but I will take it." I grabbed a couple of things before leaving my room, "Now, take me to the dungeon."

"Alrighty then, let's go," all four of them said.

We left the packhouse and headed to the dungeon. On the way there I linked my siblings. *"We just had a rogue attack, there were only about fifty of them though."*

*"What the hell, Brin!, are you okay, why didn't you link us!"*

*"I was still out of it after what happened in the office and our pack pretty much annihilated them. They were able to capture a rogue, we're on our way to the dungeon now to interrogate him."*

*"Have fun with that,"* they both laughed, *"we know how much you love to 'chat' with prisoners."*

*"Whatever, are you guys able to come here for a little while?"*

*"Not yet, Dad wants us to wait until the arena's complete so we can train together."*

*"What! That means I won't see you for six months!"*

*"I know, we weren't too happy about it either. Dad said we needed to give you space, but Sissy, remember, if you need us we can be there in minutes and Mom and Dad would be none the wiser."*

*"True, I appreciate you guys being willing to sneak out if I need you, I love you."*

*"We love you too."*

We arrived at the dungeon as I ended the link. We got here before Tate did. "Let's see what this rogue has to say for himself and why they keep attacking this pack. I also want them to know this pack has the backing of Winter Moon."

"You don't want to wait for Tate and Benjamin?" Max asked.

"Nope, I know they lead this pack, but I'm an alpha too and they are our allies, so I will head this little 'chat' until they get here."


## TATE

There were about fifty rogues who attacked us this time. I was worried because every time they attack we usually lose half the pack who fight. Not this time, this time we had backup. I had no idea the construction crew were all trained warriors. With their help, we were outnumbering them for the first time, ever.

I was surrounded by eight rogues when all of a sudden three of the Winter Moon construction workers showed up, one of them took out three of the rogues by himself, I could not believe it. With their help, we were able to kill all eight of them. When I got word we killed the majority of those fuckers, and captured one, they retreated like cowards. I notified Cecil to let everyone out of the bunker.

I was checking my pack on the field, sending those injured to the clinic, and realized this was the first time since the rogues started attacking that we didn't lose a single person. I made a pack-wide link, *"Pack members, we succeeded in holding off this attack without losing a single person, this, in part, is due to the assistance of our pack allies, Winter Moon. When you see a Winter Moon Pack member, please reach out to them and thank them for their assistance."*

I headed upstairs, and the sweetest smell hit my nose, fresh strawberries then right after the unpleasant smell of burnt marshmallows and burnt toast. I raced upstairs to make sure Brinley was okay but as I got to her room I saw a mess in there. It had been ransacked and I knew exactly who the culprits were. Brinley wasn't in there, thank goddess.

I need to have that damn conversation with Maribel and it looks like Diane now too. I don't care if they used to be the beta's and gamma's daughters. They need to know there are consequences to their actions and for going against my order. I was getting ready to link them when I got one instead that had my heart racing.

*"Alpha, this is Connor, five people from Winter Moon just arrived at the dungeon to interrogate the prisoner, four men, and one woman, just thought you should know."*

*"Thanks, Connor,"* I tried to say as calmly as possible, *"I'll link Beta Benjamin and have him meet me there."*

*"Yes Sir."*

*"Our mate is at the dungeon, we need to protect her, she shouldn't be there, go to her now,"* Chase said worriedly.

*"You're right, she shouldn't need to know what the inside of a dungeon looks like. What is wrong with her detail, she doesn't need to see the dark side of this. She is fragile and needs protecting."*

*"I agree, get her out of there!"*

*"Ben, get to the dungeon immediately. Brin is down there with her security detail. I don't know what the hell is wrong with them. I don't want MY mate and LUNA to see what we do to prisoners. She needs to be protected from that,"* I closed the link, turned around, and darted to the dungeon. Talking with Maribel and Diane will have to be put off, again. Benjamin was on my heels as I reached the dungeon. I nodded at Connor and we headed inside. We were stopped in our tracks when we heard one of the guys, Erik, I think, talking to the rogue.

"What's your name, rogue?"

"I don't need to speak with you."

"Seems you are speaking already, if you don't give me your name, then I'll make one up and give it to you, asshole."

"I'm not giving you my fucking name."

"Fine, George it is. So, George, why did you attack this pack?"

"Fuck you."

"No thanks, I can get any girl I want, I don't need to jerk myself off like you probably do. I just want to know why you guys keep attacking this pack."

"I'm not telling you shit."

"If you don't start talking, then I will turn this little 'chat' over to this lovely lady right here."

"That bitch? What is she going to do to me, she's just a pitiful she-wolf."

"So, do you want to talk to me or her?"

"I'll take my chances and let that bitch try and get anything out of me."

"My lady, how would you like to start?"

"I think I'll start with this first."

"What the hell is Erik doing, using Brin as a distraction to get information out of this rogue?"

"I don't know, but let's let this play out and see where it goes."

*"Chase and I don't want Brinley anywhere near this. I'm putting a stop to it, right now."* I was getting ready to walk in there when Ben grabbed my arm.

"Just hold on and let's see what happens if it gets out of hand, then we'll step in."

"Fine, but she better not get hurt."


**BRINLEY**

I walked over to 'Georg,e' placed my hand on his arm, and held it there for a minute. "Hi, Brent, it's nice to meet you."

He looked at me in shock, "h... how... how did you know my name?"

"That is for me to know and you to never find out. You want to have a chat with me instead of him, so let's chat." I nodded to the boys, they put restraints around his body holding him to the chair that was bolted to the cement. Once they put the restraints on his legs and arms, I set the fingernail polish on the table.

"What's the nail polish for?" he asked snidely.

"You don't need to worry about that at the moment," I said sweetly with a smile on my face. "Now, I believe my friend here asked you a question. Do you care to answer it?"

"Hell no!"

"Okay, fine." I opened the bottle, grabbed his hand, and painted his thumb. He reacted to the polish almost instantly, I was surprised, usually, it takes a few minutes.

"What the hell do you have in that polish!?" he asked while trying to pull his hand away.

"Silver," I smirked.

# Chapter 12 Interrogation

**TATE**

I was shocked, *"Silver? How the hell does she have silver and why would she carry it around with her?"*

Ben shrugged, *"Be quiet, I want to hear where this is going. I don't think she's as fragile as you and Chase think she is."*

I huffed, my face turning red as anger built up inside me. I tried my hardest to reign it in but secretly, I wanted to hear where this was going too. I just wished she wasn't the one leading the interrogation. I'm going to have a conversation with the guys on her security detail and with Jaxon. Why she is allowed to have that in her possession is beyond me. If I'd have known she brought that dangerous shit onto my pack land and into my packhouse, I would've sent her back home immediately.

I'm fuming mad, how the hell did Alpha Zane let her leave with that shit... unless he didn't know she took it. That must be it, he must not know. He will as soon as I call him.

*"What's gotten into you? You're about ready to break the table."*

I looked down at the cracks forming under my hands, *"Sorry, I'm fucking pissed she had silver on her without my knowledge. Do you know what could've happened if Maribel had found that!? I don't even want to go there!"*

*"Then we need to make sure it stays locked up. Now shut the hell up so we can concentrate on what's happening in the interrogation room."*

## BRINLEY

I had a firm grip on his hand, he was reaching toward me with his other hand but the restraints prevented him from moving it too far. "*Andi? Can you lend me some strength, I might need it. I'm not sure how long I'll last if I need to use a lot of my powers.*"

"*I'll do my best, just try not to over-exert yourself though, neither one of us is strong enough yet.*"

"*Thank you.*"

*I linked the guys, "Amanda is going to lend me some strength if I need it. I need you guys to get me out of here as fast as possible if I start to fade.*"

"*Just be careful, Alpha,*" they all replied. I chuckled because they only call me alpha when I'm either being too bossy or trying to do something my body isn't ready for.

"I'm going to ask you some questions and I expect truthful answers, got it?"

"Whatever lady."

"If I don't think you are answering truthfully, I will continue to put this on your nails." He cringed and Andi smirked as I barely laid my hand on top of his.

"What is your name?"

"What the hell, you already guessed my name, it's Brent."

"Good, I asked you that for a reason. "

"What color is your wolf?"

He rolled his eyes, "I don't know what kind of questions these are but they are pointless."

"Answer the question"

"Fine, my wolf is black."

"Wrong, why don't you try that again."

His eyes got wide, "what are you?"

"Answer the question."

"Alright, my wolf is dirty brown."

"Thank you."

"How many rogues are traveling within your group?"

"About 200."

"Wrong again, how many rogues are traveling within your group?"

He looked shell-shocked, "after today, seventy-five."

I nodded at him. "How long has your rogue group been attacking this pack?"

"I'm not answering that."

"Fine," holding his hand down I put more polish on him. He shrieked but I didn't bat an eye. "I'll ask again, how long has your group been attacking this pack?"

"More than five years," he clenched his teeth and growled at the same time.

"Why?"

"Why what, bitch."

"That just garnered you another finger getting painted. I'm a lady and expect to be treated as one."

"The hell! You ain't no lady, no lady would do what you're doing, a lady would bend down and suck my dick."

"You want me to suck your dick, do you. I'd be happy to, but first I think I need to wash it, I wouldn't want to get my mouth dirty."

"Now that's what I'm talking about!"

## TATE

I stared at Benjamin with my mouth agape, *"how the hell does she know that rogue isn't telling the truth?"*

*"Beats me, maybe they have intel on this group of rogues since they are from Winter Moon. I mean, they do have intelligence on a lot of packs and rogue camps that we wouldn't have. That is one of the reasons no one messes with their pack. That, and Alpha Zane is pretty ruthless."*

*"How do you know all this?"*

*"I'm your beta, it's my job to know."*

*"You and I are going to have a sit down when this is over."*

*"Whatever, Alpha."*

I caught the tale end of her last words, *"What the hell, she's not going down on that asshole, she is MY MATE!"* I yelled and growled through our link.

*"She doesn't know that. As far as she knows, Maribel is your mate and if you go in there she's going to be pissed at you for interrupting her. The guys are in there, they aren't going to let her do anything that will put her in any danger. You need to control yourself and Chase. They grew up with each other, remember, I'm sure this is all for show."*

*"I don't like this."*

*"I know you don't, and neither do I but you have to trust her."*

*"She shouldn't be in there,"* I gritted out.

*"And I agree, but you are forgetting one thing, she's an alpha, not just any random alpha either. She has double alpha blood, which makes her stronger than you and I put together. Neither of us was born with alpha blood it was transformed in us when we ascended to our current positions, we were born with warrior blood, she was born with alpha blood, you need to remember that."*

## BRINLEY

"Jacob, can you give me a bottle of water?" I turned around and grabbed a vile out of my pocket and emptied it into the water he handed me. I placed the water bottle on the table, being sure to 'accidentally' tip it over. I needed the silver to get mixed up in it. I stood up, walked over to Brent, and pulled his zipper down, and pulled his his cock out.

I tried not to gag from the smell of him, I gripped him and rubbed my hands on his dick to get him hard. He closed his eyes and moaned. I looked at my guys with a disgusted look on my face, rolled my eyes, and talked to him like I was into this. The guys knew exactly what I was doing, we've done this many times before when we've had to interrogate men.

I pulled away from him, and he groaned out a complaint. "Shhh, it's okay baby, I just need to clean you before I go down on you."

"Don't make me wait Sugar, Big Daddy will give you what you need," he tried to say sensually.

I looked at the guys, raised my eyebrows, and gave a gagging motion with my mouth. I grabbed the bottle of water, opened the lid, and dumped it on his dick. He screamed in pain, his dick went so soft I thought it was going to tuck inside him. I was laughing as I sat down.

"What the hell bitch! What did you pour on my dick!"

"You were dirty, I had to clean you, I may have also slipped some silver in the water first. You better start talking when I ask questions, as you can see, I'm not fucking messing around," This time I pushed my aura on him and he cowered. "Are you ready to cooperate?" He hung his head and nodded.

"Good, now answer my question. Why have you been attacking this pack?"

We were paid, okay?"

Now we're getting somewhere. "Who paid you and why?"

"The former alpha."

That threw me off. "Why would the former alpha pay you to attack his pack?"

"His daughter, Emberly, her fated mate, was a warrior. He wanted that warrior dead because he wanted his daughter mated with another alpha's son. He didn't want his daughter to be downgraded to a warrior's mate."

"That is the most disgusting thing I have ever heard. Did he succeed? I don't recall meeting anyone by the name of Emberly in this pack."

"No, he didn't succeed. She refused to take anyone but her fated mate. He was so angry with her that he decided he was going to get rid of both of them. She snuck out one night and didn't know he had someone following her. When he was told she left the packhouse, he found her, snuck up on them, and waited.

She and her mate were having sex but before they could mark each other, Alpha Frederick stabbed her in the back with a silver knife, right through her heart."

"They didn't see or smell him coming?"

"No, they didn't because they were so engrossed with each other. After she slumped over, he pulled the knife out, lifted her head, and slit her throat. her mate got out from underneath her and took off running. He was followed but was soon lost in darkness and the chase was called off."

"How do you know all this in detail?"

"Because I was the one who was informing the alpha of her every move."

"Why are you still attacking this pack if the former alpha is dead?"

"Because he wanted her mate dead. He paid us a lot of money to make sure her mate was dead and we're going to follow through with it. We would've had him too, we had him surrounded but then these other wolves came out of nowhere and tore through eight of our men like it was nothing."

*Realization dawned on me. Tate, they were after Tate. Oh, my goddess, he watched his mate die by her father's hand. He challenged the alpha and killed him. It's all starting to make sense now. Why he's so protective of his pack, why the rogues are attacking all the time, why the bunker was rebuilt the way it was, and why he was so desperate to have an alliance with my pack.* I looked at my guys, I was desperately trying to hold back the tears. They stood there in silence, not knowing what to do.

*This feels too close to home for me. Those words in the letter that was left for me about Jerod came flooding back into my mind. I had to push them away so I could finish this interrogation, but all I wanted to do was climb into bed and cry. Get it together Brinley.*

"Where is the hideout for the rest of your rogue group?"

"They are about three miles beyond the southwest border of the pack, there is a cave there."

"Why are you willing to tell me this?"

"Because I realized what we did has not been worth it. I'm tired of fighting for a pointless cause, especially since the alpha who paid us is dead and can't hold up his end of the bargain anymore."

"What bargain was that?"

"If we helped him succeed, he was going to appoint us as elite warriors in his pack and would've allowed us to take as many women as we wanted, where we wanted, and whenever we wanted." He hung his head, "I know you're going to kill me and I'm okay with that. It's been a hard life and I've done some bad things."

"You are correct, I am going to kill you, but before I do, is there anything else you can tell me about your rogue camp?"

"The self-appointed leader, Arnold, you need to take him out otherwise his reign of terror on this pack will continue. Everyone hunkers down in or around the cave at night. When you attack, it will be best to do it around 1:00 am. That's when everyone is asleep and during patrol change. Arnold's wolf is gray with a black spot above his left eye."

"Thank you for telling me." I took a silver knife we found in the dungeon and I slit his throat.

## TATE

I was fit to be tied. Hearing her saying those things to that asshole, was pulling at everything in me not to go in there and put a stop to this and mate and claim her in front of everyone. I had to get out of this dungeon before I killed someone but I couldn't move. Chase wasn't helping either because I could feel his anger rising inside him too.

I had to hold on a little longer, I had to see where this was going. Then I heard him scream like a baby, what the hell did she do this time? All I could do was stare toward where they were.

I can't believe what I heard. I was shocked, Chase was shocked, and Ben was shocked. To hear the reason why my mate was killed by her father, opened up those wounds from so long ago. I don't know how Brinley stayed so focused when she heard that but she did. I wanted to go to her, to hold her, and comfort her, but I couldn't. I pray to the goddess that one of the guys killed that man, she does not need to have blood on her hands.

I looked at Ben and we left the dungeon. There was nothing else for me to do there. We headed back to the packhouse, I linked Ben to not let anyone bother me. I went to my office, closed the door, locked it, and cried. I cried for Emberly, I cried for my lost pack members, I cried for what Brinley lost and the devastating heartache she went through, and I cried for the mate bond I have with her that she doesn't know about.

# Chapter 13 Scenting

**BRINLEY**

The boys and I left the dungeon, I needed some time alone to process everything that happened today, to say it was an emotionally draining day would be a fucking understatement. From talking about my mate and daughter, the rogue attack, and hearing what happened to Tate, I don't think I could handle one more thing. "If you guys don't mind, I'm going to my room for the remainder of the night."

"We'll walk you to your room Alpha."

"Thanks, Erik, I appreciate it." Crystal was walking towards us as we headed back to the packhouse, "Max, go to your mate, she may need to be comforted after the day's events."

"Thanks, Peanut, I'll see you later."

"Goodnight, I'll see you tomorrow," he leaned down and kissed my head. We entered the packhouse and Rose was sitting in the front room with Brayden. "Hello Rose, Brayden. How are you both doing since the attack?"

"We are good, thank you for asking. Unfortunately, we're used to hiding in the bunker. I wish I didn't have to say that, but it is what it is."

"Well, I hope to remedy that as soon as I can speak with your alpha." She nodded her head at me, "I haven't seen him, but he might be in his office. That's usually where he goes after rogue attacks."

"Thank you, Rose." I left and headed up to my room.

"Peanut, do you want us to stay with you?" Jacob asked.

"No, I'll be fine. I'm tired and just want to sleep." I opened my door and completely forgot my room had been ransacked. "Well, shit!" I stared at the mess, and then I smelled something I hadn't picked up on earlier. It didn't register with me that I smelled scents. I know those scents, but I don't recall where from.

*"Andi, do you smell that?"*

*"I do, I know that scent, I can't place it though."*

*"Neither can I."*

"Do you guys smell that?"

"Smell what?"

"It smells like something is burnt."

"Did you just say you smelled something?" Phillip asked.

"Uh, yeah why?... don't answer that, I haven't been able to scent anything since Jerod and Cassie were killed. If I can smell it, that means my body must be healing."

*"Max, I hope I'm not interrupting you and Crystal, but I need you both to come to my room, like right now."*

*"Yes, Alpha."* Yikes, I must've used my alpha tone on him. I didn't mean to. A few minutes later, they came bursting through my door.

"What the hell happened to your room!?" Max yelled.

"Fucking Maribel and Diane is what happened to her room," Crystal growled with a scowl on her face.

"Is that the burnt scent I'm smelling?" I wrinkled my nose in disgust.

"Yeah... wait, you can smell that?"

"That's why I needed you here. I think some of my senses are coming back."

"That's wonderful Brinley!" she hugged me.

"How do we test this? I want to see if this is just a fluke or if I can smell things."

"Brin, can you smell any of us?" Crystal asked hopefully.

"No, I can't. I was too excited I smelled something, I didn't think to try and see if I could smell anything else." I said solemnly and hung my head.

## CRYSTAL

I was excited Brinley might be able to smell things again. I know it's late but I wanted to test her nose. "I'll be right back. Maybe there are certain things you can smell." I ran to my cottage and grabbed a few things and ran back to her room. I put my bag on her counter. "Can one of you blindfold her, please? I want her to sniff these to see if she can tell me what they are."

"I have some nylons in my dresser, well, they might still be there if the drawers didn't get dumped too."

Erik found some and walked over to me to tie it around my head. "Let me know if this is too tight, can you see how many fingers I'm holding up?"

"Nope."

"Okay, I want you to close your eyes and concentrate. Here's the first one, do you know what you're smelling?"

"Um, it smells like cinnamon."

"Here's the second one."

"Vanilla."

"Third one."

"Pepper."

"Fourth one."

"Peanut butter."

"Okay, you can take the blindfold off."

"So how'd I do?"

I looked at the guys and then at her, running my hand behind my neck, "You got one out of four."

"Oh, that bad huh," she lowered her head and wrang her hands together. "What scent did I pick up?"

"Pepper. I think because it's a strong scent like the burnt marshmallow and toast you smelled."

"That makes sense," she sounded sad.

"Hey, you're going to be fine, okay?"

"I know, it's just, it's been a long time, I'm ready to smell things again."

"Why don't the guys and I help you clean up this mess."

"It's not that late, we could watch a movie afterward, how does that sound?"

"I guess that sounds okay."

We could watch the movie in the theatre room if you prefer. We can get our PJs on, make some popcorn, and pop in a comedy. I think we could all use a good laugh right about now. I'll even see if the alpha and betas can join us. How does that sound?"

"I would like that," she gave me a slight smile.

## TATE

After sitting in my office for about an hour letting all those emotions out of my system, I decided to head back to my room. Tomorrow is going to be a very busy day and I need to de-stress. I was just getting ready to head downstairs and go for a run when Crystal linked me. *"Hey Alpha, are you busy?"*

*"I was just getting ready to go for a run, what's up?"*

*"Brinley, her guys, and I are having a PJ party in the theatre. We figured we could all use a comedy after today's event. Will you join us?"*

As I contemplate my answer, that fresh strawberry smell invades my nose. How can I say no to seeing my mate in her PJs? *"That sounds like a fantastic idea. I sure the hell know I could use a good comedy, count me in ."*

*"Perfect, I'll link the betas next."*

*"No need, I'll let them know."*

*Okay, thanks, Alpha."*

*"Benjamin, Quincy?"*

*"Yes?"*

I heard a breathless sound coming from Quincy. *Well, shit, I think I caught them in the middle of something.*

*"When you guys are done doing whatever it is you're doing, meet me, Crystal, Brinley, and her detail in the theatre. Wear your PJs, we're watching a comedy, we could all use it."*

*"No problem."* I heard Benjamin say. I heard Quincy moaning and a growl ripped from Ben on their end of the link. I closed it quickly so they could finish satisfying each other.

*"Chase, I wish that were us and Brinley."*

*"You and me both."*

I put my PJs on and headed to the theatre. I was excited to see what Brin was wearing. I walked in and she was sitting smack dab in the middle of the couch, leaving the two love seats and single chairs vacant. "Uh, hi," I said to her while brushing my hand through my hair. She turned around and the most beautiful icy blue eyes stared back at me. She was wearing this skimpy little top and bottoms set, and her perky nipples were poking through the thin fabric.

*I could feel my dick coming to life. I would love to wrap my lips around her tits. Just fucking great, if I come any closer to her, she's going to know I'm getting hard just looking at her. I grabbed the first thing I saw, a blanket, perfect.* "Mind if I sit next to you?"

"No, not at all."

Chase was dancing in my head and preening himself. She was moving over but I stopped her, "You don't need to move over."

"Isn't Maribel coming?"

"Maribel? Why would she be coming?"

"She's your mate, shouldn't she be here too? I'm sure she wouldn't be happy seeing you sitting next to me."

Before I could respond, Ben and Quinn walked in, grabbed some drinks, and sank into a loveseat, staring at us. "Where the hell did you hear Maribel is his mate?"

"Maribel told me."

The other guys came in and sat down and Max and Crystal took the other loveseat. "Brinley", I said turning her face toward me and tingles raced up my arm, "Maribel isn't my mate."

Her eyes grew wide as confusion settled on her face. "She keeps telling me to stay away from you. What the hell is going on with that woman!" She turns to Quinn, "Her friend, Diane, told me she's Maribel's beta."

"The fuck she is, I'll take that bitch out. I'm a trained warrior, one punch in the face she'll go crying to her mommy and daddy." Quinn said, laughing.

I could see the spokes turning in Brinley's head. "What's going on in there?" I tapped her forehead as more tingles flew up my fingers.

"I'm assuming this room is soundproof?"

"Yes, it is."

"Does the door lock?"

"Yes, it does."

"Can you lock it?"

"I can."

"Good, because I have some stuff to get off my chest and some strategizing to do. Instead of watching a movie, how would you all like to take down some rogues and two self-proclaimed, egotistical, bitches by the names of Maribel and Diane, at the same time?"

I got up, locked the door, sat back down, "Let's start talking."

# Chapter 14 The Planning

**BRINLEY**

I took a deep breath in and exhaled. "I need to let you all know, that the rogue who was captured has been killed and I'm the one who killed him after the interrogation." I held up my hand as they all started talking at once. I turned to Tate before I said anything else, "I'm sorry about Emberly." I reached out and grabbed his hand he flinched so I removed my hand quickly. "Before you ask how I know about your mate, I was able to make the rogue talk before killing him."

"How did you do it?" Quinn questioned cautiously.

I looked at the boys and Crystal, and without saying a word, they nodded their heads. "I know I can trust everyone in this room, I can't tell you how I know right now but I will soon. Please trust me on that." Tate, Benjamin, and Quinn stared at me with confused looks on their faces. "I should probably explain what happened in the dungeon, but it's probably better if I show you. Can you all link hands please, you too Crystal."

Once the four of them linked hands with me, I closed my eyes and asked them to clear their minds. They saw everything from the moment we entered the dungeon until the moment we left. I heard each of them gasp and then closed the link between all of us.

"You used silver on him?" Crystal asked.

"I did, and I'm glad I did, it got him talking and gave us great intel. I honestly don't think he'd talk any other way because we tried that."

"Well, I for one am glad you were able to get him to talk I'm glad he's no longer alive," Quincy said.

Tate turned to me, "I have a question. How are you able to handle silver without it affecting you?"

"That's a great question and what I'm about to tell cannot leave this room. It starts with my maternal grandfather. When my great-grandfather was alpha, my grandfather witnessed him die at the hands of a rogue who had a silver blade dipped in wolfsbane. I think my grandfather was fifteen or sixteen years old at the time. Even though he wasn't old enough to shift, his pack thought he was old enough to take his father's place as alpha."

"He didn't want what happened to his father to happen to him and he didn't want any of his children to lose their father at a young age like he did so he experimented with silver and wolfsbane. Since my grandfather didn't have his wolf yet, he knew anything he did to his body before his eighteenth birthday wouldn't harm his wolf."

"He was able to get a block of silver and some wolfsbane, before you ask, we have no idea how. He shaved the silver into a powder and slowly added it to whatever he ate and drank. After a while, his body stopped reacting to it. He tested his skin for immunity by touching a silver blade to himself. When nothing happened, his beta cut him with the knife. Still, nothing happened so he decided to use the same tactic with wolfsbane and he got the same results."

"When he found his mate, my grandmother, several years later and they started having pups, he wanted to see if it would work on them. He convinced my grandmother to let him do the same to my mom and her siblings. Grandma says she wasn't too keen on it but she saw how it helped save my grandpa's life over and over again."

"When my parents found each other and wanted to start their family, my mom would drink a silver/wolfsbane concoction twice a day. She wanted to pass the immunity to any pups they would have. When my siblings and I were born they had our head doctor test our blood. They were told we were the healthiest set of triplets he's ever seen."

"He touched our skin with silver and nothing happened. He did the same with wolfsbane and again, nothing happened. My brother, sister and I are immune to both and I plan on doing the same thing if I ever find a second chance mate and am blessed with another pup."

"That's amazing," Crystal said, "Does anyone else in your pack have immunity?"

"Actually yes, they do," I pointed at Erik, Phillip, Jacob, and Max. When my parents noticed how close these four were to me and my siblings, they spoke with their parents and told them they wanted them raised to be Enforcers for us specifically. Since we were all inseparable, they agreed right away, until they were told what would need to happen to make them immune. They protested until they learned of the benefits then they agreed, and here we are today."

"That's the craziest thing I have ever heard," Benjamin shook his head. "Not to change the subject, but can we get back to the issue at hand... the rogue camp and what the hell we're going to do about Maribel and Diane."

"I have a few ideas if anyone wants to hear them."

"I for one would like to hear what you have to say," Tate had a half smile as he reached for my hand but pulled it back. I'm not sure why I felt disappointment overcome me when he did that and Amira whimpered.

"I can't do any physical training until the arena is built and ready for me. They just started working on it so we're still months away from completion. In the meantime, we need to strategize and come up with a plan for the rogue camp. Brent said their 'unofficial' leader is someone named Arnold. Since we have his name and wolf's color, I think we should get some surveillance cameras set up near their camp so we can see how many rogues we're dealing with."

"Brent mentioned there are seventy-five of them left," Erik told the group.

"Where do we get the surveillance stuff and who's going to install them?" Tate asked.

"I will see if my dad will send some of our IT techs with the equipment. It's something we would provide to your pack anyway since we are now allies. He hasn't had the chance to talk with you about it."

"How they are going to be installed is a little more tricky," I looked at Phillip. "Phillip and I will be installing them and getting them set up."

Tate looked horrified. Again, not sure why he has an issue with me doing something, but, whatever, that's his deal, not mine, "Why do you need to go with him?"

"Because if there is a small tree or small space I can get in and out of there without issue."

"It's not safe, I don't want you to go."

"Well, Tate, unfortunately for you, you're not my alpha nor are you my mate. You forget, I am an alpha and I can do as I please. It's not my first rodeo, I've been in dangerous situations before. How do you think we've taken down other rogue camps, hmmm? I'll tell you how. It's because of the women enforcers, elites, and warriors."

"I'm doing this and don't need YOUR permission, 'ALPHA!' Once IT gets here we'll get the CCTV setup in Tate's office. Once that's done, we'll head out to the rogue camp and get the cameras set up. In the meantime, we'll send some of our warriors to scout the area for a few days so they can track their movements, including when they change patrol. Does that sound good to everyone?"

"I don't like the idea of you going out there, you can't shift and protect yourself if it comes down to it."

"Tate, seriously, I have scent masking spray, and I'll have wolfsbane and silver on me. I've done this hundreds of times. I'm going to be fine and I'm done talking about it. Now, what are we going to do about Maribel and Diane."

"Kick their asses to next Sunday," Crystal said laughing.

"I think I should just ban them after they publicly apologize to Brinley," Tate says.

"I think we should throw them in the dungeon for a week then make them work in housekeeping around the pack," Benjamin said.

"I can have them cleaning and preparing exam rooms," Crystal said.

"Those are all great ideas, but our main concern is keeping Brinley safe," Quinn says as she points at me.

"Since she and Diane seem to be targeting me, Amanda and I talked about it. We have something we want to pass by all of you because you all will need to play a part in it. Wanna hear what we thought then we can talk about it?"

"I'm curious to hear what you talked about," Quinn said.

"You all know they confronted me in the bunker, right?"

"They did more than confront you Peanut, they hit you and punched you," Phillip said angrily. "They deserved to be punished for that. I wish you would've let me take care of them."

"I think what I have mulling around in my mind will be more effective."

"Wait, back up, did you say Maribel and Diane hit and punched you?" Tate looked like he was about ready to murder someone.

"You heard correctly, they didn't hurt me, Tate, they aren't strong enough to hurt me. Anyway, I want to screw with them."

"That's your plan, you want to screw with them, how do you plan on doing that?"

I smiled at the group, "They don't know I have alpha blood. I've been hiding my aura unless I need it. I used it a tiny bit on Diane, but I don't think she's smart enough to figure it out.

When they attacked me in the bunker, I acted like I was weak and let them hit me. The main reason I did that is because I didn't want them wolfing out in an enclosed area with a few dozen elderly, children, and others who can't fight."

"Don't get me wrong, if they would've wolfed out, I wouldn't have hesitated to use my aura on them to make them shift back, besides, I could've taken them out in two seconds flat with my hands tied behind my back. My junior warriors hit harder than they do combined." They all stared at me and I grinned.

"Our juniors are nothing to dismiss, they are strong for their ages and their favorite thing is sparring with me and my siblings. They like to take their turns trying to lay us flat on the ground. It's fun to watch them grow in their skills. To move to the next age bracket, they can either wait to age out or they can test out. To test out of their age bracket, they can challenge someone in the next group. If they succeed, we move them up. If we notice any of them showing specific skill sets, we move them to that specific training when they are old enough."

"How many age groups do you have in warrior training?" Benjamin asked.

"Our peewees are five to ten-year-olds, juniors are eleven to fifteen, seniors are fifteen to twenty, and warriors are twenty-one and up. You need to pass a series of tests to move up to elite and after elite is master elite and then enforcer. If you make it as an elite you can choose a sub-category such as IT, construction crew, border patrol, or assist with the lower classes, among other things."

"We start training the pups under five years old too, but they don't realize they're training. It's mostly hand-and-eye coordination games, relay races, and things like that. We want training to be a game with them, not work. If it becomes something they don't like then they will be resistive to training when they're older."

"When you make master elite you can do any of the previous jobs or you can choose to be security when any of the ranked wolves or their pups leave pack lands. If you want to be an enforcer, there is additional training you need to go through. Once you are an enforcer, it's your responsibility to make sure all the other age groups are training properly, you also become a master elite trainer. Enforcers are the only ones in the pack who can train the master elites."

"Dare I ask who trains the enforcers?"

I got a smile on my face, "my brother, sister, and I do."

"You do?"

"Yes, we have been training since before we could walk. We are of double alpha blood and will drop any of our enforcers in an instant."

"Then why do you need a security detail when you leave pack lands?"

"We can't be looking over our shoulders every single second, so the security detail is there to be another set of eyes."

"Hmmm, that makes sense."

"Do you require everyone to train or is it just those who want to?"

"Everyone trains up through warrior training. If they want to continue then they do. If they want to go do other things, then we fit them into jobs where we feel they will excel. We want everyone to have a job they enjoy. If they think it's not a good fit or they don't enjoy it, they talk to my mom, Brooklyn, or me and they'll be reassigned."

"If they want to go on to college, we make sure they get enrolled and have everything they need. Everyone is still required to train daily, even if they go to college. The only exceptions are if they can no longer train or if our she-wolves are due to give birth. We give our new mothers three months maternity leave before they need to return to training."

"Some of our she-wolves think they should get back to training shortly after giving birth," Jacob says while playfully glaring at me.

"That's pretty amazing. We are trying to change things up here too. Our previous alpha never required anyone to train, especially our she-wolves. That is something we've been trying to change. There is an astigmatism in our pack about the women and children training and our male pups don't start training until they are fifteen years old," Benjamin said.

"That's insane," Jacob said, "how the hell do you expect women and children to protect inside the pack lands, near the houses, and packhouse if all the men are out there fighting and the women don't even know how to hit something?"

"That's why we went to see Alpha Zane and make an alliance. We were hoping if we could be allies he might be able to help us set up training and change the minds of our pack."

"We need to get back on topic, we can talk about our training and what it entails later. Can we get back to talking about how to screw with Maribel and Diane?"

"I for one would like to hear what she has planned," Crystal said.

"Like I said, this will take everyone's involvement. We will have to continue our charade until I'm back up to snuff on my training. I'm not sure how long it's going to take me. It could be weeks or months after the arena is built. It will just depend on how long it will take me to shift."

"What I want to do is drive Maribel crazy by spending as much time with Tate as possible. I want her to have access to the packhouse again, it's the only way this will work. Tate, I'm going to need you to use some acting skills."

"Act, as in how?"

"I'm going to flirt with you whenever we're around each other and when we see her I'm going to pretend I'm coming onto you. You need to dismiss me and push me away. remember, she believes I think you and her are mates. She has already warned me to stay away from you, it will make it that much more real."

"I told her I don't get between mates, so when she sees me coming on to you, she'll come after me. I'm going to let her do her worst to me just remember, she can't hurt me, even without Amanda, I'm stronger than her. I have an ace up my sleeve but I can't use it until after I've shifted and I'm back up to strength."

"Guys, you four need to keep doing what you're doing. She knows you're here as my security detail, so she'll try to get to me when she thinks I'm alone. So do your enforcer thing and stay out of sight, even though I know you won't be too far away."

"You sure Peanut?"

"Of course I'm sure, we can do this, you know that." The guys all looked at each other and agreed.

"Where do we fit in?" Quincy had an excited look on her face.

"Well, Diane said she was Maribel's beta, so you and Benjamin are going to have a huge fight in the main dining room when she's there. I have a feeling Diane has a crush on your mate and I want to use that to our advantage."

"Why do you think she has a crush on him?"

"The way I've seen her look at him and the way she's possessive of the beta title, it gives me pause. I want her to think there is a rift between you and Benjamin to see what she does. You both need to agree for this to work and you have to make it seem real. Do you think you can do that?"

"Hell yes, I can. There are a few things I can bring up, like me not being pregnant yet," she gave Ben a side glance. "We've been trying but it just hasn't happened yet, I can blame him," she put her hands on my hips and stared at Benjamin.

"I'm on board with that, I like make-up sex," Benjamin said with a smirk and Quincy facepalmed herself.

"I'm excited, I hate Maribel and Diane and can't wait to see them knocked off their fucking high horse and taken down. I wish they would fall off a cliff and never make it home. What's my job?" Crystal asked excitedly.

"Your job is to make sure Tate and I are in the same place at the same time. You and Tate know he's not mates with Maribel so your job is to play matchmaker and try to set us up. I'll give you my cell number so you can call me when he's in the room with you or if you see me coming, you can link Tate to meet you wherever we are."

"That sounds great to me."

"I'm sorry we didn't get to watch the movie like we had originally planned, but I think this was much better than a movie. Let 'operation fuck with the asshats commence.'" We all laughed. It was 1:00 am by the time we hashed things out between the rogue camp and our 'operation.' I was happy to get to bed and sleep. It didn't even cross my mind that I had been sleeping without nightmares since I arrived at Black Diamond. When I got back to my room, I was thankful Crystal and the guys helped me clean it up. I climbed into bed and fell asleep as soon as my head hit the pillow.

**TATE**

I was lost in thought. That was a lot to take in. If she's planning on it taking a couple of weeks or months after the arena is built to get back up to her training level and shifting, that means I'll be dealing with blue balls until then, fuck my life! Maybe she'll feel the mate pull before that happens.

*"Chase, we have our work cut out for us. I think we need to try and spend as much time as possible with her."*

*"I agree, once she's able to shift, she'll scent us and we'll finally be able to claim her."*

*"I think it will be easier for her to be around us now that she knows Maribel isn't our mate."*

Her idea of the flirty, I won't need to pretend anything with her since she's my mate. My problem will be controlling myself when she comes on to me. I see a lot of blue balls and cold showers in the coming months. I hope this works.

*"Chase, what do you think? Think we can do this?"*

*"Not sure, it will be hard to keep our hands to ourselves."*

*"I agree buddy."*

# Chapter 15 Siblings Arrive

**BRINLEY**

Over the last three weeks, I've been flirting with Tate whenever Maribel was around. Benjamin and Quincy have been doing their job, pretending to be in argument after argument. So far, Maribel and Diane have torn my bed apart, punched me in the gut, tripped me, spilled sodas on me, bumped into me with chocolate pudding, poured a milkshake over my head, and somehow managed to put wolfsbane in my food, which I pretended to affect me.

I woke up to my sister linking me, *"Sissy, we'll be at Black Diamond in about fifteen minutes."*

*"What!? I didn't know you were coming! What time is it?"*

*"It's 7:30 in the morning, we left a little early so we're about fifteen minutes ahead of schedule."*

*"I'm so excited! I thought Dad wasn't going to let you come for a couple of months. I'm throwing on some clothes and I'll meet you at the door. I need to share something with you and Jax so you're updated on some stuff going on here."*

*"Sounds like a plan, see you in a few."*

*"Bye."*

I threw on some clothes, I can shower later, and ran my fingers through my curls, "screw it, messy bun it is, again." I ran downstairs to the front door, forgetting to shut and lock my bedroom door. *Oh well, not much I can do about it now. It's early enough, neither one of them should be in the packhouse yet. She's still banned from being here but that hasn't stopped her from getting to my room. I do need to be more careful though.* I swung open the door just as their SUV was pulling up.

A few of our IT crew scrambled out of the vehicle, "Hey guys," I waved. *"Jacob, IT just arrived, can you grab the other guys and Tate and escort them to his office so they can get set up."*

*"We'll be right there."*

"I'm so happy you guys are here," I squealed as I hugged my siblings. "He John, the boys will be here in a few minutes to help grab things."

"Thanks, Brin."

"We are so happy to see you Sissy, Dad said we can stay for as long as you need us," Brooke grinned.

"That's so great! Let's go to my room so I can show you what's been happening and what we have in the works."

"Lead the way," Jax said with a huge smile.

We got to my room and thank the goddess nothing was messed with. Jax sat on the couch and Brooke and I sat on both sides of him. "Okay first things first, take my hands." We linked hands, cleared our minds and I showed them what happened in the bunker, with the rogue attack, in the dungeon, what Maribel and Diane had been doing to me, and the plan we put into place. "So what do you think of our plan?"

Brooke looks at me, "Your plan? How about all the shit you've been letting these girls do to you?"

"Correction, what I've been allowing those asshats to do to me."

"Okay, fine, what you've been allowing them to do," she said rolling her eyes at me. "Sissy, I'm on board with your plan, and I think you are going to have way too much fun with this."

"I already am having fun with it. We put the plan in place a few weeks ago. Just a little flirting here and there, nothing big yet."

"Jax, what do you think?"

"I think it's a great idea too, Tate's been going along with this?"

"Yep," I said, popping the p.

"Speaking of Tate, is he around? I should probably see if he and IT need help setting up the computers so you and Phillip can get out there and set up the cameras."

"He should be, you can link the boys, they should be in his office with him."

"I'll head to his office." He kissed me and Brooke on the head and left.


## JAXON

I can't believe my sister came up with this plan. I think it's brilliant but I also think it's fucking hilarious that Tate has to pretend to push her away when she comes on to him. I'll bet he'll have blue balls until Brin realizes he's her mate. I need to check with him to see how he's handling this. I can't help but laugh at the situation as I make my way to his office.

I knock on Tate's door, still chuckling, when he opens it. "Hey Jaxon, good to see you, man."

"Good to see you too," I'm still holding in a laugh. "How's the CCTV setup going? Do you know how much longer before it'll be up and running?"

"We just started setting it up, probably a couple of hours, Alpha," John said.

"If Alpha Tate isn't needed, I'm going to have a quick meeting with him."

"He's all yours, we'll let you know when it's up and running."

"Thanks, John."

"Tate, can we go to the other office and chat?"

"Yep, let's go."

We were headed to the other office when I saw Phillip heading back upstairs with some food on a plate and a bagel shoved in his mouth. "Hey buddy, John said it'll be a couple of hours before the CCTV will be set up. Can you let the girls know, they're in

Brin's room," he nodded at me and kept on going. As soon as we walked into the office I shut and locked the door. Spinning around, I couldn't contain my laugh anymore.

"What the hell has gotten into you, you get bitten by the laughing bug or something?"

"My sister showed us the plan for the rogues and those two pesky girls. Dude, how the hell have you been able to push your mate away when she comes onto you?" I bent over laughing.

He sat down in the chair behind the desk and rubbed his hand down his face. "I'm so glad you are here. The only other person I can vent to about this is Ben, and he just laughs every time he sees me."

"I don't know if you're a lucky man or a cursed man. I saw how she was with Jerod when they first met and before their mating ceremony."

"What do you mean, how was she?"

"Nope, no way, nada, you'll find that out on your own. She said she's been doing a little flirting with you here and there the last three weeks. If this thing my sister is planning is going to work, then everything needs to be authentic, including your reactions," I patted him on the back. "I will tell you though, Maribel will be fucking pissed at what my sister does and she'll be pissed off at you for the way your body will react to her."

"Just make sure you have plenty of cold water because you're going to need it. Your balls are going to be so blue. I don't envy you, my friend. My sister can be a vixen when she wants to be and she doesn't even know you're mates. That's playing with fire. I can't wait until she gets Amanda back and they realize who you are to them." I stood up, patted him on the back, and chuckled.

"I think I need to talk with Brinley before the rest of this plan of hers gets off the ground, I'll see you later Jaxon."

"See you later, Tate."

## TATE

I went to her room. I was getting ready to knock on the door when it opened and I was met by Brooklyn's smile.

"Oh, Tate, I was just going to head to the dining room to grab breakfast for me and Brin. She's in the shower but you're more than welcome to come in and wait for her," she said, with a devious look on her face. As she skirted past me, she pushed me into the room, locked the door, and closed it behind her. I sat down and heard the shower turn off and a few minutes later the door opened. I looked over and wished I hadn't.

Brin was walking out, not paying attention, "Brooky, as soon as I...," she trailed off as her gaze met mine and a smile erupted on her face, not fazed she was standing there butt fuck naked except for the towel wrapped around her hair. All I could do was stare at her as my cock was tenting in my sweats, *fucking hell.* I need to get my quickly rising cock back down, so I started thinking about little old ladies, rogue attacks, anything.

*"Chase, stop,"* I groaned at him as he showed me pictures of me throwing her over my shoulder and making her scream my name as I ate her out.

"Tate," that sweet voice said, as my cock started twitching, "where's Brooklyn?" she asked all innocent.

"Uh, she, uh, went to grab you guys some breakfast." *Why the hell am I so speechless?*

*"Probably because our unclaimed mate is standing in front of us waiting for us to claim and mate her,"* Chase said with drool running out of his mouth.

*"Chill out bro, you need to remember, she doesn't know we're mates."*

*"Yeah, yeah, yeah."*

"Why are you in my room?" she walked over to me. Doesn't look like she's planning on getting dressed anytime soon so I stood up, removed my shirt, and slipped it over her head. She smiled coyly, reached up, and kissed me on my cheek, and the boner I had sprang to life again.

"I can't talk with you naked," was all I said. She smiled, sat down and the damn shirt rode up and I can just make out her pussy.

*"Jax warned you. This is going to be fun and the games haven't even started yet, she's just been flirting with you periodically."*

*"Chase, we are so punishing her for this when she discovers we're mates."*

*"Mmmhmm, I can't wait!"*

"Can you please close your legs, you're distracting me."

"Oh? I'm sorry, I didn't realize," she said with glazed eyes.

"I came to talk with you about this little plan of ours."

"What about it?"

"How would you feel about me not lifting the ban on Maribel and Diane and just letting them think they are pulling a fast one and getting away with disobeying orders?"

"I think that's a fantastic idea, it's not like they are obeying them now anyway."

"Good, that's settled then. By the way, the IT department said everything will be set up in a couple of hours and your sister should be back soon with your breakfast. When you're ready, come to my office with Phillip so we can be briefed on what the plan is. I want you to be as safe as possible when you and Phillip head out in a few days."

"That's so sweet of you," she got on her hands and knees crawled over to me with a glint in her eyes, and whispered in my ear, "You care about my well-being, Alpha." Then placed a small kiss on my cheek, backed away, took my shirt off of her, and sauntered away as she took one last look at me before disappearing into her walk-in closet.

I growled at her, "You are being a very naughty little girl." She peeked her head out of the closet and blew a kiss at me. *What the fuck have I gotten myself into.* I ran my hand down my face, took a deep breath, and left her room. *I need a cold shower.*

## BRINLEY

I love screwing with people. The look on Tate's face when I walked out of the bathroom naked, was priceless. Brooke linked me as she was leaving my room letting me know she locked the door and Tate was in there. I waited a minute or two before turning off the shower, I had to compose myself before going out there.

There's just something about Tate that draws me to him. I don't know what it is but I do like getting under his skin. Hearing him growl and call me a naughty girl did things to my lady bits. I wouldn't mind exploring that later and the tent in his pants didn't go unnoticed by me either. While I was dressing, I heard him leave and Brooklyn come in. She brought enough food to feed a basketball team, which is good because as soon as she put the food on the table, Jax came in with a grin on his face.

"Oh good, you brought food up, I'm starving."

"Don't mind us, we'll just eat your leftovers," I said, smacking him upside his head while giggling.

With a mouthful of pancakes, he muffled out, "Sorry, I was starving."

Brooklyn and I dove in eating before Jax could finish it all. "Phillip and I will be heading to Tate's office in a few minutes to see where they're at with the setup. Have you heard if they sent out the surveillance team yet?"

"They sent them out about an hour ago and won't be expecting them back for a couple of days. They want to make sure they note all the patrol shift times, confirm where the rogues are sleeping, and see if there are specific places the cameras should be placed."

After we finished eating, I linked Phillip to meet us in Tate's office. When we got there, Tate was sitting behind his desk. I had the urge to sit on his lap just to rile him up but decided against it. I'm pretty sure he left with blue balls this morning. I did, however, look at him and gave him a small knowing smile, as he adjusted himself in his chair.

The IT crew was finishing setting up the last of the monitors. "Have we heard from surveillance yet?"

"We just got word they found the cave but are lying low until it gets dark so they can try and get closer to the cave. They are scouting spots now for camera placements. They are going to draw a map showing where the cameras should be placed. Once they have all that done then they'll let us know when they're on their way back." John said, looking up from behind the last monitor he hooked up.

"Since there isn't anything for us to do until they get back, maybe we should check on the arena and I can show Jaxon and Brooklyn around the pack."

"Have fun and I'll let you know when they're back."

## TATE

Brinley walking into my office had me hard almost instantly. I needed to adjust myself and just my luck, she saw me and gave me a small knowing smile. Now I'm stuck here staring at her wearing a skimpy ass skirt with a shirt that leaves nothing to the imagination. After IT finished, I asked everyone to leave the office except for Brinley. I needed to have a little chat with her. "Brinley?"

"Yes, Alpha?" She said seductively.

I had to hold back a growl, "What do you think you're wearing?"

She looked at her clothes, smirked, and with a glint in her eyes, "Clothes, Alpha." Her phone rang, "Hello? Oh, hey Crys, no, I'm with him now, she is hmmm. Where are you? Got it, is she alone? Are you linking Quinn and Benjamin or do you want me to get them? No problem, I'll send him as soon as we hang up and I'll grab the other two and head down shortly. How many people are there? Okay, I'll let him know. See you in a few, bye"

She looked up at me, "That was Crystal, both Maribel and Diane are heading to the dining hall. Are you ready to amp up 'operation asshats' to commence?" She asked, with a squeal.

"Ready as I'll ever be, let's go Cupcake, let's get this show started."

"Give me one second while I link my siblings. *"Hey, I can't show you around right now, our plan is being amped up."*

*"Okay, thanks for letting us know, good luck."*

*"Do you guys want to help?"*

*"Hell yes. What can we do?"* I filled them in on what I wanted then closed the link.

She put her hands around my neck and pulled me down kissing my cheek, "Cupcake?"

"Yes, 'Cupcake,' my nickname for you," I laughed.

"Let's go, Mr. Alpha. Crystal said there are about fifty pack members in the dining room right now. You head down, I'll grab Quinn and Ben. See you down there," she wiggled her fingers and left my office.

I waited for her to knock on their door before heading downstairs. When I got down there I beelined straight to Crystal. "Where are they?" she motioned with her head. They were in the buffet line for snacks.

"You ready for this Tate? You think you can handle it?"

"Not sure, but I'll give it my best."

"Then it's show time, boss, the girls are heading our way."

"How are things in the clinic with our injured wolves?"

"They seem to be recovering just fine."

"That's good to..." I trailed off as I was tapped on my shoulder. "Maribel, Diane, what can I do for you?"

"We know we're banned from the packhouse, we just wanted some of the yummy snacks those omegas bake," Maribel said in her annoying voice.

"I don't care, Benjamin! You either go get yourself checked or you won't be getting any from me anytime soon!" I heard Quincy yelling.

"Q, calm down, I'm sure it's nothing!"

"Q? You don't get to call me Q! You know what, you can sleep with the warriors tonight, I'm done with you!"

Quincy is good. Everyone was looking at her as she stormed off. Brinley came in bouncing and stopped dead in her tracks, with worry on her face. She looked at Ben then looked after the retreating back of Quincy. She walked up to Ben and said something in his ear, he gave her a defeated look and then pointed toward me. She turned her head and looked right at me.

*"My turn,"* I said to Chase.

## BRINLEY

I was about fifty paces behind Ben and Quinn when Quinn laid into him. She did a fantastic job of gaining everyone's attention. While everyone was watching them, Brooklyn and Jaxon had their phones recording both Maribel and Diane. We wanted to record each of them together and separately, Brooklyn said she'd do recon on Maribel and Jaxon did recon on Diane.

As soon as their 'fight' was over, I put on a concerned look and walked up to Ben, "You guys did a fantastic job, that looked and felt authentic."

"It should look authentic, we've had that conversation before, civilly though, I might add. We both got checked out and nothing is wrong with either of us. Getting pregnant just hasn't happened for us yet, but it will. Anyway, it didn't take much to recall the feelings we were having back then and we just went for it."

"Well, you guys were amazing, you didn't happen to notice where Tate and Crystal are did you? Remember, stay in character as you turn around." He gave me a curt nod, turned, and pointed to where they were.

"Good luck," he whispered before he left.

I looked over at Tate and Crystal and headed toward them. As I got closer I put a big smile on my face and pushed my way in between Maribel and Diane and they looked pissed as they walked off toward the buffet.

"Can you believe that fight? I'm going to check in on them later to make sure they're okay, but not until they cool down, that was intense. Anyway, Crystal, I've been looking all over for you. Do you have any heat suppressant medication? I think my heat is due soon and I want to be prepared before it hits me."

"I have some in the clinic, I'll bring it to you later today if you like."

"Thanks, I'd appreciate it." Okay, so that wasn't an act, I do need heat suppressants. When she-wolves are mated and marked, they start their heat cycle. The heat cycle can last anywhere between two to five days, it depends on your rank in the pack. The higher the rank the longer the heat cycle lasts. Since I'm an alpha wolf, my heat cycle lasts for five days.

It's exhausting if you have a mate because you pretty much have sex the entire time you're in heat. When you no longer have a mate, like me, it's painful, unless you're on heat suppressants. The only other thing to help with the pain and fever is sex, and let me tell you, sex toys do not cut it. Being close to your mate is what helps, and when you're in heat and no longer have a mate, you need to be locked in a room with someone who can help keep you cool and fed. Unmated and unmarked males will try to get to the she-wolf to get her pregnant because the heat increases your chance of pregnancy.

"Alpha," I said with a sultry voice, I took two steps closer to him. He had a tie on so I grabbed it, and stepped closer to him. I rubbed my breasts against him, lowered my other hand down his chest towards the promised land, and right before I touched his cock, he grabbed both my arms and pushed me away.

"That is uncalled for, you DO NOT have permission to touch me, do I make myself clear!"

I stared back at him and without looking at Crystal, "Crys, I don't think I'll be needing those suppressants after all. Challenge accepted, Mr. Alpha." His eyes went wide and he stared at me, his mouth hanging open. I walked up to him, closed his mouth, and said, "Keep your mouth open like that I might put something in it." I turned around, dropped the fork I'd been holding, and bent over at the waist in my short skirt so my ass was in the air facing him. I picked up my fork and walked off. Did I mention I wasn't wearing any panties? Oops.

Jax linked me, *"That was so dirty of you to do that to him, Baby Sis. It got a huge rise out of him in a certain area, and the looks on the girls' faces, if looks could kill, you'd be dead about ten times over."*

*"Incoming, in about thirty seconds,"* I heard Brooklyn.

*"Alpha or asshats?"*

"Asshats."

*"Thanks, Sis."*

"Who the hell do you think you are you piece of shit whore!" They said as they grabbed me, swung me around and Diane's lame-ass fist connected with my jaw.

"I'm not sure what you're referring to."

"How dare you make a move on my mate! You horrid fucking bitch," Maribel said as she slapped me across the face. I had to force myself to tear up, as I held my hand to my cheek. "I told you, the alpha is mine and no one else's!"

"It must've been my wolf, I'm going into heat any day now, you know how our wolves can be. They want to find any unmarked males and take them whenever and wherever they can. As I've told you before, I would never come between a mated pair, even if they aren't marked yet. Our wolves, on the other hand, only seek out unmarked males. Surely you must know how that is," I sniffled.

"You know what bitch, I don't know what it's like yet because my mate and I haven't consummated our mate bond. You stay away from him and tell your stupid wolf to find someone else!" They both retreated and I walked to my room. When I got there, Tate was waiting for me.

# CHAPTER 16 FEELINGS

**TATE**

Pushing Brinley away from me was the most difficult thing I ever had to do. All I wanted was to pull her closer and spank that naked ass she put in my face when she bent over. When she walked away and the girls followed her, I decided to go to her room and wait for her. The first thing I need to do is find out if she is going into heat, that would be bad for both of us. Not to mention the mission to the rogue camp would be pushed back. They'd be on her so quickly, that no one would be able to get her out of there safely.

I heard her door knob turning, she looked surprised to see me in there. "Oh, hi, uh why are you in my room?"

"We need to talk."

"Oooh sounds serious."

"It is, have a seat."

"Why thank you, Sir," she sat on the couch, "what do you want to talk about?"

"You"

"Me? Why, Alpha?"

*Because you are driving me fucking crazy that's why.* Although, I kept that to myself.

"Stop calling me that, it does things to me."

"Oh, I know, that's why I like to say it."

I shook my head. "Were you acting when you said you needed heat suppressants or do you need them?"

"I was not joking, I do need them, just not as soon as the asshats think I do. I'm not due for my heat for another four or five weeks."

"That's good to know."

"Anything else I can help you with Tate? If not, I would appreciate it if you could see yourself out." She got up to walk away.

"Can we talk about this mission you and Phillip will be going on?"

"Why? What I do doesn't affect you directly so there's no sense in talking about it."

"I can't keep you safe while you're out there."

She stopped dead in her tracks, turned, and faced me, I could feel her aura change too. *Oh, shit. I think I just said the wrong thing.*

Through gritted out, "Tate, I don't need you to fucking keep me safe. I will keep myself safe and Phillip will keep me safe too."

She was irritated and angry with me, not what I was trying to do. I wanted to fuck her not piss her off. "This isn't my first goddess damn rodeo, Tate! I've done this more times than I can count so stop trying to keep me from doing what I have been trained to do! I didn't take you for an egotistical bastard who thinks women can't do shit except cook, clean, and have pups! Now, GET THE HELL OUT OF MY FUCKING ROOM!"

She was so pissed. I don't know how she went from sultry and seductive to pissed off and ready to bite my head off in seconds.

*"You better fix this, Tate, that is MY mate and YOU are screwing this up. You need to apologize to her and smooth this over."* Chase piped up in my head.

*"I don't know how to fix this Chase!"* I yelled back at him.

*"Well, you better fucking figure it out or I will prevent you from shifting until you do!"* he yelled back.

She turned around and walked towards her bathroom. I heard the shower turn on so I got up to leave when I heard what sounded like crying coming from the shower. I stopped, not sure what to do.

*"Tate, our mate is crying. You need to go to her, she needs us, she doesn't know she needs us, but she does."*

*"Chase, I'm at a loss here, I want to go to her but I'm afraid of what will happen if I do."* I got up, put my hand on the bedroom doorknob, stopped, and locked the door instead. I walked over to the bathroom and everything inside me was screaming to leave but I ignored it. She is my mate, even if she doesn't know it yet, and I need to comfort her, even if she punches me in the face. Right now, all I know is I needed to be with her.

### BRINLEY

The last thing I expected when I entered my room was Tate sitting in there. At first, I was excited to see him until he asked me questions about my heat cycle like it was any of his business. I have been worried because I forgot to pack my heat suppressants, but for him to ask me about it, was uncalled for, even if I did bring it up first. That was part of the act though, sort of.

Then he has the fucking audacity to tell me he doesn't want me to go on the mission with Phillip. Does he think I'm a weak, fragile she-wolf who can't take care of myself? I was getting pissed off at him and was starting to lose control of my emotions. The last straw was him telling me he couldn't keep me safe.

He doesn't know me, he doesn't know what I can do, even without being up to par with training or having my powers. I was exhausted from all the shit that's happened since I arrived here. I was tired of all the shit those asshat bitches were causing me, and I needed some sleep. I was so tired after getting to bed late and getting up early this morning, I needed a few hours of sleep. I know that's why I'm being so emotional right now.

My siblings know this and so do the guys. Even the IT crew knows this, and that is why they are leaving me alone. Tate, however, does not know this. I was so emotionally drained, I turned the water on, stepped into the shower, and cried. That is the best way for me to release all this since I can't train yet. I heard a knock on the bathroom door. In a quiet and concerning voice, I heard, "Cupcake, can I come in?"

"No, go away," I choked out.

"Brinley, I want to make sure you're okay."

I chose not to say anything, I didn't trust my voice. I heard him open the door and walk over to the shower, he reached in and turned off the water. He must've grabbed a towel because he climbed in with me and wrapped one around me. I held onto him and continued to cry as he carried me to the bed. He sat me down, and moved my hair out of my face, "Why are you crying Cupcake?"

"I'm emotionally drained and when I get this way I cry," I hiccuped. He held me and rubbed my back. Then he began drying me. When I was completely dry, he got up, grabbed my nightgown, and put it over my head, and pulled it down. He turned down the bed sheets, picked me up, and placed me gently in bed. Then he pulled the covers back over me, kissed me on the cheek, and started to walk away.

"Tate," I reached my hand out to him, "please don't leave, please stay with me." I don't know what came over me, I had this inert need to have him by my side. I don't know why I feel so drawn to him, but when I'm with him, I feel safe, sassy, and vulnerable. I would think we were mates the way I'm drawn to him and want to be naughty and sassy around him but I don't feel the mate pull to him. I can't scent him, I don't feel any sparks when we touch and he hasn't reacted to me to indicate we are mates.

He hasn't said anything about us being mates so maybe it's because he was there at the right time and right place when I needed someone the most. He walked back to me, "Where do you want me?" His voice was soft. I patted the bed next to me, and he laid down and pulled me into him. I curled up in his chest and fell into the best sleep I've had in five years.

I slept so well that when I woke up it was morning, Tate was still sleeping next to me and I was safely tucked in his arms. *I could get used to this.* I very carefully got up, kissed him on the head, and padded into the bathroom. I showered, dressed, and snuck out of my room, but not before leaving a note of appreciation and thanks for him on the nightstand next to the bed.

## TATE

Falling asleep with my mate in my arms was amazing. I was so tired after the argument we had, that I didn't even feel her get up and leave. Being wrapped in her scent kept me in a deep sleep. When I finally woke up and looked at the clock it was 1:00 in the afternoon. I slept all night and all morning. I jolted out of bed when realized she was no longer in her room. I grabbed her pillow, soaking in her scent when I saw a note on the nightstand.

*Dear Tate,*

*"Thank you for not leaving me when I was emotional. You could've left but you chose to stay. You staying, meant the world to me. Thank you for allowing me to come to your pack to try and heal from the wounds that are deep in my heart. I want you to know how much I appreciate you."*

*"Thank you for taking care of me last night, for drying me off from the non-existent shower I had, for not taking advantage of me, for dressing me, and for putting me in bed only to curl up into your arms. I know you have a mate out there somewhere and whoever she is will be one lucky woman. I'm happy you have entered my life, even if it is for a short time."*

*"I'm sorry if I'm coming on too strong, sexually, when we're around the asshats, but I just can't seem to control myself around you. You will be a good second chance mate for someone when Selene blesses you with one. I'm sorry for the things I said last night out of anger. There is no excuse for the words I threw at you. I know it's not an excuse*

*but reliving what happened with Jerod and Cassie finally caught up to me and adding what happened to your beloved Emberly on top of it, I think it just threw me over the edge, it was too much."*

*"I hope you can find it in your heart to forgive me but I will understand if you don't. I hope, going forward, we can grow our friendship. I will see you in your office for the mission planning. I hope when this mission is over we can continue screwing with those dumb ass girls".*

*"I wish we could be more... you make me feel safe."*

*Brinley*

I folded the note and placed it in my pocket. I went to my office, walked in and the whole crew was there except Phillip and Brinley.

"Where's Phillip and Brinley and where are we at with the mission?"

John responded, "A little late getting here, aren't you? They just left. Not sure where they went."

"So what's the plan?" John filled me in on what they talked about, "Thanks, I've got some work to do. I'll be in the other office if anyone needs me." I grabbed a few folders out of my desk and left my office.

## JOHN

Two days later Josh, our surveillance team leader, made contact with me, "We found the cave pretty easily. Their patrol shifts change about every six hours. Their shifts seem to be 6:00 am to 12:00 noon, 12:00 noon to 6:00 pm, 6:00 pm to 12:00 midnight, and 12:00 midnight to 6:00 am. Everyone sleeps in the cave or close to it and they don't wake up and come out of the cave until 7:00 am. The only rogues we saw between midnight and 6:00 am were the ones patrolling."

"When do you think you guys will be heading back to base?"

"It's 10:00 am now, so probably in the next hour or two. We want to double-check a few more spots for cameras."

"Alright, we'll see you when you get back. I'll have everyone waiting in the office when you get here."

"Thanks, John."

I opened up a link to everyone involved. *"I just heard back from Josh, I need you all in the IT office at noon."* The door opened a few minutes later and Phillip walked in. "That was fast, I just linked you but you don't need to be here right now."

"I was walking by the office when you called us. So thought I'd just stop in. So what did they find?"

"I want to wait for everyone to get here first." A few minutes later Brinley walked in. "You're here early too, what is wrong with you people?"

"Good morning to you too John. I just thought I'd hang out here for a while."

## PHILLIP

I was waiting in Tate's office talking with John when Brinley walked in. I sensed something was off with her, "Are you okay Peanut?"

"Yeah, I've just been having a couple of rough nights."

"Nightmares?"

"No, actually, now that I think about it, I haven't had any nightmares since arriving."

"That's good, the meds are working then."

"I haven't been taking my those either, so it's weird I haven't had any nightmares."

"You wanna talk about it?"

"I would."

John left to give us the office and I told him I'd let him know when we were ready for him to come back in. As soon as he left, she broke down crying.

"I don't know what's wrong with me Scout. I know I'm a strong she-wolf, I'm sassy, I get things done, but there is a part of me that just wants to curl up and let the world pass me by."

"Do you think it has anything to do with you talking about what happened with Jerod and Cassie?"

"I don't know, maybe," she sniffled back a sob, "I think that's part of it," she cried shrugging her shoulders at the same time while wiping the snot from her nose. "I have these feelings inside me like I need to hit something or I'm going to explode on someone. I need the arena built so I can train. I haven't felt like training in five years but something is bringing this out in me and I don't know what it is."

"Have you asked Andi, does she knows what's causing this?"

"No, she's just as stumped as I am. Maybe it's because I'm ready to shift but we can't until the arena is built."

"That could be. Is there anything that helps calm this down?"

"Yes, when I'm around Jax, Brooke, Max, and... Tate."

"Tate? I can understand your siblings and Max, they've always been calming for you, but... Tate?"

"I know, it's weird, right? Maybe it's because he's an alpha and promised my parents he'd protect me... and... keep me... safe." She trailed off and slowed down saying, "Oh fucking hell, I'm so stupid, Scout," she bit her lower lip.

"Why are you saying you're stupid? You're not stupid Peanut."

"Because he isn't trying to protect me and keep me safe because he likes me, he's doing it because my goddess damn parents threatened him and he made a promise to keep me safe."

We heard a knock on the door, and as it opened, John popped his head inside, "Hey guys? Everyone is here, are you okay for us to come in?"

I looked at her then my watch. Two hours passed by quickly, "Are you okay? We can wait another day to go over this if we need to."

"No, I'm good, let's get this over with. I don't know about you, but I'm ready to kick some rogue ass to the afterlife," she sniffled while trying to laugh. I wiped her tears with my thumb, leaned in, and kissed her cheek.

We stood up, "I love you, Peanut."

"I love you too Scout."

The office door opened, Jax, Brooklyn, Erik, Jacob, and Max walked in and a few minutes later, Benjamin and Quincy walked in. We were all talking about the mission, how long it should take, and checking the cameras to make sure they were all working. "Where's Tate?" Benjamin asked.

"I have no idea," I happened to glance at Peanut and she blushed. *"Peanut, do you know where he is?"*

*"He might have slept next to me in my bed last night and when I woke up he was still sleeping so I snuck out."*

*"That would explain why you slept so well,"* I waggled my eyes at her.

*"It's not like that, I was under the covers and he was on top of the covers. Nothing happened."*

*"Sure, you just keep telling yourself that,"* I smirked.

"How many cameras are you setting up?" Quincy asked drawing us out of our private conversation.

"About ten," Josh said as he walked into the office and heard her question. "We want to cover a couple of angles on the cave opening, the camp area, and some of the surrounding areas. We made a map of where the cameras should be placed. Phillip and Brinley should be able to get in and get out as quickly and silently as possible. They've worked together as a team for a long time. They know each other's strengths and weaknesses, and they complement each other. I wouldn't want anyone else doing this." He looked at Brin and smiled.

"We had two days to run our surveillance and that was all we needed. Phillip and Brin should be ready to go tonight."

"That's great, the sooner we get these cameras installed the better. Meet back here at 10:30 tonight so we can make sure you have everything you need before you leave. Until then, make sure you get plenty of rest and food. It's going to be a long night for the two of you," John said.

## BRINLEY

Throughout the day, I made sure to grab everything I needed out of my backpack. I went to the kitchen with Phillip to get some food made up for us to take and also got a nap in. It's 10:30, Phillip and I met in Tate's office. I have everything I need, concealer, wolfsbane, and silver just in case we need it. "Are you guys ready for this? Brin, did you bring the concealer, wolfsbane, and silver?" John asked me.

"Ready as we'll ever be and yes, I have everything with me."

"I have everything you need to install the cameras in this backpack," he handed it to Phillip.

Jax and Brooklyn walked in, "Good luck guys, not like you're going to need it, but stay safe. Remember Brin, if you need one of us, we will come right away. We are a team, don't forget that."

"I will and I won't forget. I promise I'll be careful, I always am." We headed out of the office, down the stairs out the front door of the packhouse, and into the trees. I looked back at the packhouse before walking off with Phillip. Something was unsettled inside me when I realized, Tate never came to see me off. My heart hurt, Amanda whimpered, and I hung my head and followed behind Phillip. *Pull up your bootstraps Brin, you've got a job to do, it's not like he's my mate.* When I looked up I realized I had slowed down, I picked up my pace and caught up with Phillip.

"Are you okay, Peanut? You look like something is on your mind."

"I was just thinking, but I'm fine. Let's get this over with," I tried to smile but know I failed miserably.

Phillip put his arm around me, "Everything will be okay, Peanut," he leaned over and kissed my head.

"Thanks, Scout.

Phillip and I just entered the tree line when we stopped, sprayed the scent concealer on us, and headed out. It took us an hour to get there and as we got closer to the camp we stopped and did some recon. When we didn't see or hear anyone we silently approached the trail. She took the first camera, scrambled up the small tree, and installed it. Once she had it installed and turned it on she linked John and he gave the all-clear so we could install the next one.

Right after we got the fifth camera installed we heard voices coming down a trail.

# Chapter 17 Going Crazy

**TATE**

It was 11:30 pm the time I ran into my office, "did they leave yet?"

"Yeah, they did, about an hour ago," John looked up from the computer, "why?"

"Shit," I ran my hand through my hair, "I wanted to see Brinley before she left."

"Is there something going on between the two of you?" He raised his eyebrows at me.

I scoffed, "No, have they installed any cameras yet?"

"They installed five of the ten cameras in the trees and bushes. We're waiting to hear back from them about the last five."

"Any issues yet?"

"None. So far they have gone undetected by the patrol. We're hoping they can get the remaining cameras attached before the shift changes at 6:00 am. Once all the cameras are installed we'll be able to monitor their every move, find out exactly how many people we are dealing with, and come up with a game plan for the attack."

"How many days do you plan on monitoring them before we make a plan of attack?"

"As long as it takes. We need to know how many people we are dealing with before we do anything."

The door opened and Jaxon walked in, "Hey, Tate, I know you were against this mission but Phillip and Brinley are the best two people for this. They know what they're doing, it's not their first rodeo. They know each other, they know how each other works and operates. They can communicate with their eyes, it's crazy to watch."

"You need to trust them as a team, they've done this time and time again. They will be back, just be patient. They are safe, I can assure you and if they need backup, my Baby Sister will link me or Brooke one of us can be there at the snap of our fingers."

Jax gave me a knowing look, he's the only one besides Benjamin who knows Brinley and I are mates. This is going to be the longest night of my life. I want to go back to her room, curl up in her bed surrounded by her scent, and fall asleep until she returns home. Home, I want her home, by my side so we can be partners, leading this pack together. I am falling in love with her and there is nothing I can do about it.

## PHILLIP

This time I took the lead and headed to what looked like another trail. We heard two people coming so we dipped behind a rock formation in hopes they wouldn't come this way. If they did, we would have to take them out. Unfortunately, they stopped directly in front of us. I looked at Brin, and we nodded at each other.

We heard them talking very carefully and quietly. She reached down and turned on the camera's mic attached to her so the team at the packhouse could hear the conversation we were hearing and I reached down and turned on the record sound portion of my camera so we could replay it as we needed.

"I don't know why Arnold wants to keep attacking this pack. The alpha is dead, his daughter is dead, and there's no reason to try and keep going after the new alpha. I wish we could just defect but he'd hunt us down and slaughter us the first chance he got."

"I know, and I can't do that, he is holding my mate and unborn pup hostage in the cave. He said if I don't follow orders he'll slit her throat and make me watch her and our unborn pup die in front of me. I'm stuck doing his dirty work unless we can figure out a way to kill him."

"Not sure how we'd do that, I think he's forcing most of us into this. I was hanging around some other rogues when he found us. One of the rogues had a mate and pup. Arnold killed his mate in front of him and threatened to kill the pup too if we didn't come with him. The man is a crazy ass bastard and needs to be put down."

"We better keep checking the parameters in case someone wakes up and sees us standing around talking."

They walked away, Brin and I blew out a breath we didn't realize we were holding, looked at each other, and turned off the mic and the recording. We carefully got up and walked to the cave and set up the rest of the cameras. Brin, being her crazy ass self, very quietly and ninja-like, went into the cave, found a secluded place to anchor a camera to, and snuck back out.

By the time we were finished getting the last camera installed, it was 3:00 am and we headed back to the packhouse and went straight to Tate's office. We were greeted by the entire IT crew, including Alpha Tate, his betas, Jaxon, Brooklyn, the rest of her security team, and Doc Crystal. Brin had a huge ass grin on her face as we waltzed in there.

"All the cameras are placed. I was even able to get inside the cave and place one there in an inconspicuous spot," she said proud of herself.

"Please tell me all the cameras are functioning properly and you guys were able to catch the conversation between the two rogues patrolling? Brin turned her mic on as soon as they started talking and I turned my recorder on in case they said anything we needed to go back and listen to if needed." We spent the next three and a half hours going over everything we saw and heard when Brin said she needed a shower and some sleep. She got up, left, and a few minutes later, Alpha Tate left, mumbling something about the training pitch. *Something is going on with them.*

## MARIBEL

I couldn't sleep, my brain wouldn't shut off on all the ways I could try and get that fucking bitch, Brinley, off-pack lands. It was about 4:00 am, I got up and decided to sneak out of the house I shared with my parents and little sister, Noelle, and head over to the packhouse. I was going to ask Diane to help me but I didn't want to wake her up.

She, Emberly, and I had always been thick as thieves since we were the daughters of the ranked members. Emberly was the alpha's daughter, I was the beta's daughter, and Diane was the gamma's daughter. Emberly was our friend until she turned twenty and found her fated mate in the warrior I had a crush on. I avoided her after that and made Diane avoid her too.

Our alpha told the pack she was killed by a rogue during one of the attacks. I was sad to lose a friend but part of me was jumping for joy inside because then I had a chance at becoming Tate's chosen mate. When he killed the alpha and took over I was excited to be the next luna. I've been doing everything I can to get him to take me as his chosen mate ever since.

Then everything changed, my dad stepped down as beta since he didn't want to fight to the death, and his beta powers were stripped, which essentially stripped my mom's, mine, and Noelle's too. Even though Tate and Benjamin didn't have a gamma to take the place of Diane's dad, he also decided to step down. They all lost their gamma powers too which didn't matter since the main job of the gamma was protecting the luna and we didn't have one.

The gamma had a way of instantly calming the luna in stressful situations. Diane and I hated the fact our authority was stripped from us just because our parents stepped down, now we're just regular pack members, at least we're not low-life omega's. Tate just had to bring that fucking she-wolf home from another pack. I don't know what makes her so special that she needs a security detail. I think it's the stupidest thing in the world.

I can't even smell her wolf, maybe that's why she needs protection because she doesn't have a wolf to help her out. It makes sense since she wasn't able to fight us in the bunker. I was wandering around the packhouse trying to think of ways I could destroy her. I mean, who the fuck does she think she is, coming into MY packhouse and trying to take over and seducing MY man.

She's no one special, she's a nobody, she's lower than an omega, you can't get any lower than that. I mean, her wolf doesn't even want her. I snuck up to the alpha floor where her room was and checked the door, it was unlocked. I quietly crept in and didn't see her sleeping nor did I hear her in the bathroom. I walked back to her door and locked it. I didn't want anyone walking into the room while I was in there and I'm glad the rooms are soundproof.

I continued looking around. I didn't see that dumb backpack I occasionally saw her carry around either so I knew she was somewhere, I just didn't know where. I wasn't sure what I would've done if she was actually in there. She's probably in her security details' room. That thought put a big smile on my face, I walked over to the dresser and pulled her clothes out, this time I decided I was going to destroy her room, not just throw things around. I extended my claws and shredded all her clothes. I walked to the bed and destroyed the comforter, sheets, and mattresses. I went to the bathroom and broke the toilet, mirror, and shower head.

I found her lipstick and left her a note on her wall. I took pictures of my handy work so I could show Diane later. I walked to the door, unlocked it, peeked out the door, didn't see anyone then snuck back downstairs, out the packhouse, and back to my house. My parents were still sleeping, I looked at the time and it was 6:00 in the morning.

I managed to do all that in two hours. I felt great and proud of myself for the damage I caused. Maybe this will make her cry all the way home, pathetic little girl. I still had time to sleep for a couple of hours before my mom woke up and made breakfast. I fell asleep with a smile on my face and my brain calm.

## BRINLEY

By the time we finished debriefing everyone and making sure all the cameras and mics were working properly, it was about 6:30 am. I excused myself to go shower and take a nap. I didn't realize Tate was following me until I opened the door to my room and heard a growl come from him. My room had been destroyed and I'm pretty sure I know who did it too, fucking Maribel.

We walked in and all my clothes were shredded, my bathroom was destroyed, and on the wall, written in big letters with red lipstick was 'GO HOME BITCH, YOU ARE NOT WELCOME HERE!' I turned and looked at Tate, "What the hell! I'm so fucking tired of that bitch! She wants to play games, she's getting games! Are you ready to step this up!?"

"Hell yes I am, bring it on Cupcake. I'll play whatever game you want and I won't hold back." He leaned down and kissed my head. "Are any of your clothes salvageable?"

"Doesn't look like it," I picked up one of my panties and showed him, "even my panties are torn to shreds. Thank goddess I brought my backpack with me, it had wolfsbane and silver in it. I don't even want to think about what would've happened if she got a hold of that stuff."

"Me either," Tate said with a shudder. "Let's get you to my suite so you can shower and take a nap. I'll have Q bring you some clothes and when you wake up I'll take you shopping."

"You don't need to do that."

"I know I don't, but I want to," he pulled me closer to him, tucked some curls behind my ear, and bopped me on the nose with his finger.

"Thank you, I appreciate it," I smiled at him.

When we entered his suite, it was beautifully decorated. The walls were light blue with light gray trim and a white ceiling. There were dark blue curtains over the windows with dark gray blinds, and french doors leading out to a balcony overlooking the front entrance of the packhouse. There was a sitting room off to one side with an office desk, a filing cabinet, what looked like comfortable sitting chairs, and a couch.

As I was looking around, he must've gone to a linen closet because he handed me two plush oversized towels and led me to his bedroom where the en-suite bathroom was. There was a California king-size bed with gray sheets, fluffy pillows, and a plush comforter. It looked so comfortable I wanted to curl up in it. His bathroom had a huge walk-in shower. There were jets on the shower wall and the shower head looked like it flowed water on you like a waterfall and a bench to sit on.

There was a huge jacuzzi-sized bathtub with jets that was filled with a bubble bath, I didn't even hear him filling the bathtub when I was looking around. The toilet had a bidet and the counter was tall with double sinks, a vanity, and a huge mirror with lights all around it. There was a ceiling fan and heat lamp, and the walls were painted the opposite of his bedroom and suite, with light gray walls and light blue trim with dark gray and dark blue accents. The tile floors were heated so when you stepped on them your feet were warm. I could live in this bathroom alone, it was beautiful.

"I added some rose scent to your bubble bath, I hope you like it," he said, tentatively. "If you need anything, I'll be in my office. When you're finished with your bath, you can use my bed to get some sleep. Let me know when you wake up and we'll go shopping. Have a good sleep, Brin." He smiled before gently shutting the door and walking away. When he left, something inside me felt empty.

I removed my clothes, pulled my hair out of my messy bun, climbed in the tub, and sank under the water to wash away all dirt and grime from the mission. Once the water turned cold,

I climbed out of the tub, pulled the drain, wrapped one towel around my hair, and dried my body off with the other. I was so relaxed and tired, that I just walked over to his bed, climbed in, and fell asleep under the soft sheets forgetting to put clothes on.

## TATE

Knowing my mate was in my jacuzzi taking a bubble bath I prepared for her, had my cock pressing against my pants so hard I had to unzip them from the pressure. I heard the water draining from the tub and knew she was going to be climbing into my bed. After about twenty minutes I walked to my room and heard her soft, even breathing. My mate, asleep in my bed, put a big smile on my face.

*"Go to our mate, let her snuggle into you."*
*"You think so, Chase? I don't want to wake her."*
*"Just be slow and gentle."*

I stripped out of my pants and shirt and climbed on the bed, the second I lay next to her she snuggled right into my arms. It was then I realized she was naked under my sheets. It took everything in me to not touch her naked body. I was in heaven and Chase was preening himself. I only allowed myself to lay with her for a short time.

I didn't want her waking up and seeing me there in only my boxers when she didn't invite me to lay with her. With reluctance, after thirty minutes, I got up, dressed, and went back to my in-suite office. It took me a little while to get my head wrapped back around work and off my naked mate in my bed, where I'd much rather be but I've put off my alpha duties for too long.

## BRINLEY

I woke up a few hours later, well-rested. There were some clothes on his bed, I'm assuming Q brought them in. I didn't feel like wearing them, and with a devious smile, I went to his walk-in closet, pulled out a pair of his boxers, slid them on, and used one of my hair ties to tighten them. I slipped on one of his button-up shirts, took one of his ties, and used it like a belt. My hair was a mess since I didn't dry it before falling asleep, just the look I was going for.

I linked Max, *"Are you with Crystal?"*

*"I am, did you have a good nap?"*

*"I did, but I'm in Tate's suite. When I got to my room it was destroyed. I have a plan, wanna hear it?"*

*"Do you seriously need to ask me that?"*

I told him my plan and he said he'd get right on it.

## BROOKLYN

Max linked us letting us know what happened to Brin's room. It happened sometime between Brin leaving at 10:30 last night and 6:30 this morning. He said she showered and took a nap in Tate's suite, and what Brin's plan was. Jax and I were on board with it. We can pretty much read each other without talking or using mind-link so this would be perfect for us.

Brin's plan is excellent and the look on Maribel's face when she sees the consequences of her bedroom massacre is going to be priceless. We just have to pull it off and pretend we don't see her when we stop to "gossip" with each other.

Crystal worked her magic in getting Maribel to the packhouse too. She asked Benjamin and Quincy to head to the dining hall and start talking about Brinley and Tate within earshot of Diane. She said Diane is there every morning for breakfast because she doesn't like to cook and her parents eat too early for her.

## DIANE

I was sitting in the dining hall eating breakfast around 9:00 am, by myself, like I usually do. My parents eat too early for me and I don't like to cook. I was sitting there minding my own business when I felt the aura of the beta's entering the dining hall. I do wish they'd split because I'd like to get my hands on him. I've had a crush on him for years. Unfortunately for me, they must've made up because they were in a deep conversation, so naturally I tuned my wolf hearing to their conversation.

"Did you hear what happened to Brinley's room?" I heard Benjamin ask his poor excuse of a mate, Quincy.

"I heard a little. Someone went in and ransacked it or something."

*Hmmm, that's interesting, I'll have to ask Maribel if she did that, it sounds like something she'd do.*

"It wasn't just ransacked, it was demolished. I heard Tate brought her to his suite, but I don't believe it. Not when her brother and sister are here. She would've stayed with them."

"We could always go up and see if it's true, I haven't seen either of them yet."

I tuned them out and linked Maribel immediately, this is news she would want to know. That fucking bitch is still trying to seduce her mate.

# Chapter 18 Plan in Motion

**MARIBEL**

I was eating breakfast with my parents when Diane linked me.

*"Hey can you meet me in the packhouse, I just overheard something you need to hear."*

*"I can be there in a few minutes, I'm just finishing up breakfast."*

*"Tell your parents hi from me, I'll see you in a little while. I'll be in the dining hall, you can meet me there."*

*"I should be there in about fifteen minutes, see you soon."*

*"Okay."*

I turned to my parents, "I'm going to meet Diane in the dining hall, we'll probably just hang out all day unless you need me."

"Thank you for letting us know, maybe you could help me out in the daycare later today?" Mom asked.

"I'll think about it, like I said, I'm not sure what Diane and I will be doing today." I finished my breakfast, put my dishes away, and left the house. I made sure to have my phone so I could show Diane my handy work from this morning.

As I was heading to the dining hall, I saw two people coming towards me talking excitedly. I think they're Brinley's brother and sister because they look like her. Not being one to miss out on some gossip, especially if it's about the person I want out of this pack the most, I hid behind a tree and they happened to stop near it so I could hear what they were saying. Lucky for me, they didn't realize I was there, I laughed to myself.

## BROOKLYN

We were waiting in an area of the dining hall watching the betas for a sign as soon as they gave it to us we headed outside. We saw Maribel heading toward us so we pretended we didn't see her. We watched as she hid behind a tree and we stopped just short of it. "Can you believe someone demolished the room Brinley is staying in?" I asked Jax.

"No, I can't. When I heard about it, I couldn't believe it. Why would anyone want to decimate a room like that."

"I heard she couldn't even use the shower, so she snuck into Alpha Tate's suite without him knowing, used his jacuzzi, and slept in his bed." I gave him a look with my eyes, saying we needed to wrap this up.

"I heard he was working in his office when she did it too. When he went to his suite and found her, he was so angry. I think they're still there too." We walked away and out of the corner of my eye, I saw Maribel leaving so I linked Brin and Max.

## MARIBEL

I was so angry. I can't believe she snuck into his suite to bathe and take a nap. How dare she do that to Tate. Now more than ever I want this bitch gone. I linked Diane and told her I needed to take care of something before I met up with her in the dining hall. I didn't give her a chance to respond before I shut the link off and put a block up. The more I thought about it the angrier I got and I was going to take it out on this pathetic girl. I marched up the stairs to the alpha floor when I stopped dead in my tracks. Brinley was coming out of Tate's room and I was fucking pissed at what I saw.

**BRINLEY**

I didn't want to do anything until I got the go-ahead from Max. He contacted my brother and sister while Crystal contacted Benjamin and Quincy and filled them in on our plan. We didn't give them any instructions, just said to play along however best they felt. Once Max linked me back saying things were in motion, I waited a few minutes before leaving Tate's bedroom. I walked over to his office, and his back was facing me. I placed my hands on his shoulders, leaned in, and whispered in his ear, "Showtime, are you ready?"

**TATE**

I felt my mate walking into my office but didn't want to turn around. When she touched me and those tingles raced up and down my arm, it was all I could do to control my urges to pull her into my lap and ravish her body. Then she leaned down and whispered in my ear. "Showtime, are you ready?" I had no idea what she had planned but I would follow and do whatever she wanted.

I slowly turned around and looked her in the eyes before pushing her away from me. I was drinking in her body and she smiled. "Ready as I'll ever be." We walked to the door, she smirked and then we walked into the hall. She began yelling at me as soon as we stepped outside the room, something broke inside me, in a good way, and I wanted to take her then and there.

**BRINLEY**

I smirked at Tate, opened the door, and we walked out. I turned around, and pointed my finger at him, "Stop yelling at me, it's not my fault someone destroyed my room! I needed to take a shower and I wasn't going to wake Jax or Brooklyn! You weren't in your fucking suite so I took advantage of that!"

"You could've found me and asked if you could use my bathroom! You made a huge mess in there, not to mention sleeping in MY bed! Then you dared to put MY FUCKING CLOTHES ON! Who the hell do you think you are!"

I walked right over to him, poking my finger in his chest, "I'll tell you who the hell I am! I'm a woman who is in YOUR pack, under YOUR protection and MY room was destroyed and you did NOTHING to prevent it! What if I would've been in that room when it happened, huh? I CAN'T FUCKING DEFEND MYSELF, ALPHA!! "

He grabbed my hand I was poking him with, pulled me closer to him, and growled, "I told YOU to stop calling ME ALPHA!"

"Are you serious right now!? What are you going to do if I continue to call you that, you fucking bastard!"

"Don't push me bitch, or you'll find out!"

"Oh, I'm going to push, ALPHA!"

He grabbed my arms, pushed me into the wall, and anchored my hands above my head. He leaned down and whispered in my ear but made sure it was loud enough for Maribel to hear. "Every time you call me Alpha, my dick gets hard for you."

Okay, I was shocked for about thirty seconds, until I felt the hardness of his cock pressing against me, I had to stay in character though. "Let go of my arms, Alpha," I said through gritted teeth.

"Oh, I don't think so. You're the one trying to seduce me! You get me all riled up and you think you can just walk away!"

I squirmed in his hold, he loosened his grip so it looked like I broke free. I decided to change tactics and put on a show, both for my messed up pleasure and to piss off Maribel. I wrapped my arms around his neck, and in a sultry voice, "I think I felt something hard pressing against me, Alpha. If I make you hard by arguing with you, I'll continue doing it."

He smiled as I whispered so Maribel couldn't hear me, "Thank you for letting me take a bubble bath in your jacuzzi. It was so relaxing and your bed was the most comfortable bed I've ever slept in, Alpha." I stepped into him so my breasts were pressed against him, I leaned into him and this time loud enough for her to hear, "I'm sorry I had to use your clothes, but mine were shredded so I had nothing else to wear."

"It's okay Brinley, just ask me first next time okay?" he said as he moved my curls behind my ear. "I do like seeing you in my clothes though. But I'd rather see you out of them."

I looked up at him through hooded eyes, "Well Alpha, that can be arranged," I removed the tie I used as a belt, then slowly unbuttoned the shirt I wore. I saw his eyes go dark, I knew his wolf was peeking through, which turned me on, and Amanda whimpered. I could feel heat and moisture pooling in my core and the boxers I was wearing were getting soaked.

His nose caught the smell of my arousal. Amanda was purring in my head, it's been a long time since a man touched me intimately. I slowly removed the shirt from my shoulders and his hand automatically reached for me. He bent his head down, took one of my breasts in his mouth, and swirled his tongue around my nipple. I let out a moan and reached to unbutton his shirt. Before I could get it off, we were pulled out of our trance by a scream. We saw Maribel storming toward us with fire in her eyes. She grabbed me by the hair and I gave Tate a look that said 'Don't interfere.' The next thing I knew, Jacob was there pulling her off of me and rejecting her as his mate. This was crazy and I wouldn't have believed it if I wasn't seeing it firsthand.

## MARIBEL

"You don't have any right to be near him, bitch," I yelled at her. I slapped her, I did some damage too, her face was turning red. I was proud of myself. All of a sudden, someone pulled me off of her and as soon as his arms touched me I felt tingles up my arms and down to my core... *"Mate!"* I heard Sally, my wolf say.

I was stunned and hopeful it was Tate, but it wasn't, it was one of the guys on Brinley's security team. I don't know his name but I knew I wanted him. "Mate" I heard him say.

"What is your name?" I asked him.

"Jacob."

"Hi Jacob, I'm Maribel."

"What is your full name and do you have a rank?" he asked me.

*Oh, My Goddess, he's going to do this right here, right now, I'm so excited.* "My full name is Maribel Elise Wood, I was supposed to be the future beta of Black Diamond, but my rank was stripped when my dad stepped down," I said excitedly.

"So, no rank then? Just a regular she-wolf, okay, not a big deal. I, Jacob Adam Parker, Enforcer of the Winter Moon Pack, reject you, Maribel Elise Wood, of the Black Diamond pack, as my mate and future wife."

I was shocked, I immediately fell to the floor and held my chest, the pain was too much. My heart was hurting and Sally was whimpering. I heard Jacob say, "The pain will go away once you accept the rejection. Now do it and if you don't I'll have Alpha Tate command you to do it!" he yelled at me.

"But why, why are you rejecting me?" I cried.

"I'm rejecting you because Brinley is one of my best friends, she's like a sister to me, and no mate of mine will be disrespectful to her, ever! Now, accept the fucking rejection!"

With a shaky voice, "I, Maribel Elise Wood, of the Black Diamond Pack, accept your rejection, Jacob Adam Parker, Enforcer of the Winter Moon Pack, as my mate and future husband."

The pain I was feeling instantly went away but I knew the memory of the mate bond and rejection would stay with me for a very long time. Now more than ever, I want to get rid of this bitch. She took the man I wanted as a mate and then made my actual mate reject me for no fucking reason other than he's a goddess-damned friend to her!

*"Diane, can you meet me outside?"* I asked crying.

*"I'll meet you outside the dining hall by the trees, are you okay? Why are you crying?"*

# CHAPTER 19 SEEKING REVENGE

**TATE**

Maribel ran down the stairs crying, but I couldn't care less. Brin moved toward Jacob, "I am so sorry you had to reject your mate."

"It's okay Brin, she's not worthy to be my mate. I've seen how she is around you and what she's done to you. No mate of mine will ever disrespect you like that. Besides, it didn't hurt when I rejected her, so I'm okay with it. Aries and I talked about it when we first noticed her. He said he wasn't getting a good vibe from her wolf and wanted to watch her from a distance before we made a decision. Once we saw a pattern with her he was agreeable with me to reject her ass. We love you and Andi and we don't want a mate like that."

Jacob looked between the two of us, "I think you guys have some unfinished business you need to get back to. I'm going to leave now and make sure no one disturbs you. I'll be posted on the stairs leading up to the alpha floor." He turned and walked away.

I looked at Brin, walked over to her with a gleam in my eyes, and picked her up bridal style. I carried her to my suite, closed the door, locked it, and took her to my bed.

I got a taste of my mate and I needed more. I know I told her I'd take her shopping but seeing her in my clothes and watching her get angry, even if it was acting, did something inside me. Then she changed tactics on me. She may have been acting when she came on to me, but I wasn't. Now I have her locked in my room with me.

"Tate, you can put me down now, Maribel isn't here so we don't need to keep acting."

"Who says I'm acting." I could feel Chase peering at her through my eyes. "You started something and now you need to finish it," I recalled the letter she left me.

*"I wish she could feel the mate bond, Chase. I need her to feel what I'm feeling and thinking for her."*

*"I want her to feel it too,"* he whimpered.

I gently let her out of my arms but before she could get away from me, I lifted her chin, looked her in the eyes, then at her lips. She ran her tongue across them. "I'm going to kiss you, if you don't want me to, you better tell me now."

When Brin opened her mouth permitting my tongue to enter, I was ecstatic. She tastes the same as her scent, fresh strawberries. She pressed harder into the kiss. I removed the shirt she was wearing only breaking the kiss for a moment. When the shirt dropped to the floor, she whimpered. I kissed her cheek, moved to her neck, then down to her marking spot.

I lingered at that sweet space between her neck and shoulder. My mouth tingled for my canines to come out and put my mating mark on her. Instead, I gave her love bites. I loved how her body was reacting to me, only the mate bond would allow that to happen. You can have sex with anyone, but it's not as intense as a mate bond. I continued to kiss and suck down her neck to her throat, down to her breasts. I gently took one in my mouth and swirled and sucked on her nipple while my other hand played with her other breast, pinching and pulling her nipple. I smiled when I heard her moaning my name.

I got down on my knees and kissed my way down her abdomen. I snapped the tie she was using to hold the boxers on her hips and slid them down her legs. I stood, picked her up, and placed her on the bed. "Lie down Cupcake," she complied, "good girl."

I knelt and kissed up her legs, then her thighs. I worked my way to her pussy, spread her open, and dipped my tongue into her.

"Mmm, you taste so good." I withdrew my tongue and circled her clit before I plunged a finger inside her.

She arched her back, "Oh, goddess Tate, that feels so good," she moaned.

I plunged a second finger inside her, "You are so tight." I growled out as I continued sucking her clit. I knew I found her G-spot when she bucked up. I pressed down on her hips to keep her in place.

"FUCK TATE!," she screamed out. I'M GOING TO CUM!"

"Yes, Baby Girl, cum for me," I pumped in and out of her more quickly, and she released her orgasm.

"TATE!," she screamed my name and came all over my face and fingers. I lapped up every last drop before kissing my way back up to her neck where I nipped at her leaving love bites all over her neck and down her chest.

## BRINLEY

Oh... My... Goddess, I was only partially acting when I came on to Tate. I thought Jacob telling us we had unfinished business we needed to attend to was for Maribel's benefit, but I guess not. When Jacob left to guard the alpha floor, I knew I was in trouble. I mean, I like playing with fire, and Tate is someone I would like to have, but I haven't had sex since Jerod. I feel like this is my first time. I can't believe this is happening. Andi was jumping for joy in my head and I smiled at her.

"I'm going to kiss you." That's all I heard, I was a goner, I wanted him to kiss me. I wanted to turn to mush in his arms, in his bed, and anywhere else he wanted me. He leaned down and brushed his lips against mine. I didn't move, I didn't breathe, all I could do was hold onto him so I wouldn't fall. His lips were soft and gentle, and his tongue asked for permission to enter my mouth, which I opened and our tongues tangled together. He kissed me slowly and softly at first then I pressed harder into his mouth.

Tate was kissing and giving me love bites near my marking spot, which drove me crazy. Then he kissed my neck and down my throat. I was so lost in lust, that I didn't even realize he removed my shirt. *"Andi, I feel things for him, I want him to be my mate. Can we take a chosen mate, would that be wrong?"*

*"I don't know Brin, I can kind of feel his wolf. I don't know what that means but I want him too."* I let out another moan. It's hard having a conversation with Andi when Tate is doing this to me.

Tate was removing the boxers I was wearing and I could feel my core filling up. I was so wet for him. He picked me up and gently placed me on the bed, when he said "Good girl" all I wanted was to please him, to hear those words again. When he plunged his tongue inside me, I thought I was going to come undone. Amanda was dancing in my head, she was so happy. When he withdrew his tongue I was wanton with more, I... needed more... more of him.

He plunged a finger inside me and a moan left my lips. I started moving when he pushed another finger inside me. When he found my G-spot I couldn't help but scream and move my hips more. He held me in place, "FUCK TATE, I'M GOING TO CUM!" I screamed out.

"Cum for me Baby Girl" was all I needed to hear before my orgasm hit me so hard. I felt him lapping up all that I gave him and he crawled up me and nipped at my neck and chest.

I reached down and realized he still had clothes on, this was not going to work for me. I grabbed a hold of him and flipped us over. I leaned down and kissed him while unbuttoning his shirt. He picked me up so I was sitting in his lap and removed his shirt. As soon as his shirt was off, I pushed him down and kissed and nipped at his neck, sucking over his marking spot. "Fuck Cupcake, don't stop." He growled out.

My gums were tingling where my canines were and I had the sudden urge to mark him. I'm sure it's because I'm just caught up in the moment, but I was able to hold back. I kissed down his chest sucking on his nipples and rolling them between my fingers. "That feels so good," he moaned and he ran his fingers through my hair.

I kissed my way down his abdomen, my hand moved to his belt then I opened them. I pulled his boxers down, his cock sprang forward and bobbed against him. He was so hard. I looked up at him, licked my lips as pre-cum was glistening on his head and I tasted him for the first time.

He tasted delicious and I wanted more. His cock was so big and the harder it got the bigger it grew. I took him down my throat, "Aw fuck Cupcake, you feel so good with your mouth around my cock." I let out a little growl and it vibrated on his cock. I swear it grew even harder. I puffed my cheeks and sucked him in further down my throat then withdrew my mouth and licked up the sensitive skin on his shaft.

I bobbed my head up and down, I wanted more, more of him, I couldn't get enough. "Shit, Brin, I'm going to cum if you don't pull off of me." I didn't though, I wanted to taste him. I could hear his breathing change. I knew he was close. I kept sucking and I started playing with his balls. I felt them tighten then I felt his cum spurt down my throat and I swallowed every last drop.

## TATE

As soon as Brinley put her mouth on my dick, I knew I was a goner. I will do anything and everything in my power to keep this girl safe. She is my life and my world, and I can't wait until she realizes it. Chase was dancing in my head and wagging his tail, he was so happy.

*"I think I can almost feel her wolf!"*

*"Really? That's amazing Chase!"*

When she swallowed my cum, that was the sexiest thing I ever felt. I watched her take me in her mouth and was watching her as she sucked me off. She is perfect and she is all mine. When she made her way back up to me, I grabbed a hold of her and flipped us over. I needed more of her and wasn't going to stop until I was buried balls deep inside her. I moved my hand down her clit and pushed a finger inside her pussy to see how wet she was and she was soaked. "Are you ready for me?"

She moaned, "Yes Alpha."

My dick just got harder, "good girl." I lined myself up against her entrance and slowly entered her. "You are so fucking tight." I let her body adjust to my size before coming halfway out and slamming back into her. She grabbed a hold of my hair, pulled me closer, and started kissing me.

I was pumping so hard and fast when I heard her cry out, "Yes, Tate, harder."

I could feel her walls tighten around my cock, "cum for me Cupcake,"

"Tate, I can't hold it much longer, I'm going to cum! She screamed out. She grabbed me around the neck and her body shuttered shortly after as another orgasm ripped through her. A few seconds later my orgasm ripped through me.

I laid my forehead on her chest, *"Chase, I love her."*

Brin was lying there completely satiated. I got up, drew a bath, came back, and carried her in. I sat behind her as I washed the sex off her body and mine. She leaned against me with a sigh of contentment escaping from her lips. I can tell how satiated she is by how relaxed she is. I want her to feel protected, safe, and loved. After our bath, I carried her to my bed and laid her down before climbing in next to her. She snuggled right into my arms not caring we were naked,

## MARIBEL

Diane was waiting for me outside the packhouse dining hall. I grabbed her by the arm, "Come on, I have a phone call I need to make." I was angry and extremely pissed.

"Can you let go of my arm, you're digging your nails into me, and what happened to make you so fucking pissed at the world? I haven't even told you what I overheard yet," Diane said as I was dragging her away from the packhouse. "Where are we going?"

"Back to my house, my parents are gone. My dad's at the training pitch, my mom's at the daycare, and I have a goddess damned phone call to make."

"Isn't Noelle home? I thought she was coming home from college today."

"No, she had to stay for another week or two, little Miss Perfect," I said snidely. She never does anything wrong and I hate her for it "Now let's go, I'm going to ruin both of those motherfuckers for trying to ruin my future!"

"What the hell are you talking about? What happened and who are you talking about?"

"MY FUCKING MATE! That BITCH made HIM REJECT ME! Me, of all people, she made him REJECT me! No one does that and gets away with it! I WILL get him back."

"Wait! What? You have a mate? When did this happen and why would he reject you? You're the best person anyone could have as a friend, you'd make an excellent mate for anyone. You're kind, generous, helpful, not to mention beautiful. What can I do to help you get your mate back?"

"Nothing, but maybe the luna of the pack he belongs to can. That's why we're going to make a phone call and maybe I can get that bitch banned from her pack and turned rogue while I'm at it," I was angry.

We reached my house, made sure my parents weren't there, and headed to my dad's office. He still had the directory of all the pack alpha's and luna's phone numbers. Since he stepped down, he wasn't required to turn the directory in. He was allowed to keep it in case of emergencies and this was an emergency. Mates rejecting each other was frowned upon because the Moon Goddess blesses each mating and to reject that mating could be looked upon as a rejection of the blessing.

After locating the directory, I scrolled through and found Winter Moon's number, and right underneath Alpha Zane's number was Luna Estelle's number. I looked at Diane, "Well, here goes nothing," I smiled, composed myself, and dialed the number.

"Thank you for calling Winter Moon. You've reached Luna Estelle's office, how may I assist you?" said a very kind voice.

I put on my best phone voice, "I would like to speak with Luna Estelle please, it's an urgent matter."

"May I ask who's calling and what the call is in regards to?"

I could feel my anger rising and needed to rein it in. I took in a deep breath, "My name is Maribel, I'm calling from Black Diamond. Some of your pack members are visiting my pack," I cried for effect. "I just found out I'm mated to one of them and he rejected me because someone told him to," I sniffled and Diane smirked.

"Oh, my goddess, can you tell me the name of your mate and the person who interfered with the bond?"

"Yes, my mate is Jacob Parker and I don't know the girl's last name but her first name is Brinley," I added more sniffling for good measure.

"Do you know why he would've rejected you?"

"No, now can I please speak with the Luna?"

"I'm sorry Maribel, she is a very busy woman. She will want all the details before returning your call."

"Okay," I'm trying to sound sad and not pissed at this lady.

"I was talking to my alpha and Brinley came up to say hello. Then out of nowhere Jacob came, he looked at me, touched my arm, said 'mate', and then looked at Brinley. She gave him a look, then he asked for my full name and if I had a rank. Then he rejected me and told me if I didn't accept then he'd tell my alpha to command me to accept it. After accepting the rejection, Brinley started hitting me and pulling my hair," I said as fast as I could while adding more crying.

"Oh my sweet child, I will pass this along to the Luna, we'll see what can be done for you."

"Thank you," I said before hanging up.

"Wow! You were amazing on that phone call, with any luck you'll get your mate back and get her kicked out of her pack for messing with the bond. Now, can I tell you what I overheard in the dining hall?"

"Yes, and I need to show you my handiwork I did in that bitch's room," I giggled.

After putting the directory back, we headed to my room. As soon as the door closed, she proceeded to tell me what she overheard the beta's talking about then I told her what I overheard Brinley's siblings say. I told her what happened on the alpha floor too, and she was as pissed as I was. Then I showed her the pictures I took after destroying the room.

"Why didn't you wake me up to help you? I would've gladly helped."

"It was very early in the morning and didn't want to wake you."

"Well, if you do anything like that again, I want to help, so please wake me."

"Fine, I will. Do you wanna spend our day at the pool? I just bought this devilishly small bikini, it might help get my mate back if he sees me in it. It barely covers my nipples and pussy but my ass is on full display. We know how possessive mates are."

"Oooh, that sounds like my kind of game, we can stop at my house on the way so I can grab my suit."

I changed into my too-small suit, left my parents a note, and headed out the door.

**TATE**

I've enjoyed laying in bed with Brin snuggled next to me the last few days. It was the most amazing feeling, her naked body pressed against me, feeling her chest rise and fall as she slept. I love this woman and I can't even tell her. I need to check on the progress of the arena. I think the sooner it's built, the sooner she can shift, and the sooner she'll realize we're mates.

Right now, I'm just going to enjoy the feel of my naked mate sleeping soundly next to me. When she wakes up, I'll take her shopping for clothes, she can't keep wearing Quinn's clothes, or mine, and I'll talk with her about the arena. I kissed my mate on her head, held her tightly, closed my eyes, and fell asleep.

# CHAPTER 20 KEEPING SECRETS

**ALPHA ZANE**

When Essie told me about the phone call that came in from some girl named Maribel at Black Diamond saying Jacob rejected her for no reason and my Pumpkin was the cause of it, I was pissed. I was pissed at Jacob for rejecting his goddess-given mate, and Brinley getting in the middle of it was out of character for her. I wanted to leave for Black Diamond immediately but we had meetings the next few days and couldn't reschedule them.

"Zane, you need to settle down. We know our daughter and we know Jacob. There must be a good reason for him to reject his fated mate."

"Essie, there is never a good reason to reject a fated mate. It's a three-hour drive to Black Diamond, I want to get on the road. I'd like to be there before it gets too late."

"Zane, it's 6:00 in the morning, I think waiting to leave until after breakfast will be fine. Besides, you need to have food in your stomach before you confront Jacob and our daughter."

"Fine! But I want to be on the road by 9:00 am sharp!"

"Yes, Dear," I saw her roll her eyes and realized I was being an asshole.

"I'm sorry, you don't deserve to be spoken to that way. I'm just upset, please forgive me." I walked over to her and kissed her.

"You're forgiven, just promise me you won't fly off the handle until you hear the whole story."

"I promise. I will hear their side first."

We were finally on the road and arrived at Black Diamond at noon. I tried holding my promise but as soon as I stepped foot in the packhouse, all bets were off... for both of us. We stormed into the packhouse and could smell Tate and Brinley upstairs. We ran immediately to the alpha floor. Jacob was guarding the floor, "Jacob, get to the Luna office now. We need to speak with you."

"Yes, Alpha Zane." We got to Tate's door and pounded on it.

## TATE

Brinley has been spending every night with me since the incident with Maribel and Jacob took it upon himself to be our floor guard. I've been working in the private office in my suite for the last few days. It's easier to work from there instead of moving my files back and forth between my main office and the luna office. We hold meetings in the luna office and when we do I need to move my files out of the way since I can't store them anywhere in that office.

I heard someone pounding on my door. *Fucking Jacob*, he was supposed to be guarding our floor and not let anyone come up here. I looked at the clock, it was noon. I'm at my desk and Brin's currently in the shower. She and the girls are finally going shopping today since I haven't had a chance to take her and I'm glad she's going with them.

I got up from work to find out who was pounding on my door, standing on the other side were Alpha Zane and Luna Estelle... *oh shit*, now I know why Jacob let them pass by. "Alpha Tate," Luna Estelle said with irritation, her arms crossed over her chest. "Didn't I tell you, that if a hair on my daughter's body was touched, you and your beta would answer to me?"

I gulped, "Yes ma'am."

"Well, where's your beta? I need to speak with both of you, immediately. I will be using the Luna office, I suggest you come to see me in the next five minutes."

"Yes ma'am." They turned and walked away.

I closed the door and linked Ben, *"We need to be in the Luna's office in the next five minutes. Alpha Zane and Luna Estelle are here and they look fucking pissed. I think word got to her about Maribel messing with Brinley."*

*"Shit, I'll meet you there."*

*"Send Q up to my suite, Brin's finishing up in the shower and they're going shopping today. Let Quinn know I want her to get a full wardrobe of clothes and I'm moving her into my suite permanently but I don't want Brin to know that."*

*"Sure, I'll let her know and I'll see you in a few minutes."*

When I got to the office Ben and Jacob were standing there. "Do you know what this is about Jacob?"

"I have an idea."

"Mind sharing it with the rest of the class?"

"I think Maribel may have called them because of the rejection and I'm assuming she said something about getting into a fight with Brinley."

"Why the hell would she do that?"

"Because it's fucking Maribel," Ben said.

Before walking in we took a deep breath, "Let's see what this is about and get it over with."

"Alpha, Luna, what brings you to Black Diamond?" I asked nervously.

"Have a seat boys, we need to talk," Luna Estelle gestured to the chairs across from the desk. We each took a seat, she sat and folded her hands on top of the desk. "I want to know why some girl by the name of Maribel called my office and told my secretary Jacob rejected her as a mate and was also in a fight with Brinley because of it. Why would any of you allow my daughter to be in a fight when I specifically told you there would be hell to pay if a hair on her body was harmed!? Jacob, of all people, you should know better than that!"

Jacob looked at Ben and then back at the Alpha and Luna. "Alpha, Luna, Maribel is not a nice person, nor does she have a good heart. She thinks she can have and do whatever she wants and she's been disrespectful to Brinley." He went on to tell her about all the things she's been doing and the final straw that made him reject her. I could see the Alpha and Luna getting angry because of the things she's done to their daughter.

"Alpha Zane, Luna Estelle, I can assure you, Brinley is safe."

Luna Estelle looked at me with fire in her eyes, "How the hell do I know that, I haven't seen my daughter yet!"

"Ma'am, Brin has been letting Maribel and her friend, Diane, attack her. She's pretending to be weak when she's around them."

"She's of double alpha blood, even without her wolf, she can do some serious damage, why is she pretending to be weak?" Alpha Zane asked, trying to keep the anger out of his voice.

"Maribel and Diane don't know she's an alpha. She's been hiding her aura since her arrival. Nor do they know you're her parents and we'd like to keep it that way," I said.

"Brinley keeps mentioning about giving them what they deserve when she's at full strength but can't do that until the arena's built. I'm not sure what that means, but with the fire and tenacity in that woman, I can't wait to see it." It must have been the tone of my voice or something because Luna Estelle stood up, walked over to me, put her hands on my cheeks, and looked me in the eye.

"Are you her mate?"

I gulped, and nodded my head, "Yes, I'm her mate."

Jacobs' eyes flew wide open, he threw his fisted hand in the air. "I knew it! Max, Erik, and Phillip owe me a hundred bucks each!"

I turned to him, "Seriously? You made a bet on whether or not we were mates?"

"Of course we did. The way you've been looking at each other, it was either mates or just lusting for each other. Don't get me wrong, I'm glad you're mates, that way I won't have to kick your ass when you stick your dick inside her."

"Boys, this is my little girl you're talking about. No one will be sticking their dicks anywhere near her. Do I make myself clear!" Luna Estelle yelled.

"Yes, ma'am," we responded.

"Does she know?" Alpha Zane grinned.

"Neither she nor Amanda realize it, but her body does. Her body reacts to mine whenever we're close or touch."

"Zane, we need to check out the arena and see how far along the crew is. I want that arena finished sooner rather than later. We will pull our construction crew off all other projects if we need to."

"Sweetheart, that's a hundred and fifty extra wolves working on that arena, we can't just pull them off other projects."

"You can and you will, because if you don't, then I'm putting a 'Do Not Enter' sign on my pussy until you do!" My mouth dropped open, I looked at the guys, then at Alpha Zane.

"Yes dear, I'll get on it right away."

"Good, now where are my pups?"

"My mate Quinn, Brooklyn, and Crystal are getting ready to leave to take Brin shopping for new clothes since Maribel destroyed them."

"What do you mean Maribel destroyed her clothes?"

"A few days ago, when Phillip and Brin went on their mission to the rogue camp, some time between them leaving and returning, Marible snuck into her room and decimated it. She shredded her clothes and the mattresses, she busted the toilet, shower, mirrors, pretty much everything she could get her hands on in that room."

"I have a crew in there making all the repairs to it. Thank goddess she had her backpack with her, I would hate to see what Maribel would've done with silver and wolfsbane she has in it," Jacob added.

"Leave it to my Baby Girl to not leave her stash behind," Luna Estelle snickered. "Since my pups don't know we're here yet, Beta, can you let your mate know I will be joining them for shopping? Don't worry Tate, I won't say anything about her being your mate, your secret is safe with me."

"Yes ma'am."

"Thank you, Beta Benjamin. Jacob, you're coming with us. We can't have that horrible ex-mate of yours thinking anything is different. She may have called my office but I didn't directly speak with her nor does she know what I look like." She looked at Alpha Zane, "Send a link to our pack members who are on-site at this pack and tell them to treat us as regular pack members. If anyone acknowledges us as Alpha and Luna, they will deal with me directly. I will play Brinley's game while we are here, and Tate, we'll be out of your hair this evening. Now, take me to my pups."

## BRINLEY

I was getting dressed when I heard knocking on the door. "I'll be right there!" I hollered, always forgetting the rooms were soundproof. I need to get clothes and I'm so happy I'm finally going shopping today. I grabbed one of Tate's shirts, threw it over my head, and headed to the door of his suite. Quincy was standing there with a knowing look on her face. "Hey girl, you ready to go shopping? I'm assuming the clothes I brought you are still in here?"

"Uh, yeah, they are. I just prefer to wear Tate's clothes," I blushed.

"Perfect, go get dressed so we can do some damage. You can't wear his clothes shopping," she held up a credit card she had between her fingers.

I let her in, walked back to the bedroom, and changed before heading downstairs. At the bottom of the stairs, I saw my parents and ran to them, jumping in my dad's arms. I know it's childish, but I have missed them.

"Hi Pumpkin," my dad laughed. "Your mom is going shopping with you while your brother, Tate, Ben, and I check the progress of the arena."

"Dad, is there any way we can have the arena built more quickly? Amanda and I would like to shift."

"We are pulling the other crews to come and help finish it so we'll have about two hundred wolves working on it, it should be completed in half the time. They've been working on it for a month and a half already so I'm hoping it will be completed in two to three months with the additional one hundred fifty crew members."

I squealed, "Thank you, Daddy."

"Don't thank me, it was your mom's idea."

"Thank you, Mom." I gave her a big hug.

"Let's go shopping," I said as I linked arms with my mom and Quincy. Brooklyn met us outside by the car with a glare in her eyes. "What's wrong?"

"Maribel and Diane were just here."

"What'd they want?"

"They said, and I quote, 'Your lame ass, weak sister better watch her back if she knows what's good for her.'" I punched them both in the face and told them to fuck off, they ran off crying. I wish you could've seen it, it was priceless." All I could do was laugh, which caused Brooklyn to laugh, and then my mom, Quincy, Crystal, and the guys laugh. We hopped in the SUV and headed to the mall.

## LUNA ESTELLE

I was stewing while we were on our way to the mall. *I can't believe the kind of person Maribel turned into, she was so sweet when she was little. I thought I was going to be ripping Jacom a new ass for rejecting his mate. Instead, I want to throw him a party. I wanted to give her a piece of my mind when I found out the truth of what happened. I need to come up with a plan to make her think she's going to get her way, maybe I can talk with Jacob, Tate, and Brin and see what we can come up with.*

*The one thing we have going for us, she doesn't know who I or Zane is, so we might be able to pull something off. I have an idea of what kind of person she is but I want to find out more about her. She made it sound like Jacob rejected her for no reason. Zane and I need to avoid her parents because they have met us before. I wonder if they know what their 'precious' daughter was up to.*

*I hope someone took pictures of Brin's destroyed room. We might be able to get the council to banish her and turn her rogue. I doubt she'll make it an hour on her own in no man's land before she's killed. I want to personally rip this girl's head off but I will respect Brin and let her take the lead on this.*

*If I had known all it would take for Brin to get better was to send her to another pack, I would've sent her to one of her uncle's packs. Although, the Moon Goddess does know what she's doing and Brin has been better since she came here. I think it all has to do with being close to the mate she doesn't know she has. I was also surprised to find out my baby girl was able to suppress her alpha aura.*

*I wanted to give all my attention to my girls, especially Brin, knowing she was mated to Tate, I'm excited for her to find out. She needs to shift, and now that she's expressed wanting to shift, I want it to happen as soon as possible. I know our construction crew can get that arena completed in a couple of months if they are all working on it.*

## BRINLEY

"Mom... Mom... Mom! LUNA ESTELLE!" I yelled and my mom was startled. "Where did you travel off to," I laughed.

"I was lost in thought with that horrid girl, Maribel. She is something else, that one."

"You don't need to tell me twice. I've been the brunt end of her shit since the day I arrived and only because I'm a she-wolf who came back to her pack with her supposed mate."

"Her mate?"

"Uh yeah, she told me she was Tate's mate and to stay away from him."

*"Like you're going to do that now that you've had a taste of him and you know what he can do to you,"* Andi snickered.

*"Damn straight, I'm keeping him, and if he ever finds his mate, I will be challenging her."* I looked out the window of the car, "She and her friend, Diane, thought they'd teach me a lesson when we were in the bunker during a rogue attack."

"Did it hurt?"

"Seriously Mom?"

"Well, they are the daughters of the former beta and gamma so they should know how to fight."

I rolled my eyes, "My juniors hit harder than they do."

"Ouch, that bad uh."

"Yeah, I don't think they've ever trained a day in their life."

"Hey guys, we're here. Let's get some retail therapy in, max out Dad's card, and get Brin some hot clothes," Brooke said, waggling her eyebrows.

Quincy had a mischievous look, "Don't forget we need to get you some matching lingerie and cute swimsuits too. The way Tate's been drinking you in, it won't surprise me if you get pregnant before the next full moon."

Brooke must've caught my look and saw my body language change.

*"Are you going to be okay?"*

*"Yeah, I'll be fine. It caught me off guard."*

*"I think you should have Max by your side, he can help you."*

"I think that's a good idea. Can you link him for me? My anxiety is picking up and I don't want to worry him."

"Of course."

"Peanut," Max said as he came over to me. "look in my eyes and take a deep breath," I stared at him. "That's it, focus on me, good girl," he rubbed my back with his eyes locked on me. "Good, you're doing so good, Peanut," I could myself calming down..

"I'm so sorry, did I say something wrong?" Quincy asked concern showing in her voice.

"She'll be fine, Max has a way of calming her when he's around. It's kind of weird actually. He's been able to do that since we were all little pups. Now, can we please go shopping, this credit card is burning a hole in my pocket and I need to look at new swimsuits with Brinley." Booklyn quirked an eyebrow and grinned.

# CHAPTER 21 GIRL TIME

**ALPHA ZANE**

My mate just ordered me to pull all my construction crew from their current sites and bring them here. She wants this arena built and completed in two to three months instead of the remaining five it should be taking and it's going to take all two hundred of them to pull it off. They will need to work around the clock, to complete it in that amount of time, as long as they don't have any more rogue attacks, but it can be done. Our crew is fast and efficient.

Jax, Tate, and I walked to the building site. I needed to see how far along they were in the process. Once we got there, I was impressed, It's been a month and a half and they have the old building demolished and the debris hauled away. The foundation has been poured, the walls are up and they're currently building the roof. My lead foreman came over, "Al... Zane, come to check up on us uh?"

My foreman caught himself before exposing who I am, we don't need Jacob's bitch of an ex-mate catching wind we're here. "Yes, we are and I have some good news and bad news. Estelle wants this completed within the next two to three months, however, I'm pulling all the other crews off their current sites to concentrate on this one. You'll be working around the clock, will that be a problem?"

"Not unless there's another rogue attack."

"Good, they should all be here within the week."

"Thank you, Zane."

"You're welcome, and don't worry, we are monitoring the rogue cave and surrounding area. We're headed to IT next, I want to see how the cave monitoring is going."

"We can head back to the packhouse and to my office, we have the CCTVs set up there."

"Sounds good, Tate."

Once we got to his office there were a bunch of TVs set up. "John, got any good intel yet?"

"Yes Sir, we've been able to get a lock on the number of wolves, there are seventy-five left. Of those seventy-five, there are two heavily pregnant she-wolves, and one we believe isn't very far along because she keeps a protective hand over her belly. They look scared out of their minds. There are also fifteen young pups, maybe ten years old and younger who look like they have bruises all over them."

"Are you fucking kidding me, who the hell would hit pups?"

"From the intel, we got from Brin and Phillips recon, the leader, Arnold, has been using the pups and pregnant she-wolves to keep the other rogues in check. If they step out of line, he beats the kids and threatens to slit the throats of the she-wolves in front of their mates or parents."

"He is one sick bastard."

"Yes, he is Sir."

"So we're looking at only fifty-seven who can fight then?"

"Yes, Alpha, although there are a few rogues who were forced into fighting for fear of their mates getting killed or their pups. That seems to be what Arnold is holding over their heads. We also gathered, through the voice record prompts on the cameras, that most of these rogues were born to rogues and they want a pack life. They just don't know how to approach packs without getting killed on site."

"That is good to know. What we need to do is figure out who wants to defect to a pack and get the she-wolves and those pups to safety."

"The question is, how do we do that?" Tate questioned.

## BRINLEY

Even though I've only been away from my pack for a short time, I've missed shopping with my mom and sister. A lot has happened since I've been here and I needed a break from it. The first place my sister dragged us to was the lingerie store.

"I think we'll stay out here while you ladies go in there," Erik said, running his hand through his hair and nodding his head toward the store.

"Why? Are you afraid of seeing ladies' panties and bras?" I laughed.

Awkwardly, he responded quietly, "I'd rather see me tearing them off someone." We all just laughed at him and walked into the store.

Brooklyn pulled all kinds of sexy bra and panty combos, black, red, white, green, blue, silver, you name the color, she pulled it. Laughing at Brooke, and holding the lacy panties and bras up, "Why do you keep pulling these lacy things for me, it's not like I have a mate to show them off to and even if I did, he'd probably just rip them off my body anyway."

"Come on Brin, I've seen how you look at Alpha Tate, I know you like him," she waggled her eyes, "Besides, didn't you use his bathroom and bed when your room was destroyed, and I heard about you coming on to him."

"That was an act and you know it."

"Whatever you say, Baby Sis, you just keep telling yourself that," she chuckled.

I blushed, "fine, I'll buy these, but I want practical ones too." She gave me a devious smile.

"Brooke, don't you think we should be getting clothes instead of lingerie and swimsuits?"

"Priorities, Sissy, the important stuff first," she laughed. All I could do was shrug my shoulders.

We entered the swimsuit shop and again, Brooklyn went straight to the bikinis. If you can call them that. They looked more like strings holding patches of fabric where my boobs and lady bits are supposed to be. With a questioning look I held them up, "I think not, my bra and panties cover more than these."

"Oh come on, live a little. Maybe you could just wear them in Tate's jacuzzi," Quincy piped in with a mischievous look in her eyes.

"Not you too," she gave me a crooked smile.

We all walked out of there with six swimsuits each. All mine complemented my skin tone and a few of them left nothing to the imagination. I'm looking forward to wearing them to taunt Tate and piss off Maribel... two stones, one bird. Much to the boys' relief, we finished shopping. I bought, at the ladies' insistence, a full wardrobe. It almost felt like I was never leaving Black Diamond. My mom even made me buy a couple of formal gowns, which was weird. I felt like we maxed out my dad's and Tate's cards.

The next stop is furniture shopping. Tate told the boys to let me pick out anything I wanted. I have a lot of furniture to replace in that room. "Do you know how you want to decorate the room? Quincy asked.

I shrugged, "Not sure, I guess I'll see if anything strikes my fancy." We spent four hours in the furniture store. I found a beautiful king-size bed, a very comfortable couch I could fall asleep on, two new dressers, a cushy chair with a side table for reading, and a nice big mirror. After dropping ten thousand dollars we headed to the linen store for towels, bed sheets, curtains, and anything I could find I might need in the bathroom.

## BROOKLYN

Do you know how difficult it is to keep a secret from your twin sister? I know she and Tate fucked, I could smell him all over her, and knowing they are mates makes it that much harder. I want to tell her but I can't take that away from her and I promised Jaxon I wouldn't say anything. I remember how excited she was when she found Jerod. I was also there to watch her fall apart and how devastated she was when she lost him and Cassie Mae. She was a shell of herself in the aftermath of their deaths.

For a long time, Jax and I thought she would lose herself and we'd have to put her down. It was about a year after their deaths when a little boy, about six years old, asked if he could train with her. She told me later, it was that day she was thinking about taking her life because she couldn't handle the pain anymore. After that little boy came to her, she decided she had to live for Jerod and she had to live for Cassie.

She started working with the peewees but only occasionally. She helped with the juniors too, but not very often. She would never train with the elites or enforcers but only watch. "Brooky, where'd you go? You looked like you were deep in thought." Brin poked me in the head. "What were you thinking?"

"Just how happy I am to be here with you, to see the spark back in your eyes, I've missed the sparkle," I grabbed her face and kissed her nose.

"I've missed my smile too. Going on that mission with Phillip, and doing something we've trained for since we were pups, I don't know, it invigorated me. I forgot how much I loved going on missions and taking chances. Amanda and I, well, me mostly, since Amanda has been ready for a long time, are eager to shift. The arena will be ready in a couple of months and I think Branson, Maya, and Amanda have a long overdue reunion."

"Really!? That makes me so happy to hear," I hugged her tightly.

*"Brooky, I've missed my sister and I know Branson has missed her too, do you think Brin will let us play with Andi when they shift?"* Maya broke into my conversation with Brin.

*"I'm sure she will as soon as the arena is built."*

*"Can you thank her for us?"*

*"You can thank her, you know that."* I felt her pull Brin into the conversation.

*"Thank you for giving us this gift Brin. We love you."*

*"I love you both too and I'm sorry for being so selfish."*

*"Brin, you are not selfish, you were hurting,"* Branson piped in.

*"Who invited you to this party?"*

*"Hey, she's my sister too, besides, Brin linked me so I could be a part of this. I'm just excited to see Andi again,"* he smiled.

By the time we got home, it was dark out and we were very tired. I was ready for bed and I know Brin was too. "Brooke, since the furniture won't be delivered for a couple of days, can I sleep in your room until then?"

"Of course you can but I don't know that Tate will allow that."

"Why do you say that?" She said as she opened the front door and as we entered the packhouse foyer, we were met with an angry and pissed-off Maribel.

## MARIBEL

I was pissed. I was pissed when I found out that bitch was sent off with not only Tate's credit card but MY MATE who was told to go with her. How am I supposed to make him change his mind and take back the rejection when she's keeping him away from me? I stomped my feet and crossed my arms as I stormed to the front door and waited for them to come inside.

As soon as the door opened, I glared at Brinley, Quincy, Crystal, and some lady I'm assuming was her mom. Then I glared at the guys. Jacob wouldn't even look at me. I was so furious. I walked up to Brinley and slapped her across the face. She grabbed her face and took off running, crying. Good, she deserves that.

"If you people don't stop staring at me, I'll punch you all in the face!" The women all sidestepped me, as they should, I am a beta after all. Then Brooklyn walked in carrying some shopping bags and I cringed when I saw her. I moved out of her way as soon as Jacob got closer to me. I reached out to touch him, I wanted to feel those sparks again. I knew if I could get him alone, I would be able to seduce him into taking back the rejection. I put on my best smile and innocent look, "Jakey poo," I batted my eyes. "Can we talk, in private?"

I reached out to touch him and he backed away from me. "I have nothing to say to you, bitch. I rejected you for a reason. You are not good enough to be my mate. My mate would never be disrespectful to other people she feels is beneath her!"

"You will not speak to me that way! I am a beta and you are just a warrior! I outrank you by... a lot!"

"Really!? Because last I knew, your family was stripped of that title and everything that goes along with it when they stepped down and retired!"

"Just so you know... mate, I put in a call to YOUR Luna and she's going to MAKE you take back YOUR rejection!"

"Do you even hear what you're saying? You called me 'just a warrior' so why would I want to be with you? If you're not willing to be with 'just a warrior' why are you trying so hard to get me back!? Give me ONE FUCKING REASON why I would take back my rejection!" He was fuming and I needed to try and change tactics because this clearly, was not working.

I decided to do the next best thing, mates can't keep their hands off each other, especially when they don't have clothes on and I'm desperate. "We'll see if you change your mind Jakey poo," I tried to sound sultry as I removed my shirt.

"What are you doing?" He asked with horror on his face. *Gotcha big guy,* I said to myself with a smirk. After removing my shirt I worked on removing my pants.

"Are you seriously stripping in the middle of the foyer?"

"Why, yes mate, I am." I finished removing my pants and then moved to my bra. I noticed his eyes weren't changing color to show his wolf.

*"Sally, can you feel anything from his wolf?"*

*"No, it's like his wolf isn't even there,"* she pouted. *"I want my mate Mar."*

*"I know and I'm doing my best to get him back."* There is no way he will resist me standing naked in front of him, so I removed my panties and I could feel myself getting horny. I felt the wetness pooling inside me. I know he can smell me but he's still not reacting. Maybe if I masturbate in front of him he'll take me away and fuck me. If I can get him to fuck me, I know I'd be able to get him to mark me.

Putting my plan in motion, I licked my lips, moved my fingers down to my breasts, pinched my nipples, and moaned. I kept my eyes on him to see his reaction, but nothing yet. I moved my hand down my abdomen and to my pussy. I circled my clit, getting even wetter until I was dripping. I slid two fingers inside me and finger fucked myself, moaning his name.

I found my G-spot and pounded my fingers into me more quickly. I was lost in my masturbation and screamed his name as my orgasm drew closer. I couldn't think, I was so caught up in it, that I knew he would be taking me to his room any second. I finally came all over my fingers and it was dripping down my legs.

When I finally came down from my orgasm and opened my eyes, I couldn't believe what I was looking at. My mate wasn't there, he was gone. Instead of looking at my mate, I was staring at four newly shifted eighteen-year-old boys jacking off to my masturbating and that's not even the worst part, my parents were right behind them staring with their mouths open in disbelief.

# Chapter 22 Reprimanded

**TATE**

I was in my office talking with Alpha Zane and Luna Estelle about the arena when she told me about the confrontation they had with Maribel in the foyer. This she-wolf is getting out of hand and I feel it is high time we bring her parents into the mix. Maribel may be an adult and living with her parents but she's acting like a teenager so if she wants to act like one then we'll treat her like one. I wish she'd be more like her sister.

"Before I link Maribel's parents, I wanted to ask if you'd like to stay here tonight so you're not traveling in the dark. There is an extra room in the alpha suite you can use."

"That would be nice, we'll take you up on that offer," Alpha Zane said.

"I just happened to buy us both clothes while shopping with the girls today too."

"Good, that's settled then and I'm sure Brin, Jax, and Brooklyn will be happy too."

I linked Cecil and Anabel when there was a knock on the door. I stood up to answer it but Alpha Zane beat me to it. "Alpha, Luna," Jacob addressed them.

"Hey Jacob, what brings you to my office?"

"Maribel."

"What the hell did she do this time?"

"After the ladies left the foyer she confronted me. She slipped saying she called Luna Estelle's office and was pretty confident I would be forced to reverse my rejection. She told me she wanted me back and would do anything to make that happen. Then proceeded to strip and masturbate thinking it would make me jealous. Can you fucking believe that!?"

"Excuse me, she did what!?"

"She removed all her clothes and masturbated right there in the foyer. I guess she thought it would turn me on and I'd take her back. What it did was cement in my mind and my wolf's mind that we truly do not want her as a mate. When I noticed her eyes were closed I walked away. As far as I know, she had no idea I left, nor do I know what happened after."

"Are you considering reversing your rejection?" Luna Estelle asked.

"Absofuckinglutely not, I wouldn't touch her with a ten-foot pole!"

"I'm glad to hear that. I linked Maribel's parents, they should be here any minute. You are welcome to stay if you'd like."

"If it's okay with all of you, it's been a trying day and I would like to turn in."

"Go right ahead."

"Thank you, Alphas, Luna, I'll let Brin know I'm turning in for the night. See you all in the morning."

"Goodnight Jacob"

## CECIL

Even though Anabel and I retired from the beta position, we still came to the packhouse to help Tate and Benjamin. We were here now because we had a meeting with them. They are still pretty new to their positions and we want to help them as much as possible until they are confident enough to run things without us. They are exactly what this pack needs. They are confident, kind, caring, diplomatic, and treat everyone with respect.

When Tate challenged Fredrick for the alpha title and won, Anabel and I were ecstatic. I knew Tate was going to appoint Benjamin as beta and I had no interest in challenging him. I wanted to retire several years ago but Fredrick wouldn't allow it. When I was given the chance, I took it.

Walking into the packhouse, there was a commotion in the foyer and people were gathering around. We saw four newly shifted male wolves jacking off and staring at a girl. Then we saw who that girl was... my daughter, butt-ass naked and we could smell her arousal from where we stood. "What the fuck is going on in here Maribel! Why the hell are you naked!? Someone better tell me why there are four male wolves in here jacking off!"

Maribel looked shell-shocked seeing us in her compromising position. Her mother went to her, grabbed her clothes, and pushed her to the bathroom. I looked at the four young men, "what the hell do you think you're doing?"

"Sir, we came in from training and she was standing there naked in the middle of the foyer masturbating, our wolves took over, and well, we're guys," they shrugged.

"Get out of here before I report you to the alpha!" They scurried out as fast as they could and I checked on my mate and insolent daughter. I knocked on the bathroom door and Anabel opened it. Maribel was standing there with a blank look but at least she was dressed. "Maribel, what hell possessed you to masturbate in the foyer!" I was trying to keep the anger out of my voice but failing miserably.

"D... Daddy, I was t... try... trying to get m... my m... mate back," she cried.

"Mate? What mate, you never told us you found your mate."

"That's because he rejected me, Daddy," she sniffled.

"So you thought it was a good idea to get him back by masturbating, in the foyer!?" That is so disrespectful to me, your mother, yourself, this packhouse, and to your supposed mate! Your mother and I have a meeting with Alpha Tate and Beta Benjamin. You WILL go straight home and stay there until we return. When we get home we will talk about your behavior. Do you fucking understand me!?" I yelled and growled out at her.

"Y... yes Daddy."

"Good, you better get out of my fucking face right now before I have the alpha place a guard on you to make sure you do as I say!"

After sending Maribel off to our house, Anabel and I headed to Alpha Tate's office for our meeting. It was getting late for a meeting but we didn't question it. When we arrived at his office we were surprised to see the Winter Moon Alpha and Luna. "Alpha Zane, Luna Estelle, it's so good to see you again," I walked over and shook both their hands while Anabel shook Alpha Zane's hand and hugged Luna Estelle.

"What brings you to our pack?"

"Our children," Luna Estelle said.

"I thought those were your pups running around here. How has everyone been? I think the last time we saw you was at your son-in-law and grand pups funeral," my voice somber.

"We've been good. It's been stressful at times but it seems Brinley is doing better since coming here. She says she hasn't had any nightmares since arriving," Alpha Zane said.

"That's wonderful to hear," I smiled at them and turned to Alpha Tate.

"So what brings us to your office Alpha?"

"Does Maribel know who the triplets are?"

"I'm not sure what you mean."

"Does she know the triplets are the Wintoer Moon triplets?"

I looked at my mate. "She should, but I don't think she remembers them. She and Noelle were very young, maybe five and three years old when they and the triplets last saw each other. It was around that time Fredrick forbade me from bringing them with me to other packs, said it wasn't good for future relations or some shit like that."

"What does she have to do with knowing who the triplets are?"

"What we are going to say needs to stay in this office. Is that understood by both of you?"

"Yes, Alpha."

"Good."

"Cecil, Anabel I'm not sure if you're aware of this but Maribel hit Brinley and we're pretty sure she's the one who destroyed her room even though the only evidence we have is her scent. Jacob rejected her because of her aggression toward Brinley and we made her accept the rejection. She went as far as to call Luna Estelle's office too, that's why they are here. They had every intention of making Jacob rescind his rejection but after they met her, they supported Jacob."

"I can't believe our daughter did all that," Anabel was on the verge of tears.

"Well, unfortunately, it's something you need to believe. She thinks the triplets are just regular pack members and doesn't realize who Alpha Zane and Luna Estelle are and we'd like to keep it that way."

"All our pack members on site have been instructed to treat us as normal pack wolves. We don't want her to know who we are because we need to see how far she's willing to take this. We need you to pretend you don't know who we are as well and continue to think the triplets are just regular pack members who are visiting."

"Alpha Zane, you have our word, we won't disclose who you are. We'll have a talk with her about her ex-mate as well."

"I'd appreciate that, Cecil."

"I know it's late and you probably need to get home," Alpha Tate stood to walk us to the door.

"Alpha Tate," Anabel said as she stood up. She gave me a nervous look, "um, you said you needed proof of Maribel destroying Brinley's room."

"Yes I did, do you have proof?"

"I don't have proof but I did hear her sneak back into the house and squeal something about showing Diane pictures of what she did. I think she may have pictures on her phone."

"Thank you for telling me. Do not say anything to her about this, we need her to think she's getting away with it."

Her voice was shaky, "Alpha Tate, I know Maribel will be punished for her misdeeds, can you tell me what that punishment will be?"

He looked at Alpha Zane and Luna Estelle, they nodded at him. "As you know, her misdeeds have been aimed at an alpha she-wolf. Her punishment will be severe, however, that severity will be decided upon by your future Luna, Brinley."

"Brinley's the future Luna! She's been doing all these things against our future Luna? That is punishable by death!"

"Brinley is the future Luna but since her wolf hasn't been able to shift, she cannot scent us. We need you to keep this to yourselves until Brinley can shift and scent us as her mate. As for what her punishment will be, that will be placed in the hands of Brinley and Brinley alone."

"Alpha Tate, we are excited you found your second chance mate. You deserve a wonderful and strong mate after those rogues took Emberly. We are so happy for you."

"Thank you." We said our goodbyes and left.

## LUNA ESTELLE

"Do you think they'll keep their word and not mention our rank and treat us like regular wolves, especially around Maribel?"

"They better or they won't only be dealing with Tate, they'll be dealing with us," Zane huffed

"Before turning in for the night, I want to look at the CCTV and check with John to see if there's been any movement at the rogue cave. Tate and I will go with you, I want to see if they've made any plans on how we can get the rogues who want sanctuary before we attack them," Zane rubbed his hands together.

We entered Tate's office our children and Brin's security detail were there. "What are all of you doing here and Jacob, I thought you went to bed?"

"We're here because John wants to send me and Phillip out again to try and make contact with the two rogues we caught on video talking about defecting and Jacob is here because he scented Maribel near his door," Brin shuddered

"Tate you need to do something about that girl, at least put a guard on her without her knowing so someone has an eye on her."

"Yes, ma'am, I will work on it."

"Baby girl, I don't think I want you out there again."

"Mom, seriously, you know I'm the only one qualified to speak with them."

"Are you strong enough?"

"With Andi's help, I am and it's only two people. Phillip and I can handle this. I'll take the wolfsbane and silver just like last time in case we need it. We were safe then and we'll be safe now."

"I know there's no way I can talk you out of this. Can we at least talk about sending one of your siblings with you?"

Tate finally spoke up, "Brin, I agree with your mom. I don't like you going out there a second time. We need to let someone else do it."

"I'm sorry Tate, but I AM the only goddess damned one who can do this."

"Why do you think you're the only one? We have plenty of warriors between our two packs who could do it."

"Because I just am!" she yelled.

Tate held up his hands and backed away from her, "Okay Cupcake, you win, I won't stop you, but I want you to be safe."

I realized at that point Brin hadn't told Tate what she was capable of. *"Zane, did you catch that? She hasn't said anything to him about what she's capable of, she's still holding back."*

*"Yes, Sweetheart, that didn't pass me by either. But this is her decision and we need to let this play out how it's going to. Let's watch her fly with her newfound confidence and wings. We'll be there to catch her if she needs us."* We looked at her, and smiled, "Your choice Brin, either Jax or Brooklyn."

"I have full confidence in Brin's capabilities but if you insist one of us go with, then I think Jax should go. I'm still getting the hang of being useful when I apparate whereas Jax can be there if she needs the help."

"Thank you for taking my side Brooky."

"You know I'll always have your back, Sissy."

Jax walked to Brinley, and put his hands on her shoulders, "I also have full confidence in my Baby Sister. I will stay here and only go if she needs me."

"Thank you, Jax."

"Always Baby Sis," he leaned down and kissed her on her head.

"We should probably get you two hooked up to body cams if you're ready. If this is going to work, you need to get out there before they change their patrol shift," John was saying as he grabbed the body cams and Brin's backpack.

# Chapter 23 Inside Allies

**PHILLIP**

Brin and I headed to the trees just like last time, "How yeah feeling Peanut?"

"I'm frustrated they can't see I'm capable and think they still need to coddle me. I'm frustrated I can't shift yet, and I'm falling for someone I can't have because he might have a mate out there somewhere."

"I'm sorry you're so frustrated, is there anything I can do to help?"

"No, just don't treat me like I'm incapable."

"Peanut, you know I would never do that."

"I know," she lowered her head and sighed.

As we drew near, we sprayed the scent concealer on us, made sure the wolfsbane and silver were ready if we needed it, and hid behind the same rock we were at before. It was midnight so we should be seeing them soon. The hardest part about this was going to be grabbing them before they alert the others. After talking it over with each other, we felt the best way to handle this was for us to sneak up and grab them from behind.

Thirty minutes later we heard them. We turned on our body cams and as soon as they passed in front of us, we snuck up behind them, grabbed them by the neck, covered their mouths, and told them not to make a sound or link anyone or we'd snap their necks. We dragged them behind the rock and Brin moved her leg so it was touching the guy I had.

She whispered to them, "We are not going to hurt you if you stay quiet and do not link anyone. Nod your heads if you will comply." They nodded, *"We can trust them."*

We let them go and they stared at us with unease, as they should. "We need to ask you some questions then we will tell you why we are here. Nod your head if you'll answer truthfully." They nodded their heads again. "Good, My name is Brinley, and this is Phillip. I'm going to keep my hands on you while we ask questions."

"What are your names?"

"I'm Jeremy and this is Francis."

"Sorry, we couldn't meet another way."

"Pfft, no one can help us," Jeremy said.

"Oh, you are wrong. We can and will help you but we need your help too."

"What can we do?"

"We know Arnold is holding three pregnant she-wolves captive along with some pups. We know he's been using them to make some of the wolves, including both of you, do his bidding. We also know some of them want a chance at a normal pack life, we are here to help with that."

"I don't understand," Francis spoke with a shaky breath, "how can you help and how do you know this information?"

"Have you ever heard of the Winter Moon pack?"

"Yes we have, we've heard rumors about them, that's why Arnold always stayed away from that pack."

"Well, we are from that pack and our alpha has sent us to see if we can help those who want sanctuary defect to our pack. But we need your help to do it," I smiled at them and patted their legs.

"We would very much like that but again, how can we help?"

"That's an excellent question. We need to know when Arnold is going to strike the Black Diamond pack again, how many of his wolves will fight, and how many wolves want to defect. Then we'll need you to get word back to us."

"How the hell are we supposed to do that?" Jeremy was irritated.

"We have CCTV back at the packhouse monitoring the cave and it's manned twenty-four-seven." I handed him an extra camera because we didn't want them to know where all the cameras were placed in case they got nervous and looked at them. "We want you to place this camera in a spot only you and Francis will know. Once you get the information we need, find the camera you set up and push this button here, it turns on the mic. Once it's turned on say 'We've got what you need' and Philip and I will meet you the following night."

"We can tell you, Arnold isn't looking to attack again for a while. The last attack threw us off because there were more warriors, we lost several of our fighters and you captured one of them. He wants everyone to recoup before we hit them again and he mentioned something about finding more rogues."

"Okay, that's perfect, it gives us time to plan, even though we have no idea how much time, and it gives you guys time to get what we need. Keep calm and if anyone in this rogue pack is loyal to Arnold, be sure they don't hear you talking to the others. We will wait to hear from you." We let them go and Phillip and I headed back to the pack.

**JEREMY**

"Well, that was interesting."

"It sure was, I wonder if we can trust them."

"I think we can, I mean, think about it. They gave us some information, they knew things about the camp, they gave us a camera, they could've snapped our necks but they let us leave. I that's good enough in my books, plus our girls will be rescued and our pups might have a chance to be born in a pack."

"I guess you're right, I didn't think about that."

"Francis, we'll be able to help save three pregnant women, our unborn pups, younger pups, and other men and women who want a better life. Who knows, if we can help pull this off, we might even be able to hold warrior ranks at the most sought-after pack out there." I had a huge smile on my face and smacked him on the back.

We decided to hide the camera behind the rock they took us behind. No one ever leaves the path so we knew it would be safe there. We did bury it just in case though. "We need to come up with a plan on how we're going to talk with the people we know who want to defect. I wish we could link each other."

"Me too."

"Let's start with telling our mates since we have a routine of seeing them after our shift is over. They'll be able to give us an accurate count of how many pups are in there. Then we can work on the others who we know will defect."

"I'm looking forward to fighting against Arnold and choosing the good side."

"I am too brother, I am too. I never wanted this life but my brother got us all kicked out of our pack because he raped a girl. I was just a young pup around five years old when that happened. Our alpha believed if someone was getting banned the whole family should go."

"That's rough Jeremy, I'm sorry to hear that. I was born a rogue. My mom told me her alpha wanted her as a concubine even though she was married. He killed my dad to force her to be with him but she was already pregnant with me. When the alpha found out, he tried to get her to abort me, when she refused, he banished her, and she became a rogue. She tried finding sanctuary but no one would take her. As the story goes, that alpha called all the other alphas and lied saying he caught her trying to murder his mate."

"That's fucking messed up, Francis, I'm sorry."

"Thanks, my mom is still out there somewhere and I'd like to find her. Who knows, maybe after we're rescued, we can find her." I shrugged and we were silent the rest of the way to the cave.

## TATE

I was a nervous wreck watching my mate walk back out to the trees and ultimately to the rogue cave. Anything could go wrong, and again, there was nothing I could do but just wait with the rest of them and hope she doesn't get injured. After three hours, they were finally walking back through those woods and back to the packhouse. Once inside, we all gathered in my office. "So, how'd it go? Did you get what we need?"

They looked at each other and big grins formed on their faces, Brin said, "We did and they agreed to help. We also found out Arnold isn't planning on any more attacks for a while. They said he wants to try and find more rogues. He was angry we got the better of him and he wanted his wolves to recoup before attacking again. The men who are helping us are Jeremy and Francis."

"They are going to find out exactly how many men, women, and pups we need to give sanctuary to and how many are on Arnold's side. We gave them the camera as planned. They are going to hide it and make contact as soon as they can give us what we need. The CCTV needs to be monitored twenty-four-seven and when they make contact, either Brin or I need to be contacted immediately."

"Thanks, Phillip, it's almost 4:00 am, get some sleep. It sounds like we don't need to worry about anything for a little while so we'll be able to relax some." I took my mate and her parents up to the alpha floor, showed Brin's parents to their room, and guided Brin to mine.

"Uh, where are you taking me?"

"To my suite, where else do you think I'd let you sleep?"

"I was going to sleep in my sister's room."

"Nope, I'm not letting you out of my site."

"Then I'll sleep on your couch."

"You've been sleeping in my suite, in my bed since your room was destroyed. What's changed?"

"I shouldn't be sleeping in your bed when you have a mate out there somewhere. Whatever this is, between you and me, needs to end Tate. I don't mind acting when we're around those asshats, but you have a mate out there somewhere and I can't do this anymore I can't do that to her, I'm sorry." As she turned away from me, I heard her say very quietly, "I wish I could be your mate." I almost couldn't hear her, even with my wolf's hearing.

*Oh, you have no idea Cupcake. "Chase looks like we have a mate to catch."*

*"That we do."*

Have I mentioned how much I love my mate? Mate and love, are two words I never thought I'd get a chance to say, ever again. I'm so thankful to the Moon Goddess for sending her to me. I will cherish her until the day I take my last breath and I can't wait to tell her I love her.

I ran after her and before she got to Brooklyn's suite, I picked her up and carried her to mine. "I'm not letting you go." We entered our suite and as soon as I shut the door I locked it. I know it's 4:00 am, but I've missed touching her body and needed her. I scooped her up in my arms, and the moment I touched her, tingles bolted straight up my arms and down to my cock. I walked to the couch, grabbed the blanket and a pillow, walked to the kitchen, set the blanket and pillow down on the table, and placed her on top.

"What are you doing?" She giggled. I could listen to those giggles all day.

"I'm having a snack."

"A snack at 4:00 am?"

"Yes, a snack."

"Okay, you get your snack and I'll take this pillow and blanket back to the couch."

"Cupcake," I put my hand on her chin, moved in closer to her, and gently brushed my lips against hers. "You, are my snack."

She blushed and I kissed her so gently I almost couldn't control myself. She melted into me and her arousal hit my nose instantly. I moved my hand between her legs, she was so wet, she was soaking through her pants. "Your so fucking wet, would you like me to help you with that?"

"What about your mate?"

"Trust me, she won't mind."

I kissed her again, slowly moving down her neck to her marking spot. My canines extended and grazed her skin and she shuttered underneath me. I gave her love bites and sucked at her marking spot, her arousal became stronger. I moved down to her chest, slowly removing her shirt and then her bra. "You taste so good."

"Alpha, mmmm, it feels so good, please don't stop." I gripped one breast with my hand and used my mouth to suck on the other. She arched her back and moaned, "Tate."

"You are so fucking sweet, I could devour you right now." I continued to suck and moved my mouth to the other breast to give it attention. I'm kissing down her abdomen when she starts to close her legs, "Keep those pretty legs of yours open, I want to see your pretty pussy."

Chase was doing the happy dance, *"mine, my mate, no one else's."*

*"Yes, Chase ours, our mate."*

I followed her abdomen to her pussy, dipped my head and slipped my tongue around her clit, and sucked. "Mmm, you taste so good." She moaned out, grabbed my head, and pulled me closer inside her. I parted her lips and slipped my finger inside her pumping in and out. "You are so fucking tight," I growled and she bucked her hips into me.

She grabbed my hair and ran her fingers through it. She was on the verge of cumming when she finally released her orgasm and my breath stilled in my chest. *I couldn't have heard that correctly, right?*

*"Chase, did you hear what she moaned?"*

*"No, I am enjoying how her body is reacting to us, so shut the fuck up and continue or I'll come out and finish it for you."*

*"The hell you will, I'll push you back so far you won't be able to find your way to the front of my mind for a long time."*

*"Tate just shut it and keep eating our snack."*

## BRINLEY

As soon as his mouth touched my marking spot, I felt more wetness pooling in my panties. My brain was telling me to stop but my body and wolf were urging me on. I felt him giving me love bites and sucking my marking spot and I couldn't help but moan. I was falling in love with this man and I couldn't stop the feelings. Tate was kissing and sucking my breasts and I was getting wetter. He moved down my abdomen removing my pants and panties. I squeezed my legs shut, "Keep those pretty legs of yours open, I want to see your pretty pussy." This man is going to be the death of me.

He sucked my clit and then plunged his fingers into me, my body reacted by bucking up. I pulled him closer to me then he stuck his tongue inside me. I was a moaning mess. I was lost in the moment and ran my fingers through his hair, pulling him closer to me. "Oh Tate, just like that. Mmmm, it feels so good. Please don't stop, I'm so close! Please Tate more! Harder! I'm going to cum! I was so close and when my orgasm ripped through me and I breathed out and cried in my head, "I love you so much Tate, I wish we were mates."

After coming down from my orgasm, he pulled me to the end of the table and made sure the pillow was under my head. "Are you ready for me?"

"Yes, oh goddess yes, please, I need you inside me." He teased the outside of my lips with his cock, are you sure, Cupcake."

"Yes, I need you!"

"What do you say?"

"Yes, Tate, I need you, please," I moaned.

"Call me Alpha."

"Please Alpha, I need you inside me." He slammed into me filling me up, after I adjusted to him, I urged him to move, I wrapped my legs around him to bring him closer to me and he started pounding into me.

## TATE

I loved the way her body accepted me. I loved watching her tits as they bounce up and down when I pound into her. She is the sexiest woman I have ever seen. *"Chase, she is perfect for us,"*

*"Yes, she is. I can't wait to see her wolf so I can mark and mate her."*

*"I'm looking forward to that too."*

I continued to pound into her. My balls were tightening and knew I was close, but I wanted, no, needed Brinley to cum first. I spit on my finger to play with her clit as I was pumping in and out of her. "You are so fucking tight and you feel so good. I reached my free hand up to play with her nipple. Don't ever tell me I can't have you, Brinley. Do you hear me?"

"Yes Tate, oh goddess yes, Tate, I hear you... I'm going to cum," she said breathlessly.

"Cum for me Cupcake." A few seconds later I felt her tightening around me and then her body shuttered as another orgasm ripped through her, and a few seconds later I filled her up not caring if I could get her pregnant or not. I pulled out of her, already missing the feel of her on my cock. I picked her up and carried her to the bathroom. I sat her on the counter, ravishing her mouth and pussy a second time. I broke the kiss, started the shower, and carried her to it. "Shit Brinley, I can't stop touching you," I said as I started sucking her tits again.

After taking her to the shower and ravishing her body two more times, I could tell she was completely exhausted and satiated. I carried her to my bed, pulled the covers over her, and just as she was about to fall asleep, I climbed into bed. I pulled her close to me, kissed her on the head, and as soon as she curled in my arms, she fell asleep. I whispered in her ear, "I love you too Brinley and I also want you as my mate," and I fell into a sound sleep.

# CHAPTER 24 CATCHING MARIBEL

**ANABEL**

*****Two Weeks Later*****

I'm still in shock at seeing my daughter naked in the foyer. The meeting with Alpha Tate and the Alpha and Luna of Winter Moon was an eye-opener. Hearing the horrible things Maribel did to their daughter and might still be doing breaks my heart. I don't want to believe she's the one who destroyed that room and has been purposefully harming a guest in this pack all because she thought Brinley was stealing the Alpha Adam away from her. Not to mention us knowing Brinley is to be our luna and not say anything, that goes against wolf hierarchy.

I understand why they're requiring us to keep their ranks and who they are under wraps, I just wish we didn't need to. My daughter has dug herself a deep hole and I don't want her to keep digging it deeper by continuing to do such stupid things. I don't know if she's forgotten what her treachery and rage will cost her or if she just doesn't care. She's my flesh and blood, as her parents we are supposed to protect our pups, keep them safe, and teach them right from wrong. We did that, we taught them both right from wrong but in the end, as an adult, she has to make her own decisions.

That's why I struggle with the reality of this. She has taken our protection of her for granted. She thinks she can do whatever she wants without consequence because we've always fixed things for her. When she was younger, she'd come home crying because the other kids were mean to her. She would tell me they were jealous because she was a beta and I would believe her. I never wanted to believe either of my girls could make bad choices. Maybe that's where I went wrong.

Cecil would always tell me I spoiled them but I brushed him off. Now look where we are, I can't brush this off, this is all her. There is no more hiding behind a wall, it's in front of me and now I'm going to lose my eldest daughter because of it. My hurt turned to anger. Anger because she put us in this position, anger at myself because I hated punishing my girls for things when they were younger, anger because it hurt me more to see them sad or cry so I would coddle them instead.

I know what must be done and I have the strength to do it. I need to find her phone and get evidence of what she has done. If she did do this and took pictures, I have to turn her over to the alpha so she can be punished for her crimes. As much as this will hurt me and as much as she will try to make us fix this for her, we can't. We can't fix this and she will lose her life because of it. That is the reality of this and there is nothing I can do but watch it play out and it breaks my heart.

I'm thankful her sister isn't here to see what she's causing. Maribel hasn't always been a wild child, she used to be kind and caring just like her younger sister, Noelle. Noelle didn't make a fuss when we were stripped of our beta rank. She went along with it and left for college once she graduated high school. Maribel on the other hand, had a very difficult time with it. Noelle may be two years younger than Maribel but she has a better head on her shoulder than her sister does. I need to do this, even if it hurts my relationship with my daughter. Standing at her bedroom door, I knocked.

"Honey, may I come in?"

"It's open Mom."

I walked in and saw her phone sitting on her bed, unlocked.

"Hi Mom, what do you need?"

"I wanted to talk with you for a few minutes."

"I was getting ready to shower. Diane and I are going shopping and to a movie, can we talk after my shower?"

"Sure Honey, is it okay if I wait in your room?"

"Sure, can you give me fifteen minutes?"

"I'll be here."

Leaving her phone on the bed she walked into her bathroom and closed the door. I waited until I heard her in the shower before picking it up. Taking a deep breath I opened her pictures hoping not to find what I was looking for. Scrolling through her pictures my heart dropped. There were pictures of Brinley with her siblings, by herself, with her security detail, with the alpha and beta, and even Crystal.

She saw videos and then pictures of a destroyed room and in one of the photos, I could make out her satisfied face in one of the mirrors holding red lipstick. I knew I had to get these pictures to Alpha Tate. I took out my phone taking pictures and videos of what I found so I could send them to him.

I heard the shower turn off and quickly put my phone away and made sure her phone was placed back on her bed exactly how she had it sitting. She came out of the bathroom a few minutes later, walked to her closet, and got dressed.

"So what did you want to talk about?"

"Noelle is due to come home soon, I was wondering if you'd like to help plan a welcome home party for her and help me decorate? Alpha Tate said we could use the common dining room."

"I would love to help! I'm excited she's finally coming home, I've missed her so much."

"I'm happy to hear that, I thought I was going to have to do this by myself," I chuckled.

"Mom, she's my sister, I would never let you do this on your own. I'll even see if Diane will help."

"Thanks, Honey. I'll let you get ready, you and Diane have fun shopping and going to the movies."

I gave her a hug and kiss and walked out of her room to do the next hardest thing, turn my daughter's infractions over to the alpha.

## BRINLEY

Tate was in his office getting some work done so the boys and I decided to check on the progress of the arena. I was excited to see they had all the plumbing finished and were working on the electrical, it's coming along and I can't wait until it's finally finished. All of a sudden I was feeling hot and it took me a minute to figure out why. *Fuck*, "Uh guys, you need to get me back to the packhouse, and stay alert."

Erik took one look at me before my scent hit him, "oh shit," he shifted immediately, *"get on my back."* The other guys realized what was happening and they also shifted. It was their best defense to keep unmated males away from me when we were outside and my heat came. Since we were raised as siblings, my going into heat doesn't affect their wolves like it does other unmated wolves.

As soon as we got to the house, Quincy was walking out. My voice was frantic, "Quincy, can you link Crystal, I'm going into heat."

"Oh shit, get her to Tate's suite, the doors are reinforced, Tate won't even be able to break them down if he tries to get to her." Erik nodded his head and all five of us headed upstairs, the guys staying in wolf form. Once we were in the suite, my heat picked up. I needed to be in cold water. They all shifted back, Jacob locked the doors and stood guard with Phillip. Max undressed me while Erik got my bath ready. Once Max brought me to the bathroom, he picked me up and placed me in the tub.

There was a knock on the suite door but before opening it, Jacob and Phillip made sure it wasn't a male. Crystal and Quinn were standing there, "where is she?"

"In the bathroom with Erik and Max."

They came inside and I heard Crystal, "I want you guys to stand guard outside and not let anyone in."

"Yes, ma'am." I heard a different kind of lock engage on the door.

"How long ago did your symptoms start?" Crystal asked as she walked into the bathroom.

"About twenty minutes ago, we were down at the arena checking it out. When I was feeling hot, that's when the boys brought me here."

"You being in heat and naked doesn't bother their wolves?" Quinn asked.

"No, we were pretty much raised as siblings, so they don't react to me."

Another wave of heat hit me and I needed to relieve it, so I stuck my fingers inside my pussy and cried out. I could feel Amanda trying to reach out to someone, anyone when Tate popped into my mind. "Amanda's trying to reach out to Tate's wolf." With him on my mind, I moaned his name as I plunged my fingers deeper into me. My other hand grabbed my nipple and I pinched and pulled until an orgasm hit me hard.

"Quinn, you stay here with Brin, I'm going to get some sex toys for her, she's going to need them. I'll also have someone bring food for all of us. Be sure to engage the door lock when I leave, we don't need Tate getting in here, especially if Amanda succeeds in calling Chase."

"But I need Tate, I need his dick inside me, I need relief. I plunged my fingers inside me again. Please let him come," I begged.

"Brin, if we let Tate in here, he will mark you and you won't be happy we allowed that."

I knew they were right and to be honest, I wouldn't be happy with myself and I would probably end up pregnant. Having sex constantly for five days with few breaks would almost guarantee that. Being in heat is exhausting and I don't like to be touched in any way for a few days after.

"We'll be here for at least five days. Quinn, you may want Benjamin to bring you some clothes as well because you aren't leaving this suite and neither am I."

## TATE

It's been two weeks since the whole Maribel debacle and talking with Jeremy and Francis. I asked Anabel and Cecil to keep Maribel busy so they decided to plan an impromptu welcome home party for Noelle, which should keep her out of our hair for now.

Alpha Zane and Luna Estelle went home two weeks ago and Jaxon and Brooklyn went with them. The arena should be finished in another month or so and they said they'd be back once it's finished. Jeremy and Francis haven't reached out yet either. All we've been getting are thumbs up in the camera. We have to assume they are still working on gathering intel.

I was in my office sitting at my desk when I was feeling uncomfortable. I couldn't keep still and Chase was agitated too. *"Chase, do you know what's going on? I'm feeling hot and can't keep cool."*

*"No, but I can feel Brinley's wolf, he's calling to me."*

*"What the hell, how can you feel her wolf?"*

*"I don't know, I just can. We need to go to her now!"* He didn't need to say that twice. I left my office, her scent was strong and coming from my suite. I was running up the stairs when I got a link from Anabel.

*"Alpha Tate, can we meet?"*

*"Not right now, there's something I need to take care of first, can it wait?"*

*"It's regarding Maribel, I found evidence on her phone of what she did to the room and she's been stalking Brinley too."*

*"Fucking hell, meet me in my office, I'll be there in ten minutes."*

*"Yes, Alpha."*

*"Make sure Cecil is there too,"* I closed the link before she could answer. I got to my suite and blocking the doors were Erik, Phillip, Jacob, and Max. "Sorry Tate, we can't let you in."

"Why the hell not! Last I checked, that's my suite." At that moment the door opened and Crystal stepped out.

"Alpha," she said nodding her head at me. Turning to the guys she said, "DO NOT, I repeat, DO NOT, let anyone in this room other than me and Beta Quincy. Especially the Alpha, is that understood?" She turned and glared at me when she said that last part.

*What the hell, it's my fucking suite!*

"Yes Doctor," they said in unison.

"Can someone please tell me what the hell is going on? Chase is ready to jump out of my skin."

Crystal grabbed my arm, "Come with me, we need to talk." She walked me into what used to be Brin's room and closed the door. "Brinley is in heat. That's why Chase is unsettled and you're looking and feeling the mate effects of her heat." She held up her hand as I was about to speak. "Before you say anything, even though neither of you has marked each other, the pull is strong because you are both alphas."

"Okay, but Chase could feel her wolf calling to him."

"Again it's because you're both alpha's. Her wolf wants to mate so she can produce pups. You cannot go to her, if you do, the pull to mark her will be too great and she'll think you're marking her out of the intense sexual drive and not out of love or the mate bond. If you do that, she may reject you when she finds out and I don't think you or Chase wants that."

"No, we don't. Why didn't she get on suppressants?"

"To be honest, we've been so busy, that we both forgot about it. She's going to be in heat for five days. If you don't think you can stay away from her, then I'll need to send her back home."

"I'll do my best to keep myself and Chase under control, but if I can't, then you have permission to send her to Winter Moon. Black Diamond is her pack whether she knows it or not."

"Understood Alpha."

I turned around and walked back to my office to see what Anabel had. My mate's upstairs, in heat, and all Chase and I want to do is fuck her until we put a pup in her. I'm sure the door locks were engaged so there's no getting in there. I linked Ben, *"Meet me in the luna's office."*

He's already in there when I walk in. "What's gotten up your ass, you look like you're about ready to punch someone."

"Quinn hasn't told you?"

"Tell me what?"

"Brinley went into heat."

"Oh man, that fucking sucks for you."

"You too."

"Why would her going into heat suck for me, she's not my mate."

"No, but Q is. She and Crystal are with her now, which means I'll probably be bunking with you until her heat is over. Which also means extra training for both of us because I'll need to get rid of this pent-up sexual frustration."

"Fucking hell, are you serious!"

"Sure am."

"Not cool bro, not cool. Did you call me to the Luna's office to tell me she's in heat, or is there another reason you needed to meet with me?"

"Cecil and Anabel are meeting us in my office."

"Your office? Not the Luna office?"

"Shit, I forgot. *Anabel, Cecil, can you meet me and Beta Benjamin in the Luna office instead?"*

*"We'll be there in a minute."*

"Why are we meeting with them?"

"Anabel was able to check Maribel's phone and found the evidence we needed on it. She also discovered she's been stalking her."

"She's what? What in the hell is wrong with that she-wolf!?"

"I don't know man, but I told them to keep her busy to keep her away from Brin. She needs a break from her, that's why we haven't seen her around the packhouse. I told Anabel and Cecil to plan a welcome home party for Noelle so they can use that as an excuse to keep her busy."

"Great idea." There was a knock on the door and Ben answered it.

"You wanted to see us?"

"Yes, please come in and have a seat. I'll get right to the point. Anabel, did you inform Cecil what you found?"

She looked nervous, "No, I haven't."

"Very well, would you like to say it or me?"

"No, I will," she dropped her head. "I was able to look at Maribel's phone this morning while she was in the shower. I found pictures and videos of her stalking Brinley and of the destroyed room."

"How do you know it was her who destroyed the room from the pictures? Maybe someone sent them to her." Cecil asked.

"Because in one of the pictures, she accidentally caught herself in the mirror, almost happy about it, holding the lipstick in her hand."

"How do you know she's been stalking her?"

"I'll show you, Cecil. Look, I took pictures and videos of what I found on her phone."

"I can't believe she would do this!"

"I don't have pups, but I can't imagine what you're going through. I know it must be difficult and I'm sorry you have to go through this."

"If you don't mind, even though she's an adult, she's still living under your roof, do we have permission to hack her phone to verify it was used to take the photos and videos? As you know, these are infractions against a future Luna who happens to also be of alpha blood," Ben asked them.

"You have our permission Beta. Our daughter needs to learn she can't get away with things like this."

"Cecil, you do understand, if she's guilty of this, she could be put to death at the hands of Tate or Brinley. Most likely, by Brinley, since the infractions were done against her and chances are she will be put to death."

"We understand. She has been out of control for a while. We were hoping once she found her mate, she'd see the error of her ways and make the necessary changes. It was too little too late for her since her mate was one of Brinley's security and the infractions were against her. As her parents and former betas, we fully understand the consequences of her actions. Whether she understands them is another thing altogether," Cecil said.

"Speaking of her mate, have you spoken to her about him yet?"

"No Alpha, we haven't."

"I expect that to be done in the next couple of days."

"Yes, Sir."

"If there's nothing else you may be excused." They got up and left. I feel bad for them but as former betas, they should've expected more from their eldest daughter. I'm thankful Noelle is the opposite of her sister.

# CHAPTER 25 OLD HABITS

**MARIBEL**

My mom has been keeping me so busy with planning and errands for Noelle's party I haven't had time to do anything to Brinley to get her back for interfering with my mate bond. I asked Diane to keep an eye on her and send me pictures and videos of her though. I found out Brinley's in heat. Diane overheard Crystal say something to the kitchen omega's and she called me right away.

I'm happy she won't be around to stop me from getting Jacob back. The last thing I tried pretty much backfired on me so I need to figure something else out. Hmm, I tapped my finger to my chin, I know she's been seducing Tate, maybe the heat pheromones coming from his suite will make him horny and want to fuck someone, like me. *I think I know what I'm going to try.* I thought with a devilish smile.

"Maribel! Are you home!?" I heard my mom yelling.

"Upstairs!"

"Can you come down here please!"

"Yes, I'll be right there!" I hope it's not more errands, I was just out shopping for three hours and I don't want to go out again.

"Aw, there you are daughter. Come sit with me so we can talk," my dad patted the couch next to him.

I walked over and sat down, "Dad, if we're going to talk about the party, Mom and I have it under control."

"It's not about the party, it's about your mate."

"Uh... my mate? Dad, with all due respect, my mate rejected me and I DO NOT want to talk about it," I huffed and crossed my arms.

"Listen, young lady, We are going to talk about it whether you like it or not, and we are also going to talk about your behavior regarding visiting pack members too," he said a little too calmly and it made me nervous.

"Which do you want to talk about first?" My mom asked gently, patting my leg.

"I didn't do anything to deserve Jacob rejecting me," I cried, hoping I could end this conversation sooner.

"Why don't you tell us what happened, Sweetheart." *Shit, since I'm not getting out of this anytime soon, I may as well make it look like Jacob and Brinley's fault.*

"Fine," I huffed, "Diane and I were minding our own business hanging out in the theatre getting ready to watch a movie when I smelled the most amazing scent, pina colada. It was refreshing and when I turned around to see where it was coming from, Jacob was standing there. He was the most handsome man I've ever seen."

"Sally went crazy jumping around and I saw his eyes darken. I walked over to him, and we each said 'Mate,' he kissed me and I didn't want him to stop. Then Brinley walked in and interrupted us." I was laying it on thick and lying about how and where it happened, but they didn't know the truth, so no harm.

"He was about to take me upstairs to mate and mark me but she stopped us. She told him he had to reject me because she couldn't have anyone on her stupid security detail having a mate. Once he rejected me, she told me I had to accept or she'd tell Tate to command me to do it." I covered my eyes pretending to cry. I think it worked too because my parents looked very concerned.

"Sweetheart, I'm so sorry that happened to you. Why didn't you come to us right away or tell Alpha Tate what happened?"

"You and Dad were busy, I didn't want to interrupt you and Tate was in a meeting. I thought I could handle it on my own."

"Okay Sweetheart, but why did you feel it necessary to masturbate in the foyer?" The disappointment in my dad's eyes was grating on me.

"Daddy, I was desperate to get my mate back. I would try anything, even if I had to humiliate myself to do it."

"Oh, my poor girl." My mom hugged me. "Is there anything we can do to help you win him back?"

"You would do that?"

"Of course we would. You're our pup, we'd do anything to help you if we can and can."

"You said he's part of Brinley's security detail. I still have the contact information for the Winter Moon Alpha and Luna. I'll go to my office right now and speak with Luna Estelle and see what she can do. I'm sure she'd be happy to clear this up and make him rescind the rejection.

*Fuck my life, how do I get out of this. If he calls her office, they'll tell him I called and what I said.* "Dad," I pulled him down to sit again, "we don't need to get his Luna involved in this. I'm sure it's just a misunderstanding, we can fix this on our own."

"Are you sure, Sweetheart?"

"I'm positive, I'll figure it out."

"Alright, but if you need us to, we'd be happy to call her."

"Thank you, Daddy, I'll let you know if I need your help." *Maybe if Jacob sees me with Tate it will make him jealous and he'll take me back.*


## ANABEL

*"I cannot believe our daughter just lied to us. It makes me wonder how many other things she's lied about over the years. To have her look us in the eye, and blatantly lie about what happened with her mate, makes me so angry."*

*"I know, I'm ready to take her to the dungeon myself and tell the alpha to handle her any way he feels."*

"She turned the offer to call Luna Estelle down real quick."

"She did, she didn't want us finding out she's already spoken to Luna Estelle's secretary."

"Are you ready for the next part?"

"No, but we don't have a choice."

"Maribel, what's been going on with not being respectful to the visiting Winter Moon pack members."

She put on a smile, "I have no idea what you're referring to, Daddy."

"We were told you haven't been nice to anyone from that pack."

"Daddy, I haven't done anything to anyone, I've been welcoming and kind."

"You sure you want to stick with that answer?"

"Yes."

"Then why did we hear you beat up Brinley in the bunker during the rogue attack."

"It wasn't me, it was Diane. I tried pulling her away but she kept hitting her. I told her to stop but she wouldn't."

"So Diane was the one who kept hitting her?"

"Yes, and I saw her pulling her hair too. She told me she destroyed Brinley's room and even sent me pictures. Do you want to see them?"

*"Is she going to show us the pictures she took on her phone and pass them off as Diane's doing? I don't know where we went wrong with this child. Noelle is nothing like her and we raised them the same. I'm so disappointed in her and her actions. I know I.T. is going to hack her phone, but I want to see if she'll give it to us."*

*"I don't know either. I'm curious to see how she's going to dig herself out of the hole she got herself into."*

"Can we borrow your phone so we can show Alpha Tate the pictures she sent you?"

**MARIBEL**

*I stared at my mom. If I say no, they might figure out I lied but if I say yes they will most likely think I'm telling the truth.* "My phone is in my room. Let me go grab it and make sure I didn't delete the pictures." I ran upstairs, grabbed my phone, and archived all my text messages with Diane. If they ask, I'll just tell them I archive messages randomly and accidentally archived the ones to Diane.

I ran back downstairs, handing my phone to my mom. "Here you go."

"Thanks, Sweetheart."

"You're welcome," I smiled hoping I was doing the right thing. Even if I get in trouble, my parents are always there to bail me out.

"Your mom and I are going to get your phone over to I.T., is there anything else you need to tell us before we leave?"

"No."

"You're sure?"

"Yes, I'm sure, I told you the truth about everything."

"Okay, because there will be huge consequences if anything is found and we won't be able to help you out."

I smiled, "They won't find anything Daddy, I was trying to stop Diane, my hands are clean." My parents finally left for the packhouse and I was alone, wondering if I did the right thing. I didn't dwell on it too long because I needed to put my plan in motion and find Tate.

**TATE**

I need to burn off some energy. Brinley's been in heat for five hours and Chase has taken me upstairs every thirty minutes. The last time I went up, the guys told me if I came up again they were locking me in a cell until her heat was over. I linked Ben and told him to meet me at the training pitch.

We'd been training for two hours when I got a link from Cecil, *"Alpha, Anabel and I need to see you. We spoke with Maribel and she gave us her phone willingly."*

*"Ben and I will meet you in the Luna's office in twenty minutes."*

*"We'll be waiting."*

*"Crystal, can you ask Max to link John and have him meet me in the Luna's office please."*

*"Sure will Alpha."*

*"Crystal?"*

*"Yes?"*

*"How's she doing?"*

*"Not good. She's doing her best to stay strong but since you are near, her heat is really bad and she's in a lot of pain. Her body's reacting to you being near but she and Amanda have never had a heat like this so they think something is wrong."*

*"Do you think having her go back to her parents' pack would help?"*

*"At this point, I'm willing to try anything. She's only getting fifteen minutes of rest between each fever spike and the sex toys I brought up aren't even touching her sexual desires. She knows you can't be in here and every time she cries out for you we remind her you'd lose control of Chase. She's been asking for Max, but Tate, he's my mate and we're not marked, I don't want him to see her like this."*

*"Crystal, you need to listen and listen carefully, okay?"*

*"Yes, Alpha."*

*"I felt the same way until I saw how she calmed down around him. They have all been very close since they were little pups. They view each other as siblings, as well as friends. He would never do anything to jeopardize that, not to mention, none of the boys' wolves react to her that way."*

*"Okay, okay, so you're saying we can trust them?"*

*"That is exactly what I'm saying."*

"I need to go. Ben and I are meeting Cecil and Anabel shortly. Let me know if Max can help with her fever. Otherwise, we may need to contact her parents."

*"Will do, Alpha."*

Ben and I showered and as we came out of the locker room, there was a butt-ass naked Maribel, playing with her tits and pussy. *"Just what we fucking need right now,"* I linked Ben. *"I'm trying to hold Chase back because he's so damn horny right now he'd fuck anything and pretend it's Brinley. My cock is getting hard just looking at her, I'm going back in to take a cold ass shower, get rid of her. I want her gone in five seconds, call a warrior if you need to."*

*"She'll be gone, Tate."*

# CHAPTER 26 TIME OUT

**BENJAMIN**

It shouldn't have shocked me to see Maribel standing in the men's locker room butt-ass ass naked playing with herself, but I was. She's back at her games and all it's doing is pissing off all the ranked members. She probably asked where to find us or overheard others saying where we were. I don't know what she's thinking but if she's not careful when Brin finds out, she's going to find herself in a world of hurt by Brin's hands and wolf and I'm bringing the popcorn.

I grabbed a towel and walked over to her, "Maribel, what in the fucking hell are you doing in the men's locker room? You know women are not allowed in here!"

"I came to see Tate. I heard that bitch is in heat and staying in his suite. I'm sure he's having a difficult time and thought I could take care of his needs. I'm not stupid Benjamin, I know when an unmated alpha wolf is around an unmated she-wolf in heat the pull is too strong to stay away. I'm hoping to help him with some release he may need," she smirked while batting her eyes at me.

I rolled my eyes. "That's Alpha Tate and Beta Benjamin to you, and Brinley being in heat isn't YOUR concern. I threw the towel at her, "You have three seconds to get dressed before I call a warrior to drag your nasty ass out of here."

"You know what Benjamin!... " She threw the towel on the bench.

I cut her off, "BETA Benjamin to you, you fucking bitch!"

"How dare you call me that," she growled, "I'm a lady and expect to be treated like one!" she stomped her feet.

"If you were a fucking lady, you wouldn't be standing in the men's locker room butt-ass naked getting yourself off and trying to hit on YOUR ALPHA so you can FUCK HIM! No wonder Jacob rejected your ass! You are not worth the oxygen you breathe!" I felt bad for saying that, I want to build people up, not tear them down but I wasn't in the mood to be nice to her.

*"Adam, Pete? Can you come to the men's locker room by the training pitch and haul Maribel's nasty ass off to the cells per Alpha Tate's orders."*

*"We'll be right there."*

Maybe if she stayed there for a few hours she'd grow the fuck up. "Ah, here's your escort now," I smiled. Adam and Pete, two of our warriors walked in and grabbed her.

"Get your fucking hands off of me, where are you taking me, let me get dressed you fucking idiots!"

"Oh and Maribel! Next time put your clothes on when you're told, you might be more comfortable." I laughed, picked the towel back up, and threw it at her as they hauled her off to the dungeon cells for a few hours.

"It's safe Tate, you can come out."

"Thank the Moon Goddess, what is her fucking problem?"

"She was hoping to seduce you."

"Not on her fucking life. Where are they hauling her ass off to?"

"The dungeon, I thought she could spend a few hours there." I laughed and smacked Tate on the back. "Let's get to that meeting, we need to tell her parents where their dear ol' daughter is."

## MARIBEL

"Where are you taking me? Get your fucking hands off of me!"

"Sorry, no can do, we have our orders."

"Where are we going!?" I keep trying to get out of their grasp but I can't, they are too strong.

"Keep struggling and I'll use wolfsbane on you, Sweetheart," one of them said.

"What are your names so I can report you to the alpha? He would never condone this!"

"My name's Adam and this is Pete, but you were told that when we came to get you. You can report it all you want, he's the one who ordered it."

"You're lying! He'd never do this to me!"

"You're probably right, but the beta would," they snickered, "and last I checked, the beta takes orders from the alpha."

We were heading toward the dungeon, which was the last place I expected. I figured they would take me home. "You can't put me in there, I'm of beta blood and I don't belong there!" I'm still struggling against them when I feel a needle stick in my arm. "What the hell did you poke me with?"

"Wolfsbane, we told you we would inject you if you didn't stop struggling. Your choices have consequences. Your wolf will be asleep for a while and you'll be too weak to struggle." I stumbled as they pulled me along, one of them picked me up and threw me over his shoulder. Then everything went black.

When I came to from my blackout out I was in the cell, naked. "Guard? Guard!" I screamed.

I heard a door open, "pipe down!"

"How long have I been down here?"

"Two hours."

"Can you let me out!"

"Sorry, alpha's orders, he'll let me know when you can be released."

"That's fucking messed up!"

"Then you shouldn't have fucking messed with the alpha! There are consequences to your actions you know!"

"Can I at least get some clothes?"

"You chose to not get dressed when given the chance, so no, you can't have any clothes, you get to be naked."

"That's so fucking messed up!"

"Again, that was your choice, not mine. I'd prefer your ugly ass to be covered."

"I don't have an ugly ass!" I screamed. "Can I have a blanket or towel at least?"

"You chose not to take the towel when it was tossed at you so no, you can't have a blanket or towel."

"You are such an asshole!"

"And you are such a bitch!"

"My parents will get me out of here when they find out where I am!"

"No, they won't, they know you're here and said you can stay and maybe learn your lesson."

"Oh, and what fucking lesson am I supposed to learn?"

"If you haven't figured it out yet, then I guess you get to keep me company until you do. I think this is more of a punishment for me than you, bitch!"

"Don't call me that!"

"Why not, if the shoe fits, wear it!" He slammed the door shut, effectively ending any human contact I'm going to have for the foreseeable future.

"HOW AM I SUPPOSED TO FUCKING KNOW WHAT LESSON TO LEARN IF I'M NOT FUCKING TOLD WHAT THE LESSON IS!!!" I screamed at the top of my lungs to no one. Then I did the stupidest thing ever, I grabbed a hold of the cell bars to shake them and burned my hands. "STUPID FUCKING SILVER! Then I kicked the cell door and burned my feet. "I FUCKING HATE MY LIFE RIGHT NOW!!

## TATE

Ben and I made our way to the office while Maribel was being hauled to the dungeon and put in a cell. I'm hoping she'll learn a lesson while in there and change her ways. I'm not holding my breath though. Cecil, Anabel, and John were waiting for us when we arrived. "Come on in. Before we get started, you should know that I had warriors take Maribel to the dungeon and they put her in a cell."

"What? Why? What did she do now?" Cecil asked, rubbing his temples.

"When Beta Benjamin and I came out of the locker room showers, she was butt-ass naked and getting herself off in front of us. Beta Benjamin said she found out Brinley was in heat and wanted to use that against me. I told Benjamin to get rid of her and if needed call the warriors to escort her. They gave her wolfsbane, she was fighting them we're keeping her there until I decide to release her."

"I can't believe what our daughter has been doing. Please keep her there, maybe it will do her some good." Cecil said.

"I will do that, thank you for agreeing to keep her there. Now, to the issue at hand, did you bring her phone?"

"Yes, we did, here," he handed it to me.

"Thank you. John, can you take it and see if the pictures and videos were taken by it or if they were sent to her?"

"Sure can, I'll be back in a few minutes."

"Thanks, John," Cecil said nodding his head.

"How's Brinley doing with her heat?" Anabel asked.

"According to Crystal, her heat is pretty bad. Her fever spikes about every fifteen to thirty minutes and nothing has been able to calm it."

"I'm sorry she's going through this."

"Thank you."

John returned fifteen minutes later. "What's the verdict?"

"The pictures and videos were taken by her phone. We also found pictures and videos that were sent to her from another phone. We traced those and they came from Diane's phone. It looks like Maribel had Diane spying on Brinley too."

"So what are we going to do with this information?" Ben asked.

"That, I haven't figured out yet, but I'm open to suggestions if anyone has something," I said, at a loss. "Well, now we know for sure Maribel's been lying and I don't want either of them to know we're on to them."

*"Mate! Go to our mate! Tate, you need to get to her now! If you don't go, I'm taking over!"*

"I need to leave, I'm losing control of Chase." I jumped up and ran to my suite and pounded on the door when Chase made an appearance and tried busting the door down.

## BRINLEY

I'm so hot my fever peaks every fifteen to thirty minutes. I need relief. I keep calling for Tate, Amanda and I think he can ease our pain so she's been calling to him his wolf. Crystal mentioned something about going back to my pack but I don't know if I'd be able to make the three-hour drive. If I can't have Tate, then I need Max, he can help me through this. I understand Crystal's unwillingness to let him help me, but I need him.

"Brinley?" Crystal asked.

"Yes?"

"How are you feeling?"

"I'm exhausted and hungry. I'm waiting for the next fever to hit me. I want the pain gone, I don't know how much more I can handle."

"How have you gotten through your previous heats?"

"I usually go on suppressants but when I forget, I have my mom and sister to help me through them. Sometimes my brother and the guys will stay with me when my mom and sister need a break. Why?"

"When you are at the height of your fever, you call out for Tate but you yell at us when we remind you that he'd mark you. Then call for Max. Don't take this the wrong way, but I was getting jealous because Max and I aren't marked yet. Please don't be angry. I talked with Tate and he said your heat doesn't affect the guys, that you're like siblings, and I should let Max help if he can."

"I appreciate you confiding in me, Max does help. I've always been closest to him growing up. I'm not mad at you. It just tells me how much you love him and don't want to lose him. Can I ask why you haven't marked each other? You need to make it official."

"We have some logistics to work out. I want to stay here since I'm the head doctor, but he wants me to go back with him to your pack. He won't mark me until a decision is made," she said quietly with her head down.

"That's bullshit, get him in here right now, I'm going to kick his ass then tell him what he needs to do or he'll have to deal with me," I huffed.

Crystal's smile grew, "You'd do that for me, talk to him I mean, not kick his ass?"

"Hell, yes I will. He's like my brother, and I'd love for you to be my sister. Now, tell Roo to get his ass in here before I tear him apart."

Crystal left with a little giddiness to her walk, and a few seconds later Max was standing in front of me. "Why the HELL, haven't you marked her yet?"

"We're seriously going to discuss this while you're in heat?"

"Yes, yes we are!"

He rubbed his hands down his face, "Look Peanut."

"Don't you 'Peanut' me, Roo! You are one of my best friends, one of my brothers, I want you to be happy and I want my new sister happy. What is your fucking problem?"

He looked defeated, "I don't want to lose you." He pushed a loose curl behind my ear.

"What are you talking about, 'lose me,' you're not going to lose me."

"She's a doctor in this pack, I can't very well take her back to our pack, I'd have to stay here. Besides, other than Jax and Brooklyn, I'm the only other one who can calm you when you need it. I can't stay here while you're back home."

"Roo, l appreciate you and I love you, but you need to put your mate bond above all that. I'm not going anywhere anytime soon, you'll still be one of my best friends, and don't forget, Brooklyn can bring me here anytime."

"You're right, but I will wait until your heat is over since she needs to be here with you."

"Roo, speaking of my heat, would you mind staying with me, maybe your being with me will help with the pain?"

"Does Crystal know I can help you and is she okay with it?"

"I talked with her, told her you're not affected by it, she said it would be okay. She also talked to Tate, not sure why, but he said he'd be okay with it, too."

A few minutes later I was in the throes of my heat again. I was in so much pain. Max grabbed me and held me rocking me back and forth. The pain was subsiding when I heard pounding on the door. Breathlessly I asked, "Roo, what is that pounding?"

"That would be Chase taking over Tate's body trying to bust the door down to mate with you." As soon as he said Chase and Tate's name, I moaned and my hand immediately grabbed a dildo, and I was slamming it into me. It wasn't satisfying me though.

"Tate, I need Tate, he would be better. Roo, I need Tate, I need him."

"I got you, Peanut, I got you, you'll be okay."

I cried out, "Roo, I can't take this anymore. I don't care if he fucks me and marks me, I fucking need him!"

"Shhh, I know you do, we can get through this. You won't be happy if we allow him to mate and mark you Peanut, you know that, right?"

"Y... yes," I sobbed.

"I think I know what will help."

"You... you do?" I asked between sobs.

He was brushing my hair out of my face, "How about I have something made for you? Would you like something that's your very own to help you through the rest of your heat?" I nodded my head as I brought myself to an orgasm while Max was holding me.

I'm sure the sight would be disturbing to anyone who walked in on me in this position, especially since Max isn't my mate. He brings me comfort and helps with the pain, so I don't care what others think. "Peanut, as soon as this fever comes down, and you've orgasmed enough, I need to go see Tate, okay?" I nodded my head.

## MAX

Helping Brin through her heat is no big deal to me. I've done it many times over the last five years. She playing with herself and having an orgasm while I'm holding her is no big deal. Neither of us is embarrassed by it. When she first asked me to help her, it was awkward, but we soon got over it. Seeing how she reacted when I told her Chase was trying to bust the door down, I'm sure there is more to this than anyone is saying. I'm almost positive Tate is her mate whether either of them knows it or not and I will find out.

*"Is Tate still out there?"*

*"Erik currently has him on the ground in a headlock, why?"*

*"I have to ask him a question but I need him off the alpha floor before coming out. Can you strongarm him to his temporary office?"*

*"Will do, I'll let you know when we're there."*

*"Thanks."*

A few minutes later, I was met with a very pissed-off... "Chase?" showing through Tate's eyes. "You smell like Brinley, why were you touching my mate!" Chase yelled. *Okay, that answers that question, I'll be keeping that to myself.*

"Chase," I held my hands out, "calm down, can you give control back to Tate? I need to speak to him about your mate." Chase took a deep breath and stepped into the foreground of Tate's mind, his eyes returned to his amber color.

"Max, what are you doing here, and why do you smell like Brinley?"

"Look, this is going to sound weird so don't get pissed off when I say it either or I'll have you in a headlock so fast you won't even know what hit you. Got it?"

"Yeah. I got it."

"I was with Brin when her fever spiked, she got very horny when she heard Chase trying to break the door down. She wanted you and the dildo wasn't cutting it. She was able to orgasm but she was screaming your name the entire time."

"So what's your point? I can't be with her right now."

"I know you can't physically be with her right now, but what if I told you there was a way to let her have a part of you?"

"What are you talking about?"

"Your dick man."

"What about my dick?"

"You can make a silicon casting of it, this way she can use your dick to satisfy her while she's in heat, she won't be using some random dildo, she'll be using yours," I smacked him in the chest.

"How do we do this and how long does it take?"

"I have the kit in my room. When Crystal bought some sex toys for Brinley, she saw the kit and got it for me. She said after we mate and mark each other and I have to leave on pack business, she'll be able to use it while I'm gone."

"Go get it, let's see what we have to do."

I ran upstairs, grabbed the kit and we read the instructions. I helped mix the molding with warm water and left so he could jack off and get hard, then came back in after he put his dick in the molding and waited for it to dry. "This is the weirdest feeling ever. I'm surprised my dick stayed hard." Once it was firm, he removed himself from the molding, then we filled it with silicon.

We waited about twenty minutes for it to dry. Once it was dry, we took it out of the bucket to remove the molding around the silicon, it looked just like his dick with veins and even his balls.

We were impressed. I grabbed it and took it to Brinley.

# Chapter 27 Secret Rendezvous

**TATE**

That was the weirdest fucking thing I have ever done, but at least it's my cock inside her and no one else's. I hope it helps her too. Max said she's been in terrible pain and I wish I could alleviate it for her. The chance of marking her in the height of her heat is too great.

"Honey, I'm home! I yelled walking into Ben's suite.

"Hey, where've you been?"

"You wouldn't believe me if I told you."

"Try me."

"Max brought me a DIY dildo."

"A what?!"

"A Do It Yourself Dildo."

"What the fuck is that and why do you need one?"

"It's not for me, asshole, it's for Brinley. You know that kit you can take a casting of your hands with and then fill it with plaster?"

"Yeah?"

"It's the same thing except you take a casting of your dick and fill it with silicon. Once it dries you peel the dildo out, clean it, and presto, you have a casting of your dick. Your mate can use your dick dildo when you can't be with her instead of some random dude's dick dildo.

"Are you serious? That's amazing! I think I need to make one for Q, she'll probably want one after she sees it too!"

"Oh fucking hell, I forgot those two are going to see my cock." I slumped down on the couch. Benjamin just laughed at me, until he realized what I said.

## BRINLEY

Two hours and four fevers and orgasms later, Max came back to the suite. I was between fevers and had enough energy to eat and have an energy drink. "Peanut, I brought you a gift," Max had a grin on his face.

I smiled, "What'd you bring me?"

"I brought you a custom-made dildo," he smirked.

"A custom... made... dildo?" How do you get a custom-made dildo? Do you go to a store and choose the size, color, and firmness of them? How exactly does that work?" I asked skeptically.

"No," he scrunched his nose. "You have someone mold their dick."

"Oh, goddess, please tell me this is not your cock, if it is, please give it to Crystal. I think she's been getting horny seeing me in heat," I laughed.

"Peanut, it is not my cock."

"It isn't one of the other boys' is it?"

"No, eww, Take the bag and open it," he shoved the bag at me.

Before I could look inside my fever spiked again. "I'm so fucking hot," I moaned. Quinn heard me and came in to fill the tub with ice water again.

"Max, carry her to the tub please."

"Yes ma'am."

"What's in the bag?" I heard her ask.

"A gift for her." Quinn raised her eyebrows. "What? She's going to like it, trust me, I know my Peanut."

"Oh, Goddess!" I yelled trying to get friction inside me with my fingers but it wasn't working. "Tate! I need him, please, he can stop the pain!" I tried reaching for the toys Crystal brought me but Max put something in my hand instead. I thrust that thing inside me and it filled me up so much I let out a moan. Once my walls stretched around it I thrusted in and out of me. It felt so good I released two orgasms in a row.

I slumped down, leaned my head on the tub, closed my eyes, and fell asleep. I was so satiated from using that dildo, that I slept for four hours before I felt the fever coming on again. I had made it through the first day, with four to go. I asked Max where the dildo came from and he whispered the answer in my ear. He didn't want Crys to see what Tate's cock looked like and he assumed Ben and Tate felt the same way.

I woke up at 2:00 am, rummaging around the fridge. I was looking for something to eat but there was nothing I wanted. Day two of my heat and I was craving brownies, yes, at 2:00 am. I didn't want to make them in the suite's kitchen because I wanted the other three to sleep. I knew it would be safe to leave the suite this early. My fevers have spread further apart since using Tate's cock. I just need to convince the guys to let me out.

Max and Crystal were sleeping in one room and Quincy took the other spare room. Using my enforcer abilities, I snuck out and walked to the door. I know there's a mechanism on the door somewhere to disengage the lock, I just need to find it. I'm feeling all around the door jam when I feel a small button and push it. I hear a click and try the door handle, it turns and the door pops open.

Luckily for me, Erik, Phillip, and Jacob aren't at their post. Knowing them, they're probably taking a break. After all, I should be sleeping and not trying to sneak out. I quietly shut the door and walked to the stairs. I don't know why I'm so afraid of someone finding me but the pull for brownies is so much stronger than the fear of being found.

I snuck downstairs, Tate's office door was open and the guys were talking with John. I listened to them for a few seconds. Jeremy and Francis showed a piece of paper with the number of pregnant she-wolves and pups being held as hostages. I quickly hurried past the office door and made my way to the kitchen where I proceeded to make my brownies.

## TATE

*"Mate, go to our mate!"* Chase woke me up at 2:00 am. I rubbed my eyes.

*"Chase, we can't go to her, she's in heat and we don't want to lose control."*

*"I promise, I won't lose control, please go to her."*

*"The guys will stop us Chase."*

*"Then sit by her door."*

*"Fine, let's go"*

I quietly got up and headed out of the suite. I decided to head to the kitchen first and grab a snack. I could've grabbed something in Ben's kitchen but didn't want to rummage around in it. I stopped dead in my tracks before I reached the kitchen. Chase was jumping around in my head. I smelled fresh strawberries and... heat. *"Chase, do you smell that? I think Brinley's in the kitchen."*

*"Yes, I smell her. Go to her before she leaves. I will, but remember, you promised to not lose control."*

*"I won't now go to her."*

I watched as Brinley finished mixing what looked like brownie batter, she turned to get a baking dish when she stopped and stared straight into my eyes. "What are you doing down here?"

"Making brownies, I was craving them. It's been a few hours since my fever spiked so I snuck out. What are you doing down here?"

"Chase woke me up and wanted me to sit by your door but I wanted a snack first."

"You want a snack? What kind of snack?"

"What kind of snack?" *I want to snack on her, that's what kind of snack.* When she turned around and smeared the brownie batter all over her, I couldn't stop myself. I walked over to her, lifted her chin kissing and licking the batter off her. I moved down to her marking spot and felt my gums tingling. Then moved down her neck, throat, and to her nipples, licking her clean. I growled as I continued to suck her nipple.

*"Keep doing that Tate, she's getting aroused. Can you smell her?"*

*"I can buddy. She wants us."*

## BRINLEY

*"Brins, are you sure about this?"*

*"Yes, I am. Please do not take control."*

*"I won't."*

I wanted him, right now. I don't care if he marks me or not. I've fallen in love with him and I want to be wrapped in his arms. I can feel my fever coming back from being near him.

This, this right here is what I've been craving. I want him and I can feel his cock pressing against me. My core is dripping and my fever is coming back. I grabbed his shirt and ripped it off him, then slipped my hand down his sweatpants grabbing a hold of his cock. I pushed away from him, and pulled him to the theatre, forgetting about my brownies. I locked the door once we were inside. I stripped out of my shirt and shorts, pulled his sweatpants down so his cock sprang free, pushed him onto the couch, and took him in my mouth.

"Awe fuck, Cupcake, you do that so well." He grabbed my hair and pulled me closer so his cock went down my throat. I sucked him hard. "Cupcake, if you keep doing that, I'm going to cum." I pulled my mouth off of him with a pop, pushed him down, and climbed on top without saying a word.

I sunk on him and as soon as I did, my fever hit me. I was burning and the pain was there. I rode him hard. "Tate, Tate, oh my goddess, you feel so good inside me. This is what I needed, I needed you inside me. I needed you to take the pain away." He sucked one of my dangling breasts in his mouth and something snapped inside me.

I bent down licking, kissing, and sucking his marking spot. My gums started to tingle and my canines were extending. They grazed across his marking spot when he flipped me over. I wanted the pain to stop, I didn't care how. I was moaning and crying out his name. "Oh, Tate, more, I'm so hot, it hurts, make it go away, please make the pain go away" I cried out. I felt it when Chase pushed him back and he took control. We were both so lost in lust, I didn't care, at the moment.

"Mine! You are mine Brinley, no one else's. Say you are mine too," I heard Chase say.

I felt Amanda push me back, I heard Chase claim me as his. Amanda responded, "I am yours, Chase, I will always be yours." Then I felt his canines grazing my marking spot when the door was flung open and Branson was baring his teeth.

## MAX

My wolf woke me up around 2:10 am nagging me that something was wrong. I got out of bed, my first thought was Brin. I needed to check on her but when I got to her room, she wasn't in there. I frantically ran around the suite thinking maybe she laid down somewhere else. I couldn't find her... anywhere. I caught her scent and followed it to the suite's main door and found it unlocked.

Oh Goddess, please let her be with the guys. I opened the door and no one was there, except her scent. I followed it downstairs, saw Tate's office door open, and stormed in there. "Please tell me you know where Peanut is?"

"She's not in the suite?" Erik asked.

"No dumbass. Do you think I'd be in here looking for her if she was in the suite? Why the hell are you guys in here and not at your post where you're supposed to be!? Her fucking scent is in the hallway!"

Before any of the guys could answer me, Ben came running into the office. In a hurried voice, "Have you seen Tate? I got up to get something to drink and realized he's not in my suite anymore."

The boys and I looked at each other and looked at Ben, when the realization hit us, "Oh shit!" We all scrambled out of the office and followed their scents. It took us to the kitchen where we saw what looked like brownie batter sitting in a bowl. We could smell both of them and Peanut's heat scent was strong.

We followed their scent down the hall and it led us to the theatre. I tried opening the door but it was locked, "Shit, they locked the door. We need to get in there and this will not be fun," I said to the guys. When two wolves are in the process of mating and you interrupt them, you could lose your life. Especially if those two wolves are mates who are not marked and the she-wolf is in heat. It will be worse since Tate knows they are mates.

"We're not getting in there. The door was made so it could only be locked and unlocked from the inside. If we were watching a movie with our mate and decided to have a little fun, we didn't want anyone walking in on us. We won't be able to break it down either, it's reinforced," Ben told us.

"I'm going to link Brooklyn, she can get in there and unlock it."


## BROOKLYN

I was woken up way too early by a mind link from Max. *"Cheese, sorry to wake you but this is an emergency. We need you to grab Jaxon and get to Black Diamond packhouse, immediately."*

*"Why, what's wrong?"* I asked frantically thinking something happened to Brin.

*"Brin snuck out of the suite and is now locked in the theatre room with Tate."*

*"And why is that an emergency?"*

*"She's in heat, that's why!"*

*"Oh shit! we'll be right there!"* I jumped out of bed, ran to Jax's room, and without saying anything, I grabbed his arm and aparated us to where Max was standing.

"What the fuck Brooklyn. I was having a great dream, why the fuck are we here? In the middle of the night?"

"Emergency" is all she said.

"Brin and Tate are locked in the theatre," Max rushed out.

"So?" Jaxon raised his hands.

"She's in heat and the door can only be unlocked from the inside. So if you don't want your sister marked, I'd suggest one of you get your ass in there and unlock it so we can stop them from marking each other!"

I could see Jaxon was stunned for about five seconds before I pulled him with me into the theater. When we got in there, Tate was about to plunge his canines into her neck. I opened the door as Branson took over and shifted. He jumped to push Tate off Brinley. Only it wasn't Brinley and Tate, it was Chase and Amanda. Branson was baring his teeth at them. I linked the others letting them know we were dealing with their wolves in human form.

## CHASE

I was tired of waiting for Tate to claim Brinley. When I saw her through Tates's eyes in the kitchen, I knew I needed to take control. I can feel her wolf on the surface I wanted to see if I could pull her out. I want my wolf mate as much as Tate wants his human mate. Tate was yelling at me not to mark her but I wasn't listening. I told him I wouldn't, but the scent of her heat was too much for me to resist. I was getting ready to mark her when I heard a growl and was pushed off of her by another wolf I didn't recognize. I could feel the power coming off of him though. I shifted and stood over her body to protect her.

## AMANDA

When I saw Tate's wolf coming forward, I wanted to mate with him. I pushed Brinley to the back and took over. I promised her I wouldn't but I couldn't resist him. Being in heat has spurred me on, I want to mark him. I tried but he flipped me over before I could. Then I felt his teeth graze my neck and I wasn't going to stop him. I was lost in the lust of heat.

I felt Branson in the room, then heard him growl and push Chase off of me. "Branson? What are you doing" I said breathlessly. Chase shifted, he's so beautiful, he's the most beautiful silver I've ever seen. "Chase, it's okay, he's my brother." He kept growling at him though.

"Chase, I'm giving control back to Brinley, please do the same. Give Tate back control." I begged him.

My brother growled and bared his teeth at him. "Branson, stand down and give control back to Jax." I gave control back to Brinley, and she walked over to Branson, petting him behind the ears. He leaned into her and licked her on the cheek. The guys and Ben came in next. Brooke came over and hugged her. Branson gave control back to Jaxon and he shifted back then he commanded Chase to shift back and give control back to Tate.

I could tell he wasn't happy shifting back but he kept control, not giving it to Tate. As soon as he shifted, he walked over to Brinley and grabbed her. "You are mine and no one will take you from me," those were his last words before Jaxon forced him to give control back to Tate. Between the guys, Jaxon, and Brooklyn, there is no way he would've been able to take them all on.


## TATE

"Brinley? What happened? One minute we were making out on the couch, the next minute Chase pushed me back and blocked me. Why is your brother standing naked in this room, and why are we naked?"

"I'm not sure what happened but Amanda did the same thing, she pushed me back and took over." Brin shook her head.

"I'll tell you what happened," Max pointed at us. "Long story short, my wolf woke me up, I couldn't find Brinley. We followed her scent to the kitchen. She must've decided to make some brownies because your batter is in the kitchen. We followed your scent in here, I linked Brooklyn, and she and Jax showed up. When Brooklyn opened the door we saw Branson shift and push you off of her. Chase was seconds away from marking her!

"Brooklyn," Jax said angrily, "take Brinley back to the suite and get her settled. I'm assuming her heat will probably be hitting her again in a couple of hours."

"Hey, what about my brownies!"

"I'll make sure they get baked and brought up to you, go with Brooke please, Baby Sis."

"Fine," she huffed. But before she left, she walked her naked ass over to me, jumping up and wrapped her arms and legs around me. She smirked at them, pushed her lips to mine, and kissed me as she moved her ass so my cock was running against her pussy.

"Oh for goddess sake, Brooklyn, get her upstairs."

"Come on Sissy, before our brother has an aneurysm." She took her by the shoulders and walked her out of the theatre.

I glared at Tate, "This isn't working out. You need to chill in the cell until her heat is over."

"The hell I'm going in the cell, you can't make me go in there!"

"I can. I'm stronger than you and can knock you out so fast you wouldn't know what hit you. So, you can either walk in there on your own, I can have Brooklyn apparate you, or my men and I will drag your ass in there. So what's the choice?"

"I think I prefer neither. I understand why you're doing it. It's because Chase almost marked her," he hung his head. "Fine, I get it, I will go until she's out of heat but the second her heat is over, I'm outta there!"

"I don't have an issue with that, let's go."

# Chapter 28 Grounded

**TATE**

From the dungeon's entrance, we could hear Maribel squawking. I completely forgot she was in there and I pray to the goddess I won't have to listen to her the entire time I'm locked in that fucking cell. I understand why I'm getting locked up, but it doesn't mean I have to like it. "You guys have got to shut that bitch up if I'm going to be locked in here. I cannot listen to her squawking voice the whole time."

"Tate? Is that you? Have you come to let me out?" She whined.

"I am not letting you out!"

"But Tate, I'm sorry for what I did, I didn't mean it!"

"Seriously Maribel? You were butt-ass naked in the men's locker room trying to get yourself off... not going to happen. Someone needs to move her to solitary confinement. Any volunteers or do I need to do it myself?"

Jacob stepped forward, "It will be my pleasure to move her."

"Good, move her to the furthest one away from me... just as she is."

He grabbed the keys, and opened her cell, "Jakey Poo, you came back to me," she squealed. He ignored her, grabbed her by the arm, and took her away while she tried to convince him to let her go.

I walked into my cell, which was fully stocked with a bed, blankets, a privacy screen around the open bathroom, and a fridge stocked with food and drinks. They even installed a TV for me. "Adam, remember, this is for your own good and the safety of both Brinley and you. You will be let out after her heat is over."

"I know, I get it, Ben. I fucked up." It was hard for me to be humble, but I screwed up and knew what the consequences were if we got out of control. Unlike Maribel, I knew the consequences of my actions and took responsibility for them. That doesn't mean I have to like it though.

*"Chase, I'm so angry at you, you caused us to be locked up because you went against your promise to me."*

*"I'm sorry Tate, I shouldn't have done that. I wanted our mate and you were taking too long and she was in heat, I lost control."*

*"I get it, buddy, I do, but we cannot let that happen again. Once she shifts and realizes who we are to her, things will be different, I promise."* He lay down and whined for the next few hours.

I'm pissed, pissed at myself. It's my fault I'm in this fucking cell. She looked so good standing in the kitchen. She smelled even better with the scent of her heat surrounding her. All I could think of was pulling her close to me and devouring her. Then she turned around and that little vixen spread brownie batter on herself. I lost it, seeing that batter on her, I had to clean her off and I enjoyed doing it too.

Chase took over my body, pushed me back and I don't know if I'm happy or angry we were pushed off of her. I was angry with him for a short time but quickly got over it because I'm a guy and I wanted to fuck my mate. We've both been holding back from marking her. I want her to know she's our mate but each day is getting harder and harder to hold back. With her being in heat, it's nearly impossible.

*"Tate?"*

*"Yeah, Chase?"*

*"I'm sorry I pushed you away. I lost it when her heat spiked. I was angry you haven't marked her yet and I wanted to claim her as mine."*

*"You cannot let that happen again."*

*"I know, and I'm sorry."*

*"I appreciate you saying that but we're stuck in here until her heat is over."*

*"For what it's worth, I truly am sorry. I hope you're not angry at me."*

*"Chase, I'm not angry with you anymore. I'm angry we let it get out of hand."*

*"Tate?"*

*"Yeah?"*

*"I love you, you're the best human a wolf could have."*

*"Thanks, buddy, I feel the same way."*

*"Tate?"*

*"Yeah?"*

*"Brinley's wolf isn't doing well, I can feel it. I don't know what's wrong but she feels lost and... so sad."*

*"Well, there's nothing we can do right now. We're locked in here for a couple of days."*

*"I know,"* he sounded sad and defeated.

## BRINLEY

I'm not sure what or how I was feeling. The moment I felt Amanda push me to the back of my mind, I knew my fever was spiking and Tate was there. All I could think about was mating him to take this fucking pain away. I thought I was still in control enough to not let anything else happen. Then I felt his teeth graze my marking spot and Amanda took control.

Once she gave me back control I saw Branson growling at Chase, who was standing over me, protecting me. Probably because I was in heat and then seeing the other guys, I knew something must've happened. Tate shifted back and so did Jaxon. Brooklyn grabbed me to take me away from Tate but my body had other ideas, I couldn't stop myself, so I ran and jumped on him.

Now I'm sitting in Tate's suite with mated guards inside and outside the suite to make sure that doesn't happen again. I'm still trying to figure out what the hell happened.

*"Brinley, can we talk please?"*

*"Amanda, I'm so angry with you right now, I don't even know if I can speak to you without banishing you to the furthest recesses of my mind!"*

*"Brins, please, please don't do this. You're to blame too, you were getting hot and heavy with Tate."*

*"Don't you 'Brins' me! I may have been getting hot and heavy, but I was in control until you pushed me back!"*

*"I'm sorry, I don't know what came over me. I felt the pull of his wolf and lost all control."*

*"Amanda! Stop! I... Hate... You... Right... Now! Please don't talk to me. I don't want to hear your excuses!"*

*"But Brin..."*

*"YOU WERE GOING TO LET HIM FUCKING MARK ME FOR FUCK SAKE, AMANDA!!! How am I supposed to trust you not to do something so stupid and without MY FUCKING permission when we're able to shift again, uh!? Answer that question!"*

*"Brin, I... I'm so sorry, please forgive me."* She curled up and I could feel her crying.

Brooklyn gently placed her hands on mine, "Brin, do you want to talk about it?"

"Not really."

"Come on Peanut," she said, trying to get a reaction out of me, I allow the guys to call me that.

"I don't want to talk about it, Brooky," I lowered my hands to face.

"Shhh, it's okay Brin, I'm here, Maya's here, we love you."

**MAYA**

*"Brooky, can you ask Brin if I can talk with Andi?"*

"Maya wants to know if she can speak with Andi."

"As long as she blocks me from it because I'm infuriated with her."

*"Brin said yes, but to block her from your conversation."*

*"Thank you Brooky."*

I think I understand why Brin's angry with Amanda but Brin needs to take responsibility for her actions too. None of this would've happened if she'd stayed in that damn room. I mean, I don't know what it's like to go through heat, I only know from listening to Brinley and Amanda talk about it and from our mom. It sounds agonizingly painful with pure sexual desire mixed in. I don't know that I wouldn't have made the same decision.

*"Andi, can we talk?"*

*"Go away Maya,"* she sounded so sad.

*"Please Sissy, I want to know how you're feeling,"* I said quietly.

*"Brin hates me, how do you think I feel?"*

I sighed, *"Sissy, help me understand what happened, please?"*

*"Why, you'll end up hating me too."*

*"I could never hate you, I love you."*

*"Brin was supposed to love me too, look how that's going. She'll probably never talk to me again,"* she was whimpering and I could feel her tears flowing out of her eyes. My heart clenched for her, *"You know sh... she told me sh... she'd banish me."*

*"She what!?"*

*"She... she... said... she'd... banish me if I kept try... trying t... to talk wi... with her,"* She whimpered some more.

*"Oh my Baby Sister, please tell me what was going through your head when you took over."*

*"Oh Maya, I miss my mate and pup so much. I miss how Jerod would hold us and when Tate held us that way I just wanted more,"* she cried. *"My heart is hurting so much, I want my mate and pup back and Brinley can't know. I'm trying to be strong for her."*

"*Wait, Sissy, I'm lost, I thought you moved past them dying.*"

"*I had to move past it for Brinley's sake. I had to be strong for her. I told everyone I was good and wanted to move on, but that was a half-truth. I do want to move on but I'm still missing them so much. That's part of the reason we haven't shifted and her nightmares, I wasn't able to stop them this whole time because I wasn't strong enough.*"

"*Oh my goddess! You were going through this all by yourself all these years. Branson and I would've been there for you.*" Now it was my turn to whimper and tears were falling down my muzzle.

"*Maya, I'm afraid to tell Brinley any of this. She's made some progress since arriving here, the nightmares have all stopped and I can feel us getting stronger, I just wish I knew why.*"

"*I wish I could answer that for you Sissy. Can you tell me why you were going to let Chase mark you?*"

"*I was so lost in the moment and I could feel Brinley's heat starting to spike. I miss the feel of the mate mark on our neck and the connection it gives. I just thought, maybe, if I let him mark us we could have that connection to someone again, and he'd put a pup in us. I know it sounds stupid and selfish but that's the truth and that's why I pushed her as far as I could in our mind. I didn't want her to try and stop me,*" she covered her head with her paws in shame.

"*You know, he might have a mate out there. If he marked you and then found his mate, you would've been devastated.*"

"*I know, you're right.*"

"*What if he had marked you and you shifted and scented your second chance mate, what would've you done?*"

"*Oh my goddess, I didn't even think of that.*"

"*Sissy, you made a mistake, we'll help you get past this, okay?*"

"Brin said she doesn't know how she'll be able to trust me if we shift."

"You need to talk with her."

"She won't listen, she'll banish me. I'm afraid of her right now and I've never been afraid of her Maya," she cried, "Do you think the Moon Goddess would come to us if we called her?"

"Maybe, but we would need Branson."

"Do you think he would?"

"We can ask him if that's what you want."

"I do, can we try?

# CHAPTER 29 SEEKING GUIDANCE

**JAXON**

I needed to check on Brinley and make sure she was okay. She was so lost in the moment and when I realized Amanda was in control, I knew I had to get to her fast before she was marked. I know he's her mate and coming between a wolf and his mate when he's about to claim her can be dangerous. The problem is she doesn't know they are mates and she wouldn't be happy he marked her without consent. She would believe she's keeping him from his second chance mate.

We finally got to Tate's suite when I was met by Quincy. "Hey Quincy, how is she?"

"Brooklyn's with her now but I think their wolves are talking. When I checked on her they were sitting there as quiet as can be."

"Thanks, I'll go check on them." I entered the bedroom and they were sitting on the bed. Brinley's head was lying in Brooklyn's lap and she was stroking her hair. Brooklyn reached her hand out for me so I walked over and sat on the bed. As soon as I sat down, Maya contacted me.

*"Jaxon?"*

*"Yes, Maya?"*

*"I'm talking with Andi, she's not doing well. She needs Branson, is it okay if he joins us?"*

*"Maya, my sweet Little Sister, you never need to ask me if your brother can join you. Of course, he can, I'm pretty tired too so he's all yours while I nap next to Brinley."*

*"Thank you Jaxy."*

*"You're welcome."*

## BRANSON

*When I heard Maya calling to me, it didn't take long for me to join her. "What's going on?"*

*"Andi, she's not well. Brinley is very angry at her, she's threatened to banish her."*

*"Oh shit, Andi, we'll fix this, you know we will."* I lowered my voice, *"Andi, I love you. We will never leave you okay?"*

*"I... I'm just so ashamed of what I've done. I feel pulled to Tate and don't understand why. It feels similar to the mate pull but I don't have any other feelings that go along with it. I just know I feel safe with him, and Brinley feels like she's falling in love with him. We're so confused because it doesn't feel the same as it did with Jerod,"* she cried.

*"Branson,"* Maya got my attention. *"We were thinking we could use our bond to try and contact the Moon Goddess to see if there is anything she can do to help Brin not be so angry. Do you think you could help us?"*

*"I'd do anything to help, you know that, let's concentrate on calling her."*

We pushed all our thoughts to the Moon Goddess. A few minutes later, a bright light shone and we bowed our heads she appeared. *"You called me little ones?"*

*"We did, is there anything you can do for Brinley? She's angry with Amanda, she's threatened to banish her,"* Maya explained.

*"Oh my precious pups, I will speak with her. She's lost right now, there are things I cannot reveal to you, but soon all will be well."*

*"Amanda, what you almost allowed Chase to do cannot happen again. Not without Brinley's permission, do you understand?"*

*"Yes, I'm sorry for my behavior. I will not repeat it."* She petted Amanda's head and kissed her.

*"Amanda, she loves you and will not banish you. You are a part of her and only I can remove a wolf from their human. I paired each of you with your humans because, like them, you are stronger together. You enhance each other's abilities and you were inseparable when you were pups. Rest easy my child, now, I must leave and go have a word with Chase."*

She was gone as quickly as she arrived. *"I wonder what she needs to talk with Chase about?"*

*"I don't know, but I hope she reprimands him for almost marking our sister,"* Maya huffed. All three of us fell asleep until we felt Brinley's heat return.

## MOON GODDESS

Things are a mess. I'm angry, I'm so angry one of my precious triplets is hurting. I'm angry Chase took over and almost marked her before she's ready, and I'm angry at Brinley for saying all that shit to Amanda. Believe me, I understand where she's coming from, but now I need to pull her out of this anger somehow without telling her they are mates.

I want to yell at her but I also need to be soft because of everything she's been through. I know she wouldn't be angry at Amanda if she knew they were mates, but she needs to discover it on her own. I cannot tell her. Right now, I will let her rest. I need to have a conversation with Chase first. I know Tate well enough to know he will go easy on him, so I will lay down the hammer on him or he will suffer the consequences.

*"Chase, we need to talk."*

*"Who said that?"* his voice frantic.

*"Chase, my child, look at me."* He blinked a few times, allowing his eyes to adjust to the light. *"M... Moon Goddess?"*

*"Yes, Chase, it's me."*

*"Why are you here?"*

*"As I said, we need to talk."*

He tried hiding his face but I pulled his head up to meet my eyes. *"I know Tate has gone easy on you, I, however, will not. Chase, what you did was forceful, unkind, uncaring, trust-breaking, unthoughtful of her wishes, and very selfish! Brinley and Amanda have NO IDEA you are mates and thanks to YOU for taking over control of TATE and almost MARKING HER... she may NEVER allow Amanda to SHIFT AGAIN!"*

*"How do you think Amanda is handling this, huh? I'll tell you how she's handling it, SHE'S NOT!"* I don't think he's ever been reprimanded like this before. *"Chase, LOOK... AT... ME!"* He slowly lifted his eyes to me. I'm sure my icy blue eyes were dark and scary. In a very stern voice, I said, *"If you EVER, and I mean EVER, DO... THAT... AGAIN... WITHOUT... TATE'S... PERMISSION... I... WILL... BANISH... YOU... FROM... TATE... FOR... HOWEVER... LONG... I... FEEL... IS... APPROPRIATE... DO I MAKE MYSELF CLEAR!!!!"*

*"Ye... yes ma'am."*

I patted him on the head, *"I love you Chase, don't ever forget that."*

I need to cool down before I speak with Brinley. If I come at her the same way I did with Chase, I'm afraid I'll lose her. That is the last thing I want to do. I have plans for her that I can't disclose and she needs to be healed. I stood inside her bedroom. She had another heat fever and now she's settled and sleeping. I entered her subconscious, blocked Amanda, and spoke with her.

*"Brinley, I know you can hear me, stay asleep child. You need your rest. I know you are angry with Amanda. What happened without permission is inexcusable. I'm not making excuses for her but she was acting on her pure animal instincts with your heat. I've spoken with her and she will not*

*let that happen again. You need to forgive her, you need each other. Rest easy my precious Brinley."* I kissed her and left.

## BRINLEY

It's been four days since the theatre incident. I'm still exhausted from my heat. Brooklyn and Jaxon left a few hours after the incident only to drive back later that day. They've been by my side since then helping me through my heat fevers and probably making sure I didn't do anything stupid like that again.

They are currently sprawled across my bed with me between them. My legs tangled in Jaxon's, my hands wrapped around Brooklyn's arms, and Brooklyn's legs were slung over both of us with Jaxon's hands in Brooklyn's hair. When we were pups, we always slept this way especially when one of us had a bad day or scary dream. I always felt protected by my older siblings when I was wrapped in their cocoons.

We were so tangled, that if I tried to move, I'd wake them, but I had to pee so badly. As I squirmed to get free, their grip on me tightened. "Stop squirming Baby Sis," my brother said as he drew me closer to him.

"Jaxy, I need to pee." He released me only after promising to come back and cuddle some more. After going to the bathroom and brushing my teeth, I looked at myself in the mirror. *"Andi?"* I saw her shine through my eyes in the mirror and I lowered mine. *"I'm sorry I got angry with you, will you forgive me?"* my voice somber.

*"Brin, you hurt my feelings. You said some mean things to me, I don't know if I can forgive that."*

*"I understand. I'll be here if you want to talk, I'm ready when you are."*

*"Thank you, Brin, I need some more time,"* she said sadly, as a tear slipped out of her eye.

I walked back to the bed crawled between my brother and sister and cried. "What's wrong Baby Sis, why are you crying?"

Jaxon asked softly as he stroked my cheeks and my sister woke up and wiped away my tears.

"I was mean to Amanda and said some pretty horrible things to her. I tried talking with her, but she's not ready yet," I sniffled.

Brooky was running her hand through my hair, "Brin, would it be okay if I spoke with her? Maybe I can help?" I nodded my head yes and closed my eyes.


## BROOKLYN

*"Amanda? Andi, I know you can hear me."*

*"Go away Brooky,"* she sounded heartbroken.

*"Will you please talk to me?"*

*"I don't want to."*

*"I know you don't, but I want to help. Please tell me how I can help mend this brokenness between you two."*

She placed her head between her paws and whimpered. *"She hurt me so much, she broke me."*

*"I know, and I'm so sorry you both hurt each other. How can I help make it better? You need each other."*

*"She needs to promise I can shift. I promise I won't take total control unless she gives it to me. I need to know she won't banish me, and... and most importantly, I need to know she doesn't hate me and she still loves me,"* tears fell down her face.

*"Oh Sweetheart, do you want me to tell her or do you want to tell her?"*

*"No, I'll tell her, but Brooky, thank you for checking on me."*

I petted her head and kissed her. *"You're welcome."*


## BRINLEY

I must've fallen asleep again, I woke up to Amanda calling me. *"Brin, can you wake up?"*

*"Andi? What's wrong, are you okay?"*

*"Yes, you fell asleep, I'm ready, can we talk now?"*

*"Of course we can. Can I go first though?"* Not waiting for her to reply I continued, *"I'm so sorry I said those horrible things. Will you forgive me? I'm at fault too. I could feel the heat fever coming back, Tate was there and I should've had more control."*

*"Brin, I never should've taken over and pushed you back. I'm sorry I did that, will you forgive me?"*

*"I forgive you, I shouldn't have gotten angry for doing something that comes naturally to you. I don't hate you, I could never hate you. We are a part of each other, I love you."*

*"I love you too Brins and I forgive you too,"* she sounded a little happier. *"Now that our heat is finally over, can we go see Tate?"*

*"Yes, we can go see him. We need to apologize to him too."*

*"I know, again, I'm sorry I stayed mad at you for so long. I never want to stop speaking to you again, that was awful."*

*"Yes it was, I hated not hearing you in my thoughts."*

I opened my eyes and noticed both Brooke and Jax had fallen asleep again. I stretched and nudged them to wake up. I felt so comfortable caged in by them. I didn't want to get up but the day will get away from us if we don't and we have a lot of stuff to do. "Time to wake up guys," I sounded chipper, as I should, my heat was finally over.

"Why? Why can't we sleep more?" my brother whined.

"Because we have stuff to do. My heats over and we need to meet Tate and the team in his office to see if Jeremy and Francis have made contact yet."

"Uh, Sissy, about Tate... we kinda put him in the cells," my brother said slowly.

"What? Why would you do that?"

"Because Chase almost marked you, that's why. The guys, Ben, and I agreed it was the best thing for him, at the time. He went willingly, although not happy. When we got to the dungeon, he put Maribel in solitary confinement so he wouldn't have to listen to her."

"Why was she in the cells to begin with?"

"Tate's been making Ben train with him to distract him from wanting to mate you. When they came out of the showers in the locker room, she was naked and waiting for them." he snickered.

"So why would that cause her to be thrown in the cells."

"It's not, it's what she was doing. She was masturbating in front of them and told Tate she would take care of his sexual frustration while you were in heat."

I felt Amanda stirring and feeling a little jealous, weird, but whatever. He's not my mate but we have been spending a lot of time together so maybe that's why. "We need to let him out of the cells first and maybe Maribel too if she's still in there. I heard her sister's supposed to be arriving this week, maybe she needs to help her mom?"

"I think Tate may only release her if she's learned her lesson."

"What lesson was she supposed to learn, Jax?"

"That there are consequences to her actions."

"Jaxon, there must be more to her getting tossed in a cell for masturbating in front of Tate and Ben. Those actions don't seem to fit the punishment," Brooklyn commented confused.

"I know, I thought the same thing. Guess we can ask Tate and Ben when we get there."

"Well, I for one, am ready to breathe fresh air after being cooped up in here for five days," I grabbed both their hands and headed for the suite door. I already linked the guys letting them know my heat was over. Crystal and Q met us in the foyer of the suite, she linked Ben to meet us in the hallway.

# Chapter 30 Releasing Maribel

**BENJAMIN**

When Q told me Brinley's heat was over, I was thankful. Tate has been driving me nuts asking about her all the time. I finally had to close the link between us and I found out Q and Crys had to do the same. Tate was relentless, which I completely understand. Being away from your mate while she's in heat can be torturous.

"Brinley, how're you feeling?"

"Much better, thank you."

"John has more information, shall we head to Tate's office?"

"No, I found out Tate's in the cells. I want to get him first, release Maribel, then we can go to his office."

Ben scratched the back of his head with a concerned look, "We can release Tate, but I'm not sure he's going to release Maribel."

"Why not? Her masturbating in front of you guys doesn't fit the punishment, she's in solitary confinement, not cool Ben." I was stern.

"You're right but there is more going on than her being in the men's locker room, that was the breaking point."

"What else did she do?" Jaxon asked.

"I think we need to get Tate and go to the office and talk about it. He may want Cecil and Anabel there.."

"Let's break him out and get this sorted. I want to see the arena too. Maybe after we meet with Tate and the surveillance team we can go to the arena?"

"I think that's a fantastic idea."

I was lost in thought on our way to the dungeon, *"Penny for your thoughts, My Love,"* Q linked me.

*"Just thinking how nice it's been getting to know everyone and how close we've become in the short time they've been here."*

*"Yes, it has been nice. I enjoy their company very much and I love Brin, she's a breath of fresh air."*

We nodded to Adam and Pete before entering the dungeon. When we made it to Tate's cell he was doing push-ups. I saw him subtlety stiffen when he caught Brin's scent and I smirked. He got up and walked to the cell door. "What are you guys doing down here?"

"Brin's heat is over so we came to let you out." I unlocked the cell door, he walked right over to Brin, took in a deep breath, and gave her a gentle kiss on her head, then whispered in her ear, "I'm sorry Chase and I lost control, it will not happen again."

"I forgive you if you forgive me for enticing you with brownie batter," she giggled.

"I will always forgive you, Cupcake," he smiled softly at her.

## BRINLEY

When I saw Tate, I got butterflies in my stomach. I know it's because of what almost happened and the stupid crush I have on him. I need to get myself under control, I can't think of him as mine. When he walked over to me and took a deep breath of my scent, I swear I could feel tingles running up my spine. I know it's wishful thinking. He gave me a gentle kiss on my head and then apologized.

"Now that Tate is out, we need to let Maribel out."

"Nope, she's staying in the cells. She's not coming out, it's for your safety."

I put my hands on my hips, "Tate, seriously? You need to let her go, her sister is due here any day."

"Brin, there is more to this than you know."

"Then explain it to me," I stomped my foot.

"Not here, let's go back to the office and I'll have Cecil and Anabel meet us there."

"Fine, but I want to know everything. There has to be more to her getting thrown in the cells besides masturbating in front of you."

"Don't worry, there is."

Cecil and Anabel were waiting for us at the office. "Alpha, Lu...Brin, what can we do for you?" Cecil asked.

"Please have a seat," I told them. "I want to release your daughter from the cells. Tate says there is more to her being in there. Can you shed some light on this?"

"Alpha Tate hasn't told you?"

"No, he hasn't." They looked at each other then to Tate, then back to me.

"I don't even know where we can start," Cecil said.

"Why don't you start with why you agreed to her being in the cells."

"We confirmed she's the one who destroyed your room."

"How did you find this out?"

"I looked through her phone and saw the pictures, and showed them to Alpha Tate. We were able to convince her to let us take her phone and we gave it to John to verify the pictures were taken with it. We realized there were other pictures on her phone that were sent to her from Diane."

"What pictures?"

"They were of you. You with your siblings. You and the Alpha. You and Beta Quincy. You and Doc Stevens. You around the packhouse and with your security detail."

"Okay, this is too much for me, I need to sit. She was... stalking me?"

"She was," Anabel said softly, reaching for my hand.

"Tell me, does she know the consequences of stalking an alpha?"

"She should, but she doesn't know you're an alpha." they lowered their heads.

"I will give her one chance and one chance only to prove she's learned her lesson. If she does one thing out of line to me or any of my family or friends, I will probably take her life. You understand that right?"

"Yes, we understand."

"Good, now before we head to another meeting, I know your daughter, Noelle, is due to arrive any day now. Do you have everything set up, do you need assistance with anything?"

"No, we are good and the party will be in two days when she arrives."

"Wonderful, Tate, will you link the two men at the dungeon and let them know Maribel's parents are coming to get her?" I looked at them, "Please do not warn her or talk to her about this. She is old enough to know what will happen if she paid attention in school, and she's old enough to know right from wrong and to suffer the consequences if she steps out of line." They nodded at me, I stood, shook their hands, and dismissed them.

That was the hardest thing I've had to do. Tell someone's parents I would kill their child if they continued this behavior towards me. Deep down, I hope Maribel and Diane did screw up so I could show them how much strength I do have. I kind of feel bad because she doesn't know I'm an alpha but that doesn't excuse her behavior towards me or my family as guests in their pack.

I looked at everyone in the room after Maribel's parents left, "before we head into our next meeting with John and his team, I need to speak with Tate in private." I glanced at him as everyone left the office. I walked over to the door and locked it.

## TATE

When Brinley was talking to Cecil and Anabel, telling them exactly what would happen to their daughter, my cock was straining in my pants. She was firm yet soft with them, exactly how a luna should be. How my... luna... would be. She told everyone she needed to speak with me in private. All these things were running through my head as to what she needed to say and Chase was being silent for once.

She locked the door after everyone left, turned around, and stalked toward me. Her hands were on her hips and her lips were pursed. *Oh shit, she's not happy*, and just like that, my cock shrank. "Tate, I heard Chase took over and almost marked me when I was in heat!?"

"Uh, yeah, he did." I felt ashamed and embarrassed.

"May I have a word with him please." The way she said that, although she was asking, she wasn't.

*"Chase, you need to come forward, our mate wants to talk with you."*

*"Yeah, no, I'm good. I'm not coming forward. She looks pissed and she's scaring me."*

I blew out a breath, "Chase doesn't want to come out. He's, um, afraid of you," I said hesitantly.

"You tell Chase, that if he doesn't show himself, then HE will learn his lesson since you guys are so caught up on teaching lessons."

I rubbed my hand down my face, "I'll try again."

*"Chase, dude, I don't know what she is capable of but, buddy, you need to come forward."*

*"Nope, not happening, she's scary when she's mad."*

*"If you don't come forward she might make you. You think she's scary now? I'd hate to see how scary she can get."*

*"I'm an alpha now, she can't make me do anything."*

*"She's also your mate, you don't want her angrier do you?"*

*"No, but I don't want to face her either."*

*"So what do you want me to tell her?"*

She tapped her foot, "I'm waiting."

*"I don't care, tell her I'm sick or something!"*

*"I'm not telling her you're sick! Grow a pair and face her. She looks like she's getting pissed."*

*"No!"* He growled at me.

"Chase doesn't want to come forward."

"Why?"

"He's afraid. You're angry and he's afraid of you. He wanted me to tell you he's sick," I snickered and shrugged my shoulders.

She stalked over to me, grabbed me by my face, and as sparks flew all over my body, she looked into my eyes. In an alpha command stronger than I have ever known, she spoke to him.

"Chase Beckman! I don't give a flying fuck how scared you are of me. I need to speak with you. I COMMAND YOU TO SHIFT, NOW!"

I felt the power rolling off her and through me. I felt Chase cowering and then I shifted. Now I was looking through Chase's eyes and at a very pissed-off Brinley.

"I'm pissed, Chase. The last thing I wanted was to use my alpha command to get you to come forward when all I wanted to do was talk and ask some questions. I'm trying to contain my anger before speaking with you. Since I forced you to shift, you can no longer participate in this conversation."

"Now you will have to listen to me and when you are man enough to join in the conversation you can shift back. Until then, I command you to stay in wolf form. DO I MAKE MYSELF CLEAR!" He nodded his head.

She huffed and sat down placing her hands on the desk. "Chase, please sit." I could tell she was trying to stay calm, she tried, but there was irritation in her voice. He shook his head no and I felt the heat of anger rising in her. "I'm not asking again, if I do, it will be a command." He huffed and stood there staring at her. I'm not entering a power struggle with him either, if he wants to do this then he will lose, every single time, I can feel it.

"Fine, have it your way."

She looked at Chase, raised her eyebrows, and forced him to sit. We could feel her energy waning then all of a sudden it picked back up again. "Chase, you will stay sitting, do you understand?" He nodded his head. "Good."

"I don't appreciate YOU taking ADVANTAGE of ME being in heat. I accept my role in that situation with Tate, but, YOU HAD NO RIGHT to take over his body. It was horrible, inconsiderate of me and Amanda's feelings, it was rude, and very selfish! I'm sorry Tate had to be thrown in the cells but I'm glad you did! That never should have happened and I hope you learned YOUR lesson. If that EVER happens AGAIN, I will personally KICK YOUR ASS UNTIL YOU HAVE TO BE DRAGGED TO THE CLINIC!! DO I FUCKING MAKE MYSELF CLEAR!"

Chase sat there and stared at her with his mouth open and whimpering. "I will give you one chance to speak unless you're not 'man enough.' If you want to say anything, shift back so you can speak through Tate. You have two minutes to decide before I walk out that door to the surveillance room. He just sat there, staring at her. I'm in shock, she made me shift. I've never felt power like that before.

*"Tate, what the hell was that?"*

*"I have no idea, Chase. The power she held, that was amazing."*

*"Amazing? Amazing!? She made me shift against my will then forced me to sit!"*

*"Yeah, how did being forced to shift and sit feel? I sure as hell didn't like it when you took over my body."*

*"I'm sorry, I won't ever do it again either."*

*"Thanks Chase. She gave us two minutes to shift back and I think we're at that now."*

Two minutes later, he was still sitting there. She waited another fifteen seconds, got up, and headed to the door. I shifted back and placed my hand on her shoulder as she grabbed the doorknob to open it. She didn't turn around, I don't think she wanted to look me in the eyes, and I didn't want to see the disappointment in hers. She took a deep breath and without turning around she said, "You're twenty seconds too late, meet me in the surveillance office in three minutes, don't be late," and she walked out the door slamming it behind her.

I was stunned, Chase was stunned. *"Who does she think she is demanding things from us, an alpha and her mate?"* Chase asked.

*"I think that was our mate asserting herself. You need to remember, she doesn't know she's our mate yet."*

*"I think I liked it better when we thought she was fragile and needed to be taken care of."*

*"Me too, Chase, me too. I don't know where this confidence of hers is coming from, but I kinda like it."*

*"You can like it all you want, I for one, do not like it when she thinks she's in control, especially of me."*

*"Chase, she didn't THINK she was in control of you, she WAS in control of you,"* I laughed. *"We need to get to my office, she gave us three minutes to get there and I'll be damned if we're late."*

We walked into the office two minutes later with one minute to spare. You could cut the tension in the air with a knife, it was so thick. "What's going on?" I asked cautiously.

Brinley, Brooklyn, Quincy, and Crystal were wiping their eyes and all the guys looked agitated. John spoke, "We got word from Jeremy and Francis. One of the rogue men tried to rescue his wife and pup from the cave. Arnold caught him and tied him up. He raped his wife and killed his three-year-old son in front of him. We confirmed it by checking the cave's surveillance camera."

"How did we not catch this before it all happened?"

"Because it happened during our shift change. We wouldn't have been able to do anything about it at the time, but we do have an idea how to get the pups out of there and it involves Jaxon."

"So, what's your idea, John?"

"Since Jaxon and Brooklyn are the only two who can get in & out of there on their own accord, we thought about sending them in to get the pups out."

"How would they do that without being seen?"

"They'll probably be seen but if we do it properly, they will only be seen by the women being held there. We will need them to distract Arnold if he's in the cave and we'll need to know which pups to take first. To do that, we need to contact Jeremy and Francis again. So we're sending Brinley and Phillip back out tonight."

"I don't like it, I think we can send someone else out there."

"No can do Alpha, they have already established contact with them and we can't send others to them. They have built up a fragile trust with them, it can only be them. Once they establish contact, they will find out which of the pups we can rescue. They did confirm there are fifteen pups and five women being held hostage; three of the women are pregnant. The pups range in age between a few months old to ten years old. We need to find out if Arnold would notice them missing."

"Phillip and I will be ready to head out. Do you want us here at the same time around 11:00 pm to get ready?" Brinley asked.

"Yes, same time would be good, or maybe a little earlier."

"If there's nothing else, we're going to head to the arena and check it out, we'll be back at 11:00 pm. See you later Johnny Boy."

"Bye Brin, see you tonight."

# CHAPTER 31 GETTING AN UPDATE

**BRINLEY**

After getting brought up to speed with John, I was excited to get to the arena and check it out. I'm hoping it will be ready soon because I know Amanda and I are ready for this. It's been five years since we've shifted, five years of being lost in myself, and five years of Amanda not being able to play with Branson and Maya, which I know I'm mostly to blame.

The arena is near the training pitch but a little more secluded. As we made our way there, we decided to stop and watch the warriors being trained by our elites. It was mid-morning, around 10:00 am when I felt something pelt me in the back while watching training. *What the hell was that?* I glanced over my shoulder and saw Maribel and Diane standing there, not fifteen feet away from us with smirks on their faces and rocks in their hands.

I linked my pack members who were around me. *"Don't react, just listen. Maribel and Diane just pelted me in the back with a rock. Let me handle this."* Max told Crystal, who then linked Ben, Quinn, and Tate. Tate then linked his pack members who were near us. I dramatically turned around and started to cry while walking toward them. "Why did you hit me with that rock, it hurt."

"You deserved it! You took my chosen mate then you made my fated mate reject me!" Maribel screamed. Diane reached out and slapped me across the face, I drew in a breath while pretending it hurt. "What was that for?"

"Maribel is my best friend, she's the best person anyone could ask for as a mate and you made her lose two of them! You messed up everything when you arrived in our pack and you deserve more than a slap in the face!" she spat.

"I'm sorry your chosen mate doesn't want you and your fated mate rejected you," I tried to sound as pathetic as possible.

Maribel continued, "You're so pathetic, your security team isn't even stepping in to stand up for you," she spat.

"I... I don't know why," I cried while linking them telling them to back away from me.

"Oh look at that, they're even leaving you," Diane said snidely.

I turned around to look at the group. I linked them to meet me in the arena and told my elites to start training again. "How can I make this up to you?"

"You can let me have both my mates so I can choose which one I want, that's what you can do!" She screamed.

I backed up as they came closer to me. I pretended to trip and landed on the ground to see what they would do. They walked over and kicked me in the stomach. *Amanda, can you believe them, they think they're hurting me. I think the toddlers in our pack kick harder than these two can.* I chuckled.

*"I know, this is ridiculous, and the worst part, they are supposed to have beta and gamma blood in them."* she laughed back.

I pretended their kicks hurt me, "please leave me alone." I forced tears to come to my eyes. When they felt they hurt me enough, they grabbed each other's hands and walked away. They turned, as I was 'struggling' to get up, and laughed at me.

"Come on Diane, Noelle will be here in a couple of days, we need to see if there is anything my parents need for the party." After they were out of sight, I got up, brushed myself off, and headed to the arena.

*"Strike three for them Amanda, wait until they find out who they've been messing with. We're going to teach them their final lesson."*

*"Yes, we are and I can't wait to sink my teeth into them."* We were still laughing as we reached the arena.

Jaxon walked up to me, "How are you feeling? What happened with those asshats?"

"Oh, my fucking goddess. I pretended to trip and fall, they came over and tried kicking me. Well, they did kick me but the toddlers in our pack kick harder than they do! I pretended it hurt and cried so they left."

"Why were they doing that to you?"

"They're still angry, blaming me for taking Tate and Jacob away from her and Diane is following suit," I shook my head. "They just crossed the line, Maribel didn't learn her lesson. I decided I'm going to let her see her sister one last time before Amanda and I take care of her."

"Are you going to banish her?" Quincy asked.

I shook my head, "No, I don't believe in banishment, I believe in capital punishment. Why make more rogues who will just cause problems for others? Besides, neither one of them would last more than an hour on their own before some rogue catches them, rapes them, then kills them. They are better off being killed. They won't be killed right away, Amanda, and I want to mess with them first. Then Amanda can have the killing strike."

*"Baby Sis, I'm glad you're deciding to end their lives, it's what they deserve."*

*"I appreciate your support Jaxy, it means a lot to me."*

*"You know I'll always be in your corner. I love you, Brin."*

*"I love you too Jaxy."*

We were looking around the arena, the drywall was up, the plumbing and electrical were installed and the crew was in the process of installing the men's and women's locker rooms including the bathrooms and showers. The windows were installed, and the skylights were being installed but there was still a lot of work that needed to be done before the arena was ready for use. The foreman walked over to us and told us the arena should be ready in another month. That makes me so happy to hear.

The afternoon is getting away from us and I needed some sleep before Phillip and I head out tonight on our mission. "Let's leave the crew to continue their work so we don't get in their way." We all left, the guys headed to the training pitch, and the girls and I headed to Crystal's cottage for a little girl time before I needed to take a nap.

By the time I left Crystal's cottage and headed to Tate's suite for my nap, it was 5:00 in the evening. I wasn't hungry so I stripped my clothes, and climbed into his bed. I must've been really tired because Phillip woke me up at 10:30 pm so we could head to Tate's office to get ready to leave.

## JOHN

Phillip and Brinley arrived a little after 10:30 pm. "How's the arena coming along?"

"Great! They still have a lot of work to do but the foremen said it should be ready ahead of time, possibly even next month."

"That must make you feel so excited. I know you have been waiting a long time to shift again."

"You have no idea, Amanda and I are excited. Are you going to come train with us?"

"Hell no, you kick my ass on a bad day, there is no way I'm going to let you kick my ass on a day you have finally shifted again. Not to change the subject but are you guys ready to head out and see what's been going on at the cave?"

"We are, it will be nice to talk with Jeremy and Francis instead of reading the notes they are putting in front of the camera."

"Let's make sure you have what you need before you head out. Did you bring the scent concealer, silver, and wolfsbane?"

"Of course I did, I'm still not taking any chances."

"Then you guys are good to go." I walked with them out the front door and watched them head to the trees before heading back to the surveillance room.

## PHILLIP

Once we got to the tree line, we sprayed the concealer on us just like we did before. "You ready to do this again?"

"Sure am, it will be nice when we don't have to keep meeting them like this though."

"I agree, it will be nice when this is all over with. Unfortunately, I don't see this ending anytime soon."

"Me neither. Let's get out there and see what info they have for us."

We arrived at our designated rock an hour later and shortly after, the guys showed up. I said their names quietly and they sat on the rock for their 'break.' Jeremy spoke up first, "Hey guys, glad to see you. I'm assuming you've been seeing the notes we've been putting in front of the camera?"

"We have, that's why we needed to come out. Has Arnold harmed or killed anyone else?"

"No, we've been keeping a low profile, and as hard as it is for the other rogues, they are holding up too. We don't want any of the other pups getting hurt and if we follow Arnold, he won't touch them or the women. The rogues who want to defect are doing a good job at keeping this under wraps. Do you know when you might be rescuing the pups?"

"No, we don't have that information yet. We are still working on it. As soon as we have an idea of when it will happen we will let you know. Phillip and I will most likely come out again and talk with you directly so you would know the plan."

"That sounds good. We'll keep watch on the camera like we have been so we will know when to expect you."

"Have any other developments been going on that we need to be aware of?"

"No, it's been eerily quiet in the camp and it has us on edge."

"Keep vigilant and if you hear or see anything you know how to reach us." I looked down at my watch and noticed two hours had already passed, "we need to get back to our packhouse and you need to get to return to your shift. Before you leave, take this marker. The ink isn't visible except under a special light. When the time comes, put a mark on the left hand of the pups we will need to rescue. Make sure you hide the marker in a safe place where Arnold won't find it."

"I will be sure to give it to my mate. It's been nice talking with both of you again. Hopefully next time you will have good news for us about the rescue."

"We do too. Take care and be safe." The guys left and a few minutes later Brin and I headed out.

## JEREMY

Francis and I walked off as Phillip and Brinley left. "So what do you think about all this?"

"I think if they can pull this off then we'll have a new pack to call home. Do you think they were serious about letting the defectors merge into pack life?"

"I do. So far Phillip and Brinley have seemed pretty honest and they haven't given us reason to question them, not like Arnold does anyway."

"Do you think they'd help find our old packs to see if some of the rogues could rejoin them or do you think they'll find another pack for everyone to join?"

"I think it will depend on the individual or each family to decide if they want to stay as a rogue or if they want that chance to be a part of a pack. For some, it will be strange to live under the governing rules of a pack and alpha, especially if they've never experienced it before."

"I know you're right, I just want to make sure those who want to defect are treated fairly and not treated as a slave. I'd hate for them to get put in a worse position than they already are."

"Francis, Brinley doesn't seem like the person who would want anyone treated as slaves. She seems like a fair and just person who puts the needs of others above what her needs are. I don't think we need to worry about the rogue becoming slaves. I think the pups will integrate into school fine and the adults will probably adjust to life in a pack more quickly than we think they will."

"I have hesitations about it. What if we aren't accepted? What if we get run out by the pack members because they won't trust us being there even though most of us were born into this life?"

"That's not something I want to dwell on yet. I want to think about getting our mates and all those pups to safety first. Then we can dwell on the fact we might have a pack to call home and what that will look like. We're almost to the cave, we need to table this discussion."

"Fine, I'll drop it for now, but we need to find out from Brinley if everyone will be treated fairly once they are under the alpha's command."

We made it back to the cave, Arnold was nowhere to be found, no big surprise there. He seems to be disappearing a lot lately and sometimes comes back smelling like burnt marshmallows, it makes me want to gag. Francis and I looked around the cave to see our sleeping mates, the other three women, and all those pups. My mate, Lydia, is pregnant, the last thing I want is for my pup to be born a rogue.

We quietly walked up to them and gently woke them from their sleep. "Hey beautiful, remember that woman, Brinley, I told you about."

"Yeah, what about her?"

"She met up with us tonight, she and the guy she was with, Phillip, gave us a marker to use to mark the orphans. Do you have a place you can hide it so Arnold won't find it?"

"I do." She held out her hand and I gave it to her. She got up and walked to a rock sticking out of the cave wall. I was in awe of her as she pulled the rock out, placed the pen inside then replaced the rock. It didn't look like anything was disturbed and looking at the rock you wouldn't realize the rock could be removed.

"Have you heard Arnold talking about anything that could be useful against him?"

"No, he pretty much keeps his talking in the cave to a minimum but I'll let you know if I hear him say anything worthwhile."

"I'd appreciate it. That way I can relay anything back to Brinley and Phillip. The more information they have the better it will help us in the long run."

"I'll do my best but you know the consequences if I'm found out."

"That I do, that is why this mission is so important to be successful." I kissed her and left the cave before Arnold had a chance to return. When I got back to my space under the trees, Francis was waiting for me. He spoke with his mate too and told her what the plan was. His mate is also expecting but she was a month behind Lydia in her pregnancy.

"Is everything all set for Lydia to mark the orphans?"

"Yes, she put the marker in a safe place and when we give her a signal, she'll mark them. How's Kami doing?"

"She's holding up. She's terrified of Arnold, but who isn't? She's ready to be rescued and be done with this. She told me she wants the safety of a pack and wants our pup raised in one. She doesn't like the uncertainty that living like a rogue has and would rather have people around her she can trust. I get it, I want the same thing too. That's why I'm sticking my neck out there."

"That's why I'm doing this too. I know pack life is way better than rogue life. I want it more for Lydia and our pup and we'll get that in a pack. Let's get some sleep before Arnold gets back and makes us train. Goodnight Francis."

"Goodnight, Jeremy."

# CHAPTER 32 FINALLY SHIFTING

**BRINLEY**

*****One Month Later*****

A lot has been happening this past month. Maribel and Diane have been trying to get to me but Tate won't allow me out of his sight, my siblings are still here and plans are coming together to rescue the pups and women. There haven't been any rogue attacks and we're on edge because of it. Jeremy and Francis still haven't heard talk of when Arnold plans to attack.

They said he keeps leaving the cave, sometimes for days on end and they can smell sex on him occasionally. They think he's meeting up with someone but it's just a speculation. We've noticed Diane leaving the pack lands at random times too. We're not sure what's going on with that but as long as she stays away from me the better.

Noelle was supposed to arrive home a couple of weeks ago but decided to stay at college for a little longer. I'm excited for her to return so I can meet her. I've heard all kinds of wonderful things about her. She seems like Maribel's polar opposite, which would be a breath of fresh air. I was meeting our group in the foyer of the packhouse so we could head to the arena and see how things were coming along. I know they are close to being completed with it but we wanted to check on it. We've been doing that every week and I'm sure the foreman is getting tired of seeing us.

"Hey guys, you ready to head to the arena?"

"Sure am Baby Sis, let's get down there and see how much longer this will take. I'm excited to start training with you again."

"I'm excited too."

We headed down to the arena and were stopped by a few of Tate's pack members before heading to the training pitches and then the arena. By the time we arrived there, it was 11:00 am. It looked amazing. Our foreman came out and told us they had finished an hour earlier. I can't believe they got it done in half the time, although I should've since we had two hundred of our construction crew working on it around the clock.

I looked around the outside of the arena before heading inside. It was as big as one and a half football fields and completely enclosed, just like the one at home. There were windows all around the building to let light in and two sets of doors. The windows and doors were reinforced and steel shutters were installed on them as well. This building is so secure that when the shutters are closed it's impossible to get in. We walked inside and saw the skylights with reinforced steel shutters as well.

I know there are shutters on the outside of the skylights as well because we have the same thing on ours back home. There are two locker rooms built inside and different flooring for training on such as hardwood, grass, turf, gravel both large rock and pea gravel, dirt, and cement. There's a swimming pool and a mud pit too. There are a couple of other rooms off to the side which I'm assuming holds all of our training weapons and an office.

"This is amazing," I told our foreman, "you guys did a fantastic job. You can all go back to the jobs you were pulled off of unless you want to stay and help with the attack on the rogues."

"We'd be happy to stay if you need us."

"I don't think we'll need all of you, so if half of you want to stay you are welcome to."

"Thanks, Brinley, I'll get with the crew and find out who wants to stay and who wants to get back to their other jobs."

"Whatever they decide is fine with us." He bowed his head and left the arena.

**JAXON**

"Well Baby Sis, you ready to do this? Are you and Amanda ready to shift?"

"We are, I'm excited. I'm feeling better, although I miss Jerod and Cassie Mae, I know I need to move on for them and me."

Brooklyn walked up to her and put her arms around her then kissed her cheek, "Let's get this show on the road. Maya is pestering me to play with her brother and sister."

"Okay, but we need everyone out of the arena except for Erik, Max, Phillip, and Jacob."

"On it," I said.

I walked over to Tate's group. "Brin's going to shift and train. We need you guys to leave the arena. You can stay outside if you want but we might be here for several hours so if you have other things to do, please feel free to do them."

"Are you sure you don't need us?" Ben asked.

"I'm sure, we can handle it from here."

"Okay, but if you need us, we'll just be outside."

"Suit yourself, but you won't hear us, the building is soundproof and we're closing the shutters so you won't be able to see inside."

As they were heading to the door, I pulled Tate aside. "Brin's going to shift, it's going to be painful for her. I know you're her fated second chance mate so you may want to seclude yourself in case you're able to feel her pain. I know you don't want a lot of people to know yet and you want her to discover it on her own."

"Thanks for telling me. I'll be able to handle it. Won't she scent me being in here though when she shifts?"

"No, we have a built-in scent extractor, that pulls out scents in the air and replaces it with forest air."

"That's amazing."

"It's how we train for tracking. We can control if there is a full scent or no scent. As our trackers train in the arena to improve their noses, we decrease the strength of the scent and where it's coming from. It's one of the games we play with our younger pups. They think it's fun to track the scent, they don't realize they are training. Our pups with the best tracking noses pick up on it fast and they enter an enhanced tracking training on top of their warrior training."

"Brin was explaining to Ben and me the different age levels you have for training but she didn't mention anything about track training at such a young age."

"It doesn't surprise me. She likes to keep our young pups safe so she doesn't normally tell people what they can do at a young age, otherwise, people might try to kidnap them." I held open the door for them and once they were out, I opened the secure control box, locked the doors, closed the shutters, and flipped the switch to clear the air. Once I couldn't smell Tate anymore. I turned to the guys and my sisters, "You all ready for this?" They nodded their heads and looked at Brin.

## BRINLEY

*"Andi, are you ready to shift?"*

*"I am but I'm afraid of hurting you, it's been so long."*

*"I will be okay. It will be like the first time we shifted, we'll be okay, I promise."*

*"Andi, Brin?"* We heard Maya and Branson, *"We're going to shift too, if it gets to be too much lean into us okay?"*

*"Okay, thank you."* I thought of Amanda and my wolf form. I saw my white coat and lilac tips, I tried to relax and recall what it felt like to have the wind in my fur and dirt under my paws. Then I felt it, the first snap of my bones as my spine snapped and stretched I let out a painful cry. Then I felt my jaw snap and change into my muzzle and tears were running down my face and I began to whimper. My legs and arms were next, they snapped and broke as they rearranged into my four legs and paws. I let

out a whimper and a painful howl, and then I felt my tail burst from me and I screamed out another painful howl.

The shift only took a few seconds but it felt like forever. When I was finally shifted and looked around, my vision was clearer, my hearing was sharper and my nose scent was enhanced. It just smelled like fresh forest air in the arena. Jaxon must've cleared the air, not sure why since it was just us and Tate's group in here. He probably wanted me to concentrate on the smells we're used to.

*"Brins, are you okay?"*

*"I'm good, how are you, Ava?"*

*"I'm good too, I want to run, can we run?"*

*"Yes,"* I laughed, *"run all you want."* She took off running around the arena and Branson and Maya joined me. We jumped, rolled around, bit each other, and played tag. I think we ran and played for two hours before stopping to rest with our heads on each other.

*"Andi?"* Branson asked.

*"Yeah?"*

*"We need to give control back to the triplets, they need to see if Brin can use her powers."*

"Okay, I'll change back."

Amanda gave me back control, and the shift back to human form was much easier and quicker. The guys came running over to me to make sure I was okay. "I'm good, I'm good. A little tired but I'm good. I'm more than good, I feel excellent!"

"We are so happy to hear that Peanut." Brooklyn and Jaxon came over to me, the three of us standing there naked, but we didn't care. We cried as we hugged each other.

"Are you ready to see if your powers are working?" Brooklyn asked.

"I am, who am I going to try this on?"

"I think you should try it on the guys," Jaxon smirked.

"Okay, which of you am I going to throw across the arena?"

Max stepped up, "Give me your best shot, Peanut." I concentrated on him and then imagined him being flung across the arena. I was able to move him about fifty feet. "Good job for your first try." I wasn't happy and it showed on my face. "What's wrong Peanut?"

"I should've been able to fling you across the entire arena."

"Seriously, you've been out of practice for five years, what do you expect? That was pretty good for the first time in a while."

"I know, but I've always been hard on myself." We practiced that for an hour and each time I used one of the guys and I got them further down the arena. "I need to practice something else."

"How about asking me questions to see if I'm being honest?" Erik asked. "The last time you used your lie detector, Andi was lending you her strength so you could interrogate that rogue."

"Sounds good, let's see if I can do this without Andi's help."

"When Max and I were teenagers we snuck into the girls' locker room to watch them change."

"Lie. You were going to sneak in there but Gunther caught you. I remember hearing my parents talking about it."

"Fine but did you know I had a crush on Megan when I was ten years old."

"What! You seriously had a crush on her? I didn't know that!"

"I did, and when she and her family moved, I was devastated. I cried in my room for a week and would barely eat anything. My mom was worried about me."

"Uh, interesting, you're telling the truth. I can just imagine you as a poor little ten-year-old crying over a little girl. She was what, like six or seven years old?"

"She was eight and she was cute. She had dimples when she smiled, her brown wavy hair reached her waist, and her green eyes sparkled. She was the prettiest little thing I've ever seen."

"Sounds like you're still crushing on her."

"Shut up, I am not."

"Ooooh, another lie." I smiled at him and he blushed. "I'm going to ask my dad where they moved to, maybe he can find out if she has a mate yet."

"Don't you dare, Peanut!"

"Oh, it's happening." I giggled.

"Can we please get back to the task at hand? I can't wait to get home to your dad's weekly home-cooked meals."

"Lie. Eric, you don't like my dad's cooking?"

"Nope, he never uses enough spices."

"Truth. I think I can say my lie detector power is working, and so is my telekinesis."

"Let's see if your telepathy and psychometry are working," Phillip said. "Can you try and link into Quinn's thoughts?"

"I don't know, she's outside, let me try." With some concentration, I was able to enter her mind and what I saw gave me the biggest smile. "My telepathy is working."

"Okay, let's check your psychometry, "here hold this, I found it in the packhouse," Jacob said.

"What is it?"

"I think it's a hair tie, here," he handed it to me, and as soon as I grabbed it I immediately dropped it.

"It's working."

"You barely touched it."

"The person who owns that hair tie is working with the rogue pack."

"Fuck!" they all yelled out.

"Who does it belong to?" Jaxon asked me.

"Diane, she's Arnold's mate."

**TATE**

Jaxon told us we needed to leave the arena, he was locking them in. I wanted to stay, I wanted her to scent me when she shifted. I wanted to be with her, during this momentous moment but knew she needed to do this with her siblings and friends. "Tate, you may feel her pain when she shifts, you may want to be somewhere secluded since you don't want people to know you are mates," I heard him say.

I can handle it, I know I can, but I decided I needed to work out, that might help. I grabbed Ben and we headed to the gym. Once we got to the gym we sparred, all of a sudden my back felt like it was breaking and I dropped to my knees. Ben came running over, "You okay?" I waved him off, then it felt like my jaw was breaking then my legs and hands and feet.

I was panting... hard, "Drink some water, Tate. The pain will end shortly, I'm sure she's fully shifted now." Just like that the pain was gone and I could breathe again.

"That was rough and painful, I hope her shift isn't that painful going forward."

"I'm sure it's only because she hasn't shifted in a long time," he patted my back.

## JAXON

"Well, I didn't see that coming. It makes sense now. I've seen her leaving pack lands every once in a while but didn't think anything of it since it's normal for pack members to leave."

"I think we need to check the security gate CCTV for the days and times she left the property and see if it matches when we noticed Arnold leaving the cave and rogue camp," Phillip piped in. "Now that I think about it, I've seen her trying to hang out around Tate's office too."

"We'll need to be extra vigilant when we're doing things and talking. Now that Brin can enter minds, she'll be able to link with anyone in Tate's pack. Okay guys, we've been training for three hours, it's 4:00 pm. Let's get cleaned up so we can fill everyone in on what we just discovered."

"Sounds good, I could use a nice shower," Brin said.

"Me too," Brooklyn replied. We all hit the locker rooms. As I was showering I realized we forgot to test Brinley's scent factors.

*"Brin?"*

*"Yeah, Jaxy?"*

*"We forgot to test your nose. I'm linking Max to have Crystal bring her scent jars."*

*"Oooh, great idea."*

Once we were out of the showers, we met Max and Crystal in the middle of the arena.

"Let's get this show on the road and see what happens."

"Jaxon, can you put this blindfold on her please? I put twenty of my scent jars in my case. I'm going to hold them up to you, you tell me what they are and we'll see how many you get correct, sound good?"

"Sounds good."

"I'm going to start now, okay?" After twenty minutes, we finished with the scent jars.

"You can take your blindfold off. You got all the scents correct. I have no doubt your nose is working properly."

I saw Erik sneaking up on her and without missing a beat, She whirled around, grabbed him by the neck, flipped him over, and held him down. "Well Peanut, your senses are working now too. No more sneaking up behind your back and scaring you," he laughed and she was unamused.

"It's 5:00 pm, we need to head back to the packhouse. Crystal, is everyone still outside, or did they leave?"

"They left, they decided to get something to eat since the last time they ate was breakfast."

"Let's get the arena locked up and head back." Once we were all outside, she stiffened next to me.

"Are you okay?"

"Yeah, I'm good."

I smiled at her then used the retina scanner to lock up the arena and we headed to the packhouse.

"Why do you have a smile on your face?" No reason.

We got to the packhouse and I saw Ben, "I need to ask Ben a question, I'll meet you in the dining hall."

"I'm going up to Tate's room to change my clothes first, so I'll see you in there when I'm done."

"Alright, I'll see you sooner or later."

"What did you just say?"

"I just said I'll see you later," I smiled at her.

I ran over to Ben, "Hey, do you know where Tate is?"

"Yeah, he's in his suite, why?"

I got a big-ass grin on my face and whispered in his ear, "Brin can smell things again."

"No shit," he got a big grin on his face.

"She's heading to his suite to change her clothes. Looks like you'll officially have a luna in a few minutes," I slapped his back.

"It's about damn time too."

## BRINLEY

I made my way through the packhouse, and Andi started pacing back and forth. *"Andi, what's going on, what's got you so on edge?"*

*"Can you smell it, can you smell him?"*

*"I can smell rain and forest and it smells so good."*

*"Mate, that's our mate!"*

*"Andi, we need to get to him. I wonder who he is."*

*"I don't know Brin, but I want our mate."*

*"I do too. I can't believe we were given a second chance mate and he's here, in this pack."*

*"I know!"*

We followed the scent through the dining room, through the kitchen, and to the stairs. We walked up the steps, past the offices, and the beta and gamma floor. When we got to the alpha floor the scent was strong. Tate, Tate is our mate. I linked my brother and sister, *"Tate is my mate!"* I heard laughing on the other end of the link before I closed it off.

I ran to the suite and stood outside the door. My heart was beating fast as I reached my shaking hand out and grabbed a hold of the knob, turning it slowly. I pushed it open, *"Andi, what the hell are we doing?"*

*"We're going to our mate, that's what we're doing. Now is not the time to be all shy, now scoot and get your ass in there, go claim our mate!"*

*"I'm going, I'm going."* I closed the door, locked it, and leaned against it. I'm so nervous and scared. *Why the hell am I scared? I don't know why I am, maybe because this whole time I've had a crush on him, trying unsuccessfully to keep my distance. Thinking back to all the times my body was drawing us closer. I can see it now, always wanting to be near him, not getting enough of his touch.*

*It's because my body knew we were mates but Amanda and I didn't because I was lost in myself. It makes sense now, how my nightmares stopped as soon as I was around him. How I was feeling stronger and more confident in myself. It's all because of the mate bond, without realizing it, he was healing me, and I was finally home again.*

As I'm having this internal dialogue, I'm taking small steps toward his bedroom. I can hear the shower running, *he's in the shower, he's my mate, you can do this Brin, get a hold of yourself.* I slowly remove my clothes as I walk to his room. I kicked my socks and shoes off by the couch. I dropped my shirt next to them and removed my pants leaving them on the floor between the couch and his bedroom.

My bra came off next to his bedroom door, and I stepped out of my panties as I got near his bed. I can feel my pulse quicken and my core tightens with anticipation. I can feel my pussy getting slick as I step closer to his shower, our suite, our bedroom, our shower. He is mine and I am his. I walk into his shower, placing kisses on his back. As soon as I touched him, I felt the tingles of the mate bond on my lips. He stiffened, then relaxed as I wrapped my arms around him and sparks flew all over my body.

# CHAPTER 33 MATE! PART 2

**TATE**

I was in the shower and smelled her as soon as she reached the suite. I heard the door open, close, then lock. I don't know what she's doing but my cock is getting hard. Does she finally know we're mates? She must, she's here, then I hear something hit the floor, shoes? Did she remove her shoes? Then I heard something land on the floor, was she... undressing?

Chase is bouncing around my head. *"Buddy, calm down or you're going to give me a headache."*

*"Sorry, I'm excited our mate is here."*

*"I am too buddy, but we do this at her pace and comfort level. So you need to contain yourself."*

*"Okay, okay, okay."*

I heard her enter the bedroom, I took a deep breath and slowed my beating heart. She came into the bathroom and walked into the shower. I felt the lightest kisses on my back and tensed a little before relaxing as soon as I felt her hands wrap around me. The sparks were igniting all over my body. I turned around in her arms, looked into her eyes, and heard her say, "Mate" for the first time.

"Mate," I smiled at her then leaned down and brushed my lips against hers. She tasted better than I could've imagined. I brushed my tongue against her lips asking for entrance, she parted her lips and I slipped my tongue inside, tasting her more deeply. Our tongues glided against each other as our kiss grew more deeply. I could feel her nipples harden against my chest and my cock grew harder between us.

I don't know how long we were kissing in the shower, but when the water turned cold, I turned it off and grabbed towels. I wrapped one around my waist and one around her. I picked her up and carried her to my bed, our bed. I laid her down gently, "Lay still Cupcake." I was going to worship her body as it should be. This feels so much more intense with her knowing we're mates. I kissed her lips again, then kissed down her cheek to her marking spot.

I nipped but didn't mark her, I don't know how she'd feel about that yet. I kissed down her neck, removed the towel, and sucked in one of her nipples. I ran my tongue over it while my hand gripped her other breast and was playing with her nipple. "Mmm, Tate, it feels good," she moaned.

She moved her hand down to her pussy to rub and play with her clit, I removed her hand, "Mine, all mine, don't touch Cupcake." I slipped my finger between her folds, she was dripping wet. I kissed down her stomach and when I reached her pussy, she grabbed my hair and ran her fingers through it.

"Please Tate, I need more."

I plunged my tongue inside her, licking and sucking her sweet nectar. I couldn't get enough, I wanted more. I pushed my finger inside her and she let out a moan. "Please, Tate, please. I need to feel you inside me." I replaced my tongue with my finger, found her G-spot, and thrust into her hitting it each time. She moved her hips closer to me, I could feel she wanted more. I added another finger to stretch her and get her ready for me.

"Cupcake, you are so wet and tight, are you ready for me?"

"Mmm, yes, my Alpha, please, I need you inside me," she moaned.

I lined myself up with her opening and pushed in. "Fuck, you are so tight, are you ready for me?"

"Yes my Alpha, please, make me cum."

"Let me get a condom."

"No Tate, I want to feel you, skin to skin."

"I'll pull out, I don't want to take a chance of you getting pregnant."

"Tate, please move."

I growled and thrust slowly. She scratched my back and dug her nails into my skin, trying to pull me closer to her. "Tate!" She screamed, "harder, I need it harder! Please!"

I slammed into her, "Look at me Cupcake, I want to see your eyes. You need to watch me slamming my cock into you. I want you to see how much pleasure you give me." I moved my hand down between us and played with her clit.

"Oh goddess Tate! I'm going to cum!"

"Cum for me, I want to feel you tighten around me."

She came so hard, her breathing was labored, and she was trying to catch her breath when her body began to shake. I didn't stop thrusting inside her, I was on the verge of my own release. "Cupcake, I'm going to cum!" My balls tightened, and as I was seconds away from my orgasm she flipped us over and rode my cock. Her mouth moved to my neck, I felt her canines graze my marking spot when she bit down deep to my bones. I couldn't hold back, I released my seed deep inside her. She withdrew her teeth and licked the wound to seal it so it would heal.

I growled out and flipped her back over. I was slamming into her again, I wanted to pull another orgasm from her. "Tate! I... I'm," she's trying to be coherent, "I'm about, mmm, oh Tate!" I felt her walls clenching around me, my canines lengthened and I sunk them into her marking spot, going just as deep as she did on me. As soon as I sunk my teeth in her, her walls clenched around me as her orgasm ripped through her. Her pussy was so tight and slick as she came all over my cock.

I leaned to her ear, "I love you, Brinley."

"I love you too Tate." Then she cried.

"Why are you crying?"

"Because I'm so happy. I'm happy you are my mate. I'm happy because I think my body knew you were mine. That's why I always felt pulled to you. You are why I no longer have nightmares and why I was feeling stronger, I was near my mate. I'm happy because I never thought I'd find love again. Now that I have you, I'm never letting you go."

"I'm never letting you go either, but why do I feel like there is something else bothering you? You can talk to me Brin, please open up and talk to me, I'm not going anywhere." I wiped her tears away with my thumb.

"We didn't talk about marking each other. We just got caught up in the moment and let instinct take over. We haven't accepted each other and, I love you Tate, but I still love Jerod too. How do I move on and give you everything when I still love him? It's not fair to you."

"Oh Brin, you just being by my side gives me everything I need. It's okay to still love him. I'm not jealous of him, I understand, he was your first mate. You had a pup together. I know how devastated you were when they died and I don't ever expect to replace him. If you ever want to talk about him, you can. I will always listen," he kissed the top of my head and wiped my tears away.

"Thank you for understanding."

"Let's take this one thing at a time, okay?" I nodded my head. "I know it's too late now but, Brin, would it be okay if I marked you?"

"Yes, please, I would like that very much." I leaned down and kissed my mark and her body shuddered beneath my touch.

"Tate, would it be okay if I marked you?"

"Yes, please for the love of the goddess mark me." She leaned in and didn't kiss my mark but bit down then licked the wound closed. Sparks went straight through me and to my dick. "Mmmm, that will get you in trouble." I leaned in and kissed her. I grabbed her by the cheeks, and looked into her eyes, "What's your full name?"

"Brinley Khrystyne Jameson."

"I, Tate Isaiah Beckman, Alpha of the Black Diamond Pack, accept you Brinley Khrystyne Jameson, alpha and master elite enforcer, of the Winter Moon Pack and former mate of Jerod Jameson, an elite warrior and mother to Cassandra Mae Jameson as my second chance mate and luna."

"I, Brinley Khrystyne Jameson, Alpha and master elite enforcer of the Winter Moon Pack and former mate of Jerod Jameson, an elite warrior and mother to Cassandra Mae Jameson, accept you, Tate Isaiah Beckman, Alpha of the Black Diamond Pack as my second chance mate and alpha. Thank you for including Jerod and Cassie Mae in the mate acceptance, it means a lot to me."

We leaned into each other and I gave her a passionate kiss. We felt the mate bond snap into place and a rush of emotions flooded over us. We were connected more intimately and could hear each other's thoughts and feel each other's emotions: something I've never experienced before and something I will need to get used to.

She pulled out of our embrace, "how are you feeling?"

"A bit overwhelmed. I've always heard about the mate bond but didn't realize how powerful it is. It's like we're connected on a deeper level. I never had this with Emberly because we hadn't marked each other yet. How are you feeling?"

"It feels good to have that connection again. I missed it and didn't think I'd ever have it again."

"Is there a way to keep you from reading all my thoughts and feeling my emotions?"

"Why? Do you not like it?"

"I love it, but if I ever want to surprise you with something I won't be able to if I can't block you."

"Blocking our mind link is the same as blocking the pack link, so don't worry, you can still block me, sort of," she smirked.

"Why are you smirking?"

"Because I need to tell you something about me but it needs to wait."

"We've been in our suite for a couple of hours, are you ready to shower and get something to eat? You and Phillip will need to leave in a few hours." She nodded her head. I scooped her up and carried her to the bathroom. I placed a towel on the counter and sat her down. I pushed her legs apart and stood between them, my cock coming back to life. I leaned in and gave her a gentle kiss, backed away, and started the shower before I picked her up, and carried her to the shower. I set her down and washed her hair.

## BRINLEY

Tate was so gentle with me. His understanding of my feelings of still loving Jerod while loving him and trying to sort those feelings out was more than what I expected. It was more than I could handle, the tears kept coming. I felt so comfortable in his arms that I never wanted to leave. Now we're in the shower and he's washing my hair. I turned around to face him as soon as the shampoo was rinsed grabbed the loofa, put body wash on it, and began to wash him.

As my hands got closer to his cock, it twitched. I placed my hand around it and stroked it up and down. "Cupcake, what are you do... ooooh, yeah, that feels good," he moaned. There's a bench in the shower so I sat down and brought him closer to me then wrapped my mouth around him. I stroked the underside of his cock with my tongue then nibbled on the tip before taking him as deep as I could.

"Mmmmm, Alpha, you taste so good." I bobbed my head up and down. I sucked on his balls before sucking him into my mouth again, while playing with his balls. I couldn't get enough.

"Cupcake, if you don't stop, I'm going to cum down your throat." That only spurred me on. I continued sucking and stroking his balls faster. I felt him go stiffer in my mouth and a few seconds later his seed was squirting down my throat. I swallowed every drop then licked him clean. He picked me up, I wrapped my legs around him and he carried me back to bed. We spent another hour ravishing each other's bodies before going back in the shower. This time we were able to make it out of our suite without being distracted, sort of.

**PHILLIP**

Tate and Brinley walked into the office where we were all waiting for them. The first thing I noticed was a new mark on her neck then looked at Tate and saw a mark on him. I smiled, "about time, congratulations. Are you excited to see what your marks will look like?"

"We are," Brin smiled at me, looked up at Tate, and leaned into him.

I walked over to Brinley and clasped her face in my hands. Tate growled at me, I looked at him, "Seriously Tate, she's like my sister."

"Mine," he said, as he grabbed her out of my hands.

"I know she's yours." I chuckled, grabbed her back, and placed my hands on her face again, "I'm so happy for you. You deserve all the happiness in the world after everything you've gone through." I gave her a bear hug and kissed her on the forehead. "We have a mission to complete and now that you can shift, we can get to the rogue camp more quickly."

# Chapter 34 Rogue Allies

**JOHN**

I was happy for Brinley, she's been miserable since Jerod and Cassie died. I hope she'll find happiness with Tate and his pack, although we are going to miss her terribly when we leave without her. Our packs' little pups will feel her loss too, they love her so much. "Now that you can shift, we need to make sure the bags won't be too tight. I'll also spray the concealer on you before you leave. The concealer will last several hours."

Brooklyn and Jax walked in a few minutes later, "Perfect timing, can you guys help me and Tate move a couple of things? I want each of them to shift so we can adjust the straps on their bags."

"Sure can," Brooklyn turned to Brin and gasped when she saw the mark on her neck. "Brin! I'm so happy for you!" She hugged her, "Let me look!"

"Brooky, the design won't show up until tomorrow, silly."

"I know, I'm just excited to see it! Mom and Dad are going to go ballistic when they find out."

"I know."

"Mom's gonna want to start planning your Luna ceremony right away."

"I know that too, but we need to keep it quiet for a little longer, so no telling Mom or Dad, got it?"

"Yeah, I got it," she smirked. "Why and how do you plan on hiding your mark? I'd ask how you're going to hide Tate's scent on you but since you've been sleeping in his suite, his scent was already on you, now it's in you," she covered her mouth trying to hold back her laugh.

"Sis, Really? You had to go there?"

"Well, yeah, I had to go there," she giggled.

"I haven't figured out how to conceal our marks yet. That can wait until tomorrow."

If you ladies are finished with your side conversation, I need them to shift. "Sorry John," Brooke blew him a kiss.

"Alright, who's shifting first?"

"I'll go first," Philip said removing his clothes and shifting into Sam. I strapped the bag to him and adjusted the straps on his back.

*"Sam, does the pack feel too tight or too loose?"*

*"It's a little tight around my waist, can you loosen it a little?"*

*"Yep, how's that?"*

*"Much better, thanks."*

*"No problem, close your eyes so I can spray your face and body."* After spaying him I rubbed it into his muzzle around his eyes. *"Okay, all done, you can shift back.* Brinley, your turn." She stood there and stared at me.

"What? Is something wrong?"

"Um, I've never shifted in front of Tate. He doesn't know what Amanda looks like," she said hesitantly.

"Shit, do you want to shift without him in here or do you want to just go in human form?"

"It will be faster for us if we go in wolf form and he is my mate. He'll see what she looks like eventually, may as well be now." She removed her clothes and shifted ignoring the look on Tate's face. I put the bag on her and adjusted her straps.

*"Amanda, how do the straps feel? Too tight, too loose?"*

*"They feel good."*

*"Close your eyes, I'm going to spray you."* I sprayed her down then rubbed the concealer around her eyes like I did

for Sam. *"You can shift back when you're ready."* When she shifted back her eyes were locked on Tate.

## TATE

Brinley was nervous shifting in front of me, not sure why, I've seen hundreds of wolves shift. Then she shifted, and I was speechless. She was beautiful. *"Chase, she's beautiful."*

*"Yes she is and I can't wait until I can shift and run with her in the forest, lay next to her, and mate and mark her. I want to put pups in her right away."*

*"So do I buddy, so do I."* Her coat is white with a hint of lilac brushing the tips of her fur and her icy blue eyes, made her more beautiful. I wanted to bury my face in her coat but knew we had a schedule to stick to. No wonder they locked her in the arena to train, people would be shocked to see her color. When she shifted back, our eyes were glued to each other.

"You and Chase want to put pups in me?"

"Huh? What? Did I say that out loud?"

"Nope."

"I must've because I blocked my thoughts from you." She and everyone in the room laughed. "Why are you laughing?"

"You'll find out at our next training session."

"Now that you've marked each other, your training has just amplified," Jaxon said, still laughing. I was so confused and so was Chase.

## BRINLEY

We got a late start but now that I can shift we can make up for the lost time in wolf form. Once we got to the tree line, we stripped, and put our clothes in the bags, strapped them to our backs, and shifted. We arrived at the designated rock in half the time, shifted back, and dressed. A few minutes to midnight, we heard Jeremy and Francis coming up the trail.

I concentrated on them and Phillip then linked all of them. *"Don't make a sound, this is Brinley. Phillip and I are at the rock. Is anyone following you?"*

*"No, no one is following us."*

*"Good, when you get to the rock, sit down."*

About a minute later the guys came. "Jeremy, I think I want to sit a minute before we continue patrolling, are you good with that?"

"Sure am."

I reached my hand out and barely touched them. *"We have some questions for you and we hope you have answers. Only talk through the link, we don't want anyone to overhear us if they are out and about."*

*"Brinley, how are you able to link us when we're not connected to you in a pack?"* Francis asked.

*"I'll answer that question at a later time. Are you or any of the other rogues aware Arnold has a mate?"*

*"He hasn't come out and told us but we all kind of figured it out. We would see him sneaking off and coming back smelling of burnt toast and sex. He also stopped raping the women he's holding hostage,"* Francis said.

*"Do you know who his mate is?"*

*"No, we've never seen her but assume she's from a pack since she has a pack scent and not the scent of a rogue."*

*"She is from a pack, ours. His mate is the former gamma's daughter and we suspect she's working with him. Giving him whatever pack information she can."*

*"That would explain why he told us we wouldn't be attacking for a couple of months. He said something about finding intel on the pack. He intends to take over the pack and make it the largest rogue pack in the United States."*

*"How would he do that? Rogues get banished from packs because they don't like the rules or do something horrible within the pack."*

"*He wants to find rogues who want to be in packs because they were born a rogue or forced to be a rogue because of a family member.*"

"*Most of us in this rogue camp were born a rogue or banished because of what our parents or siblings did,*" Jeremy said.

"*Take me and my mate for instance. I was born a rogue and my mate was forced out of her pack because her brother attacked their pack's gamma. Their alpha banished the whole family. My mate was ten years old when it happened, just a young pup. Most of us in that situation want the security of pack life. That's how he's found most of us, but he keeps us here by killing our pups or raping our mates. If we get out of line he will kill the pups' parents because they try to escape.*"

"*He's even killed some parents and their pups when he sees them trying to run.*"

"*That's horrible. We'll do everything we can to get everyone out who wants to live in a pack. I think the best way to make sure we don't kill any of those who want sanctuary is to have them run to a specific area when they cross pack lines. We'll inform you of where that location will be once we figure it out.*"

"*If he's not attacking for a couple of months then we have time to get the pups out. Have you figured out which pups we need to take first?*" Phillip asked.

"*When Arnold allowed me to see my mate, I linked her asking about the pups,*" Jeremy responded. "*She said Arnold never pays attention to the youngest pups. Three of the youngest are orphans because Arnold killed their parents when they tried to escape with them. They are two-month-old triplets. It's very sad, they were only in the camp for three days when Arnold separated them from their pups to try and get them to do his bidding.*"

"*They snuck into the cave, grabbed the babies, and as soon as they made it to the opening of the cave, one of the babies cried. Arnold happened to be returning to the cave from a run at the same time. If they had been five minutes earlier, Arnold wouldn't have been none the wiser and they would've escaped.*"

"*They weren't here long enough for us to find out what their story was, where Arnold found them, what their names were, or their pups' names. We only know they are two months old because my mate heard their mother screaming it when Arnold grabbed the babies away from them.*"

"*That is horrible!*" I said as a tear slid down my face.

Phillip spoke up, "*Do you still have the marker I gave you?*"

"*I do, I gave it to my mate, she put it in a safe place until we needed it.*"

"*Perfect, ask your mate if she can mark the pups, I think we're going to try and get them sooner rather than later. Possibly even tonight.*"

"*Once the pups are marked, find one of the cameras and give us a thumbs up. We will send someone to get them. We will come at night in case anyone sees them missing, we want natural responses when they notice the pups are missing. There is a possibility of the women seeing us, please tell them not to make any sounds if they see the pups being taken.*"

"*Our hope is no one notices so Arnold won't be suspicious of missing pups.*"

They looked at each other, "*We have other orphaned pups who range between eight months to ten years old. Do you think you could get them as well?*" Jeremy asked.

"*It depends on what night we rescue them. If it can be done without raising suspicion then we'll do it,*" Phillip said.

"*You said there were fifteen pups and five women with three of them expecting?*"

"Yes, about half of the pups are orphans now. The others either have one or two parents."

"We will get the orphaned pups out first but before we take the other pups, we will need their parent's permission. We will also need the pups' ages and birthdates, rank if they have one or no them, names of their parents, and their former pack names if they know them. If the parents don't make it out of this attack, we will do our best to find their extended family before placing them with new families."

"We will also do our best to place the orphans with families who can care for them. We can test their blood to see if they have any ranking in their bloodline. If they do, we will be sure to place them with families of the same rank. If we have other pups who have no rank in their bloodlines, we will place them with wonderful families. Just to give you peace of mind, all of our pack members are treated with respect regardless if they have a rank or not."

"Thank you, that makes me feel better," Jeremy said.

"Can I ask a question before we need to leave?" Francis asked.

"Sure, what's your question?"

"Is it possible to test the blood of the adults too? Like we said, a lot of us were either born a rogue or were banished because of a family member. Those who were too young to recall would probably like to know something about their bloodline."

"I don't see why not, Phillip, do you think that would be possible?"

"I agree with you. I don't see why Doc Carter or Doc Stevens would have a problem doing that."

"Looks like whoever wants their blood tested, we'll test it."

"We need to get going, we've been here for forty-five minutes already and you need to get back to your shift."

"Remember, when you use the marker, you won't visibly see the mark you place on the pups just make sure your mate *makes it large enough. Ask her to make a filled-in circle on the back of their left hand. If she's able to, have her mark all the orphaned pups, we'll get them out first, before we remove the other pups. Be sure to get us the information we need about them and make sure the parents are on our side and are aware their pup will be rescued so they won't ask Arnold if they can see them."*

*"That won't be a problem. Arnold doesn't allow them to see their pups unless they are being defiant. Only then does he bring the pup out to torture them until the parents are submissive."*

*"He is a horrible person, he will get his just reward in the end. Once all the orphaned pups are removed, place marks on the other pups we need to rescue and we'll try to get them out as soon as possible. We'll work on getting the expectant women out next, then the other two women. Hopefully, we can get them out right before the attack breaks out. We will be in contact soon."*

*"Don't forget to give us a sign when the marks are put on the pups."* They left to continue their patrol and as soon as we were alone, we shifted and headed back to the pack house. *"Were they honest?"*

*"They were, I found no deceit in them whatsoever."*

*"It's very sad about those orphaned pups."*

*"Yes it is, I'm curious what their blood tests will show. You don't hear of triplets very often. I was going to ask if they are boys or girls but in the scheme of things it doesn't matter. I think I want to know because I'm a triplet and feel connected in that way."*

*"I agree, in the scheme of things, it doesn't matter. All that matters is getting them out of that situation."*

# CHAPTER 35 DEBRIEFING

**BRINLEY**

By the time we got back to the packhouse, it was 1:30 in the morning. We headed straight to Tate's office for debriefing. "You guys did a great job. We'll have eyes on all the cameras from here on out so we don't miss anything," John was saying as we handed him our bags.

"Crystal, are you able to run the necessary blood tests on the pups and adults we'll be bringing over?"

"I am, but I'm going to need assistance and was wondering if your doctor might be able to come and help?"

"I can check with him and my dad, but I don't foresee any issues with it."

"Did you ask them how many rogues will be defecting? We will need to get that number so we'll know how many people to expect," John said.

"Should we go back and ask them or do you want me to link them?"

"I want to keep your going out there to a minimum, the more we send you the better chance of you getting caught. Especially now that we know Diane is his mate. Do you think you can link them instead?"

"I can or we can have Jax ask them when he rescues the pups. That should give us enough time to know how many we'll be giving sanctuary to. We know he'll be bringing three pups back probably in the next couple of days or weeks and we need to find a family to care for them, any ideas?" I asked.

"Could we send them to Mom and Dad's pack for now, for safety? I'd hate to see all these pups get hurt when the attack comes and there's less chance of Diane finding out and kidnapping them again just for them to end up with Arnold again."

"Brooke, I think that's a brilliant idea. Jaxon, when you rescue them, do you think you can teleport them directly to Mom and Dad's?"

"I can manage that. I might need Brooklyn's help though, I'm not sure how I'd transport three infants at the same time."

"I can help, that wouldn't bother me at all."

"John, do we have eyes on Diane?"

"We do, with Tate's permission I put Pete on her and I also pulled Arlene and put her on her tail too."

"Arlene's a great choice, especially if Diane goes places Pete can't."

"Who's Arlene?" Tate, Ben, Quincy, and Crystal ask at the same time.

"She's one of our master elite warriors and one of Brinley and Brooklyn's best friends. She's amazing and the tracking nose on her is almost as good as the triplets and Matt's noses," John beamed.

"She also happens to be John's mate," Jax, Brooky, and I said as we laughed and shoved him.

"It's been a long day and we have a big day ahead of us tomorrow. We need to leave so John and his team can do their thing. I'm taking my mate," I looked over at Tate with a blush on my face, "upstairs to shower and get to bed. I will be expecting all of you," I pointed to Tate, Ben, Quincy, Crystal, my four guys, and siblings, "in the arena by 9:00 am sharp. I need to talk with everyone."

"It's almost 2:30 am so get some sleep because you're going to need it. We have a lot to go over and I want everyone awake and alert for it," I said before heading out the office door myself, only to catch a burnt toast smell lingering lightly around the hall. *"John, Diane's scent is all over the hallway, keep the door locked."*

*"Thanks for letting me know, locking it now."*

Later that morning, when Tate and I made it to the arena, it was ten minutes to 9:00. Jax, Brooke, Erik, Phillip, Jacob, and Max were already waiting for us. "Good morning everyone," I gave them all hugs and Tate fist-bumped them. "Tate, can you link everyone else and find out where they are?"

"Cupcake, they still have ten minutes to get here." I stared at him while the others tried holding back a laugh, but not succeeding, I glared at them. "Why are you laughing?"

"Be..because," Erik was holding his stomach while trying to talk, "you don't know Peanut very well," he tried breathing between laughs, "she," he held up his finger while sucking in air, "she thinks ten minutes early is on time and the actual time she tells people is too late," he and the others are bent over laughing now.

I'm standing there staring at them, my mouth agape, "So rude!"

*"It's so true."*

*"Seriously Andi? You're laughing too?"*

*"Of course I am, it's funny and it's so true, you know it is."*

*"Fine, it is true,"* I joined them, doubled over laughing.

Ten minutes later the rest of them showed up and we calmed our laughing. "Let's head inside, we need to have a conversation." We headed inside, sealed the arena, and sat down at one of the tables we had in there. "What do you need to talk with us about?" Tate asked as he kissed me on the forehead.

"Brin, before you start, can we address that mark on your neck and Tates's neck," Brooklyn said.

I blushed, "we have other things that are more pressing we need to talk about."

"Nope, first things first, we're talking about your beautiful marks. Let us see the entire thing," she crossed her arms and stared at me.

I looked at Tate, and he smiled and shrugged, *"Not helpful."*

I pulled my shirt away from my neck. Our marks are placed where the neck and shoulder meet. The ladies gasped, "It's so beautiful."

"Thank you, I was excited when I saw it this morning. My mark has an outline of a Diamond with Tate's wolf in the center of it and Tate's mark has a Diamond inside a full moon with my wolf in the center of it. Since I'm an alpha by birth, my pack is represented on Tate's mark.

"Tate, we need to see yours too." He pulled his shirt to the side. "They are so pretty," the girls gushed.

"Okay, now can we have this conversation?"

"Sorry," they all said, "the table is all yours."

"Thank you." My siblings and the guys know I'm going to have this conversation and they also know how nervous I am. I really should have had this conversation with Tate before we mated and marked each other but we were caught up in the moment, if you know what I mean. "I'm only telling you this because I know I can trust everyone in this room."

"When I met each of you for the first time and shook your hand in greeting, I did a quick scan of you."

Tate interrupted, "What do you mean you scanned us, scanned us using what?"

"My mind."

"Your mind... yeah, how does that even work?" Ben asked.

I looked at my group and they gave me an encouraging look. I took a deep breath and blew it out. "I have... the ability to see if someone is being truthful. If they are a reliable and trustworthy person. In a sense, I can read their minds." I blurted out then covered my face. I felt someone kneel in front of me and pull my hands from my face.

"Peanut, it's okay, you don't need to hide," Max's melodic voice calmed me down almost instantly.

"They don't hate me?"

"No Peanut, they have nothing but love in their eyes for you so open yours."

"Tate, you look stunned."

"I am, I can see how this can be useful in a pack, no wonder you keep quiet about it. The secure arena makes more sense."

"I apologize for not saying anything sooner."

"It's okay, I get it. When you were in the dungeon speaking with that rogue, is that how you knew he lying?"

"It is, but Andi lent me some of her strength."

"How does it work?"

"I need to touch the person directly or a piece of their clothing or an item of theirs. That's actually how I knew Diane was Arnold's mate. When you left the arena so I could train, I was handed a hair tie and it happened to belong to Diane. When I touched it, I knew."

"This is amazing! Crystal, isn't this amazing?" Quincy turned her excitement to Crystal, "Why don't you look surprised at this?"

"Because she already knew. She was given my full medical file before I arrived which also has everything I'm able to do," I smiled at Crystal. "I have a few other things to fill you in on."

"There's more?" Tate asked tensing beside me.

"There is. I can mind link with anyone I want whether they're pack members or not and once I link someone, I will always be able to link with them and vice versa unless I choose to cut it off. They, however, cannot link me first and the only ones who can link me directly are my pack members, unless I already establish that link bond of course."

"Holy Moly! That's fucking incredible!" Ben's hand flew in the air.

"With it, I can link someone without their knowledge and look at their memories. I can also..."

"Wait, there's more?" Ben interrupted

"Yes, just one more, with me anyway. You already know what my brother and sister can do. I can also move things with my mind."

"How do you mean?" Quincy asked.

"Ask Chase, he was on the receiving end of that," I laughed. "Q, I do need to talk with you in private, if it's okay?"

"Um, yeah, sure."

"Let's go into the weapons room and shut the door, they won't be able to hear us. We'll be right back," I told everyone else hesitantly. I closed the door when we got inside the room.

"Whoa, this room is amazing, there are a lot of weapons. Do you know how to use any of them?"

"I do, I'm an expert with all of them."

"That's incredible."

"Q, the reason I wanted to talk with you is because, well, I'm not sure how to say this," I said rubbing my hand down my face.

"Hey, it's okay whatever it is you can tell me."

"When I was training, I had to test my powers. Remember when I said I can enter a person's mind without their knowledge? Please don't hate me for this, I chose your mind," I said cowardly.

"YOU WHAT! WHAT THE HELL BRIN!"

"I know, I felt horrible for doing it too, that's why I needed to come clean. There's something else I'm not sure you're aware of."

"What?"

"I connected with your wolf while I did it, and, do you, um, oh man, I don't even know how to say this so I'm just going to say it, do you, um, do you know you're pregnant?"

"I'M WHAT!!?? Did you just say I'm pregnant?"

"I did, is, uh, that okay?" I asked hesitantly.

"Brin! I'm so happy right now! I don't like that you entered my mind without permission but I'm kinda glad you did. Now when I go see Crystal I can tell her why. I thought there was something wrong with me because I've been feeling weird lately. I'm in shock, I'm pregnant. Benjamin's going to be so fucking excited!"

"We've been trying a long time for a pup, I can't believe this. Thank you for telling me," She gave me a bear hug.

"You're not mad at me?"

"I was until you said I was pregnant, but with this news, absofuckinglutely not," we hugged again.

"Q, I want you to consider going to my parent's pack when we raid the rogue camp. I don't want to take any chances of you getting hurt or losing the pup if anything goes wrong during the attack."

"Brin, you know I can't do that."

"Please, just think about it?"

"Fine, I'll think about it, but I'm not promising anything."

"As long as you think about it." We left the weapons room and when we got back, all eyes were on us and Quinn had a huge smile plastered on her face.

"What?" she asked as we got closer and Ben stood to pull out her chair.

"You have an awfully big smile on your face."

"Well, I should, 'Daddy.'"

"We need to keep discus... wait, did you just, are you, Q, please tell me this isn't a joke."

"It's not a joke, Benjamin, we are going to have a baby!" she squealed jumping in his arms.

He wrapped his arms around her and twirled her around. "How far along are you, do you feel okay, do you need anything to eat or drink, don't lift anything, I'll get it for you, what do you need, do you need your feet rubbed, can I carry you when we go back...?"

"Whoa, calm down, I'm pregnant, not an invalid."

"Ben," Crystal got his attention, "I will have her come to my office later today or tomorrow to check her out and I will answer any questions you have at that time. We have a few things we need to discuss right now so stay focused."

# CHAPTER 36 IMPROMPTU RITUAL

**BRINLEY**

"Thank you, Crys. I am also excited you are pregnant. I don't want to take away from your celebration, but Crys is right, we have big issues to figure out so the baby celebrating will have to wait."

"I agree with that, what we need to figure out is much more important," Quinn said.

"Have we found anything out about Diane?"

"John gave Erik a list of things he's found," Phillip looked at Erik.

"Erik, care to expand on that?" He pulled out a piece of paper from his pocket and read it.

"She has left the pack lands twenty times in the last three weeks. She's been shopping with Maribel the majority of those times and they correspond with the times Anabel sent those asshats shopping for Noelle's party supplies. We are guessing it is one of those times she met Arnold. John's team said Arnold left to get supplies and one of his first trips was the same day the girls were shopping. We have to assume that's when they crossed paths."

"There have been a few times she's left in the evening and hung out at the gates guard shed. One of the guards noticed her making a copy of the shift change schedule but didn't think anything of it because she told him they needed a copy in the warrior common room. We usually keep a copy in there but she told the guard someone shredded it in error. Since she's the former gamma's daughter, they didn't question it."

Tate interrupted, "Jaxon, can you link John and ask him if he can remake the patrol schedule and change the start and end times of the shifts? Let him know the current one has been compromised but only give the new schedule directly to those who will be patrolling. If Diane is taking copies and giving them to Arnold, then I want him to have the wrong schedule. Be sure to tell him not to post the new schedule."

"Sure will, give me a second. He asked why you couldn't do it, I reminded him were in a meeting and that we placed the patrol schedule on his plate since most of the patrols consist of Winter Moon warriors. He'll take care of it within the hour."

"Thank you."

"He said there were a few times she left in the middle of the night wearing all black. Even her hands and face were covered in camo. Those nights also correspond with the times we noticed Arnold leaving the cave. We know they are meeting up because Jeremy and Francis confirmed they smelled her on him."

"We need to keep an eye on her, she's been lingering around Tate's office. She knows we're in there, but she hasn't had access to find out what we're doing in there. We've moved everything to the luna office but she hasn't figured that out yet, and we're keeping it locked. Arlene and Pete are still on her tail so hopefully, we'll have more information in the next day or two."

"Do they say how often she leaves pack lands?" Benjamin asked.

"Looks like she leaves in the morning on Mondays, the evening around 7:00 pm, so after dinner on Thursday, and late night/early morning on Saturdays."

"I'm sure Pete and Arlene already know her routine so we'll leave it for now," Benjamin said.

"I think we should let Pete and Arlene follow them for at least a week so they can gather enough information before sitting down and talking with was about what they've found out," Erik said.

"I think that's a great idea."

"We need to get something concrete on Diane. We need to make sure Arlene and Pete have cameras with mics on them somehow. Do you know if John and his team can do anything like that?" Tate addressed Erik.

"They do, they're pretty inventive," Jaxon said.

"Good, have him do that as soon as possible. Now, what about Maribel?"

"I don't want to show my cards with her until after Noelle's party," I said. "She's been warned to stay away from me but she isn't. When the time comes to punish her, Andi and I will do it."

"Maribel has enough infractions against her and we already have the evidence we need to either banish or take her life," Ben commented.

"I'm taking her life, it's the most humane thing we can do. I don't believe in banishment, rogues just create more issues and we have dealt enough with that."

"Do you know what you're planning on doing?" Jacob asked.

"I'm hoping she'll follow me in the arena. She thinks I'm a weak she-wolf and I want her to believe I am. When she gets inside I'm locking the door before showing her my true self. If you want to be present, you'll need to hide somewhere, maybe in the weapons room. That's what I'm hoping for, but we'll see what happens. Noelle's supposed to arrive tomorrow. I don't know her at all, how do you think she'll react to all of this?"

"Noelle and Maribel were close when they were younger. She knows how her sister is and won't be surprised to hear what she's been doing. Noelle has been the brunt of some of Maribel's nonsense, that's one of the reasons why she left for college," Quincy said.

"So you don't think she'll protest what's going to happen to her?"

"I don't see her doing that."

"Jaxon, any idea how you plan on getting the pups out of the cave?" Jacob asked.

"I'm thinking Brooklyn will apparate in the cave before me to make sure everything is quiet. Then I'll biolocate in there and grab two of the pups while Brooke gets the third. I've already spoken with Mom and Dad, they said they will be ready to receive them when we get there. If all goes well, we'll take them directly to the packhouse, go back, and get the other orphaned pups. Drop them off, then come back here."

"That sounds like a good plan."

"Tate, how's the training been going with the warriors?" Erik asked him.

"Great, everyone is getting stronger. They have more endurance, and learning a lot more than I could ever teach them."

"I know this subject came up a long time ago, but have you put any thought into who you might ask to be your gamma?"

"I have, I talked with Ben about it not too long ago as well."

"Care to share with the rest of us?"

"Since Brinley's my Luna, we wanted to find someone who has the qualities of a gamma and would treat her with kindness and respect. We also want someone who will be themselves around her and who she'll be comfortable with. Since he's mated to our head doctor, Max would you take the role of gamma?"

Max was taking a sip of water when he spit it out, "what? did you... did I... gamma? You want... me... to be... your gamma?"

"Well, you and Crystal." Crystal was sitting there staring at Tate with her mouth hung open.

## JAXON

"You want Max as your gamma?"

"I do. He has the qualities of a gamma. He calms Brinley down when she panics, he grew up with her, so he knows her very well. They will have each other in a new pack so there will be someone comfortable here for them. You even said there are only a few who can spar and train with her which includes Max. This way she'll have someone she can train with as well. Besides, he's mated to my head doctor and we cannot be without her, so he makes the best choice. Are you okay with that?"

"I would be honored as the future alpha of my pack to have one of my best friends become your gamma and the gamma to my sister. Max, do you accept the gamma position at Black Diamond?"

"Um, I, uh," he looked at Crystal and she grabbed his hand and smiled at him. "Um, if Peanut wants to be around me all the time, I will accept."

"Brin? How do you feel about Max staying on as gamma?"

I looked at her and she had tears welling up in her eyes. "I... I get... I get to keep Roo, here, with me?" She got up walked over to Max, pulled him out of his chair, and hugged and cried into his chest.

"Hey Peanut, why are you crying?" Max asked, resting his chin on top of her head.

"I'm just so happy right now. I thought I was going to be left here alone, without any family," she sniffled.

"How could I ever leave you Peanut, I was going to stay regardless. I couldn't leave you if my life depended on it. Besides, my mate is here too and I can't take her away from this pack." Max looked up at Tate, "How soon can you initiate me into the pack?"

"We can do it right now if you want. I just need to find an elder on short notice to oversee it."

I linked my sisters, *"Do you think the Moon Goddess would initiate him?"*

*"We could ask her,"* Brooke said.

*"Brin, do you want to see if she will?"*

*"Absolutely."*

"What if we had someone who might do it for us?" I asked Tate.

"That would be great, who would you get?"

The three of us looked at each other and in unison, we said, "Selene."

"Selene, as in the Moon Goddess," Quinn choked out.

"Yes, Selene the Moon Goddess."

"How in the hell do you plan to get her here?" Ben asked.

"Well, there is one more thing we haven't told you, we are blessed by her." We all lifted our shirt sleeves and showed our wrists.

"I saw that mark on Brin and thought it was a tattoo," Tate commented.

"It's not a tattoo, Selene put it there," Brooklyn told them.

"How do you contact her?" Tate asked.

"We'll show you."

"Looks like we shocked you again Tate."

"You've met the Moon Goddess, and not only met but have been blessed by her. How do you think she'll react to me knowing I killed one of her children?"

"As long as it was in self-defense or to protect another, she won't have an issue with it. Don't look so nervous, Tate, you'll be fine."

"I am a nervous."

Brin, Brooklyn, and I shook our heads at him as we sat in a circle and held hands. We closed our eyes and were very quiet while we were calling the Moon Goddess. We could feel three sets of eyes on us, curiously watching. After ten minutes, we felt her presence and we opened our eyes, there was a bright light in the center of the arena that drew closer to us. When the bright light disappeared, in its place was the Moon Goddess. As always, she was beautiful, her white dress billowing around her, her white wavy hair flowing down to her waist, and her icy blue eyes taking us in.

**MOON GODDESS**

"My precious triplets, you called me?" She asked, her voice melodic.

"We have," Jaxon said, "Tate asked Max to be his gamma and we were wondering if you could perform the ritual. He doesn't want to wait for us to find an elder."

"I would be delighted to perform the ritual. Max, come here," I called him. He got up and wandered over, "Please bring your mate." He went back to get Crystal but had to carry her because she was frozen in place with awww just like the others.

"Tate, please come here as well, I can't do this without the alpha." Tate's eyes were trained on me as he slowly walked toward me. "Brinley, Sweetheart, please stand, I'm going to make you Luna first. I can't very well make Max gamma without his Luna, now can I"

"No ma'am," she stood next to me. I pulled a chalice out and a silver knife to hold open the wound a little longer. "Jaxon, will you hold the chalice please," I handed it to him. "Tate, your hand please," I held out my hand to him and he placed his hand in mine.

"Alpha Tate Isaiah Beckman, Alpha of the Black Diamond Pack, do you accept Brinley Khrystyne Jameson, alpha daughter of the Winter Moon Pack and former mate and mother to Jerod and Cassandra Jameson as your mate and Luna? Do you promise to protect her, honor her, treat her as your equal, and give your life for her?"

"I accept Brinley as my mate and Luna and promise to protect, honor, and treat her as my equal and give my life for her."

"Brinley Khrystyne Jameson, alpha daughter of the Winter Moon Pack and former mate and mother to Jerod and Cassandra Jameson, do you accept Alpha Tate Isaiah Beckman, Alpha of the Black Diamond Pack, as our mate and Alpha? Do you promise to protect him, honor him, treat him as your equal, and give your life for him?"

"I accept Tate as my mate and Alpha and promise to protect, honor, and treat him as my equal and give my life for him."

I took their hands and sliced their palms. "Jaxon, place the chalice under their palms so the blood drips in it. Tate, Brinley please place your palms together." I placed my hand on theirs, "by the power of the moon, I link these two together forever as mates." A white thread wrapped around their wrists and sunk into their skin making a white glowing heart show up on their wrists by their palms.

I summoned wine into my hand and poured it into the chalice. "Each of you take a drink of this wine. Once you do, you will both be linked together. Brinley, you will also be fully linked with all of the Black Diamond Pack members. I must caution you, do not let them know you are linked yet, otherwise, your plans for Diane and Maribel may be discovered."

"It is my understanding your wolves have not met yet, is this true?"

"Yes, it is. We've seen each other's wolves but they haven't seen each other yet."

"Please shift" They looked at each other, undressed, and shifted. *"Chase, Amanda, please step forward."* I placed my hands on their heads, closed my eyes, and blocked Tate and Brinley. Then linked Chase and Amanda, *"Do you both accept each other as mates? Do you accept each other as Alpha and Luna? Do you promise to take care of each other, protect each other, and treat each other as equals?"*

*"We do."*

*"You need to seal your bond, I don't think I need to tell you how to do that. When we are finished here I will send the others back to the packhouse and I will have the arena sealed for you. I will trust you both to tell Tate and Brinley you have sealed your bond. Please shift back."* While Tate and Brinley got dressed, I asked Max to step forward. "Max, Crystal do you accept the position of Gamma to the Black Diamond Pack? Do you promise to protect and guard the Alpha and Luna with your life?"

"We do."

"Tate, Brinley, do you accept Max and Crystal as your new Gammas? Do you promise to protect and guide them and treat them like family?"

"We do."

"Tate, Max, please hold your palms up. Once I slice your hands, place them in each other's palms and squeeze blood into the chalice." I placed more wine in the chalice and had them each drink from it. You are now linked to each other through the pack bond. Max and Brinley, I have not closed off your links to your former pack. I will keep them intact, if at any time you no longer want those links, all you need to do is ask."

"Normally once you are moved into another pack, the link you had with your former pack, is cut off. Max, Crystal, you need to seal your bond by mating and marking each other. You have both accepted the Gamma title and have accepted each other. Now that Max is a part of this pack, there is no need to hold back any longer."

"My precious triplets, get your rest, there is more to come. I will leave you now, but you know how to contact me if you need me. Everyone must leave this arena except for Tate and Brinley. You're wolves will explain to you. Max and Crystal, I will expect you to be fully mated and marked the next time I see you." I walked over to Quincy, placed my hand on her belly, and smiled, "Congratulations my child, please listen to Brinley when the time comes." I kissed my triplets on their heads and disappeared.

## QUINCY

"Did that just happen? Did the Moon Goddess just appear before us? She touched my belly, she... she called you 'her precious triplets.' What is happening right now?" I was so giddy.

Brin placed her hand on my shoulder, "It's okay Q, she was here. She did touch you, and she has called us that since we were pups."

"You've been speaking to her since you were pups?"

"We have, I think we were around two years old when she first appeared to us."

"That's... incredible."

"She made you our Luna, my Luna, without a ceremony," I said in disbelief.

Brooklyn snorted, laughing, "Mom's going to be so bent out of shape she missed this."

Brin smirked at her, "What mom doesn't know won't kill her. Let's just keep what happened here between these walls. We'll figure out the whole Luna, Gamma ceremony later."

## ERIK

The guys and I have only seen the Moon Goddess a few times so we weren't shocked like the rest of them. What had us standing quiet was the fact she did the Luna and Gamma rituals herself. She kept their pack link connected to Winter Moon while simultaneously giving them the pack link to Black Diamond. I mean, she is the Moon Goddess and has the power to do that.

"Max, how does it feel to have two-pack links?"

"Like I need to take a bottle of Tylenol. My head hurts from the impact of receiving the second pack link. It's giving me a migraine and Hudson's passed out."

"I'm sure Jax, Cheese, and Peanut could help with that."

I looked over at them, and they were caught up in a conversation about how Luna Estelle wasn't going to be happy with Brin getting the Luna title without the ceremony. I had to chuckle because our Luna loves to throw parties. I looked at Max again but he didn't look so hot.

"Hey, guys?... Guys!... Alpha Triplets!" I finally hollered at them, snapping them out of their conversation. All three of them looked up at me and glared. "What? I tried getting your attention, but you weren't responding. I had to resort to something," I smirked and shrugged my shoulders.

They hate it when they're called that. The only people they allow to refer to them as 'alpha triplets' are the elders and the council. Mostly because there isn't anything they can do about it. Everyone else immediately gets corrected. You can call them 'the triplets' just not 'the alpha triplets' not sure why, it's just always been that way.

## JAXON

Being referred to as 'alpha triplets' grates on us, we hate it. When we were little, before we started hanging out with the four guys, people would only call us the 'alpha triplets' never by our names, never as individuals, ever. As we got older and our personalities began to shine through, we would hear, 'They're alpha triplets, they should be the same,' 'They're alpha triplets, why are they so different from each other, they should be the same.' They always thought of me as the outgoing one, Brooke as the mischievous one, and Brin as the quiet one.

They couldn't fathom us being different from each other, they even thought we'd be co-alphas together. That's why we hate it. It groups us as one person, not three individuals. We may look alike, well, the girls are identical. They sometimes get it worse, but we are three people with our own thoughts, bodies, strengths, and weaknesses. I mean, sometimes we say the same thing at the same time and sometimes we dress in the same colors, and there've been many times the girls will wear the same outfit without talking with each other.

"Erik, what is so fucking important you had to call us that?" I gritted my teeth. He ignored me, as usual.

"Max needs you. He said he has a migraine from receiving the second pack link."

"Oh, shit, why didn't you say something, Max?"

"I didn't want to bother you, I can take a bottle of Tylenol."

"Why isn't Hudson healing you?"

"Because getting the second link was too much for him and he passed out."

"Get your ass over here so we can do our thing," Brinley scolded him.

"Yes, Luna."

"Max, do not call me that, we are friends first and always will be."

"Sorry Peanut."

"Sit down, close your eyes, and try to relax, you know the drill." We placed our hands on his head and concentrated on him. White light emanated from our hands and into his head. We could feel Hudson stirring and when we felt Max's body completely relax, we removed our hands. "How're you feeling Roo?" Brin asked.

"So much better and Hudson says thank you."

## BRINLEY

"You're welcome, now can you take your mate back to your room and fully mark and mate her, please? I need my Gammas at full strength, not being fully mated will drain you."

"You don't need to ask me twice, Peanut." He leaned over, gave me and Brooke each a kiss on the head and slapped Jaxy on the back, turned around, picked up Crystal, and left the arena.

"What just happened?" Ben asked.

"Oops, sorry. When the three of us are together, we become healers."

"That explains the comment Doc Carter made when we were visiting their pack. He said something about a young pup not wanting the triplets to touch his arm and something about a scar," he said to Tate.

"That would be one of our junior warriors, if we healed him, the scar would've disappeared. Without us healing him, he'll keep the scar for the rest of his life. As for the rest of you, Amanda wants to fully mate and mark Chase, so I'll be sealing the building behind you."

I walked them to the door, Jax turned around, "You're not the quiet one anymore are you?" he gave me a side smirk. I laughed, kissed him on the cheek, pushed him and the others out the door, and sealed the arena.

I turned to Tate, gave him a rye smile, and said, "Shift!"

# CHAPTER 37 CLAIMING

**CHASE**

Brinley walked over to me, *"Chase, you are very handsome. Your silver coloring is a perfect shade, I love your black-tipped ears; you're so soft. I love you.* She leaned in and kissed me on the muzzle.

*"I love you too Brinley,"* she immediately shifted.

*"Amanda, you are beautiful. I've never seen a wolf of your color,"* she gave me a wolfy smile and licked my muzzle. *"Amanda, will you accept me as your mate?"*

*"Chase, I have loved you from the moment I saw you. Brin and I didn't know how to process our feelings for you and Tatc. I will accept you as my mate, every day of my life, I will accept you and love you. Will you accept me as your mate?"*

*"I will accept you as my mate, even through death, I will love you."* I walked over and licked her muzzle.

She backed away looking me in the eyes. I swear she was looking directly into my soul, I could feel her love for me seeping into me and I knew I would do anything to keep her safe for the rest of my life.

*"Chase, can you give me back control? I want to see her through my own eyes."*

*"I will but I want to claim her so don't take too long."* I shifted back and he looked into her eyes, those beautiful icy blue eyes.

*"You are so beautiful."* he ran his fingers through her fur, *"Your fur is so soft like feathery down."* He leaned in and kissed her muzzle. She licked the side of his face and wrapped his arms around her, *"I love you."*

*"I love you too, you can call me Andi though, that's my nickname."*

Before he could respond, I took over and shifted back.

*"Tate,"* I heard Brinley in my head, *"we need to close our links to them and each other so they can get acquainted. They need their privacy."*

*"I'll see you when they shift back, I love you, Cupcake, so very much."*

*"I love you too."*

## AMANDA

When Brin told me she was giving me complete control, I knew what was coming, I could feel it and Chase's beautiful amber eyes went black. I looked at him with a sparkle in my eyes and ran. He's not getting me that easily, he needs to prove he's able to catch me first. Little does he know, I'm fast and can outrun the best of them. After running around the arena for thirty minutes and successfully avoiding him, I decided the foreplay was over and let him catch me.

*"You're fast, faster than anyone I've ever met."*

"Do you want me to slow down?"

*"No, I like the chase. You are my prey, I'll wait until you wear yourself out."*

After an hour I decided he'd had enough, I slowed down so he could catch me. He walked over to me nuzzling and licking me. When I flipped my tail at him he lost it. He licked between my legs and a whine slipped out. *"You taste divine, my Little Butterfly."* He mounted me, slipped his cock inside me, fucking me. Right before I came, he bit my neck, marking me as his, his cock swelled, locking us in a tie. Once his knot released us, I turned around and marked him too.

'My Little Butterfly' he called me, I like the nickname. Something overcame me, my thoughts went to my past, and I became quiet. *"Amanda, Little Butterfly, what's wrong, why did you go still?"* I could feel tears well up in my eyes.

*"I'm so happy but sad at the same time. I never processed the loss of my mate and pup. I had to be strong for Brinley."*

*"Can you tell me about him and your pup?"*

*"Taylor, Jared's wolf, used to call me 'Sunshine.' He said I always brightened the room I was in and always shined bright in his heart. They were always very attentive to us. Jerod always opened doors, always let us have the last bite of whatever we were sharing, and was always giving us back rubs and foot massages, especially when we were pregnant."*

*"He carried Brin everywhere when she was heavily pregnant and had a hard time walking. He was kind, generous, thoughtful, and loved my family. He always made sure I knew how much he loved us every day. When Brin told him we were expecting, he and Taylor were so excited. They wanted to be a father more than anything. He and Taylor were always rubbing our bellies, and talking to the baby, and Jerod would even sing to the baby."*

*"The day we went into labor, he was a nervous wreck. We didn't want to know what we were having, we knew we'd love the baby regardless if it was a boy or girl. It drove everyone crazy. They wanted to know so they could buy things for the baby ahead of time. We decorated the nursery in neutral colors and woodland animals. Her nursery was so cute and Brin would rock in the chair for hours just rubbing our belly and talking with the baby."*

*"When she was born, it was the happiest day of our lives, aside from our mating ceremony and wedding. She was a beautiful baby. We named her Cassandra Mae, Cassie for short. Cassandra is my mom's middle name and Mae is*

*Jerod's mom's first name. She was such a good baby, only cried when she needed something, and she wasn't colicky like some babies are. She took to nursing right away and had a good appetite."*

*"Jerod would lay her down on a blanket on the floor so Taylor could lay next to her and even though she was just an infant, she would grab for his fur, like she knew he was her daddy. Taylor would scoot closer to her and she'd fall asleep next to him. Brin would let me shift and I'd lay right next to her too with Taylor by my side. We would surround her with our bodies to keep her safe. Jerod and Brin knew how important it was for us to bond with her. They were never jealous of the time we spent with her."*

*"Sometimes, when they were sleeping and she'd cry, Taylor and I would put up a block and take over their bodies so we could get up and take care of her and they could get some much-needed sleep. I would get the chance to nurse and connect with her more intimately while Taylor would watch us. About three weeks after Cassie was born, Brinley started running again."* Tears filled my eyes as I thought about the day they were murdered.

*"Hey, Little Butterfly, you don't need to continue, if it's too hard,"* Chase rubbed his nose against me.

*"It's okay, I need to talk about it, it's a part of my past, regardless how much it hurts."*

*"Take your time then and if it's too much we can always finish the conversation later."* I nodded and pushed my head into him.

*"The day of their murder, Brin kissed Jerod and Cassie and told them she loved them. She told him she was blocking the link, she wanted to run without anyone interrupting her. She let me shift and it felt so good to feel the dirt under my paws. After running for a while, I got a weird feeling and suddenly stopped. I let out a blood-curdling howl, turned around, and ran back to our house."*

*"It was then a pain shot straight through our chest and a sickening feeling overcame us. I'm glad we were in wolf form otherwise Brin wouldn't have been able to move. We ran back as quickly as we could and saw black smoke. Dread filled us and when we saw our house was engulfed in flames, we knew it was too late. Brin dropped the block knowing he would never answer. I shifted back because Brin was trying to get to them. We hoped they escaped but we knew knew they were gone, we knew in the depths of our bones they died in the fire."*

*"Our lives changed forever that day. We were never the same. Brin... was never the same. The nightmares started soon after. I wasn't able to heal her from them. I had to be strong for her when I was dying inside myself. I was never able to talk with anyone about it because she never wanted to, it was too painful, for both of us. I miss them, Chase, I miss them so goddess damned much it hurts. I love you, but I miss them and wish I could have them back."* I shifted but kept Brin blocked and sobbed.

## CHASE

That was gut-wrenching, I don't know how to comfort her. I love her but she is hurting so damn much I want to take her pain away but I don't know how. I remember Tate holding Brin as she cried and hearing him tell her she could talk about Jerod and Cassie anytime she wanted or needed to. I watched Amanda shift back to Brin but didn't feel her so she must've kept her blocked so I did the same thing.

She was sobbing, I wrapped my arms around her and held her. *"Amanda, I promise you, you can talk about Taylor and Cassie anytime you want. I love you and they are a part of who you are. I wish you could've talked to Brin about this but I understand how you felt. You needed to be strong for her. You both lost a mate and pup that day and I'm so sorry that happened to you."* I continued holding her and let her cry into my chest. I felt a presence around us and when I looked up, the Moon Goddess was standing before us.

*"Chase, what happened, why is Amanda crying?"*

*"She was telling me what happened with Jerod and Cassie. Did you know she never talked with anyone about it, said she had to be strong for Brinley. It breaks my heart. Did you know that was going to happen?"*

*"I knew Jerod was being hunted and that's why I sent him to Winter Moon, for protection. I didn't know they found him until it was too late."* She touched Amanda on the head, "Look up my child."

She lifted her head, "Moon Goddess, what are you doing here?"

"I'm here for you, my precious girl. I felt your pain and needed to come. I know how much you love Jerod and Taylor and how much you love and miss Cassie. I'm sorry for your loss and I wish I could've prevented it from happening." Amanda leaned into the Moon Goddess and held onto her. "Shhh, my sweet girl. I'm here for you, you are one of my chosen, don't ever forget that."

She wiped her tears and looked at us. "I chose the four of you to be second-chance mates to each other because of the tragic way you lost your first mates. I knew you would cherish each other because you know the strength of the bond. Chase, I'm sorry you and Tate were not able to mark Emberly and her wolf and feel the full mate bond, you have that now and I know you'll love them for the rest of your lives."

"I love you both dearly, love each other, be kind to each other, cherish each other, be there for each other, you are equals and partners. I must go, but take your time to be present with each other in the here and now. Chase, I know how hard-headed and stubborn Tate can be, please remind him to not be an ass to Brinley. She is a gift I'm blessing him with and he needs to cherish that gift. Brinley may be soft-hearted but she is a force to be reconned with, especially if she is feeling threatened, pushed around, or coddled too much."

"Yes ma'am, I found that out the hard way."

## AMANDA

After the Moon Goddess left, I looked up at Chase, "Thank you."

"For what Little Butterfly?"

"For letting me talk about what happened, for not interrupting me, for holding me and loving me, and being here for me."

"Little Butterfly, I wouldn't want to be anywhere else." He leaned in and kissed me on the head. I was feeling better after I spoke with him and after the Moon Goddess spoke to us. I placed my hands on his face, touched my lips to his, and kissed him passionately. He wrapped his arms around me and pulled me closer to him.

Since we were still naked, I could feel his cock stiffen against me and my pussy was getting wet. He slipped his hand down and rubbed his thumb on my clit. He wrapped his mouth around my nipple, caressing it with his tongue, and when he sucked it, I let out a moan which enticed him more. He laid me down kissing my stomach until he reached my core. He dipped his head between my legs and pressed his tongue inside me. My core was dripping wet as he lapped up my juices.

"Little Butterfly, you taste so good."

"Chase, please don't stop, it feels so good when you do that." I grabbed his hair and wrapped my fingers in it pulling him further into my core. He let out a growl and the vibration sent shivers up my spine as I felt a gush of wetness spill out of me.

## MAX

*I can't believe the Moon Goddess performed the Luna and Gamma rituals. Having a divine goddess perform it meant more to me than having a formal ceremony. I've only seen her a few times, being around the triplets and all. As soon as the gamma essence washed through me, I could feel*

*Brinley's emotions, actually feel them. I almost felt called to her like a mate bond, but different.*

*I've always wanted to protect her and calm her but now I have an innate pull to do so. I will need to check with Gunther to see if this is normal. I mean, I've always seen him around Luna Estelle and when he'd place a hand on her when she was anxious, she'd calm down. I don't know anything about being a gamma except we are the right-hand person to the luna.* I was lost in thought when I felt a nudge on my arm. I looked over and saw Crystal watching me.

## CRYSTAL

I'm lost in thought as we're walking to my little cottage. *I can't believe I saw the Moon Goddess or the fact she performed the Luna and Gamma rituals. Wait, I'm the female gamma... to Brinley. I can't believe I'm a gamma and a doctor. I don't even know the first thing about the gamma or what the gamma does, I hope Max does.* I tapped him on the arm but it looks like he's in deep in thought. "Max?" I tap him again. "Max?" this time I nudged him.

"What?"

"Can I ask you a question?"

"You can ask me anything, Baby."

"Did that just happen? Did the Moon Goddess make Brinley Luna and us Gammas?"

He wrapped his arm around my shoulder, "She did Baby."

"Did you feel anything... different... when she did our ritual?"

"I did, like something washed over me, you felt that too?"

"I did, I also feel this weird pull to Brinley, almost like I can feel her emotions."

"You can Baby, it's the gamma essence in us. I don't know much about what the gamma does so I'm going to ask Gunther. He's the gamma at Winter Moon. I know he works closely with Luna Estelle and when she's feeling anxious or worried, he can calm her with a touch or talking calmly to her."

"It makes sense you're a gamma, I've noticed she's a little calmer when you're around her. I think you were always meant for the position." We were almost to the packhouse when I veered off to my cottage but Max pulled me towards the packhouse. "Where are we going? My cottage is over there," I pointed.

"I know it is Baby, but we are gammas now, our place is in the packhouse, in our own suite." He waggled his eyebrows at me and I giggled.

"We have a suite? I completely forgot we can move into the packhouse," I squealed.

"We will only move into the packhouse if you want to."

"Can we look at the suite before we decide?"

"Of course, maybe we can christen in the bed while we're in there," he picked me up bridal style, kissed me gently on the lips, and carried me to the gamma suite.

Once there he opened the door and my mouth dropped open. I scrambled out of his arms to look around. He closed the door behind us and locked it. The suite had a large living room a kitchen and a bathroom. There were three bedrooms, the master had an ensuite with a large walk-in shower and jetted tub. The toilet was behind a door so you could close it off and as soon as I stepped on the tile flooring it heated up. The vanity was the length of the bathroom with two sinks, cupboards, drawers, and a mirror the same length.

The counter was higher than a regular counter. The other two bedrooms had a connecting bathroom. They all had king-size beds and walk-in closets. The bathrooms were fully stocked with toiletries and towels. The suite was all white, like a blank canvas ready to be painted. I'll need to check with Alpha Tate and Luna Brinley, about painting and adding color to the suite. I felt arms snake around me as Max pulled me into him and kissed my marking spot.

## MAX

Watching my mate looking around the suite, gave me shivers up my spine. I can imagine her underneath me, screaming my name. In the shower pressed against the tile wall while I ravish her body. In the tub when I sink my fingers between her folds and make her cum. Lying on the bed squirming beneath me as she screams out my name. I need to change my thoughts because my dick is getting hard and pressing against my zipper, I think it's going to leave a mark.

I walked up to her as she was taking everything in and snaked my arms around her waist. I leaned down and kissed her marking spot. She turned around in my arms, I leaned in and kissed her very gently on the lips as a small moan left her mouth and a growl left mine. I scooped her up and placed her on the bed.

I deepened the kiss as my hands slipped under her shirt and found her breast. Her hands went straight into my hair and she pulled me closer. "Mmmm, Max, please I want you closer." I moved away from her, grabbed her shirt, and removed it. I unclasped her bra and her breasts fell out.

I pushed her to lie on the bed and kissed down her luscious body until I reached the top of her pants. I opened her pants and slid them down her legs along with her panties. I kissed up her legs until I reached her center. "Spread your legs for me, Baby." As soon as my mouth touched her core, she bucked her hips into me. I pushed her back down and held her there while my tongue thrust inside her.

"Fuck, Max," she moaned. She grabbed my hair and ran her hands through it, pulling me closer to her core.

# CHAPTER 38 ACCEPTANCE

**CRYSTAL**

"Fuck, Max! Keep doing whatever... Oh Goddess, Yes!.. That... Keep Doing That! It feels so good!" I don't know if it's more intense because I know we'll be marking each other or because we both have gamma essence running through us now. What I do know, is I don't want this to stop. I love the feeling of Max's lips on me and his tongue inside me. He pulled away and I instantly missed his touch, until he placed a finger inside me while running his tongue over my clit. I feel like I'm floating on a cloud, I can't help it but I keep moaning.

"Max, please keep doing that." He slipped another finger inside me and my walls clenched around him. He found my G-spot and I saw stars right before my orgasm ripped through me "Max, Oh Max! Oh goddess, yes!" He didn't let up, he kept going.

He didn't stop pleasuring. He pulled away from me and kissed up my stomach until his cock reached its destination. He lined the head of his cock up to my opening and pushed in. My body jerked before relaxing. My walls burned as he stretched me to my breaking point. A growl left his throat and a moan left mine. "Fuck Baby, you're so tight."

"Max, please move." He pulled out and slammed back into me. I grabbed his back and felt my claws dig into him. The coppery scent of blood hit my nose and I broke his skin. I wrapped my legs around him allowing him to sink further into me.

His cock grew harder as he thrust in and out. My body was his to take and take he did. He sucked in one of my tits, biting down on my nipple and pulling a moan from me. "I'm going to cum!" I could feel it building up inside me. He flipped me over, pulling my ass in the air before sinking into me once more. I knew he was on the edge and about to cum, I felt a tingling sensation inside me. He grabbed my hair and pulled my neck up to him, leaning over me he sunk his teeth in marking me as his for the rest of our lives.

The second he broke my skin, my body shook as the heavens opened up and my orgasm ripped through me. He pushed in one last time, holding himself there as he emptied his seed deep inside me. He pulled out and flipped us over so I was on top. I slid onto him and found my pace. My breasts swung in his face as he took one in his mouth. I felt my gums tingle as my canines extended, I bent over and sank my teeth into him as another orgasm ripped through us.

He carried me into the shower and massaged my ass, my breasts, and slipped a finger inside me. "Maxe, goddess, you make me feel things I've never felt before." He kissed and nipped at me leaving love bites all over my body. He pulled my legs up and impaled me, "goddess, yes!" I threw my head back relishing the feel of him inside me.

He hit my G-spot, I wasn't expecting it and my body jerked in reaction. "Baby, you are so tight and so wet. You are mine Crystal, your body, your tits, your pussy, your ass, they are all mine to pleasure whenever I want." My hands tightened in his hair and I pulled him closer to me again.

"I'm yours Max, all yours, whenever you want, I'll always be yours" I managed to say breathlessly.

He was holding me against the shower wall and slamming into my very wet pussy. It didn't take long before another orgasm was ripping through my body. It was so strong my body shook. His orgasm came right after mine, filling me up with his seed, and just as he came I heard, "I love you, Crystal."

"I love you too Max."

## MAX

When she said she was going to cum, I told her to wait. I'm right on the edge myself but I want to mark her first. I leaned down sucked and nipped at her marking spot. When I felt her about to explode from her orgasm, I bit down and sunk my teeth deeply into her. Her pussy released its juices all over my cock, making her even more slick.

I released my bite and licked it, sealing it closed. I flipped us over so she could ride me. I sucked one of her tits into my mouth and she moaned again. I released her tit, "Fuck Baby.". She bounced up and down on me grinding her pussy into me. "You feel so good, Baby. Keep grinding on me." My balls tightened and I knew it was just a matter of time.

"Oh goddess I'm going to cum!" She rocked on my cock. "Cum for me Max, I want your seed inside me!"

That was intense. I still needed more of her. After resting with her in my arms for a little while. I scooped her up and brought her into the bathroom. I sat her on the counter and turned on the shower. Letting the water warm up, I walked back to her, spread her legs apart, and settled between them. I kissed her, picked her up and she wrapped her legs around me. I walked us into the shower, set her down, and washed her hair. I grabbed a loofa, loaded it with body wash, and rubbed it all over her body, washing the smell of sex off of her. My hand wandered down to her pussy and I slipped a finger inside her.

That was a turn of events in the shower. I was going to have my way with her, instead, she went down on me. I'm not complaining, feeling her mouth wrapped around me, there is no better feeling in the world. "Oh goddess, Baby, whatever you just did, keep doing it," I growled out. I could feel her smile around my cock. I grabbed her hair pulling her mouth further onto my cock. She scraped her teeth very gently up my cock and it sent shivers up my spine.

"Fuck Baby, keep doing that and I'm going to cum down your throat. Baby I... oh goddess, fuck, I... I'm," my breath hitched in my throat, "Baby, I'm going to... fucking cum," and as soon as that left my lips, I spurted down her throat and she swallowed every last drop. She released my cock and worked her way back up kissing my abdomen on her way up.

I grabbed her head and slammed my lips to hers and shoved my tongue in her mouth tasting my essence in her mouth. My dick went hard as a rock, again. I pushed her against the shower and sucked down her neck to her tits. I sucked on one while massaging the other. Then working my way down, I sucked on her clit and pushed two fingers inside, hitting her G-spot and making her gasp.

"I love you, Crystal." those words left my lips before I could stop it, did I want to stop it? No, I didn't, I wanted her as mine, forever. The shower was getting cold so I turned off the water and grabbed two towels. I wrapped one around my waist before wrapping one around Crystal. I picked her up, carried her to the bed, and laid her down. I brushed her wet strand of hair behind her ears and looked her in the eyes.

"I, Maximus Eugene Katz, Gamma of the Black Diamond Pack, accept you, Dr. Crystal Renae Stevens, Gamma and doctor of the Black Diamond Pack as my mate."

"I, Dr. Crystal Renae Stevens, Gamma and doctor of the Black Diamond Pack, accept you, Maximus Eugene Katz, Gamma of the Black Diamond Pack as my mate."

I leaned in and kissed her. Hudson was going crazy in my head.

*"Hudson, settle down dude, why are you so worked up?"*

*"I want my mate, you had Crystal, it's my turn for Kiara."*

"Hudson wants to mate and mark Kiara, are you okay with that?"

"Mmhm, I am, if Hudson is anything like you, Kiara will love him as much as I love you." We both shifted into our wolves and let them get acquainted with each other. Four hours later, they relinquished our bodies back to us. Feeling exhausted, we fell asleep until we heard someone pounding on our door.

## TATE

Brinley and I made it back to the packhouse later that evening. With everything that happened earlier in the day and Chase and Amanda mating in both forms, we were exhausted and ended up falling asleep in the arena. We only woke up because John kept trying to link Brinley and when he couldn't get her to respond, he sent Jaxon to come get us.

"Jax, did John say what was so important that he needed us?"

"He did, but I'm not going to have him repeating himself. He needs the entire team, I came and got you first. I'm heading to get Max and Crystal, everyone else is in your office."

"You can head to my office, we'll get our gammas," I told him patting him on the back. Brin and I headed to their suite, we tried linking them, but they must've worn each other out too because they weren't responding. We had to bang on their door. After pounding on their door for fifteen minutes, Max finally opened the door.

"What the hell, why!..." he started to yell then realized who it was. "Oh sorry Tate, Peanut."

"It's fine, we're needed in my office. Can you and Crystal be there in five minutes?"

"Sure can."

"I'm happy to see a mark on your neck finally," I smiled at him.

"Roo!," Brin squealed, hugging him, "I'm so happy for you!"

"See you in five."

Brin and I left for my office. On the way there we were stopped by Cecil and Anabel. "Alpha, Luna, we wanted to let you know Noelle's arrival has been delayed. She said something about another one of her professors needing some assistance from students and she volunteered to stay. We'll let you know when we expect her to arrive."

"Thanks for letting us know, keep us posted."

"We will. You may want to figure out how to cover your marks," we overheard Maribel talking with Diane. She's still unaware you are fully marked and mated. We heard her planning another way to try and seduce you to make Jacob jealous enough to mark her out of lust."

"Thanks for the heads up, we'll work on covering it up and inform Jacob too. Keep us informed if you hear anything else. Now if you'll excuse us, we have a meeting to get to." When we arrived everyone was there except Max and Crystal. "Jacob, be on the lookout for Maribel. We just ran into her parents, they overheard her talking to Diane about seducing me to make you jealous enough to mark her out of lust."

"Like that's ever going to happen," he scoffed, "thanks for letting me know."

## JOHN

Once Max and Crystal arrived, we locked the door. "Now that we're all here, we've got some intel on a few things. Josh, you want to take over, it was your discovery after all."

"Sure. After our last meeting and finding out Arnold and Diane are mates, we decided to bug her room. We already know she's been sneaking into the guard shed at the gate and making a copy of the patrol schedule. We changed the schedule and rearranged the shift change times. We sent a visual of the new schedule to the warriors through the pack link and their phones and put a bogus paper schedule in the shed to see if she'd copy it again."

"Through the bug, we heard her talking to Maribel about distracting the guards and trying to get their attention while she slipped into the guard shed and pulled a prank on them. Maribel, from what we can tell, has no idea what Diane is doing. We've already retrained the guards on how to be more aware of their surroundings and told them what plans are and to not stop her. They aren't happy about it, but they understand there is more going on than we can disclose to them."

"Maribel and Diane are supposed to hit the guard shed tonight. We want to see where she takes the schedule. We were monitoring the cave and turned on the mics so we could hear if anything was said on Arnold's end. At the same time, Jeremy sent us a signal so we checked the camera at the rock and Francis was there."

"We turned on the mic and Francis said Jeremy's mate will mark the triplet pups along with five other orphaned pups. Arnold commented on leaving the cave for a few hours to 'get supplies.' We suspect he will be meeting up with Diane. Francis asked if we could get the pups about thirty minutes after Arnold left. I linked Brooklyn and Jaxon, they already agreed to it and told our Alpha and Luna the pups would be coming."

"Did he say how old the other pups are?"

"Yes, eight months, two years, five-year-old twins, and an eight-year-old. He also said they received permission from the other pups' parents to take them as well but he informed them they may have to be rescued a different day. He also wanted to know if Jeremy's mate could be taken, she's a few days away from delivering their baby and he'd like to have her in a safe place."

"That's a lot to take in and process. Jax and Brooklyn, are you both okay to rescue the orphans tonight?" Tate asked them.

"We are, Brooke and I have been training and we discovered when she aparates she can only go from point A to point B. Brooke can bring the pups here and then apparate to our pack. She's not able to go from here to the cave to our pack then back here. So whoever she rescues, it will be a two-step process for her. For me, I can take the pups from the cave to my pack and then come back here. We're not sure how many times we'll be able to do that without running out of energy."

"Jaxy, Brooky, remember before I came here we spoke with the Moon Goddess and she put these marks on us," she lifted her shirt sleeve. She said we'd be stronger together. "I wonder, if you guys brought me with you, we might be able to get all the orphans in one go. We could bring them back here first then transport them to Mom and Dads."

"Cupcake, how would you get eight kids between the three of you?"

"Tate, four are babies, we could put baby packs on our front and back to carry them. We have a two-year-old, two five-year-olds, and an eight-year-old. We can hold their hands easily."

"I don't like the idea of you being in that cave, but I know you're going to do what you want and I can't stop you. The only reason I'm agreeing to this is because Arnold isn't going to be there."

"We'll be in and out before you know it."

"Okay, next thing, Diane and Arnold. What are we going to do about them? It doesn't sound like she told Maribel she found her mate and from what we can tell, neither one has fully claimed, mated, and marked the other. Do we still have a tail on them?" Tate asked.

"We do and we've got something better, Arlene was able to 'make friends' with her. She gave her a sob story about me rejecting her after marking her and told her some other shit about how she wanted to get revenge on me. Diane ate it up and told her she had a mate who refused to mark her. She said he wanted to wait until after he attacked Black Diamond. He was promised the alpha position or some shit and will make her luna once he kills Tate. Of course, my mate, such a good actress, got us the details. I'll have to reward her later," I said, waggling my eyebrows.

"Diane is supposed to meet up with him to give him the patrol schedule, which we already knew. What we didn't know is he's planning on using Wolfsbane darts to subdue the gate patrol before he attacks so they can access the front gate without anyone knowing. If that's the case, then we'll either need the triplets or Erik and his guys on guard duty since Wolfsbane doesn't affect them. We're assuming she's meeting up with him tonight because all signs are pointing that way."

## JAXON

"I don't think we'll need to change out the guards, since we know when he's not planning on attacking for a while, we can strike them first at the cave. We already know they are confined to a small area because Arnold wants as much control as possible. Taking the fight to them makes more sense. We will need to get word to Jeremy and Francis when we are going to attack so the people who want to defect can make their way to the arena."

"You want them in the arena?" Tate asked.

"Yes, it's the best place. They can be sealed inside until we can get to them." Tate nodded his head at me in acceptance. "John, can you let us know when it's time to head out? Brin, Tate, Max, and Crystal need to get food in their bodies before we do anything else."

"We can, it will be a couple hours at least. Oh, Tate and Brin, we found some concealer you can use on your marks. It will make them disappear but they'll still be there, so don't worry."

"Thank you, we appreciate your help."

"Okay, let's get that concealer on your marks then get you guys something to eat before tonight's mission."

# CHAPTER 39 NEW FRIENDS

**DIANE**

I'm on my way to the dining hall to meet up with Marible and all I can think about is my mate. I'm so excited I found him. I was in town shopping with Maribel, getting supplies and decorations for Noelle's party when the most amazing scent hit my nose, sandalwood. He grabbed me, and we acknowledged we were mates. We have been meeting secretly for a while. I met a new friend too. I've been seeing her around the pack and she looked really sad. I thought I'd cheer her up by bringing cookies to her one time when she was sitting in the dining hall.

***Flashback***

"Hi," she jumped, startled, "my name's Diane, I've been seeing you around the pack, are you new here?"

"I am," she sounded sad, "I just transferred from another pack, my name is Arlene." She stuck out her hand for me to shake.

"You look so sad, do you want to talk about it?"

"You're the first person to come talk with me," she said, lowering her eyes. "I would like someone to talk with."

"I'll link you so you can keep it private if you like."

"I still can't link, Alpha Tate has accepted my transfer, but he hasn't been able to initiate me into the pack yet."

"I understand, he's been pretty busy with just recently taking over the pack and all. We can go somewhere quiet if you'd like."

"I would like that very much, thank you for your kindness." I smiled and led her to a pond we have on pack lands that's kind of secluded. We sat on a bench by the water.

"Why are you sad, does it have to do with your transfer?"

"It does," she wrung her hands together. It's a couple of things. I found my mate and after we fully claimed, mated, and marked each other, he rejected me. He said he fully claimed me in the heat of the moment. He was in love with someone else, my best friend. Well, she was my best friend. She also happens to be the daughter of my old alpha."

"I couldn't handle the rejection or her betrayal so I asked my alpha if I could leave. He told me about this pack so I thought I'd come here. It's the furthest from my old pack," she started crying and my heart ached for her. I don't usually care about other people and I think the only reason this was hitting me is because my mate hasn't wanted to 'seal' our mate bond yet.

"I would like to find a way to get revenge on the both of them but I'm so tender-hearted I wouldn't even know where to start. I don't even like training because I don't want to hurt people."

"I would be willing to help you get revenge if you want to. I have a friend who would help too."

She looked up at me with tear-streaked cheeks. "You would help me?"

"I would, and I'll ask my friend to help too if you want."

"Who, who's your friend?"

"His name is Arnold, he's really good about getting revenge."

"Does he live here?"

"No, he's from another pack so we'd have to meet him somewhere. Would you like to meet him?"

"I don't know, can I think about it?"

"Sure," I said, patting her leg, "I'm meeting him in a couple of days, let me know if you want to join me."

"Thank you, I will."

*****End Flashback*****

## ARLENE

I was looking for Diane, after talking with John, I need to meet Arnold and see where his mind is at. I'm so glad my acting skills are on point. She took my story, hook, line, and sinker. Now, to convince this asshole so we can put him ten fucking feet under for what he's doing to this pack and those poor rogues he's been recruiting. Crystal said Diane is usually in the dining hall so that's where I'm heading first. It's been a couple of days since I last spoke with her. I walked in and spotted her right away sitting with Maribel. Here goes nothing.

"Diane?"

"Hi Arlene," she gave me a small wave and motioned me over.

"This is my very best friend, Maribel. Maribel, this is Arlene, the girl I was telling you about."

"Hi, I'm Arlene," I stuck my hand out, "it's nice to meet you."

She grabbed my hand and shook it. "Diane was telling me your mate rejected you and then ran off with the alpha's daughter who was your best friend."

"Oh, she... did?" I said hesitantly.

"I hope it was okay I told her. She went through something similar."

"You did?"

"I did. I was supposed to be Alpha Tate's chosen mate until he brought home a fucking whore from another pack. She weaseled her way into his pants. He hasn't looked at me once since that bitch arrived."

It took everything inside me to not knock this asshat from here to next week, talking about Tate and Brin that way. "That's horrible."

"The worst part is I found my mate. Turns out he's one of her security guards and she told him to reject me before even getting to know me," she said angrily.

I reached out my hand to her, "I'm so sorry that happened, you seem like a very nice person." I wanted to barf in my mouth saying those words.

## MARIBEL

"Diane's going to help me try and get revenge on my mate and that whore he claims to love. Maybe I can help you with something?" Arlene asked me.

I eyed her skeptically, "I think I might be able to use you actually, and not just for that."

"How else can I help?"

"Alpha Tate's been having secret meetings in his office. Maybe we could use you to try and sneak in there. You're new here and Diane said you don't have the pack link yet. You could use that as an excuse to hang around his office and see what you can find out."

"What if I get caught?" She asked nervously.

"Just tell them you wanted to see Alpha Tate about the pack link."

"Okay, I'll give it a try," she shrugged her shoulders.

"Is there anything else I need to know about the people in this pack or anything else of importance since I'm new here and all?"

"Actually, yes there is. That whore, Brinley, we're trying to get her to leave so I can either get Tate back or get my mate back."

"You said your mate was one of her security guards, which one?"

"Jacob, he needs to take back his rejection and mark me... hmmm, maybe you can help with that too. I'll have to think about that. In the meantime, do you want to have some fun with us tonight?"

"Uh, sure, what kind of fun?"

"We're going to mess with the guards at the gate shed this evening. I usually distract them while Diane goes inside the shed and messes with their stuff. They're none the wiser and by the time we get out of there, they have no idea what happened. I walk right up to them dressed very seductively while Diane wears all black and sneaks in the back to go inside."

## DIANE

"We'll meet at 6:00 pm. I have to meet someone at 8:00 pm so I'm free for an hour and a half."

"Who do you have to meet?" Maribel wiggled her eyebrows at me. I laughed at her, she knows I've been hooking up with a guy, but she doesn't know who.

"That guy I told you about, Charlie, duh." I looked at Arlene, praying she wouldn't blow my cover. I don't know why I trusted her and not my best friend, but I did.

"How long will you be out with Charlie?" Maribel asked me.

"Probably until midnight, why?"

"I wanted to have a movie marathon with you tonight, but it can wait."

"Sorry, maybe this weekend?"

"That would be better, we can start in the morning and go all day and night. Arlene? Are you in for a movie marathon day?"

"Sure, sounds fun."

## JAXON

We were in the dining hall when Brooklyn, Brinley, and I got a link from Arlene. "Alpha's, I just met with Diane and Maribel, can you meet me in the arena?"

"We'll be there in a few minutes, do we need to bring anyone else?"

"No, more people might be too suspicious."

"We're on our way."

"Thanks, Alpha's."

I looked at everyone sitting at our table, "my sisters and I need to head to the arena to meet John's mate. She didn't want anything to look suspicious so just asked for the three of us. When we get down there I'll have Brin open the link to everyone involved so you can hear what's being said. If everyone's cool with that, we'll head out now."

Since no one said anything, we got up, Brin kissed Tate and we headed to the arena. As soon as we got there Brin opened the link. We went inside and sealed the arena closed. "Hey Arlene, Brin opened a link to everyone else so they can hear what's going on."

### ARLENE

"Hey, Alphas. Alpha Brin, thank you for opening the link so my pesky mate won't keep bugging me," I laughed because I knew he was listening.

"I heard that Princess," he responded.

"I know you did my Prince," I said smiling. "I just met with the asshats. They are planning on heading to the guard shed at 6:00 pm. Diane said she's meeting someone by the name of Charlie at 8:00 pm, I'm assuming it's Arnold. She's taking me with her, she said he can help me get revenge on my mate who rejected me."

"I told her he left me for my best friend, the alpha's daughter. She bought my story and said 'her friend' could help me get revenge. Anyway, she isn't planning on returning until midnight. You'll have at least three hours to rescue those pups."

### JAXON

"Good work Arlene. Try to keep your link open while you're with them so we can take any precautions we need. Would you feel comfortable wearing a small camera or mic on you while you're meeting with Diane and Arnold?"

"I don't have a problem with that."

"John, do you have something we can put on her?"

"I do, I have a camera and mic we can attach to the button on her shirt. They won't know anything is different."

"Arlene, make sure you stop at Tate's office with the shirt you're going to wear so he can get the camera attached. Just make sure you aren't seen."

"Really Jaxon, next to Brooklyn and Brinley, I'm the next best female master elite warrior you have. I know how to be stealthy."

"Fine, whatever, let me unlock the arena so you can leave."

*"Jax, someone is lurking outside the arena, don't unlock it yet."*

*"Thanks, Branson."*

"Problem guys, Branson just informed me someone is lurking outside."

"On it," Brooklyn said as she aparated outside to see who it was before returning. "We're in the clear, it's just some young pups trying to look in the windows but they don't realize they're sealed shut."

"Tate's sending a warrior out to gather all the kids, they should be leaving in a few minutes," Brin said.

"I'll pop back out there and make sure." She came back a couple of minutes later. "They're gone, the coast is clear, I'll lift the sealing so Arlene can leave."

"Thanks, Alpha's, I'll be sure to keep the link open, good luck with the rescue tonight."

## DIANE

I'm excited to get this show on the road and get my mate to mark me. I'm sitting in my bedroom and decided to call him, I miss him so much. I have him on speaker so I can gather the clothes I need to wear tonight and shove them in a duffel bag. I know I'm going to see him in a couple of hours but I just need to hear his voice.

"Hi Arnie," I said as soon as he picked up.

"Hi Buttercup, how's my beautiful mate?"

"I'm good but missing you so much."

"Me too Buttercup, but I'll be seeing you tonight. Are you bringing me anything?"

"I am, the new patrol schedule for the next couple of weeks," I giggled.

"Good girl, I will reward you dearly when I see you."

"Oh, I'm also bringing a friend with me, she needs to get revenge on her mate and her former best friend."

"Did she say why?"

"Her mate fully claimed her then rejected her and left her for her best friend."

"That's horrible, why would anyone do that? You let her know I will help her any way I can."

"Thank you, Arnie, you're the best mate anyone could ever have."

"Thanks, Buttercup. When I destroy Tate and become alpha and you become my luna, we'll make our pack more powerful than any other pack."

"Have you decided what day you're going to launch the attack?"

"Two months from now because I want to try and gather more rogues for our cause. I'm thinking early morning, before the sun rises so I can do a sneak attack and they won't see it coming. I want you away from the fighting. Do you think you can make an excuse to be away overnight when the time comes?"

"I'll see if Maribel wants to have a girl's night out, that way she won't be in harm's way either."

"That sounds like a perfect plan."

"Now, it's getting close to the time you need to leave, so I'll see you and your friend in a couple of hours."

"See you then, Arnie, I love you."

"I love you too."

## JOHN

As soon as Diane entered her room we knew it. I had a couple of team members sneak into her house a couple of nights ago when she and her parents were out and put a sensor in her room. We were able to hear her entire conversation with Arnold. That motherfucker is planning on attacking the pack before dawn in two months and she's helping him. All we need now is proof she's giving him the patrol schedule and we'll have all that we need to confront her.

At least we have a timeline to work with now. Arlene came in a little bit ago to make sure the button on her shirt would work with the camera and mic I have. I'm not happy with her choice of shirt but she is undercover and she's good at what she does. I'll just punish her later for wearing it, that should be fun. I need to let the rest of them know Arnold's timeline as soon as I can.

## MARIBEL

It was 5:15 pm, I was in the dining hall waiting for Diane and Arlene to get here so we could grab a quick bite to eat before we headed to the guard shed. It's about a twenty-minute walk to the guard shed from the dining hall so we wanted to get something to eat beforehand. I was unsure about Arlene when Diane first introduced me to her but after hearing her story, I was heartbroken for her.

I know how much being rejected hurt me and we hadn't even accepted each other. She was fully claimed by her mate then he rejected her. I can't even comprehend the pain that bastard put her through. Then to hook up with her best friend! I just can't fathom how she survived that. She must have very strong family ties to help her through it.

Then to be strong enough to leave the only family and pack you've ever known to come to a new pack. Her resolve to show her ex-mate how strong she is is amazing, maybe I could learn something from her. Maybe I can ask how she handled it in the beginning. Maybe I could do the same. Instead of trying to force Jacob to take me back, maybe I should show him I could go on without him... who the hell am I kidding, that is not how I do things.

I need and want my mate, he hasn't moved on like Arlene's mate did. My mate is still here guarding that fucking bitch. Nope, I will start flaunting my best ass-sets and boobs at him. Mates don't like it when you wear skimpy clothes, they want you covered up. What's theirs is theirs, they don't like it when other males look at their females. That's what I'm going to do, of course, that didn't work out well for me the last two times. Maybe this time it would.

*"I want our mate back Mar, do whatever you need to get him back,"* Sally whimpered.

*"I'll do everything I can, Sally."* Sally's been very quiet and somber ever since Jacob rejected us. I try talking to her but she mostly just whines. She's very depressed and I wish I could help her. I was brought out of my thoughts when the girls showed up.

**DIANE**

"Hey girl, how long have you been waiting for us?"

"Only a couple of minutes."

"Good, I thought we were running later than expected. Have you checked the buffet line to see what's for dinner tonight?"

"I did, it's Italian night, baked ziti, lasagna, manicotti, alfredo, caesar salad, bread sticks, Italian wedding soup, and assorted desserts."

"Wow, that sounds amazing," Arlene said.

"Arlene was able to make it to Tate's office but it was locked so she couldn't get in."

"Were you able to hear anything at all?" Maribel asked her.

"Unfortunately not, but," she raised her finger, "I hid around the corner and saw one of the guys come out. He was pretty cute and made my wolf alert, I think he might be someone I will try to get close to. Maybe I could seduce him and get some information out of him," she was blushing. "I was hoping you guys might want to go shopping so I could buy some sexy bras and panties and maybe some clothes that will show off my ass and boobs. You know, try to entice him a little," she giggled.

"That sounds like a great idea! Let's get you back in the dating scene and maybe your ex-mate will feel the pain when you fuck this new guy," I wiggled my eyebrows at her.

"I don't know if I'm ready for fucking yet, but I can at least flaunt myself around this guy and see where it goes."

"Oh, Arlene, if your wolf is interested, she will probably make you fuck him," Maribel said laughing.

We got up, grabbed some food and by the time we got done eating it was 5:45 pm. We still needed to change so we were a little off on our time, but that's okay, I'll still be able to get me and Arlene to Arnold on time for our 8:00 pm meeting. We each stashed the clothes we were going to wear in duffle bags behind a tree. We stripped and put on our clothes of choice.

I wore all black since I'm the one sneaking into the shed. Maribel wore a short, very short I should say, and revealing dress. The thing barely covered her ass and her boobs were about to fall out. Arlene didn't have anything revealing like Maribel because she left her old pack with only a few things. She did bring some short shorts, that just covered her ass, and the shirt she wore was an off-the-shoulder button-up shirt. She only buttoned enough of them so her boobs were front and center without actually falling out. She looked really good.

"Ready ladies?"

"We are!"

"Let's do this."

We walked to the shed, and as we got closer, we saw Steve, Gage, and Wren at the post. I left the girls, headed towards the back side of the shed, and waited.

## MARIBEL

As we got closer, I adjusted my boobs and hiked up my dress just enough for part of my ass to show. I looked at Arlene and she had her hands in her bra pulling her boobs up to make more cleavage show. Once we were done adjusting ourselves, we walked seductively toward the guys, giggling like we said something funny.

"Ladies, can we help you?" Gage asked.

"Hi, Gage, we were wondering what time you guys are finished with patrol, we are looking for a good time," I started walking to him and reached my hands out, "I'm a little lonely and need someone to take care of my needs." I ran my hands down his chest and to his cock, where I started rubbing him up and down to feel him getting hard underneath my hands.

**ARLENE**

*"This is so degrading, John, I do not appreciate this assignment."*

*"I know Princess, I don't like it either but you know how to work assignments."*

*"I know, I also know how horny you get when I come home from one of these. By the way, I told the asshats, my wolf caught sight of 'one of the guys' in Tate's office and she was drawn to you. So if they see us together, they will think I'm trying to seduce you."*

*"Princess, you can seduce me anytime you want, now, get back to work."*

*"Yes, Daddy,"* I said sarcastically.

*"You can 'yes daddy' me in bed tonight Princess,"* he laughed and closed the link.

I walked over to Steve, "Hi, I'm Arlene," I leaned in close and whispered in his ear quietly enough for only him to hear, "Play along. Link Gage and Wren, tell them Diane is making her way to the shed and to keep their focus on me and Maribel. Squeeze my hips and pull me closer after you passed the message along."

A second later he pulled me to him. I patted his back and looked at Wren, "do you want to play with us?" I started to unbutton my shorts as Maribel hiked her dress up to her waist.

I slipped my shorts off and opened the link back up to John. I might as well get him off while I'm doing this. I smirked to myself as I was sending him visuals of what I was about to do. I ran my finger down my stomach and slipped it inside my panties. I began to finger myself and moan.

*"What the hell Princess? I'm in the office going over stuff with the triplets and have a boner in my pants, not cool."* I giggled at him through our link.

I looked back at Steve and his eyes were wide. Wren walked over and looked between me and Maribel. Since I'm a fully claimed she-wolf, my actions aren't affecting them so their eyes are trained on Maribel to get them hard. They'd look at me when she'd look up. It was pretty awkward, but I did what I needed to do.

I was watching Diane as she snuck into the guard shed and was rummaging around. When I saw her stand up and leave the shed, I knew she had what she was looking for. I pulled my hands out of my panties, "well, boys, if you want more of this, come find me later," I winked at them. I grabbed my shorts and started walking off with Maribel in tow.

*"You're in so much trouble when you get back Princess,"* John linked me.

*"Ooh, can't wait, my Prince,"* I snickered at him.

# Chapter 40 Arnold's Past

**DIANE**

"You were amazing Arlene, I had no idea you had that in you."

"Yeah girl, you were amazing."

"Thanks, ladies. I channeled my inner slut and went with it. You didn't do too bad yourself Maribel."

"Thanks, girly. We should do that again, it was fun!" She giggled.

"Well, you ready to head out Arlene?"

"Do you mind if I change first?"

"Of course, but make it fast, it's a thirty-minute drive to where we're going."

"I'll be right back."

"Who're you going to meet again?" Maribel asked.

"Charlie, I met him when we were out shopping that one time. I told you about him, remember?"

"Is he that guy who pulled you into the store?"

"Yes, that's him."

"He's really cute, are you mates?"

I looked around making sure we were out of earshot, "we are," I giggled.

"He hasn't marked you yet?"

"No, I told him I wanted to get to know him better since he's not from our pack."

"That's so romantic," Maribel clasped her hands together and brought them under her chin.

"It is, isn't it," I squealed.

"When will I get to meet him? It's not fair Arlene gets to meet him first. We've been besties since we were little," she pouted.

"You'll meet him soon. I'm only taking Arlene because he might be able to help her get revenge on her ex-mate and ex-best friend."

"Now hush, she's coming back."

## ARLENE

When I got back to my room, John was waiting for me. "Strip Princess," he said sternly. He didn't have to ask me twice.

"I only have ten maybe fifteen minutes at most before I need to get back."

"That's all I need, now lay down, ass in the air," he demanded.

"Was I naughty, Daddy?"

"You were so naughty, I'm going to spank that pretty little ass of yours." Swat, he spanked me then rubbed the sting away, "Don't," swat, "you," swat, "ever," swat, "do," swat, "that," swat, "again," swat. My pussy was dripping wet, he pushed three fingers inside me, hitting my G-spot. I was on the edge, he pulled his fingers from me, dropped his pants, and slammed his cock into me.

"Oh goddess, Daddy, harder please, harder."

"You like that Princess?"

"Yes!" I screamed. He kept slamming in and out of me.

"How much do you like it, Princess."

"I... I want... I want more!"

"What do you say, Princess?

"Please John, I want all of you! Oh goddess, please!"

"Fuck Princess, you're so tight, I'm going to put a pup in you right now Princess. Do you want me to put a pup in you?"

"Ye... yes."

"Yes, what Princess."

"I want you to put a pup in me," I said breathlessly.

He slammed into me one more time before my body convulsed so hard, he grabbed my hair, pulled my head back exposing my mark, and sunk his teeth into me. My orgasm hit me so hard that we both came together when my walls clenched around him. After he emptied his seed deep inside me, he waited a few minutes before pulling out.

"Princess, don't ever link me with visuals when you're on assignment, or I'll have to punish you again, understand?"

"Yes, my Prince." *If he punishes me like that again, then there will be a next time, that was delicious.* I gave him a quick blow job before cleaning myself up, kissed him, and promised to keep the camera, mic, and mind link open while I was with Diane and Arnold. I ran back to where I left the girls.

"Sorry, that took longer than expected. My mom called to see how I was adjusting to my new pack and I couldn't get her off the phone."

"It's okay, we still have time, I'm just glad you made it back. You're wearing the same shirt?" Diane asked me.

"Yeah, I just wanted to change out of my shorts, this shirt can be adjusted to look like a regular button-up."

"Shall we go then?"

"I'm ready when you are."

### ARNOLD

It was 7:30 pm, I told my rogues I was going out for a little while to gather supplies and I'd be back around midnight. They know not to disobey me because they know the consequences. Most of my warrior rogues are male. If I find male rogues with pups and or mates I take them and put them in the cave. I've found they become compliant with what I want if I have control over their mate or pup.

I've gone as far as to threaten the lives of their mate and pup if I feel anyone, especially her mate, stepping out of line. There are few pups in the cave, I don't keep track of how many I have in there, it doesn't matter, they'll be left for dead anyway. I've acquired my rogue following by promising a better life for them. My real goal is to take over Black Diamond, kill those pack members who won't bow to my ruling, and bring in rogues who want to be in a pack who will bow down to me.

I've come to find out some of the rogues in my pack were born into this fucking up life. Others were forced into it because of what a family member did. A few of them became rogues because of what they did in their packs or decided pack life wasn't for them. As for me, I was born into it but not because a family member did anything wrong, but because my father raped my mom. I'm the son of an alpha. He raped my mom and banished her to rogue life when he found out she was pregnant with me.

About five years later he found his fated mate. They had a baby together, his mate eventually died, and my mom never did tell me how. She did keep tabs on him though. She would meet up with her friends from the pack occasionally and they'd tell her about pack life and give her pictures of people she knew.

They even gave her a picture of the new alpha she-wolf as she grew. Looking back, she wanted me to have pictures of my sister. She didn't tell me everything though. I know I have... or rather... had a half-sister. I wish I had known her, she sounded like a sweet and gentle person. I became very bitter and angry because of my fucking father. Especially after my mom died. She was my glue and my rock. She kept the evil at bay in me.

When she died, I fucking broke and I became who I am today. I don't care what I do or who I have to fucking hurt. My only goal is to take back what should've fucking been mine by birthright. My father didn't even know who I was when he fucking hired me. The last time he saw me I was a scrawny fifteen-year-old. When he hired me I was twenty-five, I'm thirty now. No one knew I was his son, not even my mom's friends in the pack. They just assumed she was banished because she thwarted my so-called father's advances.

They have no idea he raped and eventually killed her. He killed her the day I turned fifteen. I know it was him because he tried to fucking kill me too, the bastard. He wanted the pack to go to my sister, she was ten at the time he killed my mom. He would only give the pack to her if she eventually married the person he wanted her to. Not the person she was fated to be with unless he happened to be an alpha. All he cared about, if you can even call it that, was his daughter.

She was five years younger than me. She had no idea I even existed. From what I could tell, she was kind and generous and loved life. I wish I would've known her. Now I'm going to kill her mate because he didn't protect her from our father when he killed her in cold blood and took my rightful position as alpha of Black Diamond. Alpha Tate won't even know what hit him until it's too late.

At 8:00 pm sharp, my beautiful mate, Diane, came walking into the cafe with another girl in tow. This must be the girl she was talking about who needed my help. I may be a ruthless person, but then there's next-level evil and what this bastard did to this she-wolf, is fucking uncalled for. "Diane," I said, getting up and walking to her. I kissed her and tipped my head in greeting.

"Hi, I'm Arnold, and you are?" I held my hand out to shake hers.

"I'm Arlene, it's nice to meet your acquaintance."

"Diane says you need some help with your ex-mate and ex-friend?"

"Yes, what they did to me was unspeakable and unforgivable. I barely made it through the rejection. I'm just thankful to be healthy and feeling like myself again."

"Do you still have your mating mark?"

"I do, I was told it takes a while before it starts to disappear. Why do you ask?"

"Do you feel it every time he fucks or kisses another she-wolf?"

"If it's that stabbing feeling I get in my stomach almost every night and sometimes during the day, then yes, I feel it."

"That's good to hear."

"Why is that a good thing?"

"Because it means if you fuck or kiss someone he'll feel it too. Have you fucked anyone yet?"

"No, but there is someone at the pack I'm interested in and so is my wolf."

"Good, let's start there. The next chance you get, seduce the man and do it knowing you're hurting the man who hurt you."

"Thank you, Arnold."

"Don't thank me yet, this is just the beginning of what we'll be doing. Eventually, I want you to tell me what pack you're from and we'll go after him."

"Really? You can do that?"

"I will be able to in a couple of months."

"A couple of months?"

"I, don't understand."

I looked to Diane, "I trust her Arnold, you can too."

"The alpha of the pack you just joined is not a good person. He may present himself as good, but he allowed his fated mate to be killed." *I'm not one hundred percent sure Diane knows Alpha Frederick killed his daughter or that he's my father so I'll keep that information to myself for now.*

"What? That's horrible!"

"It is. I'm going to strike an attack against the pack in two months. The reason you, Maribel, and Diane went to the guard shed tonight was so Diane could make a copy of the patrol schedule."

"Oh my, I had no idea," she sounded shocked.

"When the day arrives, Diane and Maribel will be going into town for the night. I don't want them around the fighting and since you are friends with them, I want you to be with them."

"I would like that, I don't like fighting. May I ask a question?"

"Sure."

"There are a lot of pack members, you must have a lot of pack members too, to fight them?"

"I don't have as many, only about seventy-five right now, but they are ruthless fighters and won't stop until I tell them to."

I turned my attention to Diane. "You brought the schedule with you?"

"I did, I looked at it, the only thing that's changed is who's working the shifts. They haven't changed the times of the shift changes only who's working the shifts."

"They are idiots, aren't they? You'd think after our last attack, they would've changed the schedule. That's okay, it works to our advantage.

"What time are you going to start the attack?" Arlene asked.

"We'll launch the attack at 2:30 in the morning. It's during a shift change and the only people who will be awake are the people on patrol. My dear Buttercup, it's almost midnight. I need to get back to my pack and you need to get home. Two more months my love and we can make everything official." She squealed in delight and giggled. "You're so fucking cute, I can't wait until we're fully claimed to each other." I kissed her goodbye and left.

# Chapter 41 Orphan Rescue

**BROOKLYN**

Jax, Brin, and I were in Tate's office getting ready to leave for the cave. At 7:30 pm Arlene sent a link letting us know they were on their way to meet Arnold. John confirmed Arnold's leaving through the cave's camera. Arlene contacted us once they arrived where they were meeting Arnold then again before they sat down with him. John was monitoring the camera and mic she had on her in case anything imperative to us was mentioned. We waited until 8:30 before leaving for the rescue mission.

We strapped two baby packs on Jaxon and one each on me and Brin. Jaxon's taking two of the triplets and the eight-year-old. I'm taking one of the triplets and the two five-year-old twins, and Brinley's taking the eight-month-old and two-year-old. Once everything was strapped on, Brin and I held hands and I aparated us to the cave with Jaxon right behind us. Jeremy was in the cave waiting for us along with his mate. Once there, Brin linked us.

*"Hi Jeremy, these are my siblings, Jaxon and Brooklyn, we're triplets."*

*"It's nice to meet you. This is my mate, Lydia."*

*"It's nice to meet you too, Lydia."*

Before we took the orphans we scanned the marks Lydia put on them. *"Can you put two of the triplets in Jaxon's baby packs, he'll also take the eight-year-old. I'm taking the other triplet and the twins, Brinley's taking the other baby and two-year-old. Once we get them to safety, either myself or my brother will come back for Lydia if we're able to, sound good?"*

*"Yes, thank you, Brooklyn. She could go into labor any day now and it's not safe for her to be here."*

*"Do you think Arnold will notice you and the pups gone?"*

*"I don't think so, he hasn't paid any attention to us since he found his mate. He doesn't even know how many pups he has in here."*

*"Will the other women or older pups in the cave say anything about the pups or you missing?"*

*"No, they know their lives depend on them keeping quiet. They know the consequences if Arnold finds out anyone is missing."*

*"Alright, then we will do our best to come back and get you."*

*"Brooklyn, we need to get moving,"* Jaxon said. *"We don't know how long we have before Arnold returns. We need to do this as quickly as possible."*

*"You're right. Brin and I will see you at Mom and Dad's."*

*"Do you think you have enough energy to make it directly to Mom and Dad's?"*

*"I do, touching Brin is giving me extra energy."*

*"Okay let's go."* Brin grab my arm with her free hand, I concentrated on Mom and Dad's packhouse and the next second we were standing in the middle of their foyer.

"Mom, Dad! A little help here please!" I yelled. Our parents came running.

"Oh my dear heavens," Mom said.

*"Mom, don't scare the pups,"* Brin linked her.

*"I'm not going to scare them Baby Girl."*

Jaxon spoke to the eight-year-old, "This is Luna Estelle, our mom and that's Alpha Zane our dad. You will be safe here okay?" He shook his head and clung tighter to him. "Mom, Dad, can you grab the babies out of my packs?" Once they grabbed the babies, he knelt and spoke to the little boy. "What's your name?"

"Grayson"

"That's a nice strong name, Grayson. Can you tell me what happened to your parents?"

"Alpha Arnold killed them," he was trying to hold back a sniffle.

"I'm sorry that happened buddy, do you know what pack you're from?" He shook his head.

"Thats okay bud, have you always been a rogue?"

"Yes, mommy and daddy said their alpha kicked them out when they were little, but I don't know why. I'm afraid Alpha Arnold will find me."

"You're safe now Grayson, no one will hurt you ever again, I promise. Do you know the baby's names?"

The twins are Emily and Emery, their mommy and daddy were killed too and he's," pointing to the two-year-old, "Magnum and that baby on her boobies," he pointed to Brinley, "is Arrow, he didn't have a mommy and his daddy was killed when Alpha Arnold made them attack that pack one time."

"Grayson, do you know anything about the triplets?"

"No. They came a little while ago. Their mommy and daddy tried running away. Alpha Arnold grabbed the babies before killing their parents in front of the adults. We've been calling them Bryce, Camden, and Kinsley. Two boys and one girl. We don't know their real names so we gave them names. They are too little to know what their real names are anyway, that's what Mama Lydia told us."

"Who's Mama Lydia, Grayson?" My mom asked him.

"Papa Jeremy's mate. She's going to have a baby. She said I could help name it because I've been a good boy. I always help her," he smiled big. "I like Papa Jeremy and Mama Lydia, they are very nice to me and the other kids. Even the kids who still have parents."

"That's good, Grayson, would you feel better if Mama Lydia were here with you?"

"She can come?"

"Yes, I need to leave so I can bring her here. Do you think you can be strong and brave while I'm gone?"

"Yes, I can."

At some point, my dad gave the baby he was holding to my mom and left the foyer. She gave the babies back to Jaxon and knelt next to Grayson. "Grayson, would you like to help me in the kitchen? I have some fresh fruit and ice cream, would you like some?"

His eyes lit up and so did Emily and Emery's. "Can they have some too?"

"Of course, they can sweetheart, come on, let's get some for everyone, okay?" My mom held out her hand and he grabbed it while they walked to the kitchen. Dad walked back in, "Tobias is on his way here. He's going to check the pups' health and draw blood." He took the two babies from Jaxon and headed to the kitchen with me and Brin following with the other pups while Jaxon left for Lydia.

"Your mom and I decided it would be best and safer to keep the pups in the packhouse until Arnold is captured. We turned one of the guest rooms on the alpha floor into a nursery. We have everything we need there from furniture, toys, and clothes. As you can see, we have baby swings, toddler chairs, and high chairs in here. We are set up to care for these little ones for as long as it takes. We have families volunteering to open their homes to them when we're at that point," Dad reassured us.

"This is why I love our pack, they are always willing to step up and help out without question," Brin beamed.

The door opened and in walked Doc Carter, "I came over as soon as Alpha Zane linked me. He said some of the pups were here. I want to get started on their blood work right away, knowing I'll be running a lot of tests in the next few weeks. I want to start with the babies first since they'll be easier to get blood from. The toddlers might struggle since they'll have an understanding of what's happening but won't understand why."

"Grayson, this is Doc Carter. He's a nice person and wants to make sure everyone is healthy. To do that he needs to draw blood from you and the other kids. Do you think you could be a big boy and help us with the little ones?"

"Will it hurt?"

"You may feel a tiny pinch, but he's so good you probably won't even feel it."

"I will be a brave big boy. Mama Lydia says it's good to help with the babies. I won't cry."

"You're a good boy, Grayson. Can I take your blood first to show the others how brave you are?"

"Yes, but can I have ice cream first?"

"Sure, you can have ice cream first."

Grayson ate his ice cream and then put on a brave face as Doc Carter drew his blood.

## JAXON

The second I returned to the cave, I walked over to Jeremy and Lydia. "The kids are getting settled, we don't have much time and I need to get you to the packhouse before Arnold shows up. You need to say your goodbyes, and Jeremy, you know you will most likely miss the birth of your first child. We will do our best to get word to you when she goes into labor, I can have Brinley link you. If it's safe, and only if it's safe, either I or Brooklyn will take you to Lydia."

"That would be amazing, thank you!"

"Don't thank me yet, I don't know if it will be possible."

"That's okay, knowing she and our baby are safe, is all I can ask for."

"Please, say your goodbyes, we need to get out of here." He turned to his mate, gave her a passionate kiss, and told her how much he loved her and to never forget. He also told her to move on if he didn't make it out alive. He leaned down and kissed her belly and told him or her that he loved it and the baby kicked him in response.

I took Lydia by the hand, "this may feel a little weird, but it will only last a second." I concentrated on my parents' packhouse again and when we opened our eyes we were standing in the foyer. We heard giggles coming from the kitchen, walked in and the older kids were chowing down on fruit and ice cream. The babies were being fed by the kitchen staff and everyone was laughing and giggling.

"Mama Lydia, you came!"

"Of course, I came, my sweet boy. I couldn't leave you," she ruffled his hair and kissed him on his head.

"Mom, Dad, we need to get back to Tate's pack. I know these guys are in good hands but let us know if we can help in any way. We'll let you know when we bring the rest of the pups and women. Lydia, my parents have set up a nursery in the guest room for the pups and there is a connecting guest room for you. We thought it was best to have the kids close to someone familiar. Please let my parents or one of the house staff know if you need assistance. This is a cell phone you can use to contact them since you don't have a pack link. Their numbers are preprogrammed for you."

"Thank you?" she said questioningly.

"Is everything okay?"

"Um, I've been a rogue for far too long, I don't know how to use one of these."

"I am so sorry, I didn't even think to ask you if you knew how to use one. My parents will explain it to you. My sisters and I need to get back before our energy is drained."

"Can I ask a question before you leave?"

"Of course."

"How come you're helping rogues? How do you know you can trust me?"

Brinley stepped up, "I trust your mate, therefore I can trust you. We know not all rogues are bad, some are rogues because of other people's actions. This pack always gives the benefit of the doubt, we have a way to know your true intentions. You, my friend, are a good person."

My sister smiled at her, "Lydia, you are safe here, your pup will be safe here and if you like it here, you can become a pack member here."

"May I ask what pack this is?"

"Lydia, my name is Alpha Zane Winter, this is my mate and wife, Luna Estelle Winter, you are in the Winter Moon Pack."

Her face dropped and her body shook, my mom walked over to her, "My dear, what's wrong?"

"I... uh, my brother... my mom..." she said, "when we were little she and my dad got kicked out of the pack because of something my eldest brother did. My older brother didn't want to be a rogue, so he left us promising to let us know what pack he ended up in, he was twelve years old. I heard my parents talking one night and I remember hearing the name. The pack name, Winter Moon, is... does... do you... know my brother?" Tears were forming in her eyes.

"Lydia, who's your brother? I do recall us taking in a twelve-year-old boy years ago."

"His name is Tobias but we always called him Toby."

We heard something crash to the floor. We all turned around and Doc Carter was standing there with tears in his eyes and shattered vials around his feet.

"Lia? Lia!, is it you, Ladybug? Is it really you?" He was shaking.

She turned around, "Toby? Oh My Goddess! Toby!" They ran to each other and held on as if the other would disappear if they let go.

"Let me look at you, you were ten years old the last time I saw you." He hugged her again before looking at her belly. "You're pregnant, wait, are you the one they brought from the rogue cave?"

"I am," she said shyly.

"Mom and Dad, are they still alive?"

She became somber, "I have no idea, Toby. When I found my mate, Mom and Dad told me to go with him and be safe. I didn't want to leave them but they wouldn't take no for an answer. We've been searching for them. Arnold found us, he grabbed me and forced Jeremy to help him. He's threatened Jeremy with mine and the baby's lives if he didn't do his bidding."

"Ladybug, you are safe here, no one will harm you and I'm going to make sure your baby is delivered safely."

"Will you be in the delivery room with me if my mate can't be here?"

"Ladybug, I'm going to deliver the baby."

"You mean you'll help deliver the baby right?"

"No Ladybug, I'm going to deliver the baby. I'm the head doctor here."

Her eyes grew big, and she gave him another bear hug. "You are? I'm so proud of you. I know Mom and Dad would be too."

"Come on Ladybug, let's get you something healthy to eat. From what we were told you're due any day and I want some nutritious food in your belly for my future niece or nephew."

"Well, that was exciting," Brinley said, "but we do need to leave. We'll be in contact and Doc, let us know when labor starts and we'll try to get Jeremy here." The triplets held hands and disappeared.

## BRINLEY

We arrived back at Tate's packhouse, well I guess it's my packhouse now too, around 12:30 am. By the time we said our goodbyes to my parents, the pups, and Lydia, we were exhausted. We knew we needed to get back and debrief everyone on what happened and find out what happened with the meeting Arlene was at. When we aparated inside Tate's office, John was gone but Josh and Daniel were in there along with Tate.

He did not look happy. I walked over and kissed him, he grabbed me. "I'm so fucking happy you're back and nothing happened to you," he kissed me again.

"I love you too," I patted him on the chest as I pushed away from him with a giggle. "Where's John?"

"Arlene linked him, she and Diane are on their way back. He went for a 'run' to see if he could intercept them sneaking back onto pack lands. He had me take his place in here," Daniel said.

"Good idea, he's been spending the majority of his time in here and needed to get out," I muffled out through a yawn. I'm taking my mate and going to bed. I'm exhausted from today's and this evening's events, we can debrief in the morning. "Goodnight boys," I walked to my siblings and gave them each a hug and a kiss, "goodnight, love you both."

"Love you too," they said in unison. I grabbed Tate and we headed upstairs. As soon as my head hit the pillow, I was out like a light.

## ARLENE

It was 12:30 am, Diane and I were almost to pack lands so we stopped running and began to walk as quietly as possible. Well, me silently, her not so much. "How are you so quiet? I can't even hear you stepping on the ground, it's like you're floating or something," she asked in a hushed tone.

Damnit, I forgot to not be so quiet while walking, damn training. "Oh, well, I have brothers. They're way too protective of me so I had to learn to be as quiet as possible to sneak out of the house without waking them," I lied.

I could smell John, he was close. I stepped on a twig right after Diane did, she's like a bull in a china shop. She's so loud for someone wanting to be sneaky. A few seconds later, we came face to face with a brown wolf with white front paws, Clyde, John's wolf. I acted startled and grabbed Diane's arm, "do you know that wolf?" I whispered to her.

"No, I don't," she grabbed my arm back.

"Can you shift?" I asked with hesitation in my voice. Clyde shifted and I drew my breath in surprise, "It's you!" I said in amazement. He went behind a tree and found some clothes stashed in a duffle at the base and put on shorts.

"What are you ladies doing out this late and so close to the border?"

"We went for a walk."

Diane whispered in my ear, "Do you know who that is?"

"That's the guy I was telling you about," I whispered back to her.

"Really?" I nodded my head at her.

"You ladies shouldn't be out this far, not with rogues on the prowl. They could grab you and hurt you. I'll notify someone you're out here so you can be escorted back to your homes."

"No need Sir, we can get back on our own."

Diane leaned into me, "Girl, you need to work that magic, seduce him, and try to get him to talk about what's happening in Tate's office."

"Are you sure?"

"Yes!"

"On second thought, can you walk us to the packhouse, that's where I'm staying until Alpha Tate finds a place for me. We can escort Diane home, I can make it worth your while," I made a kissy face at him then brought my finger to my mouth in a seductive way."

"I, uh, guess I could do that," John said scratching his head, then adjusting himself in the shorts he was wearing. We walked Diane back to her house before heading to the packhouse until we reached our room. Only then did we drop the ruse. "Did you hear the link from Brinley? We're going to debrief in the morning."

"Sounds good to me, I'm tired, do you mind if we just go to sleep? That was a stressful meeting."

"Not at all, you did well tonight Princess. Get some rest and we'll talk with everyone tomorrow." I changed my clothes, climbed in bed, and snuggled close to John before falling asleep.

## ARNOLD

I got back to camp around 12:30 a.m. All was quiet when I got there. I looked around and everyone was sleeping, including those in the cave. I looked at the pups, I could've sworn there were more pups in there, but I would know if any were missing. I also thought I had five women in there until I remembered I put one on patrol, so all the women are accounted for as well. If the women I place on patrol died, no harm no foul. It's not like they'd be helpful in the attack anyway.

Women are weak creatures and have no business fighting. Take my mate for instance, she shouldn't have to worry about anything other than shopping and having babies. I plan on having her barefoot and pregnant every chance I get. I missed out on having siblings so I plan on having at least a dozen pups, regardless if Diane wants them or not. If she says no, I'll tie her up and keep fucking her until I put a pup in her and when that pup is born, I'll do it again until I'm done with her having pups. I own her body and will do what I want with it.

Patrols won't be changing for another thirty minutes so I went into the cave, turned my flashlight on, and looked at the patrol schedule my mate gave me. This is perfect, they're so fucking stupid, they haven't changed the scheduled shift change times. I compared it with the last schedule I was given. All these fuckers did was add someone to the patrols like a third person is going to stop me.

I stashed the schedule away and looked at the sky, quietly I said, "Mom, Emberly, I promise to avenge your deaths by killing Alpha Tate and taking over the pack. I'll make you both proud of me," I sighed. I found another rogue camp not too far from here so I'm going there tomorrow to see if I can get them to join my cause, if they don't, I'll just kill them. With that thought, I removed my clothes, changed into my wolf, curled up, and went to sleep with a clear conscience, nothing was going to stop me.

## BROOKLYN

It's been three days since we rescued those pups and Lydia. Jaxon and I have been training with Brin and the guys six hours every day ever since the arena was finished. She's getting stronger and surprisingly she's almost back to where she was before she delivered Cassie. "I'm so proud of you Sissy," I hugged her.

"Thanks, Sis. I've been working hard to get back what I've lost these last five years."

"Well, you'd never know you missed a day in training, Peanut, I think I need a massage," Erik rubbed his neck.

"Sorry Erik, I didn't mean to throw you so hard," Brinley grimaced.

All of a sudden Jaxon went still and looked over at us. "What is it?"

"Lydia's in labor, Mom just linked me."

"Oh shit! what time is it? I asked, I forgot to wear my watch today.

"9:00 pm, I'll see if Jeremy's able to get away," Brin said.

*"Jeremy, are you on patrol?"*

*"I am, we're training another wolf, he's on our side."*

*"Good to know, do you know where Arnold is?"*

*"He left a few hours ago and said something about trying to find more rogues to join his cause. Told us he'd be back tomorrow, why, what's going on?"*

*"Lydia's in labor, do you think you can get away?"*

*"Please, come get me."*

*"Can you get to the rock in five minutes?"*

*"I'll be there in two."*

*"Perfect, I'll send Jaxon."*

"Jaxon, Jeremy's going to be at the rock in two minutes, can you take him to Lydia?"

"I'll be back after she gives birth and I get Jeremy back to the cave. I hope she gives birth quickly."

"Me too Jaxy." We both hugged him and he was gone.

# CHAPTER 42 MEETING NOELLE

**ARNOLD**

I've been away from camp for a little over six hours. The first rogue camp I came to only had five rogues, they were all older, and not useful to me. I left them after taking some of the food they offered me. They told me about another rogue camp about ten miles away so I went there next. That was more useful. Some men and women, a few pups. I convinced the men to join me, I had to kill one of their women and two of their pups, but they saw the light eventually. Now they are under allegiance to me, mostly because I have one of their pups strapped to me and told them I'd make the pup an orphan if they didn't.

We went to another rogue camp about twenty miles from their camp. I did the same thing there. It's amazing how quickly they bend to my will when their women and pups are threatened. They don't know me at all, I'd do it just for the fun of it if I felt like it. No one can stop me now. I've gathered fifteen more men. I decided to stay away for a couple of days, so I could recruit a few more rogues and so far, it's paying off.

**TATE**

"Cupcake, are you finished training?"

"We just finished, what's up?"

"I know it's late but Cecil and Anabel want to meet with us, are you available to come to your office?"

"Let me get cleaned up and I'll be right there."

Thirty minutes later Brinley walked into her office, Cecil and Anabel were inside with me. I got up so she could sit in her chair. "Cecil, Anabel, why such a late meeting?"

"We wanted to let you know that Noelle just called, she'll be here tomorrow, we thought you should know." They looked at each other, then back at us. "We also wanted to know how things have been going with Maribel?"

"Thank you for informing us about Noelle's arrival. As for Maribel, she has continued to do things and say things to Brinley and we don't see it stopping anytime soon. Brinley has already decided she will be put to death. We will give her the liberty to see Noelle one last time. Do you have any questions regarding this?"

"Yes, we do. Will Maribel be put to death immediately or will this be done traditionally?"

"She will be told what her charges are and who Brinley is to me and this pack. Then it will be done traditionally."

"We understand and have come to terms with this. We don't know where we went wrong in raising her and we're sorry it has come to this. Thank you for your time, Alpha, Luna," they bowed and left Brin's office.

The next morning Adam linked *"Alpha?"*

*"Yes?"*

*"Thought I'd let you know Noelle Wood just arrived, she's being escorted to the packhouse."*

*"Thanks, Adam, Brinley and I will be down in a minute."*

"Cupcake, time to wake up and get dressed. Noelle just passed through the gates, she'll be at the packhouse in ten minutes. We need to get up and get dressed."

"What time is it?"

"8:00 am."

She rolled over and groaned. "Okay, let's get this day started."

We made our way down to the front door just as Noelle's car pulled up front. Brooklyn, Benjamin, Quincy, Brinley, and I were waiting on the steps. Jaxon was still at his pack, otherwise, he would've been here too. Noelle climbed out of the car and ran to me. She jumped in my arms and I twirled her around. I heard Brinley growl, *"Would you stop, she's like a little sister to me and she's been in college for a few years. I'm happy she's safely home."*

*"That wasn't me, that was Amanda growling,"* she giggled.

I set her down, "Noelle, this is Brinley, my mate, and Luna."

"What? Tater Tot, you found your second chance mate! Wait, did you say Luna?"

"I did. I challenged Alpha Frederick to the death, and here I am."

"I've been gone a long time, neither my parents, sister, or anyone else told me about this. I'm shocked and was wondering why you were greeting me instead of Alpha Frederick."

Brinley looked at me, 'Tater Tot?' I blushed.

"Yeah, Tater Tot. He used to eat them every chance he got growing up and that's when I started calling him that. He ate them so often, the kitchen had a hard time keeping them in stock. I always teased him and said he'd turn into one," she laughed.

"Oh, I think I'm going to like her," Brin whispered in my ear.

"This is Brooklyn, Brinley's twin sister, they are triplets but their brother is back at their parents' pack right now. Do you remember Benjamin and Quincy? They are my Beta's."

"I do, how have you been?"

"We've been great, we heard you graduated from college. Are you ready to come back here and help in the clinic?"

"I am. I'm so happy to be back and can't wait to see everyone."

"This is Max and you know Doc Stevens, they are mates and my gammas."

"Doc Stevens it's good to see you again. Max, it's nice to meet you."

"I'm so excited to have you home, it will be nice working with you in the clinic."

"It's nice to meet you, I look forward to getting to know you better since you'll be working with my mate." Max smiled at her.

"Let's get inside, you're parents and sister will be here soon and we need to fill you in on a few things before they get here."

"Oooh sounds ominous," she giggled. When she realized we weren't laughing she looked at me, "Oh hell, what the fuck did Maribel do now," she shook her head.

We went to Brinley's office, closed the door, and filled her in on all the shit Maribel's been doing since Brinley's arrival in the pack.

"I can't believe she did all that shit, okay it's my sister, maybe I can. Luna, I'm so sorry you had to go through all that. I know the consequences of what she's done and I'm assuming you'll bring all her infractions and criminal acts toward you to her attention? I'm also assuming she'll be put to death because of it."

"You assume correctly Noelle," Brinley said. "Your sister also found her mate, he happens to be one of my very best friends. He rejected her because of her actions against me and Tate and we've been keeping our mate bond a secret from her."

"I'm not going to ask why, I can figure that out myself. My sister has been a thorn in my side ever since I can remember. She drives me crazy and I've enjoyed my time away. I have a secret of my own. I've been making excuses to stay at college to help my professors so I could postpone my return. I didn't want to deal with Maribel," she shrugged.

There was a knock on the office door. I walked over and opened it. Cecil, Anabel, and Maribel rushed in and engulfed Noelle in a hug. "Can't breathe," Noelle tapped them on their backs.

"Sorry Baby Girl," Cecil said to her.

"Hey, Little Sis it's so good to have you back. I can't wait to catch up with you, I have missed you so much. You're a big veterinarian now, what are you going to do now that you're home?"

"I'm going to help Doc Stevens in the clinic. I kept it a secret, but I double majored in human medicine and veterinary medicine. This way I can help whether the pack members are in human or wolf forms."

"That's wonderful!" Anabel embraced her, kissing her on the head. "We were going to have a surprise party for you, but you kept postponing your return and we didn't have enough time to get your party set up."

"That's okay Mom, we can have a party this weekend. It's only a couple of days away, this will give us time to decorate and get food made," Noelle said.

"Alpha Tate. do you mind if we take our daughters home and visit for a little while?"

"That's fine but Brinley and I will need you, Anabel, and Maribel, to come back to the office around 3:00 pm. Noelle, you are welcome to join us if you'd like."

"Thank you Alpha Tater Tot, I think I'd like to be a part of that meeting."

"Go and enjoy your family and we'll see you this afternoon."

On the way out of the office, Maribel turned around and flipped off Brinley, mouthing the words 'bitch' as she slammed the door shut behind her. "I cannot wait to give her what she has coming to her and the best part, she has no idea what's in store for her," Brinley mumbled.

"Come on Cupcake, we need to go to my office to discuss Diane's treasons. Her actions will end up with her in the same position as Maribel, the only difference is we haven't breathed a word of this to her parents and we need to have that talk with them first."

"That's not going to be fun," she grimaced.

"No, it's not. That's why we needed to have as much proof as possible of her treason, with her parents being former gammas they will know the laws forward and backward. I can see them trying to stop her execution but they won't be able to once they see the mounting evidence we have against her."

"Who's going to execute her and how are we going to do that?"

"That's a great question and one we need to figure out."

## BRINLEY

We met our core group in Tate's office, we needed to find out if Arnold was still gone and to discuss Diane's treason. Jaxon still hasn't returned Jeremy to the camp, so I linked him and asked what was going on.

*"Jaxy, why hasn't Jeremy returned to his camp yet?"*

*"Lydia just had the baby yesterday morning, we decided to give them until this afternoon to be together. Josh told me Arnold hasn't returned yet so I know we have a little time. I will be returning him in a couple of hours though."*

*"Okay, I wanted to make sure because we haven't heard from you."*

*"Yeah, sorry about that. Mom needed help with the babies since Lydia wasn't there. They won't let anyone else touch them, they somehow bonded to Mom, Dad, and I."*

*"That's so sweet. How is Lydia? What did she have and did they let Grayson help name the baby?"*

*"Lydia and the baby are doing well. Her labor and delivery went without any complications. Doc Carter is beside himself and is enamored with his niece."*

*"That's wonderful to hear, I'm so glad they were reunited. She had a girl! What did they name her?"*

*"Samantha Brinley."*

*"They gave her my name?"*

*"They did, they said it was in honor of you helping them."*

*"That is so sweet."*

*"Grayson wanted to call the baby Sam, he said it could be for a boy or a girl. They decided if the baby was a boy, he'd be Samuel, and if a girl Samantha. Grayson's in love with her already. He's always asking to hold her and refers to her as his sister. I have a feeling when this whole rogue situation is*

*over, Jeremy and Lydia will be adopting him. Oh, one more thing, they asked Mom and Dad if they could join the pack."*

*"They did? What'd they tell them."*

*"They told them yes since you scanned them already."*

*"Has Doc gotten any blood work back yet?"*

*"Nope, he's been busy tending to Lydia and the baby but hopes to get it completed in the next couple of days. The blood he drew is still good, he's kept it cold."*

*"That's good to hear. We'll see you when you get back Jaxy. I love you."*

*"I love you too Baby Sis."*

"Lydia had her baby girl yesterday, they named her Samantha Brinley. She and the baby are doing well and it sounds like Grayson hasn't left her side since she was born. Jax says he's referring to her as his sister."

"That is the sweetest thing I've ever heard," Brooklyn, Quinn, and Crystal said in unison.

"They let Grayson name her and said he wanted to name the baby Sam regardless of the gender. I think that was the sweetest gesture, they are smitten with him and the baby. Jax also said he will be taking Jeremy back to the camp in a couple of hours."

"Uh, Brin," Josh piped up, "you might want to get him to do that now." He turned on a speaker.

"Hi Arnie, I miss you so much, when can I see you again?"

"Tonight Buttercup, I'll be back at my camp in about twenty minutes. I was able to recruit thirty more rogues."

"What's our final total on fighting wolves now?"

"If my calculations are correct we're at a hundred and five. I need to let you go, when I get back to camp, I need to let Jeremy and Francis know they have more recruits they need to bring up to speed. I love you Buttercup, it won't be much longer before I'll be able to avenge my mom's death and kill Alpha Tate for letting my sister die. Then I'll be able to fully claim you and announce you as the next Luna of Black Diamond. I'll be able to take my birthright as Alpha."

"I'm so excited to finally be your Luna. My first act is to make Maribel my beta and Arlene my gamma."

"I like your plan. I'll see you tonight." The phone call disconnected.

## TATE

"What... the fuck... was that!?"

"That," Josh said, "was a call we intercepted between Diane and Arnold."

"Please tell me you recorded that fucking call."

Josh smiled, "we've recorded all their calls, this one, just gave us the ammo we needed to sink the nails in Diane's coffin."

"I want to know why he thinks he's the rightful alpha of this pack and what the hell happened to his mom and who the fuck his sister is." I was pissed and I could feel Chase close to the surface. "Brin, get Jaxon to take Jeremy back to camp immediately."

"I already did," Jax said, popping up in the office. "Brin opened the link to me and Jeremy as soon as she realized what you guys were listening to."

"The good thing about this, since they aren't fully mated, when we kill Diane, he won't feel it," I said with disdain seeping through my voice.

"Ben? Brin and I have a meeting with Maribel and her family this afternoon at 3:00 pm, it's 11:00 am now, can you let the Christopherson's know I need to speak with them in the Luna's office at noon? I also want Elder Myles and Councilwoman Brenda in attendance along with the treason evidence we have against Diane."

"Yes, Alpha, if you'll excuse me," Ben said, reaching for the door.

"Beta?"

"Yes, Alpha?"

"You are under alpha command, do not tell them why I need to see them, and use your beta command if you need to."

"Yes Alpha, anything else?"

"No, you may be excused."

## BENJAMIN

My first stop was Brinley's office to call Elder Myles and Councilwoman Brenda. I made sure the door was locked before placing the calls. Every pack has an elder and those elders speak directly to the council. On occasion, like this one, we can reach out directly to the council, and that's what I'm doing now. I called Elder Myles first though, more out of respect than anything.

"Elder Myles speaking, how may I help you?"

"Elder Myles, this is Beta Benjamin."

"Oh, yes, Beta Benjamin, how can I be of assistance?"

"Alpha Tate has requested to speak with you at noon today, the meeting will be held in the Luna's office. I know it's short notice but this is a very urgent matter."

"May I ask what the meeting is in regards to?"

"I'm sorry Sir, I'm under alpha command, I can't say."

"If that's the case then this must be of the utmost importance."

"It is Sir."

"Let him know I will be there."

"Thank you, Sir." My next call was to Councilwoman Brenda.

"Hello, this is Brenda."

"Councilwoman Brenda, this is Beta Benjamin, from Black Diamond."

"Oh, hello Beta Benjamin, how can I help you?"

"I'm sorry this is such short notice but Alpha Tate is requesting your presence at an urgent meeting he's having at noon today. The meeting will be held in the Luna's office. I'm under alpha command so I'm not able to tell you the details of the meeting, he will explain when you arrive."

"I see, have you notified your elder?"

"I have and he will be meeting us as well."

"I will see you at noon, please let your alpha know."

"Thank you, Councilwoman, I will inform him."

Now, I need to go see the Christopherson's, this is not going to be pleasant. They don't deserve this, they are good people. This is going to crush them. I calmed my heart the best I could before walking to their home. I would link them, but they deserve the formality of this. Diane was seen going over to Cecil and Anabel's home. Most likely to welcome Noelle home, so I knew it was safe to do this in person even though it's going to be very difficult. I knocked on their front door and Wilma answered.

"Hello Beta, I'm sure you're here to see Carl, why don't you come in and I'll get him for you," she said as she opened the door more for me.

"Thank you, Wilma, but I'm here to see both of you."

"Well in that case I'll link him."

*"Carl, Beta Benjamin is here, he needs to speak with both of us."*

*"Let him know I'll be down in a minute."*

"He'll be down in a minute."

"Thank you." I looked at my watch and it was already 11:30. *"Hey Tate, I'm going to have Carl and Wilma come for the meeting at 12:30, that way you'll have thirty minutes to speak with the elder and councilwoman before bringing Diane's parents into this."*

*"Thanks, Ben, that's a good idea."*

Carl finally made his way downstairs. "Hi Beta, what brings you to our home?" Carl stretched his hand out and we shook hands.

"I'm afraid I need to request your presence for an urgent and private matter with Alpha Tate. I'm unable to say what it's regarding as I'm under alpha command."

"Oh my, this must be serious if you're being commanded to not speak about it."

"It is a very serious matter. He will expect the both of you by 12:30 pm sharp this afternoon. Please do not say a word to Diane."

"But she should know where we're going to be."

"I'm sorry, alpha's orders, you are not to tell anyone of this meeting and I have been permitted to use my beta command if you choose not to follow it."

"No need, she is over at Cecil and Anabel's anyway, she probably won't be home for several hours. Please let Alpha Tate know we will be there."

"I will pass it along to him. I must go as I have another meeting to get to in fifteen minutes. Again I apologize for the inconvenience." I left their home and went back to the packhouse and straight to Brinley's office.

# CHAPTER 43 PUNISHMENTS

**TATE**

Brin, John, and I were in Brin's office when Ben walked in, "Is everyone coming?"

"Yes, Elder Myles and Councilwoman Brenda should be here any minute and Carl and Wilma will be here at 12:30 pm. Diane is at Maribel's."

Five minutes later Ben answered the door letting Elder Myles, and Councilwoman Brenda in. "Thank you for coming on such short notice." I shook their hands. "First and foremost, I would like to officially introduce you to my mate and Luna, Brinley Jameson, and her head of IT, John. They are both from Winter Moon."

"It's nice to meet you." They both said as they shook Brin and John's hands. "Alpha Tate, we hadn't received word you found your fated mate," Councilwoman Brenda sounded surprised.

"Sorry ma'am, we've had other, more pressing matters going on."

"It's fine, but we need to make this official before too long."

I didn't comment on her statement because of our situation, and they didn't need to know the Moon Goddess already blessed us. "The reason I called you here and why John is joining us is because Diane Christopherson is committing treason towards our pack."

Both their mouths were gaped open. "What did you just say?"

"She's committing treason. We have proof of this, and her parents will be here in thirty minutes to discuss this. Diane isn't aware that we know. The other reason you're here is that another pack member, the eldest daughter of our former beta, Maribel, has committed acts of crime against my mate."

"I think I need to sit down," Councilwoman Brenda said.

"Councilwoman Brenda..."

She held her hand up, "Please, just call me Brenda, there is no need for formalities when no one else is present."

"Yes ma'am. John, please tell them what Diane Christopherson has done to commit treason."

"Brenda, Elder Myles, to make a long story short, Brinley came here to heal from a tragedy that affected her tremendously. Shortly after she arrived, there was a rogue attack on the pack. Out of concern for their daughter, Alpha and Luna Winter sent a crew of their warriors to set up surveillance to keep their daughter safe. In doing so, we set up CCTV and sensors around the pack, both inside and outside of the border. We were able to capture one of the rogues who attacked us and we got vital information out of him before he was killed. With that information, we were able to locate where they were hiding and installed cameras and mics."

"John, how does this prove treason?" Elder Myles asked.

"I'm getting to that Sir, I just needed to set the scene."

"Continue then, I'm sorry for the interruption."

"One evening my head of surveillance and I noticed someone leaving pack lands at an odd hour. She was dressed in black and kept checking to see if anyone was following her. We watched her for a couple of days before discovering who it was. Her behavior seemed off to us so we decided to bug her bedroom and put sensors in there to see if we could confirm a few things. We also sent my mate undercover to see what she could find out."

"We discovered she is mated to Arnold, the self-proclaimed "alpha" of this rogue pack. She's been sneaking into the guard shed at the gate, making a copy of the patrol schedule, and giving it to him. He plans on killing Alpha Tate then taking over as Alpha and making her the Luna. They have both spoken openly about it and she has named Maribel Wood as her future beta and my mate as her future gamma. She's planning on taking herself, Maribel, and my mate to safety right before Arnold attacks. He's planning his attack around 2:00 in the morning so they won't be caught in the crosshairs of the attack."

"Wait, can we backtrack a second," Brenda asked. "Do you know why this rogue is focusing on this pack and not on other packs?"

"We do, we're not sure what it all means, we're still figuring that out. He said he's getting revenge for his mom's death and wants to kill Tate for allowing his sister to be murdered when he was supposed to protect her. Like I said, we're not sure what he's talking about but we're hoping we can capture him and find out before killing him."

"I see, and how do you plan on capturing him?"

"We are planning a counterattack before he steps foot over the border of this pack."

"Thank you, you may continue."

"This brings us to Maribel Wood. Maribel has committed criminal acts against the future Luna of this pack and Diane has assisted her in those crimes. Before you ask, she does not know Brinley is the Luna, nor does she know Tate and Brinley are fully mated to each other either. They have hid this fact from her and very well I might add. Maribel has been began aggressively towards Brinley the moment she arrived."

"She ransacked the room Brinley was staying in, destroyed her personal belongings, impersonated a Luna, and said she was mated to Alpha Tate. She's physically harmed her on multiple occasions, one of which was when they were locked in the bunker during the rogue attack. Maribel's actual fated mate, who happens to be one of Brinley's best friends and security detail team members, rejected her because of how she was treating Brinley. When Alpha and Luna Winter came for a visit,

Maribel treated them with disregard, even though they were hiding their auras as well."

"May we ask why they were all hiding their auras?" Elder Myles asked.

"We thought it was the best thing at the time. Brinley wanted to be treated as a regular she-wolf which legally she can do when visiting another pack. When the Alpha and Luna arrived, Maribel was being cruel to Brinley. They wanted to see for themselves so they hid their auras and instructed their pack members, who were in our pack at the time, to treat them like a regular pack member. They witnessed firsthand what Maribel has done to her."

"I see, that would make sense. I'm assuming you wanted us here to help decide or at least approve of their punishment?" Brenda asked.

"Yes ma'am, we would like to proceed with the death penalty for both of them. Since it's well within our right to do so considering they have not only endangered our pack but also attacked their luna."

"You have the blessing of the council to proceed how you see fit, Alpha Tate. I will inform them, but please understand, that Elder Myles and myself or one of the other council members may need to witness the judgment and execution."

"I understand, ma'am."

"The other reason your attendance was requested, we have a meeting at 12:30 with Carl and Wilma, Diane's parents. They should be here in a few minutes. As far as we know, they have no idea their daughter is committing treason. We're going to enlighten them and see how they react. After speaking with them, we will bring Diane into the meeting."

"Tate will have an alpha command in place so they cannot link anyone while we're in this meeting as well, on the off chance any of them try to contact Maribel."

"Won't she try to warn her mate?" Elder Myles asked.

"No Sir, they are not fully mated to each other so he won't even know she's been executed."

"But won't he want to meet with her one last time before he attacks your pack?"

"No, from conversations we've intercepted and what John's mate has reported back, they don't plan on speaking again until after the attack."

"I see. Well, that is in your favor then."

Before we met with the Christopherson's, Brin and I talked about her tapping into their emotions, checking for deception. This was of utmost importance considering the acts that were committed against her and the degree of punishment they held. There was a knock at the door, Ben opened it and let Carl and Wilma inside. I looked at Brin right before they entered, she looked lost in thought but seemed to recover pretty quickly once they entered the office. "Carl, Wilma, please come in."

"Thank you, Alpha."

"Before we tell you why you are here, I want to let you know your link has been blocked from anyone outside of this office." They gave me a strange look but I didn't acknowledge it. "You already know Elder Myles and Councilwoman Brenda, this is John and Brinley, they are guests in our pack, for now." I didn't disclose she was my mate, that will be disclosed if needed.

"Hello, it's nice to meet both of you," Carl said.

Brin linked me, *"they're nervous."*

"You are probably wondering why we called you here?"

"We are, it's very odd you'd call us for a meeting and then block our link to others," Carl stated.

"There is a reason for this and I'm not quite sure how to bring this up so I'm going to just rip off the bandaid and we can go from there."

"Alpha Tate, you're scaring me, please tell us what this is regarding," Wilma said.

*"She's telling the truth."*

"My intention is not to scare you, however, we have evidence of Diane committing treason against this pack," I stated matter of factly. Carl jumped out of his chair so angrily that his chair slid across the floor. Wilma is trembling, trying to hold back her tears but not succeeding.

"What the fuck... did you just say!?" he screamed at me. "How dare you accuse MY CHILD of such a heinous crime!"

"I won't believe you until I can see it myself. What kind of evidence do you have!?" Carl was pissed, it's understandable, I would be too. Wilma looked like she was going to faint but she needed to hear it as much as Carl does.

"If you calm down Carl, we can show you," John said as Carl looked at Wilma again.

"Can I at least have Wilma go somewhere else, she's in no condition to be hearing this."

"I'm sorry Carl, she must stay in this office, she needs to hear and see this as much as you do."

"I... I can't bear to see anything against my daughter, she's a good girl, she would never do anything like this," Wilma cried out.

*"Hmmm, interesting."*

*"What's interesting?"*

*"She's lying, about what, I don't know. I think she knows more than we think she does."*

"Wilma, why don't you believe she would never do anything like this?"

"She's my daughter, Alpha, she tells me everything, she can't hide things from me."

*"Keep questioning her then show the evidence, I'm curious about something."*

*"Curious about what?"*

*"That's what I'm trying to figure out, something is off."*

"Carl, Wilma, we need you to watch and listen."

"I can't be in here when you play it," Wilma said.

*"She's telling the truth, she's scared, but I know she's hiding something"*

"I'm sorry, you can't leave no matter how uncomfortable this makes you."

"Honey, it will be okay, we'll get through this together," Carl said, rubbing Wilma's back.

*"He's telling the truth and he's very concerned."*

Her eyes darkened, "I need to see MY DAUGHTER!, DO NOT tell me everything will be okay!"

Brin was intently watching Carl and Wilma's reactions.

*"What are you up to?"*

*"Do you trust me, Tate?"*

*"With my life, my love."*

"Wilma, can I ask you what kind of a child Diane was?" Brinley asked her.

"What does that have to do with anything?"

"A lot. I'm just wondering if she came to you with only the good things, the bad things, or if it was a mix of things."

"Diane comes to me with everything in her life. We have no secrets, she trusts me explicitly. She's only ever hidden things from her dad, never me."

*"It's odd she would be dishonest with Carl but not Wilma."*

"So what I hear you saying is she never did or does anything without you knowing, she talks with you about everything going on in her life."

"Yes, I know everything that child does."

*"She's telling the truth."*

"How many times does she hang out with Maribel?"

"I don't understand why you are questioning my mate, Brinley."

"Carl, I'm a visitor in this pack, I'm just trying to get an understanding of Diane."

"Fine, but don't cross the line."

"Again how often does she hang out with Maribel?"

"All the time, they're always together, they're best friends and have been their entire lives."

"How often does she leave pack lands?"

"A few times a week."

"When did that start?"

"About five or six weeks ago."

"Not before?"

"No."

"How long has she been seeing Arnold?"

"About the same time," she slapped her hand over her mouth.

*"Gotcha."*

"What would you say if I told you we bugged her room?"

"I'd say you're lying."

*"Tate, something isn't sitting well with me about her. She hiding something and doesn't want us to know what it is. I could look into her memories, she wouldn't know."*

*"Let's wait for now and if you feel you still need to look into her memories then you may do so."*

"John, will you please play the videos and voice recordings you have."

"Yes, Alpha."

## WILMA

While the videos and voice recordings are playing, I'm lost in my thoughts. I'm getting irritated with this Brinley girl and her goody-toeshoe ways. She has no fucking idea what she's getting herself into. She is exactly how Diane told me she was. She needs to leave this pack and let things get back to normal. Everything was falling in place and now, I have a lot of shit to fix.

That goddess damned insolent daughter of mine. I told her to be careful when sneaking off pack lands, I couldn't have her father finding out what she was up to. He would reject me the first chance he got and would disown Diane and I can't have that. It's bad enough he gave up our gamma title after Tate took over. I worked hard to get a ranked member to take me as a mate. Slipping that little bit of wolfsbane in his drink that one night about twenty-six years ago, just enough for him to be out of it but not enough to completely fall asleep. I needed a ranked wolf to take responsibility for my stupidity in getting pregnant by another wolf.

The alpha and beta already had mates, but Carl, Carl didn't so I set my sights on him. I managed to get him to bed, stripped both our clothes off, sucked him off and when he was about to cum, I slid his cock into me making him cum inside me. When he woke up, he'd smell his scent inside me, not knowing the baby wasn't his. When he woke up in the morning, I was lying next to him, naked. He rolled over and looked at me, I put on my best innocent face and he kissed me, still a little woozy from the wolfsbane.

He fucked me again and as his cum spilled inside me, I enticed him to mark and claim me. He marked me but that was it. I marked him back and verbally claimed and accepted him as my mate. He never claimed me back though and that's angered me ever since. But I've had to learn to live with it. For the most part, he's been a very doting mate and I've fallen in love with him over the years. I'm pretty sure he's fallen in love with me too. We never had a child together, so Diane is it.

He never found out she wasn't his. I know who her real father is, he was my fated mate but he wasn't a ranked wolf and he wasn't from this pack. I never looked back except a few years after Diane was born, Carl ran into his fated mate. Since he never claimed me, he felt the mate pull to this woman. I saw the gleam in his eyes when he was talking with her and I knew I had to do something so I killed her. He has no idea I did that either and it will stay that way if I have anything to say about it.

Yes, I know who Arnold is. He's the son of my best friend. She was banished from the pack, I don't know why, I just know she was there one day and gone the next. I was able to find her and we stayed in touch. I brought her updates about the pack and pictures when I could. When Emberly was born, I told her and gave her pictures of her growing up. She always wanted to know about the pups, especially Emberly, it's like she had a weird obsession with her.

I've never actually met Arnold, I know of him. I know she was always so proud of him and the man he was becoming. I reached out to him several years ago. My goal at the time was to have him become my daughter's mate for two reasons, one: he's my best friend's son, and two: he's going to kill Tate and become alpha. When Diane told me she found her mate and what his name was, I was ecstatic because my plan worked better than I could have imagined. I could have a piece of my best friend back and my daughter will become Luna. Carl brought me back from my thoughts, and I didn't hear or see anything they showed us.

## CARL

I'm so angry, my poor mate is just a shell inside herself. I can't even imagine what must be going through her head right now. I know she's going to fall apart at any moment. I can't believe my daughter did all those things. "Sweetheart, are you okay?" I jostled her out of her thoughts.

"Hmmm, what Honey?"

"I asked if you were okay."

"I'm not, I need to talk with our daughter and find out what she's been thinking. This is so unbecoming of her and so out of character."

"I know Sweetheart but they have her on surveillance, there is no disputing this."

## BRINLEY

I walked over to Wilma. I know something is up with her and I intend to find out what it is. "Wilma," I hugged her so I could place my hands on her even though I didn't need to touch her to do this. "I'm so sorry this had to be brought to your attention like this."

"Thank you, Brinley. I don't understand why she would do this." She pushed out some tears and sniffles.

*"She's forcing her tears."*

"We'll be here if you need to talk, however, you must know, she will be put to death due to her treasons." She stiffened in my arms but tried to play it off with crying. While I had her in my embrace, I scanned her memories and what I found horrified me.

"Mr. and Mrs. Christopherson, if you'll excuse us for a minute while we mind link," Brenda had a stern look on her face when she spoke with them.

*"What are your thoughts?"*

*"Wilma knows more than she's saying and I think Carl is in the dark and doesn't have a clue what's been happening."*

*"How do you know this Brinley?"*

*"By her answers, did you see and hear how she was answering them?"*

*"We did, and we feel she's just as guilty as her daughter,"* Brenda said.

*"I want them both executed, if we let her go, she will run and we can't have that,"* I told them.

*"I agree with Councilwoman Brenda,"* Elder Myles said.

*"If this is the decision then they will both be put to death."*

*"Would you mind if I spoke directly to her first, I want to confirm what she knows. I would just ask you and Elder Myles to step out for a moment while I do."*

*"I don't have an issue with that if you don't,"* Brenda looked at Elder Myles.

*"I have no issues with it."*

*"We will wait outside, let us know when we can come back in."*

# CHAPTER 44 REJECTION

**BRINLEY**

After they stepped out of the office we closed and locked the door behind them, I turned around and set my sights on Wilma and Carl. "I'm going to ask a series of questions, and I will expect the truth, don't try to fool me either, I will know if you are lying to me."

"Carl, I will start with you."

"What's Diane's full name?"

"Diane Elizabeth Christopherson."

"How old is she?"

"Twenty-five"

"Is Wilma your fated mate or chosen mate?"

"Chosen."

"Why do you have a chosen mate instead of your fated mate?"

"I had a night of drinking and must've gotten a little tipsy, I woke up with Wilma in my bed one morning and a week later she told me she was pregnant."

"How long did it take you and your wolf to accept her as your mate?"

"About two years."

"Try again."

His eyes got wide, "about ten years."

"Last chance, please be honest, you won't like the results if you're not. How long did it take you and your wolf to accept her as your mate?"

He looked at Wilma then back to me, "Never, my wolf and I have never accepted her as our mate. He hardly accepts Diane as his pup and I don't know why. I'm assuming it's because she's always back talking and not doing as I ask her."

"Thank you for answering truthfully."

"Do you know anything about Diane's treasons or was this the first you heard of it?"

"This was the first I heard of it."

"I don't have any more questions for you."

"Wilma, you're turn."

"This is so stupid and uncalled for."

"I'm sorry, but I need to ask these questions. Who was Diane named after?"

"My mother."

"Where is your fated mate?"

"I don't know, I never met him."

"Try again."

"I'm not lying to you, you fucking bitch," her true colors were coming out.

"You are lying so tell the fucking truth or I'll check for it myself!"

"I don't need to tell you shit, I know the truth!"

"And what truth is that, Wilma!"

"You low-life piece of shit, my daughter was correct about you. You ruined EVERYTHING! If you hadn't shown up here, my daughter would've become the next Luna of this goddess-forsaken pack and I would've become the mother of the Luna! Now that's ruined because of YOU! I set my daughter up with Arnold, low and behold, they were fated mates! My best friend was his mother! I knew he was a rogue, I wanted better for my daughter. I wanted her mate to be a ranked wolf just like I made Carl choose me!"

I glanced at Carl and his mouth fell open. "What the hell are you talking about, 'you made me choose you' Wilma!" Carl yelled at her.

"Diane's real dad wasn't good enough for me, or her, so I had him killed. I made a deal with Arnold, I told him Diane and I would help him defeat the pack if he'd make Diane his Luna. He agreed, so we devised a plan. I found out he had a personal vendetta against Tate. I didn't care what the hell he did as long as MY daughter became his Luna." She was so pissed off, I don't think she realized what she said.

Carl was fuming and about to say something when I linked him. *"Now's not the time or place if you're going to do what I think you are. Can you hold it together for a little longer?"*

*"How are you linking me right now, you're not even a part of this pack."*

*"That is not important. We need to deal with the mess Wilma and Diane have caused first so hold it together."*

"What vendetta does Arnold have against Alpha Tate?"

"I don't fucking know, bitch."

*"Hmmm, she doesn't know"*

"Did you know we bugged Diane's room?"

"No, I would've found them and destroyed them," she glared at me.

"Did you know Carl's wolf never accepted you?"

"No, I thought he had it makes sense why we never had children together!"

"Did you know or ever meet Carl's fated mate?"

"I'm not answering that question."

"You will or you will be commanded to do so. I'll ask again, did you know or ever meet Carl's fated mate?"

She wrung her hands and moved further away from Carl. "I have seen her before. A few years after Diane was born. Carl was talking with her, I saw how he looked at her and wished he'd looked at me that way," she was gritting her teeth.

"Did you see her after Carl saw her?"

"Please don't make me answer that," she teared up.

"Did you see her after that?"

"Yes," she lowered her head.

"Where did you last see her?"

"I don't think she was from around here."

"Not what I asked."

"I followed her one day when I saw she was alone, I killed her so he would never again go to her."

"Ben, can you bring Elder Myles and Councilwoman Brenda back in, please?" He opened the door for them. "Elder Myles, Councilwoman Brenda, we can proceed with the sentencing of Wilma Christopherson. She is guilty of two murders and helping Diane commit treason."

"We will need proof of her confession," Brenda said. I walked over to them and touched my hand to their heads pushing the conversations we had with Carl and Wilma into them. "Very well, Wilma, we regret to inform you, that you will be put to death as an accomplice in committing treason toward the Black Diamond Pack. You will be remanded into custody in the Black Diamond Pack dungeon cells until your execution."

"You can't fucking do this to me! I'm the gamma female of this pack! Carl, say something!"

"You want me to say something! My life has been a lie for the last twenty-six years! You stole my life, you lied to me, you killed my fated mate! You made me believe that good-for-nothing, worthless, selfish bitch of a daughter was mine! You deserve EVERYTHING you have coming to you!" He turned around heading to the door.

"Carl, you have to believe me. I didn't do any of this on purpose, I love you, my wolf loves you!" Wilma was hysterically crying.

Carl stopped in his tracks, turned around, and stalked back to her. He glared at her, "I, Carl Exzavior Christopherson, former gamma of the Black Diamond Pack, reject you, Wilma Michelle Christopherson, former gamma of the Black Diamond Pack, as my mate and wife!"

She fell to the ground and clutched her chest. "You can't do this to me, Carl!"

"I can and I did, now, accept the rejection before I ask Alpha Tate to command you to!"

"I'm not accepting it! You can't make me!"

In a calm voice, he turned to Tate, "Alpha Tate, will you please command this woman to accept the rejection?"

Tate looked at Wilma and with his alpha voice said, "Wilma, Carl has rejected you, as your Alpha, I command you to accept it."

She looked horrified, "I... I..." she was crying while trying to fight the command. "I, Wilma Michelle Christopherson, former gamma of the Black Diamond pack, accept your rejection, Carl Exzavior Christopherson, as your mate and wife." She let out a loud howl, fell to the ground, and cried.

*"Jaxon or Brooklyn, can one of you come to my office? We need Wilma Christopherson aparated to the dungeons and locked in the cells."*

*"I can do it, Jax is still at Mom and Dad's."*

*"Thank you Brooky, you'll need to come to the door though, the elder and councilwoman are with us. You might want to bring one of the boys with you just to make it look good."*

*"I understand Sis, see you in a minute."* A couple of minutes later, there was a knock on my office door.

"Brooklyn, Erik, can you escort Wilma to the dungeons please."

"We can do that."

"Thank you. *Once you're away from the office, you can apparate her into a cell. Make sure she is in a solitary confinement cell. I'm not taking any chances of her getting out.*"

*"You got it."*

I walked out of the office behind Carl. "Carl, I'm so sorry you had to witness all that."

"I needed to hear it and I'm glad I did. I always felt something was off and now I know what it was. She has put on a good disguise all these years. If you'll excuse me, I think I need to have a few moments."

"Carl, before you go, we will be speaking with Diane next. Do you want to be a part of that meeting?"

"I think so, I don't want to, but I think I should," he turned to walk away.

"Alright, please be back to my office in ten minutes."

He stopped in his tracks, "your office?"

"Yes, Carl, my office, I'm Tate's mate."

"Oh... my... goddess, you're my Luna."

I giggled, "I am, please don't say anything to anyone and treat me as a regular she-wolf."

"Don't worry, my lips are sealed, your secret is safe with me."

After he left, I headed to the dining room to grab some food for me and Tate before our next meeting. We still have the Wood family to meet with after Diane's meeting but I don't think I can handle another meeting after hers. I need to talk with Tate to see if we can postpone the meeting their meeting. I need to shift and train and I can feel Amanda getting restless.

*"I'm not getting restless, I AM restless. I feel like I haven't shifted in forever. I need to get out and I want to shift with my mate,"* Amanda sounded grouchy.

*"Andi, why are you being so grouchy?"*

*"Oh, I don't know. It might have something to do with getting tired of not being able to punch Maribel and Diane in the face. Especially after hearing what Diane and her mom were up to."*

*"I understand, I'll check with Tate and hopefully we can reschedule."*

## BENJAMIN

All these years I've known the Christopherson's, I've never known Wilma to have a mean bone in her body. She had us all fooled. To find out she's been assisting Arnold all these years, I can't wrap my head around it. I need to push my disgust for her aside. We have Diane to contend with next then Maribel and her family.

Not sure how we're going to handle her, we need to keep her alive long enough for Arnold not to get suspicious of us. Especially since he changed his time frame from two weeks to two months. We have a little bit more time before Diane is brought into the office.

I headed down to the dining hall to grab some food for me and Q and ran into Brin. She looked like she was arguing with her wolf. "Brin," I tapped her on her shoulder.

"Yeah?"

"Is everything okay?"

"No, Amanda needs to get out and I need to train. She wants to spend some time with Chase but with all the meetings today, there just isn't any time. Do you think Tate would postpone the conversation with the Wood family for a few days?"

"There's only one way to find out, come on let's go," I grabbed her hand and we headed back to her office.

## TATE

Brin left to get us some food, and now that we've fully claimed each other, I can feel her emotions and what I'm getting from her is frustration.

*"Amanda wants to shift, I can feel it. I haven't had nearly as much time with her as I've wanted to. Can we postpone the meeting with Cecil and Anabel?"* Chase asked me.

*"I'll check."*

*"Thank you, Tate."*

*"Cecil, Anabel?"*

*"Yes, Alpha Tate?"*

*"If you're okay with it, I'd like to postpone our meeting for a couple of days. Brinley is worn out and I need to release some pent-up anger."*

*"Just let us know when and what time and we'll be there."*

*"Thank you for your understanding."*

*"You're welcome Alpha."*

A few minutes later, Ben and Brinley walked in with food. *Thank the fuck because I am starving.*

"Oh thank the Moon Goddess, you brought me some food. I'm so hungry, wait, I need to pee. I'll be right back," Quincy jumped up and ran to the bathroom. We laughed as she ran to the office bathroom. "I heard that, you try having a pup sitting on your bladder and see how funny it is!" She yelled at us. When she finally joined us we were eating a sandwich, chips, and some chocolate cake. Next thing we knew she was running back to the bathroom, vomiting.

"Ben, get rid of those chips, or I'm going to hurl again."

"Yes, Dear."


**BRINLEY**

I feel so bad for Q, I know she's in her early stages of pregnancy, but I couldn't help chuckling when she told Ben to toss out the chips.

*"Brin, I need to shift, can you please talk with Tate."*

*"Yes, I'm sorry Andi, I'll do that right now."*

"Can we postpone the meeting with Maribel and her family for a day or two? I'm drained from that last meeting and Amanda says she needs to shift. I would like to hit something too. Besides, the Elder and Councilwoman already told us they don't need to be here for that meeting."

"I think that sounds like a great idea. I could use the shift too. I already contacted Cecil and Anabel about postponing their meeting. I'll reach out to them with the new date and time when we decide on it. After the meeting with Diane, we'll head to the arena."

"Thank you, I appreciate it and so does Amanda," I kissed him. There was a knock on the door, I opened it and Carl walked in.

"You ready for the meeting with Diane?"

"No, but I am ready to get this over with."

"I'll link her and tell her she's needed in my office on an urgent matter."

We waited while Tate linked her, it was taking a little longer than it should have.

"Sorry, that took a minute. Can you believe she had the fucking audacity to ask me what it's regarding?"

"What did you tell her?" Brin asked.

"I told her something happened with her parents," I looked at Carl.

"Well, something did happen with her parents, just not what she's probably thinking," he said, uncaringly.

"Are you ready for the fallout of what's about to happen?"

"No, but whatever happens, she's already chosen the repercussions of her actions. Let's just get this over with."

## DIANE

I was hanging out with Maribel and Noelle. We were catching up with her and what she's been up to the last few years while she's been in college. I got a link from Tate saying he needed to see me as soon as possible on an urgent matter.

"It's been great catching up with you Noelle, but Alpha Tate just linked me. He needs to see me in his office on an urgent matter. I'll catch up with you more tomorrow."

Maribel rolled her eyes, "did he say what it's in regards to?"

"No."

"Don't you think you should ask him first?"

*"Alpha Tate, may I ask what this is in regards to?"*

*"Not that I need to explain myself since I am your alpha, but it's in regards to your parents. Something happened."*

*"Alpha, are my parents okay?"*

*"I'll see you in my office, make that the Luna office, as soon as you get here."*

*"Yes, Alpha."*

"I need to go," I panicked, "something happened to my parents."

"Oh my goddess Diane, I hope it's not serious," Noelle said.

"Me too. I gotta go."

# CHAPTER 45 FACING DIANE

**DIANE**

Anxiety slammed through me as worry and panic guided my feet to the packhouse. I haven't felt our family bond break so they must still be alive. The only explanation is they must be unconscious or something. I rushed into the packhouse, ran to the luna office, threw open the door, and stopped dead in my tracks. I didn't even hear or see the door close and lock behind me.

"What the fuck is going on? Daddy, I tried to link you, why didn't you answer? Where's Mom? Why isn't she here? Why can't I link her? Daddy? Daddy!" He's not answering me and everyone is staring at me. *I don't know why no one is saying anything. I try to link Maribel but she's not responding to me either. Is my link broken? It can't be, Alpha Tate linked me, so I must be able to link, why isn't it working? I can feel myself panicking.*

**TATE**

"Diane, your link has been blocked, the only people you can link are myself and Brinley, my mate."

Her eyes got big and her mouth dropped open, "what did you just say?"

"I said, you can only link me or Brinley."

"No, what did you say after that? Did you say she's your fucking mate!"

"I did, and we've fully claimed each other too. Now, please have a seat."

"I don't want to fucking sit down, what the hell is this about!" she screamed and stomped her feet.

"Sit... down!" I ordered her. She slinked in the chair and clamped her mouth shut.

"I don't understand. Why am I here?"

"John, would you like to take the lead on this?"

"Sure."

"Diane, it has been brought to our attention that you have been sneaking off pack lands at odd hours of the night. Care to shed any light on that?"

"You're the guy Arlene has a crush on! Does she know you're a part of this!?"

"You're not in a position to ask me questions. Do you care to explain why you've been sneaking off of pack lands?"

"I have not been sneaking off of pack lands!"

"Really? Care to explain why we caught you on video?" He turned on the CCTV that's linked up to the TV in Brin's office and her face went white.

"I, that, uh, that's not me. I'm not saying another word to you. Daddy, don't just stand there, say something," she whined as he stood there staring at her with a blank look on his face.

"You are... no daughter... of mine," he gritted out. "Your mother is no longer my mate and you are no longer my daughter!"

"What! I... I don't understand, what did you do to my mom!?"

"Diane, I'm only saying this one time so listen carefully. Your mother's fated mate impregnated her but she did not feel he was worthy of her, or you, so she had him killed. She wanted to be with someone with rank, so she found me and tricked me into thinking the baby was mine! I never fully claimed your mom, we may have mated but my wolf and I never marked or accepted her."

"When you were a few years old, I ran into my fated mate. Your mom was with me, she saw my reaction to her. She didn't like it so she followed her and killed her without my knowledge!"

"What the hell are you talking about? What do you mean you're not my dad? Is she even my mom? How could she kill my real dad and your fated mate? Why the hell am I just now finding out about this?"

"Because I just found out about it!"

"My life has been a complete lie!? She lied to me!? What else has she lied about!? After all the things I've done for her!"

"May I continue!?"

"I'm sorry," she dropped her head.

"My wolf never accepted you as our pup and now that I've recently found out what you've been up to, I'm glad he never did."

"What are you talking about, what have I supposedly been up to?" her voice quavering.

"Carl, if you don't mind, I think I'll step in here," Brin said.

## BRINLEY

Carl linked me and Tate, *"If you don't mind, I'd like to leave. I can't be in here anymore. Can you let me know when the executions will be taking place so I can be there? I'm going for a much-needed run, if I'm needed, link me."* We nodded at him and he left.

"Diane, I'm going to pull the band-aid off. We found out your mom helped commit treason against this pack. About thirty years ago, one of your mom's best friends was banished from pack lands. We don't know the reason behind it but she gave birth to a son not too long after but we'll get to that later. Your mom met with her friend many times.

When the alpha's mate had a daughter, she brought her pictures of the baby and kept her updated while the child grew. It's unclear why she was interested in that child. At some point she made a deal with someone who wanted to take over this pack, Tate's Pack." I'm watching her face as the realization hits her. "I have some questions for you, and I expect you to tell me the truth."

"I have no idea what you have to question me for. I have done nothing wrong and I don't need to answer your questions. Where the hell is my mother?" she said smugly. I ignored her and continued.

"What is your full name?

"Diane Elizabeth Christopherson"

"Why did you help Maribel commit criminal acts towards me?"

"I didn't help her commit anything against you!"

"Stop lying, do you know some of the things you did to me were physical?"

"You stole Tate from her! She was supposed to be the next Luna of this pack! I needed to help her get rid of you!"

"Why have you been sneaking into the guard shed?"

"What! I have never done that!"

"Stop lying Diane, it will only make it worse for you."

"I am telling the truth, I don't know what you're talking about."

"Then tell me this, why were you caught sneaking into the shed and grabbing the patrol schedule?"

"I... I never did that."

I linked John, *"Can you have Arlene step in here please."*

*"Absolutely Alpha."*

"You sure you don't want to answer that question truthfully?"

"I'm innocent of that."

"You keep telling yourself that."

"Who did you give the patrol schedule to?"

"I didn't take it nor did I give it to anyone. I don't know what you're trying to imply, you fucking bitch!"

"That's a lie and it's LUNA to you!"

*"Arlene's outside,"* John linked me.

"Who's Arnold?" Her face dropped and she paled.

"I've never heard that name before."

"Stop... lying, you're not helping yourself by doing so. Maybe there is someone who can help us?"

"Maribel is innocent, she knows nothing, good luck getting her to talk."

"John, would you mind opening the door? I think whoever is out there might be able to shed some light on this."

Arlene walked in and smirked at Diane. "Hello Diane, how are you?"

"I... what... who... how are you here?" she stuttered

"Diane, can I introduce you to Arlene, John's mate, and one of my master elite enforcers." I smiled at her and the look on her face was priceless. I laughed to myself. "Arlene, Diane was just telling us she didn't take the patrol schedule and also doesn't know anyone by the name of Arnold."

"Really? Because if I recall, we met with him at a diner not too long ago. I believe she calls him 'Charlie' when she's talking about him with me and Maribel"

"You! You were a part of this?" Diane angrily pointed a finger at her.

"Yes, actually I am and thanks to you, we know Arnold's plan."

"Impossible, you don't know everything!"

"Oh, but we do," John said. "You see, we bugged your room and put a sensor in there. Every time you stepped in and out of your room, we knew. Every time you talked on your phone, we recorded it. We know everything."

## DIANE

*I can't believe this, this is too much. I can't believe my mom killed two people, one being my real dad and one being my dad's fated mate. What the hell was she thinking? I need to find a way out of this, unlike Maribel, I know what will happen to me. As soon as I leave here, I'm running straight to*

*Arnold and telling him he needs to attack as soon as possible. Preferably before they can execute me.*

"Diane," Brinley brought me out of my thoughts, "did you know your mom made a deal with Arnold to take you as his mate, and low and behold, you turned out to be fated?"

"How, do you know that?"

"Your mother told us. We have proof of you and your mother's treason against this pack. There is nothing you can do or say to get out of this. I'm sure you know the consequences of your choices if you were to get caught or do you need us to explain it to you?" I glared at her. "You will be detained in the dungeon under solitary confinement, just as your mother is. You will be brought to justice, by fighting."

"I can't fight! I was never allowed to learn to fight!"

Tate glared at me, "That isn't true. You were raised to be one of the princesses of this pack if my memory serves me correctly. You always had the option to join us in training, you just chose differently," he said matter-of-factly. "We have not decided when you will be put to death or who will be the one to do it. You need to know, not only do you have the treason crimes against you but you also have the criminal charges from what you did to Brinley against you as well."

"I hope Arnold figures out what's going on. He'll get suspicious if he doesn't hear from me. He'll come looking for me! You fucking bastard!"

"He won't, I'm going to meet up with him and tell him you went on a trip with your parents to visit family out of state and won't have phone contact. You can't mind-link either since neither of you carries the mate mark, he won't suspect a thing. You forget, he wants you in a safe place and said he would talk with you after the attack with Black Diamond is over. He won't be expecting to see or talk with you until then," Arlene said smugly.

"I hate all of you, you can all go to fucking hell!"

## BRINLEY

*"Brooke, can you come in here and take this bitch to a solitary confinement cell, please. Make sure it isn't near her mother's cell either."*

*"Will do Sis, want me to have one or two of the boys assist me?"*

*"Yes, please, just in case she gives you trouble, not that you can't take care of her yourself. After you're finished come to the arena so we can train, I have a feeling Arlene will be joining us too."*

*"You got it."* Brooklyn, Erik, and Max showed up a minute later and took a kicking-and-screaming Diane with them. I looked at Tate, "Can we please go to the arena? I need to hit something and shift. Anyone else in this room is welcome to join us."

Arlene got a big smile on her face, "It's been a very long time since I've been able to shift and spar with you 'alpha triplet' Let's see what you've got."

I laughed as I linked my arm with hers and leaned into her. "I've missed sparing with one of my best friends and I'm sorry I was so lost in myself all these years."

"You don't need to apologize, I've missed my best friend too. Although I don't know firsthand the devastation you felt, I do understand. If roles were reversed and I lost what and who you did, I can imagine I would've been locked up inside myself too," she squeezed me in a side hug as we left my office.

"Thank you for always being there for me Arlene. I know I was a walking zombie for most of it. I do realize you were there for me, even if I wasn't able to acknowledge you or what you've done or tried to do to help me." I smiled at her. "By the way, I linked Brooklyn and the guys. I told them we were heading to the arena to train. I also told them you were joining us, they said they'd meet us there."

"Good, let's go kick the boys' asses," we laughed together as we walked out of the packhouse. It feels so good to feel like myself again, laugh a real laugh, and to be able spar with my friends.

## TATE

Watching Brin take the lead in those meetings had my cock getting hard. She is amazing and I'm so happy she is all mine. I thought it was going to take me months of courting her and flirting with her to like me. Thank you Goddess for mate bonds, the minute she shifted, she knew I was hers and she was mine. Seeing her friendships being rekindled is heartwarming.

She was so lost in herself after everything that had happened to her, but seeing her push through all of that and persevere makes me warm inside. Hearing her genuinely laughing with Arlene, I want to hear more of that. I think confronting Wilma and Diane and getting them secured in the dungeon cells has lifted some of the stress from both of us.

Plus I haven't had a chance to watch her train so I'm looking forward to that. She's going to need to do it too, especially with these executions coming up. I want her to be a part of them as my Luna. I know she and Amanda will be in charge of Maribel's execution, that one is all hers. We'll deal with Maribel in a few days. I caught up to the girls as we walked to the arena, "did you guys find it odd how quickly both Wilma and Diane could go from hot to cold and vice versa in those meetings?"

"It was weird how sweet and innocent they acted before their claws came out, like mother, like daughter," Brin shook her head and shrugged her shoulders.

"Let's get a workout in. We can talk about what to do with those three asshats later." Arlene commented.

# Epilogue

**TATE**

It's been two weeks since we placed Wilma and Diane in solitary confinement and two weeks of hell for Brinley. Our reprieve was short-lived, we only got a couple of days before the shit hit the fan with Maribel again. She has been on a rampage ever since. Every chance she gets she's destroying things that belong to Brinley. She dumped a whole plate of spaghetti all over her, walked past her with a milkshake in her hand, and tossed it at her. She found one of Brin's sweaters draped across a chair and shredded it. We've had to repaint the outside of the arena because she was caught, on tape, writing derogatory shit on it.

One time, Brinley was showering in the women's locker room after sparring in the training pitch and Maribel had the nerve to walk into her shower stall while rinsing shampoo out and dumping glue in her hair. Some of her crap has been so petty like cutting Brin's hair ties in half when she sets them down. She's tried tripping her, hitting her, stabbing her, that's a story in itself and she was even caught trying to break into our suite.

She knows I've permanently moved Brinley into my suite, but she still hasn't figured out we're mates. She's acting like a fucking three year old and it's getting old. Today's the day we're talking to her and her family. She's also angry because she was asking where Diane was. Carl told her Wilma and Diane would be gone for a while visiting family in another pack and they'd be out of cell and linking range. He had to tell her something otherwise she'd get suspicious about why Diane hadn't been around.

# About the Author

Karsyn Joy is an author who was raised in the Pacific Northwest. Since she was a teenager, she's always wanted to write but never felt confident in pursuing her dream. After forty years and some personal struggles, she found solace in reading, which helped he develop ideas for her first book.

Her debut novel, Second Chances, is the first book in The Goddess's Beloved, A Winter Moon Trilogy. It's a paranormal romance novel that explores themes of love, loss, vengeance, and hope. Karsyn's writing is imaginative and creative, and her books are set in a world of paranormal fantasy and romance where anything is possible.

Find Karsyn on social media:
Facebook: Karsyn Joy Stories
Instagram: @karsynjoyn_author
Email: karsynjoystories@outlook.com